tennessee

lost series book 1

Anita DeVito

Entangled Publishing, LLC
2614 South Timberline Road
Suite 109
Fort Collins, CO 80525
Visit our website at www.entangledpublishing.com.

Select Suspense is an imprint of Entangled Publishing, LLC.

Edited by Laura Stone
Cover design by Sara Eirew
Cover art from iStock

Manufactured in the United States of America

First Edition October 2015

To my husband, for not cringing when I said, "I have an idea," and for giving this Master of Science girl the chance to play on the liberal arts side of the road. I love you every bit as much today as I did when we started twenty-one years ago.

To Kyra Jacobs, for being the foot that kicked me, the ear I ranted to, and the shoulder I whined on. Wouldn't have gotten here without you.

Chapter One

"Smooth as a baby's bottom." With his eyes closed, John McCormick, Jr. could have sworn his fingers ran over the sleek lines of his favorite Taylor guitar instead of his granddad's old work bench. His granddad had always called him Butch, and to his family and friends, he was still just Butch, easy-going with fast hands and a killer smile. Here in his granddad's workshop in the old barn, he was still a boy with big ideas and no responsibilities.

To the rest of Tennessee and the country-music-loving world, he was Butch McCormick, country music star. Last month, he released his third album since "hitting it big." He'd already had a single reach number one on the charts, and two more were climbing like cats up a tree. He had to hand it to his manager and agent, Landon Finch. He could sell water to a drowning man. Finch demanded Butch grow his hair and use a trainer. Finch bullied Butch to make the latest video without a shirt. Finch transformed small-town

Butch into a heart throb the ladies loved to download.

Butch looked up at the sound of shuffling boots on gravel. He'd know the sound of that stride anywhere. "Hey, Daddy," Butch called through the open barn doors.

The senior John McCormick stepped onto the wooden floor. "Whatcha doing in here?"

Butch ran his hand over the worn wood again. The familiar shape and texture felt like home, something he hadn't had for years. Just touching it soothed the part of him that craved reconnection with his family, his roots, his true self. "Thinking about fixing the place up a bit. Things seem to be inching their way toward hell. Even started a list." Butch had come home to find a shutter on the house hanging cock-eyed. Paint had flecked off the barn doors, weathered wood filling the gap. The downspout hung limply on the side of the house, pulled away from the gutter and doing nobody any good. The house seemed to need him as much as Butch needed the house.

"Well, I guess I have let things go a bit since your mama and I moved up to the big house. Don't put yourself out. Fixing and tinkering were never your things. Play your guitar. Write your songs. I'll get to the rest in good time."

A faint smile brushed Butch's lips. The first album he made after signing with Finch made money. Real money. Butch used a good chunk of it to build a new house for his parents on the corner of their three-hundred-twenty-acre farm. A nice house and well built. Not showy or ridiculous, but enough the king-sized bed he bought could fit with room to spare in the big house. That's what his parents called it. The big house. His grandparents' farmhouse, the one he grew up in, became the old house. Butch felt like a success the day he held his mama's hand and led her into her new home. Was it really only four years ago?

Butch kept his hands busy taking stock of the tools spread over the bench. His fingers danced over a gap where wrenches lay in a row. No, he wasn't the handiest man in the family. His hands were better suited to driving tractors instead of fixing them, but he pulled his own weight. Always had, always would. Now more than ever. "I'm not helpless, and I have time. I need to do something. You know, something that matters."

"You've been home nearly two weeks now. We respect your privacy, but other than coming to the big house for dinner, you haven't left the old house. Your mama notices things like that and she worries." John laid a hand on Butch's shoulder. "You all right?"

Butch felt the squeeze in his heart. He'd never been good at hiding things from his parents. While his father's gesture might have seemed understated to some, that simple squeeze on his shoulder said Butch's mama wasn't the only one worried, and so he confessed. "I went into Nashville and filed the papers yesterday. I started the divorce proceedings."

John's grip tightened. "That's it then? It's over?"

"No, it's just the start. Fawn isn't going to make this easy." Butch's heart raced. Adrenaline gave it a nasty little punch when he thought how the college-educated actress would react to the fact that small-town Butch hadn't played his role as the awe-struck husband. When it came to drama, Fawn Jordan was a natural.

"Maybe she wants to try again. You know, marriage isn't supposed to be easy. I figure there are more days when your mother tolerates me than when she loves me."

Butch couldn't keep the teasing grin from shining through. "She wouldn't get so riled at you if you would stop erasing her shows." His mother had chirped in his ear for thirty minutes about how the best parts were missing from all her favorite programs.

John crossed his arms over his chest, leaning against the tractor that sat like dinosaur bones on a museum floor. "I can't stand those damned gadgets. Why can't she just watch the program when it's on television?" He went quiet for a few moments. "You've only been married for two years. You've barely had a chance to get to know each other."

The smile slid from Butch's face. He'd wrestled with facts of his marriage over the year they had lived apart. Over the last two weeks, he'd come to accept those facts. Still, it humiliated him to say it aloud. "Fawn married me because she thought she could ride my coat tails into a career. And she was right; she did. The producer from one of the videos made introductions for her, and voila, another soap star is born. Fawn never cared about me, not really. She wanted the life, the fame, the money. I was just the price of admission. She was already giving me crap, because she didn't want the separation to become public. With that good-girl character she plays, Fawn didn't want a scandal to hurt her ratings. She's not going to be happy when she's served."

"What comes next?"

"I'm going to stay here for a while, if you and Mom don't mind. Just slow things down a bit. I'm thirty-three years old, I've been married three times, and I have nothing to show for it." Butch ran a hand over his face, squeezing eyes that burned from sleepless nights. "I have the tour starting up in June. That gives me about three months to fix shutters, scrape paint, pound nails, and ponder life." *Three months to figure out what I want out of life.*

"I don't think you could call those gold records nothing."

"I guess heartache does make for good country music."

John pushed off the tractor and shoved his hands deep into the pockets of his jeans. "Come up to the big house for dinner. Your brother's coming, and your mother's making a casserole."

"All right. I'll be over in an hour or so." Butch pulled a heavy canvas tarp off an impressive chunk of wood. "After I hang Granddad's old sign."

Fences framed the lush, green, rolling hillside as hedges stood sentry, separating the working fields from the roadway. Early April in northern Tennessee looked a world away from southern Michigan, where the daffodils were only starting to poke their heads above ground. Here, color burst wildly against a vibrant green pallet. The sun hung proudly in a cloudless sky, bathing the farmlands in rich sunlight, but the tranquility of the picturesque country scene eluded Kate Riley.

"How in blazes can I be lost?" Furious with herself, Kate leaned over the steering wheel to peer down the road, praying for a sign that would direct her to the highway.

She had returned to Michigan two days before, trying a new strategy for dealing with a father that thought her too young, too inexperienced, and too female to handle a project like Cicada. The only ones who thought youth a liability were old farts who thought anything invented, created, or born after they turned thirty-five to be unnecessary and overdone. Ed Riley had been thirty-six when his only child was born. Nearly thirty years later, the degrees that hung on her wall and awards parading across her mantle had done nothing to convince the old man his daughter could stand on her own two, competent feet.

Hating the near-daily debates about the details of the construction project, Kate made the eight-hour drive home to have a civil conversation with the man.

The civil part lasted ten minutes.

Her father's inside voice required ear plugs, and his vocabulary would render the conversation one long beep under FCC regulations. Kate sunk to his level. Despite the hours of pep talk she had given herself, she sank right down to the bottom of that black pit with him. The man got to her like no one else.

The silver lining had two electric blue stripes over a cotton white body. Her 1966 Shelby G.T. 350. Her baby. Her spirit raced with the speed and the freedom of driving on the open road.

Or it normally did.

Now, so lost she didn't know if she was still in Tennessee, Kate's spirit had more in common with a dung beetle than a mustang. The cherry on top of her day? The battery on her cell died, taking her phone, contact numbers, and GPS with it.

"How did people do this before smart phones? I followed the freaking detour. Where did it go?" She glanced at the clock. It had been twenty minutes since Kate saw the last detour marker. The narrow road ahead barely let two cars pass each other. This couldn't be right. "Damn it. I don't have time to be lost."

Up ahead, a man in a nice pair of Levis wrestled with a big sign on the side of the road.

"All right, handsome, you're the first human I've seen in miles. I hope to God you know your way out of this maze." Kate pulled off the road a car length back. She measured the man as she walked to him: good-sized with broad shoulders and muscles worth noticing. His knees bent, sagging under the weight of wood in his arms. Forgetting her own issues, Kate raced the remaining distance and grabbed the dropping end.

"I got it. I got it." Kate said as a means of introduction, taking part of the weight against her shoulder. "Let's set it down. Nice. Solid oak, right? Four-feet wide, three-feet tall, as thick as my thumb and made to last a lifetime."

Dusty blue eyes, cloudy with confusion, looked at her as though she were an alien. "It's oak. My granddad made it."

She admired the lettering, hand carved and well pre-served. "Do you want some help getting her back where she belongs?"

Butch crouched, mirroring the woman until the weight of his granddad's sign rested safely upon the earth. He rose slowly, measuring the interloper. She didn't belong here. Something about her didn't fit in. Something in her stance. In her demeanor. The redhead with peaches-and-cream complexion stood facing him with hands propped on denim-clad hips. Her stretchy little T-shirt showed off femi-nine curves. Her blue eyes were sharp, vivid, not muted like his own. By the set of her full mouth, he doubted those eyes missed much of anything. But that didn't answer the most pressing question. "Who are you?"

"Kate Riley." She held out her hand, an inviting smile on her lips.

Butch took her hand, surprised by her grip. She shook hands like a man, hard and dominant, but had soft-as-a-lamb skin. His hand engulfed her smaller one, his thumb caressed the back of her hand, liking the feel of it. "Nice to meet you, and I'd appreciate the extra set of hands. I need some things from the barn."

Butch headed up the long drive, his stranger bouncing beside him. He glanced at her as they walked. Did he know her? No. He didn't know her, he was sure. She didn't giggle and bounce like his fans often did. She just quietly walked next to him in quick strides to keep pace, looking left and right across his family's farm. "Is there something I can help you with?"

One of the dogs his parents kept poked his head out from behind the house. The monster black Lab broke into a loping run down the driveway tail wagging, ears flopping, and tongue lolling.

She sighed heavily, her shoulders sagged. "I got off I-65 for gas and couldn't get back on because of construction. I followed the detour but haven't seen a sign for a while."

The dog slid to a halt at her feet, sending the stone of the gravel drive flying.

She held out both hands, palms up and gave the command. "Stop."

"Easy, boy." Butch reached for the dog but was side stepped in favor of the small woman. Coming just up to his shoulder, she didn't have to stoop to rub the dog's ear. "I'm sorry to be the one to tell you, but you're lost."

She walked sideways a bit, the dog putting much of his weight into her hip. She not only didn't mind, she encouraged it by rubbing the spot the dog liked the most. Inside the barn door, she leaned down to talk to the dog.

"I was afraid of that. Would one of you know how to get me found?"

The dog exhaled long and hard as he leaned in to the rubbing hands. Butch doubted at that moment the dog was capable of a thought beyond *Aaahhhhh.*

She lifted her head and looked around the building. "Nice workshop. Vintage."

Butch picked up the drill, bits, and hardware he'd set out.

She stopped rubbing the dog's ear to pull open six dusty drawers in the wooden chest on the bench. She grinned up at him with all the satisfaction of a pirate. "This is going to be fun."

"You know how to hang Granddad's sign?" Butch laughed when the dog nearly knocked the woman over, trying to get her to pet him again. Pound for pound, he guessed the dog weighed more.

She flashed a devilish little smile. "I am a woman of many talents. Unfortunately, one of them is not finding the highway. My phone died and took my GPS with it. I'm not even sure I'm still in Tennessee."

"You are. Prettiest part, if you ask me. Where are you from?"

She built a small collection of hardware. "Michigan. Detroit area."

Butch let out a slow whistle. He'd played a few shows in

Michigan. Grand Rapids. Battle Creek. Good people, even if the land was a bit flat for his taste. "You really are turned around. You're about forty-five minutes from the highway. Where are you going?"

All expression fell from Kate's face. "Forty-five? Oh, jeez. Ah, toward Chattanooga."

Butch raised an eyebrow. "Toward?"

She nodded, her tongue darting out between contoured lips. There was more to the story, Butch had no doubt, but he let it lie.

"What's your name?" she asked.

"Butch." He said it without thinking. Would she recognize him now? She certainly hadn't acted like she knew who he was. Butch left the barn, knowing she would follow.

"Huh. You don't meet many Butches these days." Arms full, she jogged until she reached his side.

"No, I guess you don't." Butch's long strides ate up the couple of hundred yards to the road. He wrestled again with the sign, hefting it to his legs, and worked to suspend it while he lifted the drill to the thick beam. From behind him came the exasperated sigh of a woman.

"Please. Let me help. It will go much better if we work together. How about I measure, you drill?"

"All right. I can work with that plan."

Kate measured and marked both the beam and the sign, moving effortlessly with a fluidity that only came with experience. She measured twice, asked him to lift the sign, checked again, then stepped back as she moved in with the drill. She didn't speak, just worked with the materials they collected from his granddad's old chest of drawers. "Okay, up she goes."

Butch lifted the sign again while she maneuvered it into place and made the final connection.

Kate stood back and cocked her head. Then her face lit up, and she raised her hand for a high-five. "Nice team work. It hangs evenly. You shouldn't have any problem with it, even in storms. Elderberry Farm. Very nice."

"Thank you." Butch looked as the sign swung gently, back where it belonged with a lot less pain and suffering than if he had done it alone. He slapped his hand to hers, returning the pride shining in her face. "Let's get you some directions."

Butch's mother stood at the kitchen counter, her back to him as she wrapped left overs. "This should keep you for a few days."

"Thanks, Mama. I forgot how much I loved your cooking."

She turned around then. "As long as you don't forget how much you love your mama." She held her arms out.

Butch filled them, resting his chin on his mother's shoulder. "I could never forget that. Thank you for the fried chicken." He knew she had made his favorite dish instead of the forewarned casserole after his father told her about the divorce. "Jeb appreciated it, too."

"That brother of yours." She sighed heavily, pulling back until she could look at Butch's face. "Marriage is about finding your partner in life. The one who makes high times higher and the low times worth remembering. What do you want in a wife, Butch?"

Butch looked into his mother's eyes but didn't have an answer.

Her gaze drifted away then widened in happiness.

Butch's father had walked into the room. "That program's on you like. The one with the dogs."

"Oh. Is it that late already?" His mother pulled Butch down and kissed his cheek. "You take good care of my baby boy. I love him."

Butch smiled, embarrassed by her attention but treasuring it. "I'm heading back to the old house. G'night."

Butch's brain rattled on the ten minute walk along the bumpy dirt road that skirted the fields. He wasn't happy to be divorcing Fawn. He hadn't married with the intention of divorce, not this time nor his other two marriages. He wasn't proud he hadn't been able to make a marriage work. He had come to terms with the feeling that divorcing Fawn was right. His life had been on hold for the last year, waiting for some sign telling him what to do. While he waited, Fawn partied and shopped and traveled. Without him. Fawn didn't love him, if she ever had.

The second and maybe more painful realization was it didn't surprise him. It didn't really hurt. His pain stemmed from the fact that for all his professional success, he failed spectacularly in the pursuit of love. A private pain that would become public fodder. He wanted to start living again. He finished the circle, coming back to where they had met and married to turn the page on this chapter of his life.

His mother had asked him what he wanted in a wife. Butch hated not having an answer to give her. Then his father came in, and his mother's eyes lit up. They had been married for thirty-five years, and she still stood a little straighter and smiled a little brighter when the love of her life walked into the room.

That's what Butch wanted. He wanted to be the light in a woman's eyes. *The light in her eyes. The spring in her step. The reason she laughs. The one she reaches for. The one she holds on to.*

With a song on the verge of birth, the thought of going into the old house made him feel claustrophobic. He needed room to breathe. Butch detoured to his granddad's shop with a tune on his mind. Like a good whiskey, Butch found his songs needed time to ferment, and the best way to do that was not to try too hard. To give his hands something to do while his mind worked, Butch tinkered with the John Deere that stopped working his second day home. It had added insult to injury. He wanted to do something simple. Something he could accomplish. He had taken the tractor out to start working an empty field when something locked up, and the tractor growled like a poked bear. He took a hammer from the workbench, thinking he might not be able to fix it, but he couldn't break it any worse.

Somewhere nearby, the Lab barked excitedly. Butch felt a twinge of sympathy for whatever animal the dog played with to death. He crouched low to look through the under-body. The green-painted metal framed slim legs wrapped in denim and finished in leather.

"You're back." Butch stood, wiping his hands on a cotton rag.

The dog danced around the little redhead, dying to get her attention. Her brows pressed low, and lines cut deep rills around her eyes and mouth, but she handled the dog gently.

"What happened?"

Kate slapped her palms against her thighs. Her voice quivered. "How do I know? I followed the directions." She tossed the paper to him. "I never found the highway."

She lost that confident air she wore as close as skin just hours ago. Half her hair had escaped her braid, her cute tee was rumpled, and her petal-pink lips drooped toward the ground. She looked defeated, a feeling he understood.

Butch took the paper and read his own writing. There it was. Left on Route 431. It should have been a right. He looked at her out of the top of his eyes and shoved the paper into his pocket.

Kate paced across the open door, her shoulders curved inward. The dog moved as surely as her shadow, oblivious of the tension. She stopped suddenly. The dog ran into her legs. Her hand found his thick neck while her eyes took in everything in the barn and settled on the tractor. When she finally spoke, her voice was steady and laced with something that sounded to Butch like curiosity.

She cocked her head to the right. "What are you doing?"

"Tractor decided to stop running. The engine turns over but she won't go into gear." He tossed the rag on the seat. "But that's my problem, let's take care of yours. I'll get a map and meet you at your car."

When Butch came out of the front door of the farmhouse with a large map crumpled in his hands, Kate paced next to her car, shaking her hands as if to wake them up after they fell asleep. The dog, changing his tactic, sat near the fender, watching Kate with adoring eyes.

"Are you all right?"

Kate jumped when he spoke, collected herself, and turned to face him. "Physically, emotionally, or psychologically?"

Butch stopped short and let out a clear, low whistle. Shredded rubber wrapped around the front passenger wheel where the tire should have been. "Looks like you got a problem."

"What? What?" Kate walked around to the place he pointed at with his chin. "No. No, no, no, no. Why can't one thing, just one thing, go right today?" Kate walked around to the trunk, opened it and began emptying it. "Have you ever had a day when you feel like a fish swimming upstream, and you keep thinking if I can just get around the next bend, I'll be home free, but the only thing waiting for you is a hungry bear with good hand-eye-mouth coordination?"

Butch nodded, as that pretty much described his marriage and impending divorce. He joined her behind the car and began taking boxes from the trunk and stacking them on his gravel driveway. "I've had months like that. What is all of this?" The boxes made for reams of paper were full, based on their weight. Smaller boxes and bags were tucked in every gap, completely filling the trunk.

"Work." She didn't elaborate as she pulled another box from the trunk and stacked it on the growing pile.

Butch took a heavy one before she could. "What do you do?"

"Not enough, if you believe my father." She stopped suddenly. Kate's arms went rigid, and her head hung heavy, her hair flopping forward. "This cannot be happening."

Butch realized the problem. No spare tire. Kate took a deep breath and let out a long, heavy sigh. Butch felt responsible for that sigh. His mistake got her nowhere, with a flat tire.

"I know a mechanic. He'll set you up with a spare, but

as late as it is, you aren't going anywhere tonight. I have a bed you can use." When she shook her still hanging head, he quickly added, "A spare bed. I have a spare bed." His cell phone rang. "I need to answer this. Just relax. We'll take care of this. What did you tell me with the sign? Let me help. It will be better if we do it together."

Butch walked into the farmhouse and fell into the old couch his parents brought from the big house. "Evening, Finch."

"Everything is set for the tour, Butch." There was no preamble with Finch. The man got straight to it, no hellos and no good-byes. "I'll see about adding a few smaller venues to fill in the gaps, but all the major venues are set. I have your road crew set and I have a surprise for you." In classic Finch style, everything was done big. He had hired the top concert designer to work with Butch on the lighting. A hard-drinking, hard-playing band the audience would eat up would open the gigs. Then it would be Butch and the band he toured with. People would come and come big. Coliseums, ball parks.

"Nice, Finch. You are the master." Butch took a breath and broke the news. "I filed the papers yesterday."

Something heavy came down on something solid. Glass on wood? "It's about time you cut off that ball and chain. I'll handle the press statement. How has the soon-to-be-ex-Mrs. McCormick taken the news?"

"I don't expect she knows yet." Butch ran his fingers through his hair. He stayed away from social media, not wanting to see himself depicted as a villain, a jealous man, a cheat, or whatever else the person posting thought others would "like."

Finch gave a rare, real belly laugh. "Just keep your legs crossed, and protect your balls."

Butch snorted with amusement but crossed his legs. "I thought that was your job."

"Damn straight. Now I got something to look forward to this week. Fawn Jordan may play the lamb on that sex-opera of hers, but she's going to go out like a lion."

Butch cringed. "Yep, I know."

Finch snorted, the audio equivalent of an eye roll. "Don't sound so worried. Just remember, there's no such thing as bad publicity."

Butch didn't believe it but had no interest in debating the point. He didn't do this for the publicity. He wanted his life back. He wanted to feel like him again. "Finch, I need a piano."

A moment of silence preceded a question that was more an accusation. "What happened to yours?"

Butch draped his arm over his eyes. "I left it in California. I couldn't pack it in the truck like my guitars." He had moved the necessities of his life to his cabin in the hills, but his piano had stayed in the house he and Fawn shared. He could buy his own piano. Maybe he should, but he wasn't in the mood to shop. He wanted to play. That little realization made Butch sit up tall. He wanted to play. Hot. Damn.

Ice clinked against glass, then Finch spoke using the badass voice that showed his New York roots. "Fine, I'll get one ASAP but don't you let that unsophisticated wench keep that piano." Finch walked in detail through his plans for promoting the tour, including appearances on *Saturday Night Live,* a fleet of morning shows, and a spread in *Rolling Stone.*

A dull roar rolled into the living room, sounding like a

brawl breaking out outside his back door. Butch leapt to his feet. "Finch, I've gotta run. I've got trouble."

Finch dropped the business tone for concern. "Trouble? Do you need cops?"

A sharp metallic *ping* had Butch breaking into a sprint. "I've got to go. Call you later."

Butch ran into the barn and stopped short when he saw the guts of the big, green tractor spewed across the dusty floor. A computer sat on his Granddad's workbench, a disembodied voice cheered on the ruckus. Tractor parts were spread out in parallel lines against the wall. In the middle of the floor, Kate wailed on the tractor with an old sledge hammer.

"What are you doing?" Butch had to scream to get above the noise. "Kate. Kate! What the hell are you doing?"

"Yes! Who's your mama?" Kate held a mangled piece of metal triumphantly over her head.

"You got it?" an amplified voice asked. "What is it?"

"A wrench. A big-ass wrench." She reached out, handing Butch the prize.

"Who is that?" Butch frowned at the weight in his hands.

"Clayton. My gearhead," Kate said. "He's the man with the plans. Thanks, Clayton. Bill me for your time."

"This one's on me, Kate." Butch heard the admiration and more than a little interest in the voice over IP. "Just remember my name the next time your father goes shopping."

"Please, Clay. My father loves you more than me most days. He doesn't need to be reminded of your name."

"I just had a backhoe come in. Only five hundred hours on the engine. I'll make him a deal."

Kate laughed. For the first time, Butch saw her really

smile. It lit up the barn, lit up the night. Happy, carefree, proud. The smile went ear to ear and took years off her pretty face. The dog reared up, planting his front paws on her belly. Kate rubbed his ears enthusiastically.

"I'll let him know. First chance I get. Take care, Clay."

The dog refused to let her walk, making her laugh again.

"Can you disconnect the call, Butch? I seem to be a prisoner."

Butch used the finger pad to end the call. "What are you doing, Kate?"

She kissed the dog on the center of his flat head. "I couldn't solve my problem, so I solved yours. There's your culprit." She lifted the dog's paws, letting him fall to all fours and joined Butch on a clean patch of floor.

Butch turned the wrench over in his hands. The hard metal had stood up to the tractor, gouging but not breaking. "Last time I saw this wrench was two weeks ago. My first full day home. It was here, on the work bench with the rest of the tools. How'd it get in the tractor?"

Kate tapped his cheek. "I have no idea, muscles, but I think getting it out makes me your hero."

Butch returned the gesture, smiling when she laughed. "Almost. You still have to put the tractor back together. I suppose that can wait 'til tomorrow. Come on inside, hero. You can have some of my mother's coveted fried chicken before I take you to meet your mechanic."

Without the ambient light from a city, night was as it should be: dark. The full moon painted the edges in silvery shadows, bringing life to inanimate objects. Butch steered his truck into a long, asphalt parking lot, lit by warm, yellow light spilling from the adjacent building. Kate blinked until her eyes adjusted to the light. This would be an adventure, she decided. In the months she'd been working in Tennessee, she'd kept to herself. Once she had her wheels back under her, she'd keep to herself again. So what would be wrong with one night of fun? Butch held the door.

"The Sly Dog." Kate ducked under his arm to enter the local hang out. "Have you been coming here long?"

"Since I was a gleam in my Daddy's eye." Before the door closed behind them, Butch's name had been called out from across the bar.

Butch knew everyone, and everyone knew him. Kate ran her fingers through her hair, smoothing the curls that tended to run free as every one of his friends looked over the newcomer. Kate had changed into fresh jeans and pulled a white blouse over a tight, midnight-blue tank, leaving the blouse hanging open. She had dismantled her braid and let her long hair hang tousled over her shoulders. She returned the warm smiles and kind words offered as Butch introduced her to a few dozen family, friends, and acquaintances.

Kate instantly liked the small-town bar. Years of good times marred the hardwood floor. Pictures of high school football championships, framed jerseys with illegible signatures scrawled in black marker, fishing poles, a canoe, and a stuffed marlin cluttered the walls. Music from a live band brought the whole place together in a non-stop party.

Butch swept his arm around her, leaning close to be heard over the music as they finally reached the bar at the back of the room. "What do you drink?"

"Whatever you're having is fine."

The bartender set two bottles of beer on the bar. As an afterthought, he added a glass next to Kate's. Kate took the beer, left the glass, and followed Butch to a corner table crowded with laughter and empty bottles. A slim blonde with baby-blue eyes bounced into Butch's arms. He wrapped his arms around her and lifted her off the floor.

With a squeal of delight, the woman laid a kiss on Butch's jaw. "Butchy! It's about time you left the house, not that I minded having you to myself." The woman giggled and cooed until her gaze found Kate. "Who's this?"

A wave of uneasiness flowed through Kate. Butch was somebody to the people in the bar. She was nobody with a northern accent. She took a deep breath, figuring her play under the heavy gaze of the woman that had to be Butch's girlfriend. This was, after all, an adventure, and what was adventure without an element of challenge? When Butch set the woman on her feet, Kate flashed her friendliest smile.

"Hi, I'm Kate."

Butch stepped away from the blonde and guided Kate to an empty chair with a hand on her back. "This is Trudy Williams, my good friend since second grade. Trudy, this is Kate Riley. Is Hyde here?"

"I'm your best girl, Butch. Don't pretend like you don't know it." Trudy looked Kate up and down.

Kate felt the censure. Of what, she wasn't sure. Her sensible boots, well-worn jeans, and makeup-free face were less out of place here than at the bar she and Tom frequented in the Detroit suburbs. Likely, it was *who* she walked in with more than what Kate wore.

Trudy didn't dress like most women that night. She

looked like something out of a magazine. Tall and lithe, her shape came from sculpted muscles on display by the sleeveless print dress. The tucked in waist showed off her Barbie-doll figure and miles of leg. Kate envied the graceful hands tipped with fancy red and white nail polish, so different from her own calloused, short-nailed fingers.

Butch made introductions around the table of high-school friends that never lost touch. Kate admired the camaraderie of the group. The way she grew up, her family had always been her world. She grew up in her uncle's house. Her earliest memories were of construction sites, power tools, and running with the boys. While she couldn't regret what she had with her family, a part of her wished for a group of friends that accepted her without all of the baggage family brought with it.

Trudy waved to a man at the bar. "Here comes Hyde."

Kate looked around Butch at the bulldog of a man walking toward the table, a beer in each hand. Hyde Spence wasn't tall, but he had big arms and a barrel chest.

"That's your man," Butch said. "Best damned mechanic in the county."

Kate stood as Hyde reached the table and put on her brightest smile again. "Butch says you're my man."

Hyde looked her up and down and up again. He turned to Butch and wrapped his arms around him, pouring cheap beer down Butch's back. "I love you, man."

Butch pushed him away. "She needs a spare tire. Her car got a flat in my driveway."

Hyde looked her over again. "What kind of car?"

Kate let the leer slide. She needed the spare. She'd already lost more time than she could afford. "1966 Shelby."

Hyde's eyebrows were lost in his shaggy, brown hair. "No shit? What happened?"

Kate shrugged. How do these things ever happen? "I ran over something. It wouldn't have been a problem except my spare tire is missing."

"When was the last time you used it?"

"Never. I've owned the car three years and never had a flat."

Hyde whistled long and low. "Buy me a beer, and I'll bring you a spare tomorrow afternoon."

Kate sighed. "Make it tomorrow morning, and I'll buy you a good beer."

Butch snorted. "I told you that stuff you drink is crap. It even feels like crap running down my back."

Hyde took a long drag from his bottle. "You've turned into a goddamned beer snob."

Butch shook his head. "I have taste, pure and simple."

With the deal made, Kate could focus on other needs. "Gentlemen, where is the ladies' room?"

With Kate out of earshot, Butch's friends bombarded him. "I was telling y'all the truth. She got lost in construction then pulled into my driveway with a flat. I've known her for a few hours."

"You're not sleeping with her?" Hyde asked.

Butch rolled his eyes. Hyde perpetually expected Butch's fame to mean he could and did bed anything in a skirt. His friend never believed that for Butch, the good life meant wife and kids. "I just met her."

Trudy draped her upper body over Butch's arm, dancing her painted nails on his shoulder. "And he's married."

Butch took a long drink of the cold beer. It didn't do anything to loosen the knot in his stomach. It embarrassed him, admitting it to the people that mattered to him that his marriage failed. Best to do it fast. "I filed the papers. Fawn and I are getting a divorce."

The table sat in stunned silence for a full minute. Hyde slammed his bottle down so hard beer erupted out the top. "Goddamn it. It's about time. To the ex-Mrs. McCormick. May she rot in Hell!"

A roar went up from the table as bottles kissed in celebration.

"We need something else." Hyde pushed to his feet, slapping Butch on the back. "Be right back."

That knot loosened. Butch didn't expect, didn't deserve, the support but admitted he needed it. He listened to the celebration on his behalf, holding on to it like a life preserver in turbulent waters.

Trudy leaned into the table, cupping her mouth to screen her words. "Speaking of ex-Mrs. McCormicks."

A honey-blonde with streaked hair made her way through the crowd, her gaze locked on to Butch. Angie Russell McCormick had been Butch's high-school sweetheart. A lifetime ago, she had come to him, telling him she was pregnant. He did the right thing and married her. Weeks later, she lost the baby. The marriage didn't survive long after. While Butch traveled and made a name for himself, Angie stayed home, helping her widowed mother and volunteering in the community. He helped her out when he could and later, against Finch's loud objections, began giving her a monthly allowance. The courtesy checks gave Angie enough to live on, but it never seemed to be enough. Butch slunk down in his chair trying to be inconspicuous.

"Too late," Trudy said. "She's spotted you."

"How did she know I was here?"

"I'm sure a dozen people posted to Facebook, Instagram, and Twitter. She would have heard."

"Butch! Butch!" Angie called out as she elbowed her way through the sea of bodies. She broke free near the table and stood tall, giving Butch the smile that always got her what she wanted. "Nobody told me you were back in town."

"Hey, Angie. You look good." Butch muttered the compliment manners compelled him to give.

"Why, aren't you sweet for noticing? I did just have my hair done."

Trudy leaned into Hyde but didn't quiet her voice. "And her tits."

Hyde snickered while he leered at Angie's shirt. More of her was out than in the tight, black, knit cotton.

Angie leaned against the table, turning her back on the hecklers and giving Butch a full view of what his money bought. He knew the minute she got down to business. Her mouth pursed, and her bottom lip went pouty.

"Butch, did you know that the way of life of the Northern Pine Snake in Tennessee is being threatened? Construction and development is ruining the poor little snakey's habitat. A group of us are working to save the cute little snakes from mass destruction. All we need is a *tiny* donation for medical bills and foster care."

Trudy rolled her eyes.

Hyde choked on his beer. "Foster care? For snakes?"

Butch looked Angie in the eye. He wasn't giving in. Not this time. "You just got your check, Angie. If you want to save the snakes, use that."

Angie leaned into Butch, brushing her new and improved tits across his shoulder. "But, Butchy, you know I have expenses. After paying for basics, I'm lucky I have enough left to buy the occasional drink."

Butch tilted his chin toward her. "How could you have spent all of the money?" A blur of red flashed across the floor, barreling straight at him. Butch saw the accident before it happened. He spun out of his chair and caught Kate around the waist as her feet slipped out from under her on a puddle of beer.

"Crap." Kate clung to Butch's shoulders as her legs imitated Bambi on ice.

"Are you okay?" Butch lifted Kate, set her on her feet on dry ground.

"Excuse me. We were having a conversation," Angie said, rolling her mascara-lacquered eyes.

Butch narrowed his gaze on his ex. "Cut it out, Angie. She slipped."

"Besides, you weren't having a conversation," Trudy said. "You were trying to sucker more money out of Butch."

Angie glared at Trudy. "Saving the Northern Pine Snake is *important*."

Butch closed his eyes, knowing when Angie got something stuck in her craw, there would be no end to the nagging until she got her way, but was he ever tired of it. He opened his eyes and gazed down into the blue eyes of the woman who dismantled his tractor. He found strength there. Determination. "Angie, this conversation is over. You have to live within your means. If you need more money, get a job like everyone else."

"About damned time." Trudy bobbed her head, emphasizing each word. "Go find another gravy train and crawl under it."

"Trudy," Butch said without taking his gaze from Kate.

"If your conversation is over, can you come with me?" Kate looked up at him with a fire burning in her eyes, her little body nearly vibrating with energy.

He found himself nodding and let her pull him away from the table. He smiled and looked over his shoulder.

Angie's mouth hung open, a hand on her cocked hip. "This isn't the end, Butch McCormick."

The threat didn't faze him. Butch knew Angie would be on his case tomorrow and the next day. But for the first time in a long time, he really didn't care. Kate had his hand in both of hers, dragging him across the dance floor and into the game room.

"You gotta see this; you gotta see this; you gotta see this!"

Chapter Two

A dog barked…somewhere. Kate raised heavy eyelids, drawn by the noise from the bottomless pit where she had sunk. She rolled her aching head, and arms tightened around her. Her eyes snapped wide open. Seconds passed before she made sense of the scene. She and Butch lay on his living room floor, twisted together like two strands of yarn. Her head lay on his shoulder, and his leg trapped her thigh. Hands were everywhere. A blue and white blanket lay at their feet.

The heart pounding in her chest matched the banging in her head. Flipping through mental images, the crisp pictures of the early evening blurred and then just ended. Kate had no idea how she ended up with Butch on the floor. She still wore her jeans and the scoop neck tank top, but her feet and arms were bare. She would have been cold if not for Butch's body heat. Kate moved back a judicious few inches, waking Butch. She rubbed her head and pried her tongue from the roof of her mouth. "What the hell happened last night?"

Butch moved his legs, freeing her, and propped himself on his elbow. "You don't remember?"

"Of course I remember." Kate rolled her eyes, lying her butt off.

"Uh huh. Tell me your favorite part."

"Riding the bull." Kate remembered pulling him across the bar to the black monster sitting in a quiet corner, just waiting for someone to notice. She sat up high, her thighs spread wide while the room spun. True, it may be the only thing she remembered, but that didn't mean it wasn't her favorite.

The ends of Butch's mouth curled slowly into an easy smile. "And after that?"

Kate narrowed her eyes. He knew something she didn't. A shit-eating grin like that could only mean she'd done something she wouldn't be proud of. God, she hoped she hadn't done something stupid. Embarrassment in a room full of strangers was one thing; stupidity something else. "Sure, and after that."

Butch climbed into the armchair, stretching his long legs in front of him. "No, what did we do after that?"

Kate pushed up and sat tailor style, combing her hair with her fingers. "I'm a little foggy on most of the night."

"That's not surprising. You had more than your fair share of the local spirit. It's distilled just south of here at Cloud Nine. The shot is one of Hyde's favorites, called Slice of Heaven."

"It went down smoothly, but now I feel like I licked a cat." She stuck her tongue out for his inspection.

"If that's all you feel, you handled it better than most."

He obliged her and looked at her tongue. "No fur. You're good."

"I've got that going for me." Kate went to the kitchen and turned on the faucet.

"Pain killers are in the cabinet above the sink. Grab a few for me, will you?"

Kate opened a couple of half-empty cabinets, trying to remember where she'd seen Butch's glasses the night before when he'd invited her in for his mother's fried chicken. One cabinet had enough dinner plates to share a meal with friends, a handful of bowls and small plates. A second cabinet had the glasses. On the top shelf, holding court over the rest of the cabinet, were four glass in a deep cherry red. While she admired the pretty glasses, she took a glass from the bottom shelf that looked like a Mason jar with a handle. She downed three pills and half a glass of the most refreshing water she had ever tasted. Her rusty throat loosened, like the tin man after a good lube. She returned to the living room and handed Butch the ice water and pills. Kate had never shied away from keeping up with the boys, but the boys had always been family. She had been out for an adventure, not to get drunk. The holes in her memory bothered her, really bothered her.

Butch drained the glass, washing down the pills, then pressed the cool glass to his head. "What are you thinking about so hard? I can see the steam coming from your ears."

"There, uh, may be a few gaps in my memory. I don't know what happened. Maybe I should have eaten more."

"Oh, I wouldn't be too hard on yourself. Hyde plied you with shots. I think he wanted to impress you."

"Impress me?" An image flashed. Little blue glasses

etched with a dog pointing and filled with a sweet liquor. Had she bought the drinks? "The shot glasses. I thought they wcre cute."

"You stole a few."

Her mouth fell open. "No. I wouldn't do that." She pulled her purse close and opened it wide to find two blue shot glasses. "Will you return these? I don't know what I was thinking. I remember we were celebrating…something." Alcohol snuffed out the spark of a memory. "What was it?"

"My third divorce. Your first bull ride." Butch chuckled, but the sadness lingering below the surface ruined the effect. Laughter brought out the twinkle in his eyes, dimples in his cheeks, and made him beautiful. He laughed on the surface and only on the surface.

Kate thought he needed a reason to laugh. While she would only be here for another few hours, she would spend the time she had making this good man happy. She kicked companionably at his foot. "Why is that funny?"

"Do you remember the mechanical bull?"

She bit her lower lip, watching still images flip through her mind. "Yes. His name was Rip. It was written on the blanket."

Butch snickered. Kate imagined manners kept him from laughing outright at her. "That blanket was like a burial shroud. R.I.P. Rest in peace. The owners had to permanently pull the plug on it when the insurance shot through the ceiling."

"But…I remember riding it." She vividly remembered the feeling of her legs on the wide leather.

"You tried. Oh, Lord you tried. We explained to you that the bull didn't work. You were bound and determined to fix it. You crawled underneath it, asking us to hand you wrenches and things. A crowd gathered around you, cheering you on." Butch sat up, acting out parts of the evening, laughing to his core, laughing until tears wet his eyes. "It took Hyde and me to pull you away."

Kate turned to the picture window, listening to the story. She wished it didn't sound so damned believable. Who in their right mind would crawl around a bar floor to re-wire a mechanical bull? Butch seemed to get a kick out of it, there was her silver lining. "I don't know what to say. I'm sorry?"

His arms spread across the back of the chair, Butch looked very satisfied. "Don't apologize. It would ruin the best night I've had in a long time."

Kate leaned against the arm of the couch and patted Butch's hand. "In that case, you're welcome. Why did we sleep on the floor last night? My back aches like I fell down a flight of stairs."

"I didn't think I could carry you up the stairs without both of us taking a tumble."

Kate froze with her hand on his. Her sudden fever meant her face would soon be the color of a tomato. "Excuse me. Did you say you carried me?"

Butch covered her hand, and captured and held on to it. "It's been a long time since I've slept with a woman. I forgot how nice it could be."

The intimacy of her hand in his made her heart flutter. A tragically few number of men had incited this type of physical reaction, and ensuing experiences proved disastrous. Short story: the sex hadn't been worth it.

Kate extracted her hand to break the contact and changed the subject. "Nice is not how my back would de-scribe it. I need to stretch out." She inhaled, reaching her fingers to the ceiling, and let her hands fall to the floor in a graceful swan dive. She moved through the sun salutation poses, taking the time to work the kinks out of her back, hips, and shoulders. She looked to the heavens and then floated down to earth.

Butch pulled the blanket out of her way and tossed it on the couch. "There's only one bathroom. Do you want to shower first?"

"No, you go ahead. Hopefully when I finish this, I'll feel human again."

Kate loved the lines of the farmhouse the first time she'd walked up the long drive with Butch. She knew the inside would be just as spectacular. The height of the farmhouse made it appear narrow where, in fact, spacious rooms could house a crowd. Windows on the front and on the left side above the staircase lit the large entryway, bare except for a worn rug in the middle. Straight through, a spacious kitchen with miles of counter contained a table for four under the window to the back yard.

Thick wood fully trimmed every room, a detail sinfully omitted in most new homes. The craftsmanship of generations gone by lived on in each window and doorway, in the infinite trail of baseboard, in the crown molding that encircled the living room.

The soft gray of the living room's wood floors nearly matched the color of Butch's eyes. A long couch, comfortable armchair, and a few mismatched tables filled the room. The pale walls sported darker patches where pictures used to hang. The brickwork of the fireplace and woodwork of the mantle could be photographed and featured in one of her architectural magazines.

Kate checked the phone that sat on the floor, plugged into an outlet. She had lucked out that Butch had the same model of phone and an extra charger. With her battery full, the screen lit up, announcing she had missed twenty-one calls. Tom left most with a few from her uncle and cousins. Notably—but not surprisingly—none belonged to her father.

Kate unplugged the phone, pacing as she dialed. "Hey, Tom, it's me."

"Kate." Tom said her name in a long exhale. "Where have you been? I called you a dozen times. You know your father didn't mean the things he said."

"It doesn't matter. The project is only a few days behind schedule. I can make that up. It will come in on budget and be the show place of the county. I don't need my father's approval. Just his money." Maybe if she said it often enough, she would believe it.

"Don't say that. You know he loves you. He's just worried." Newspaper rustled. Sunday morning. Tom would be sitting on the couch reading.

Most Sundays, Kate sat across the room in her favorite chair, sharing the newspaper sections with him. Though they spoke every day, she missed him and the little habits they shared as cousins, roommates, and business partners.

Kate walked the length of the room, then the width, not speaking until she returned to her starting point. Tom never understood the double standard Kate lived under. If she didn't perform as well as the boys, her father dismissed it as girls not being as capable as boys. If she out shined them, her father chastised her for showing off. Tom made excuses for her father and didn't understand that by doing so, he enabled her father's attitudes.

"He would never have said those things to you. He never would have said them to me if I were a boy. Look, that's not why I called. I've had car trouble."

"Where are you?" His voice tightened.

"I'm at an inn—"

"What's it called? I'll come get you."

"It's called Elderberry Farm, and you are not driving down from Michigan to get me. I got a bad flat, no big deal. A mechanic is bringing me a spare tire. What I need is a recipe. I want to make dinner for Butch to thank him for his help."

"Butch?"

Kate rolled her eyes at the wealth of suspicion poured into the name. "He runs the inn."

"Why do you need to thank him? Aren't you paying him?"

"He's gone out of his way to help me with the car. I thought I would do something nice."

Tom paused before answering. "You're not there alone with some strange man, are you? Haven't you seen *Psycho*?"

Kate couldn't admit she liked Butch. Statements like that would bring her cousin down to Tennessee in a state that would make the Tasmanian Devil look calm. She had been a little girl when Tom, older by four years, had appointed himself her guardian. There were plenty of times when having a headstrong guy like Tom on her side worked in her favor. For the times that didn't, Kate learned that discretion, along with exaggeration and avoidance, could get her to her desired end. "Jeez, Tom. Give me a little credit. Butch is older, he's going through a divorce, and he's nothing to look at." Kate crossed her fingers behind her back to cover her fib. "Now, are you going to give me a recipe or not?"

"Fine, but if you really want to show your thanks, take him to a restaurant. I say that as someone who not only loves you but has eaten your cooking."

"Oh, you're so funny. Just wait until the next time you bring a woman home. I'm breaking out the baby pictures." Kate sat on the chair and scribbled Tom's recipe for chicken parmesan on a scrap of paper she found in her purse. A shadow fell over her. She looked up into Butch's flat stomach. Her eyes followed the hair from the tapered hips to the trim waist to the defined chest and finally settled on a very bitable mouth. Kate moistened her lower lip, wondering what he tasted like.

Tom barked in her ear. "Kate? Are you still there?"

Kate flinched. "Yeah, I'm here."

"Bake it at three hundred fifty degrees until the cheese is browned and bubbly. Do you have it?"

Kate looked into Butch's eyes. They laughed at her as he pulled on a navy blue T-shirt. He had seen her reaction to him, and now he laughed at her. She gave him her meanest glare, the one that made her cousins run. Instead of retreating in fear, Butch reached out and touched his index finger to the tip of her nose. The friendly gesture left her with her mouth hanging open.

Butch settled against the door frame and unabashedly watched while Kate finished her conversation.

She shifted to business mode under those too-watchful

eyes. "I'll be back at the motel tonight. I have a call with Cicada at nine in the morning. Follow up on the veneer submittals for me. The panels have a long lead time, and we can't afford a delay."

"I know, Kate. I'll take care of it. I'll see you soon. I love you."

"I love you, too, Tom." She stowed her phone and the makeshift recipe in her bag and walked out of the living room.

Butch stopped her with a hand on her arm. "Tom?"

Kate nodded, keeping her eyes neutral. "My partner. I'll shower now."

Butch dropped his hand. "I left fresh towels in the bathroom."

B utch whistled as he whipped ten eggs into a frenzy. Upbeat and sassy, the ditty had his bare feet tapping a beat. Words and phrases flooded his head.

Long nights, cool nights, hot nights. No. Dark nights. In the dark of night, that big moon high made me believe she could be mine. In my truck, her pretty little smile made me want to lose my way. Right turn, left turn, right turn, wrong turn, doesn't matter which way I go. They all lead straight to you.

Kate's version of fun centered on action. She sat and listened to the glory day stories, encouraging the storytelling until the trout reached the size of a whale but then that high-energy body of hers wanted to play. He would never forget the sight of her on that dead bull. There had to be a song in there somewhere. After bull riding, they played pool and darts. Of course, every stud in the barn took a look at the new filly, but Kate didn't oblige. Each one she turned away left with a smile on his face. After each one, she came back to him. She would turn a little phrase with her Michigan accent and ask him to translate a local saying or a dozen other things that made him laugh. The band rocked the joint, and Kate bounced to the beat in her seat or behind a cue stick, but she didn't dance. Getting her onto the dance floor, now that would be an experience. He would have to think on how to do that. Wait, what was he thinking? She was leaving when her car was fixed. He'd likely never see her again. But still, a man could hope. Couldn't he?

"Wow, this smells great. What can I do to help?" She pulled her hair back into a wet pony tail, leaving her freshly scrubbed face exposed.

Butch turned the eggs into the frying pan he'd used to fix the bacon. "There's orange juice in the refrigerator. You can set the table. We're minutes away from breakfast."

Kate rummaged through his cabinets for the place settings. She hadn't bother to ask Butch where things were kept. She already knew where the glasses and plates were, and she poked around for silverware as though she were on a treasure hunt. "This stemware is gorgeous." Kate held up a delicate, rose-colored wine glass like it was the Holy Grail. After a moment of admiration, she selected a second glass, set them on the table and filled them with orange juice.

Butch flexed his biceps and took the frying pan to the small table where he dished out the eggs and bacon. "That was one of my grandma's good glasses. We weren't ever allowed to touch them as children."

Kate picked up her plate and pushed half of her portion back onto his. "With good reason, I'm sure. Are you an only child?" She sat down and dug heartily into her breakfast.

"I have an older brother, Jeb. How about you?"

Kate slathered jelly on thick toast. "I was raised with my three cousins, who are more like my brothers. We all lived together: my father, uncle, cousins, and me."

Butch tried to read her face, but she had closed down. "What happened to your mother?"

"It's just me and the boys. Your friends are nice. Is Trudy your girlfriend?"

"No. We've never dated. She's been one of my best friends—"

"Since second grade," Kate finished with a grin. "That part I remember."

"Her family owns the farm next door. She, Hyde, and I ran together all through school. How are your eggs?"

"Fantastic. Do you eat like this every day?"

"No. I usually just have coffee."

"Did you do this for me? I appreciate it. Really. I'll cook dinner, if you don't mind if I hang around for a little while. I need to put your tractor back together. I can make chicken parmesan. My specialty. Is there a grocery store nearby?"

Butch made breakfast because he wanted to. He'd laughed more in the day he'd known her than he had in a year. Cooking breakfast for a beautiful woman, even one he hadn't slept with, was a simple pleasure. He liked feeding her. He liked the way she bounced in the chair and her little humming over the sustenance he provided. He liked the idea of her staying around but yesterday she had been so determined to get on her way. Why the change? "Aren't you in a hurry to get home? Yesterday it seemed like you were pressed for time."

"I'm not going home. I'm working on a project nearby. I lost a few days last week and needed to catch up. I couldn't afford to lose the day yesterday, but then I decided screw that. Work is going to wait for me whether I get to it today or tomorrow. I really appreciate you helping me and I'm going to take the time to show you. Well, unless you already had plans for the day. Then I can hit the road once I change my tire."

"Stay. I enjoy your company." Butch said it faster than he meant to. He prepared to backpedal when he noticed her wide-eyes.

Color tinted her cheeks. She tried to hide it by ducking her head. "That's the nicest thing anyone's ever said to me. I enjoy your company, too."

Pretty, vivacious, smart. Butch couldn't believe her. Every one of those boys last night had to say something sweet to her. She hadn't hidden from them, the way she did now.

The front door slammed, and Hyde called out. "Butch? Kate? Y'all here?"

"Kitchen," Butch yelled back. "You eat yet? I can put on a few more eggs."

"Nah, I'm good. Well, maybe a glass of juice." He poured a glass and leaned against the counter. "I took a look at your car."

"Did you find a spare?" Kate asked.

"I did but I'm afraid it's not gonna get you back on the road. When the tire shredded, it damaged the wheel well. Even with the spare, you can't drive her."

Butch watched Kate's face fall. All the expression

leached out, leaving her blinking. Butch squeezed her hand, letting her know he wasn't going to abandon her. "Can you fix it, Hyde?"

Hyde nodded. "I'll tow her back to my garage and see what we got. I'll have to work her in around my other customers. Likely take a few days."

"She's my baby, Hyde. I'll pay for the parts and labor to get her fixed right." Kate squeezed Butch's hand, turning her gaze to him. "Can I ask you for another favor? Would you drive me to my motel? I can catch a ride to work and then use my company truck. I brought the Shelby down for after hours, not as my primary vehicle."

Kate held on and Butch didn't believe she did that often. He didn't think she noticed they held hands but she didn't hesitate to turn to him. Her trust and confidence soothed his damaged ego. "No problem. Hyde, what do we need to do?"

"I brought the tow truck so I can take her now. Anything you want out of her?"

Kate pulled her hand back and sighed. "Those boxes. I guess we shouldn't have bothered to re-pack them."

The second floor of the old house contained four bedrooms and a single bath. Butch slept in the largest room his first night home but the sun lit the eastern-facing room and made sleeping through the early morning hours impossible. He did his best song writing after the sun set and had no interest in being awake before lunch. The second night, he slept in a smaller but western-facing bedroom and made the biggest room his studio.

With a pencil in his mouth, he picked out the melody he heard in his head. He had to get it out. The tune rattled around his brain like a pinball game, lighting up cortexes and lobes as it tried to find an out. He picked a few bars, then scribbled on the lined music sheets. Pencil back in mouth, he re-picked the bars, then added another couple notes to the sheet. Working and reworking weren't chores. They were joys.

Creaks and footfalls came from the stairway, announcing company. No one snuck up those stairs. Butch had tried and Jeb before him, but you couldn't get from bottom to top without stepping in at least one spot that ratted you out.

Trudy stepped into the room in a sunny pink dress. "Morning, Butchy. I didn't think you'd be up this early."

Just hours after Butch returned to Tennessee, Trudy appeared on his doorstep. She had been out visiting a friend when she saw his truck. The California plate stuck out, even if the truck didn't. Trudy came by most days just to check on him. She did that, took the time to check on people. He often wondered why she chose to be single. She had offers, Butch knew that because he'd gotten his shoulder cried on, figuratively speaking, when Trudy said no. If she had an aversion to a husband, she had a good reason for it. Her childhood had too many nightmares and not enough fairy tales. It had been a blessing of sorts when her father fell into the creek, drunk, and drowned. Trudy had been fifteen.

Butch stretched his back, still sore from the night on the floor. "What time is it?" The room didn't have a clock. It didn't have a bed or a phone. It did have three guitars, an equal number of music stands, one amplifier, a folding chair, a torn up bar stool, and a table covered with paper, picks, and capos.

"Just ten. Do you want to head into town with me today?" Trudy made herself at home, looking over his shoulder at the music.

The music demanded his full attention. The lines of the paper beckoned him with a siren's call. "I need to do this. Then I need to help Katie."

Trudy tapped the toe of her patterned pump on the bare floor. "She's still here?"

"For a bit. I'm going to take her to her motel later." Then he would ask her out. He didn't think she'd say no. She said she liked his company. And she blushed when she said it. That was genuine.

"Well, good. The last thing you need is a woman like her around."

Butch focused on Trudy. "A woman like her?"

Trudy rolled her eyes. "People who aren't from here have, well, different values. Look at Tessa and Fawn. Neither of them understood God, family, and country."

Butch dismissed her with a shake of his head and looked back at his music. "If you left our little corner of the world every now and then you'd find that people everywhere are more the same than not, God, family, and country included."

Trudy flicked the idea away. "Everything I've ever needed is right here. Same for you. You just haven't realized it yet."

Butch turned the discussion off. Trudy long held the opinion that the useful world ended at the Tennessee border. Before his marriage to Fawn, Butch had flown Trudy, Hyde, and a few others to a concert in Atlanta. The hustle of a big city, even a Southern big city, did nothing to change Trudy's opinion. Eventually, Butch stopped trying. He had better things to do than bounce his head off a brick wall.

Trudy flicked the pages from the music stand. "You're tuning me out. If that's the way you're gonna be, you can just walk me out."

"Damn it, Trudy." Butch gathered the sheets from the floor, set them aside and hustled Trudy out of the room, wanting his quiet back. He walked her down the stairs, knowing it was the fastest way to get her going, his head already turning back to the music. She talked at him, her voice nothing but white noise behind the melody that had all but finished. On his front porch, she popped to her toes and kissed his cheek. His friend could frustrate him, but she also charmed him. Trudy cared as few did.

"Enjoy the day. See ya soon."

"You will. I promise." With that, Trudy walked down the two stone steps and across to the small car parked on the gravel drive.

Butch didn't wait for her to back out but went into the house for something to drink. He stood at the counter, filling a glass with sweet tea when gleeful barking erupted from the barn. The overweight Lab chased a ball that bounced randomly over the gravel. Pleased to have caught the ball, the dog trotted back into the barn only to run back out moments later in pursuit again.

Butch filled another glass with the sweet drink and brought it to Kate. The barn floor was clean, but not so the woman who had put the array of parts back together. Kate sat on the floor wearing jeans, a once-white T-shirt, and grease smears. She had one on the side of her nose where it must have itched.

"How's it coming?" Butch offered her the glass.

"Perfect timing. I was just cleaning up." She climbed to her feet, accepted the glass, and drank down three healthy swallows. "My god, that's good. Are you ready for the moment of truth?"

"What truth?"

"The truth of whether I put it together correctly."

"You have doubts?"

Kate chuckled. "Not really. Lack of confidence isn't one of my issues. Let's start her up."

Butch climbed onto the tractor and did the honors. The engine turned over, sounding happy to see him. "What did you do? It sounds great."

Kate petted the tractor with nearly the same affection she showed the dog. "I figured as long as I had it apart, I'd do a mini-tune up."

"Let's go for a ride." Butch held out his hand, inviting her to join him. A ride would be fun and give them time alone to get comfortable with each other. He watched the emotions play across her face. Hesitation first, then intrigue, and finally curiosity.

"Can I drive?"

"Later. Let me show you the farm first."

Kate ignored his hand, climbing up on her own and stopping as she realized the situation. "Where should I sit?"

Butch patted his lap. "Only one place to sit, unless you're chicken."

The challenge wiped the fear from those sapphire eyes. She sat on his left thigh, her feet between his. She shifted on his lap, finding a comfortable position.

Butch hadn't thought this through. He wanted to get closer to her, getting her comfortable with him in close proximity. That required him being comfortable with her in close proximity, which was getting harder by the second. Butch took a deep breath, filling his senses with the strawberry scent that surrounded her.

Kate shouted over the engine. "Is something wrong? Am I too heavy?"

Butch reached around her to the steering wheel, trapping her in. "I was just waiting on you to get settled."

Butch put it in gear, and they rolled out of the barn and around to the dirt road that ringed the property. The black Lab abandoned the ball to follow.

Kate looked around the small cab, reaching for knobs that controlled the hydraulics.

Butch slapped at her hands. "No touching."

She frowned but didn't reach again. "Doesn't it go faster?"

"Sure, but there's something to be said for taking your time."

"That something is that it's freaking slow." She put her foot over his and pressed.

The tractor lurched forward, giving them both a good knock. "Stop that."

"When can I drive?"

"Later. McCormicks have farmed this land since the 1800s. The crops have changed, the farm has grown, but this place has always been ours."

Kate listened to the history of the land Butch loved. He never actually said he loved it, but he didn't have to. It was there in every building and tree and rock that had a story. Butch had a way of talking that drew her in. She wanted to know what his crazy great-uncle did during that full moon. She cared about the men who worked the land while their sons fought a war a world away.

Butch parked the tractor close to a pond fed by the creek that cut through the property. It had rained two days prior, leaving the pond filled high and the low spots in the road muddy. Kate extracted herself from Butch's lap and hopped to the ground. It was an experience, riding like that. Being that close made her heart and stomach flutter. She worried that he noticed what he did to her, but how could he know that whenever his hand brushed against her, a thousand butterflies batted their wings?

"My grandfather built this pond and stocked it. My grandmother complained about him running off to God knew where to fish, so he built this pond. That way, she knew exactly where he was. Do you fish?"

"I'm not much of an outdoors girl. We didn't camp or any of that kind of stuff."

Butch took her hand, leading her out onto the wood pier. "Maybe we'll try it. There's nothing like camping out under the stars."

Kate didn't know what to make of the comment. She didn't expect to see him after today, so why talk about anything beyond dinner? "Maybe," she said noncommittally before changing the subject. "What kind of fish do you stock? Anything that tastes good?"

Butch rattled off a list of fish that Kate had never heard of, offering to take her fishing.

"Maybe," she said again. "Can we walk? It's such a pretty day. I don't get to just be outside too often."

As if understanding English, the dog raced ahead down a footpath.

Butch took her elbow and led the way. "You never did say what you do for a living."

"I'm an architect."

Butch cocked his head as though the answer surprised him. It forever frustrated her that it didn't surprise anyone when Tom said he was an engineer, but when she said she was an architect, people acted like they didn't know what the word meant.

"What? You've never met a female architect before?"

Butch stroked her arm. "Don't get ruffled. I don't know that I've ever met any architect, male or female."

She backpedalled, physically and verbally. "Sorry. I thought you thought, uh, sorry."

Butch took her wrist and tugged, giving her no option but to walk with him again. "I expected you to do something mechanical."

"Oh. I've always loved tinkering with machines, but buildings are my passion. The idea that something I imagine today will be around hundreds of years just, well, fascinates me. Like your house."

"Not much to look at."

Kate bumped into him, admonishing his disrespect. "Don't you dare talk about her that way. She's strong and beautiful with twice as much grace as ninety percent of the houses built today."

Butch bumped her harder, using the grip on her wrist to pull her back. "I've always thought of the house as a 'her,' too. Do you design homes?"

Kate twisted her wrist, gaining her freedom but then

lamented the loss. Could she reach out and take his hand? He had taken hers, so he probably wouldn't protest. But she couldn't. Her hand wouldn't move. "No. My company, Riley Architects and Engineers, specializes in commercial, industrial, and institutional buildings."

"You have a partner? His name is Tom?"

Kate nodded. "He's a major pain in the ass. He has been his whole life."

"Why are you with him?"

"When he's not a pain in the ass, he's brilliant."

Spring raged around them in brilliant greens. Birds called through the air, creating a tapestry of sound. The black Lab, whose name she now knew was Bullet, but she'd come to think of as Chubsy, added to the sounds by rustling under the brush and bramble.

The path followed along the creek until a drop off, where it turned and connected back to the road. Kate could see the tractor a short walk away, but a mud puddle the width of the road and just as long stood in between. A perfect spot for a little fun.

Kate bumped Butch with her shoulder. "Betcha I can clear that puddle better than you."

Butch snorted. "That's not a puddle, it's a pond."

"Chicken? Loser buys lunch." Ten feet from the edge of the water, Kate made ready to run.

"You're on. You first."

Kate shook her head. "Together."

Butch matched her at the starting line. "On the count of three. One…two…three!"

Chapter Three

Feet digging into the soft earth, they both bolted from the starting line. One step before the leap, Kate stopped. She saw that instant of confusion when he tried to stop, but he was too far committed, and the ground too soft. He slid into the puddle like a runner stealing second.

Covered in mud from his toes to his chest, Butch punched at the fluid surface. "You cheat!"

He looked spectacular. Raw and earthy and riled.

"I don't know what you're pissed about. You won. I'm buying lunch." She couldn't keep up the innocent act and broke into laughter. She picked her way around the edge of the puddle, looking for high ground. "It's supposed to be good for you. I hear spas charge a lot of money to wallow in mud."

Instead of looking for the high ground, she should have been looking for the hand that snaked over. "Then, why don't you join me?"

And just like that, she flew sideways into the puddle. The afternoon temperatures had reached a comfortable seventy degrees, but the water temperature crested closer to fifty.

"Bastard!" The cold water shocked her warm skin. Instinct made her pop up, but gravity put her right back in the water. The harder she fought, the wetter she got and the harder she laughed.

Butch sat at the edge of the puddle, his back to the winter wheat growing in the spring sun. Kate thought he looked a little too clean.

"I know what you're thinking. Don't."

Kate put on the innocent face she'd perfected as a teen. "What?"

"Kate. Katie. I'm serious."

Kate launched herself at Butch, wrapping her muddy arms around his shoulders. He rolled them into the wheat, alternating laughing and cursing her.

"You muddy…little…brat."

Chubsy ran thought the wheat, hopping around their prone bodies, barking his head off.

"Busted," Kate said, filled with so much joy she couldn't contain it.

Butch stood first and offered her a hand. "I can't believe you did that."

Their hands slipped, but Butch caught her wrist and pulled her to her feet. "I can't believe you fell for that."

Butch swatted her behind. "I'm going to have to keep my eye on you."

Butch leaned against the counter, ankles and arms crossed, as he watched the dinner preparations. Kate handled farm equipment like a pro. She couldn't skip a stone across the pond but had the arm of a left-handed relief pitcher. Put a tool or piece of equipment in her hands, and the woman moved with the air and confidence of a queen.

Here in the kitchen, she was a fish out of water.

"Is the chicken supposed to be that color? It is chicken, right?"

She wrinkled her nose and glared at the skillet. "Of course it's chicken. Haven't you ever heard of blackened?"

"Blackened is not the same as burned."

Kate covered the skillet with a lid and pointed at him with a wooden spoon. "Since when did you become the chef? This is my specialty. Don't you have farmer work to do?"

"Farmer work?"

"Aren't you a farmer?"

Here it was, the perfect opportunity to tell the truth. But what would happen then? He liked this woman. The one he washed down with the hose. The one denying dinner was burning. He just needed a little more time with her, a little more time with the real her and the real him. "I'm a songwriter. I just help my father with the farm."

Kate shifted her focus from the skillet to the pot. She used the wooden spoon to stir the red glop he suspected of being a kind of sauce.

"That's a cool job. Have you written anything I would have heard?"

"Maybe. Do you listen to country music?"

Kate shook the bottle of basil over the pot until the

mystery contents were greener than the lawn. "I don't listen to much music at all. Sometimes the guys will have the radio on in the trailer, but I never really notice it."

Butch winced when she took up the salt shaker. "We grew up with music in the house. My mother plays piano, and my father sings. Jeb and I both have played piano and guitar since we were big enough to handle the instruments."

"I grew up on construction sites. I drove a Bobcat when I was twelve. By sixteen, I was a better backhoe operator than most of the guys on my father's crew. This has about twenty minutes yet. Will you play a song for me?"

"You want to hear one of my songs?"

She adjusted the temperature on the stove. "Yes. This has to simmer for a little while so we have time."

Butch winced at the thought of the chicken "blackening" for twenty more minutes as he took her hand and led her upstairs. He sat on the bar stool and lifted his favorite guitar into his lap. Kate crossed her legs and sat tailor fashion in the middle of the floor. She rested her chin on her folded hands and looked up at him with wide, blue eyes.

Butch saw those eyes and forgot his name. He dropped his pick, fumbling it again when she handed it to him. She pulled the band from her ponytail, letting her hair fall around her shoulders like a sinful rain. The guitar slipped from his leg. Good thing the strap around his shoulder caught.

Butch swallowed a lump in his throat and began a sultry ballad accompanied by his acoustic guitar. Kate never looked away. Those amazing eyes focused on him so intently he nearly forgot the words. He sang to her, willing her to understand that the words he sang, he sang just for her.

When he finished, she sprang to her feet. "You are

amazing! How are you not, like, King of Nashville?"

His fingers picked out another tune. He sang with a joy he hadn't felt in a long time, fueled by the carefree happiness displayed as his audience spun in circles in the intimate space.

The alarm on Kate's phone rang. "Time flew, didn't it? You are amazing. I can't believe you haven't won an Oscar or Tony. Which one is for music?"

"A Grammy." He knew, because he had one. Vegas had good odds on him getting another.

"Yeah. A Grammy. Come on, let's eat dinner."

They set the kitchen table with white cloth, real napkins, two red candles, and the good glasses. The sunlight waned as night began to rise, providing a backdrop of cotton ball clouds for the candlelight dinner.

Kate plated the chicken and pasta at the stove and set the two dishes on the pretty table.

Butch opened the bottle of wine and generously wet the glasses. "This is nice."

"It makes me feel like a grown up, eating off of something you don't throw away." Katie accepted her glass. "What should we drink to?"

He raised his glass to the things that brought her to him. "Construction zones, wrong turns, and flat tires."

She guffawed and raised her glass high. "Your granddad's sign, a John Deere tractor, and a mud puddle the size of Delaware."

Glass kissed glass. Lips touched glass while gazes met.

"I hope you're hungry," Kate said. "I made enough for you to have leftovers for a few days."

Butch inspected the green-speckled sea of red on his

plate. He poked at the rubbery lump of flesh, wondering how something could be raw and burned at the same time, and stabbed at the pile of mushy pasta with his fork.

Kate sliced the bread that had come from the bakery. "It's not a field mouse, and you're not a cat. Stop playing with your food and eat it."

Butch raised his eyes. "You first, Katie."

"Chicken." Kate put the bit of chicken into her mouth. She chewed once, twice, and snapped the napkin from the table to discreetly spit out the wad of macerated flesh.

Butch roared with laughter. "Your specialty, huh?"

Kate rolled her eyes and blushed. "I'm better at building things."

"Come on, Chef Boyardee, I'll buy you dinner before I take you to your motel."

"You'll buy me dinner?"

"Yeah, well, don't get your hopes up too high. All you're getting is mediocre pizza and cold beer."

Kate gave him a dazzling smile. "A vast improvement. I'll provide the stimulating conversation."

Kate delivered, regaling him with colorful tales from her life. She claimed to be a homebody, but her body seemed to be everywhere but home. She traveled where her work took her, collecting stories along the way. Butch listened, encouraged her, drawing out the night as long as he could.

Their easy conversation ended when he pulled into the shit hole of a motel. An inferno waited to happen in the single-story building, where half-dead scrub brush grew from wide cracks in the pavement. Litter blew like tumbleweed across the fractured asphalt, and bruised and battered vehicles lay like corpses left after a battle.

He looked at the five-and-a-half foot tall, hundred-and-nothing pound woman who held her chin up as though they parked in front of a posh salon instead of this reject from the penal system.

"You're not staying here, Katie."

"I know it's nasty, but there aren't many options. Maybe my next project will be designing a nice hotel with crown moldings and pest-free carpet."

She had to hate the roach motel. Butch couldn't imagine anyone who spoke lovingly about his old farmhouse enjoying one moment in this joint. Just looking at it made his skin crawl.

She sat in the passenger seat, a sour look on her face quickly hidden with a shrug of her shoulders. "It's not as bad as it looks."

Pride. Butch squeezed the steering wheel and shook his head. It had cost her a lot of pride to let him bring her here. "You're coming back home with me."

Kate blinked twice. "Home with you?"

"I have plenty of space." Butch looked around. "It's only a twenty-minute drive, and my house has everything."

She sat still as a statue for a long moment. "Are you serious?"

Butch looked back at the Bates Motel. "Absolutely."

In an instant, she erupted in full motion. "I'll pay rent. I can fix things. I'll do half the cooking."

"You don't have to pay rent. Hell, I don't pay rent. And you are not cooking…ever. I don't need you fixing things, either. I can hire somebody if I need to."

Kate's shoulders sagged, her hands fell into her lap, her gaze on her feet. All that life, all that energy vanished. "Then

I can't stay. I want to. I really, really do, but I have to earn my way. I can't explain it. I just have to. Sorry."

The respect Butch had for her grew ten times in that moment. Since he had "made it big," too many people were too ready to let him pick up the bill. He'd gotten used to it along the way. Otherwise, it wouldn't have surprised him that Kate would need to stand on her own.

"All right. I started a list for myself. I'll appreciate any help you can give me. But just so we understand each other, you're welcome without it."

She snapped her face toward him. Her blues eyes wide and shining. "Thanks. Thank you." She leaned into him and laid a shy kiss on his jaw.

Butch inhaled her scent as she leaned in close. Strawberries. She smelled like summer strawberries, and dear Lord, he was hungry.

"You're welcome." That soft kiss went all the way to his toes. He ran his hand up and down her smooth arm, soothing his need. "Let's get your things."

Kate unlocked the door with a little shimmying, opened it, and flipped on the lights.

"Holy shit! How long have you been living here?" Twenty bucks a night would have been too much for the dump of a room. Every piece of mismatched furniture was broken or dented, and the fluorescent light in the bathroom flickered like a bug zapper in July.

"About three months." Kate stuffed files into a paper box. "Glamorous, isn't it?"

"I'm going to need a tetanus shot." Butch lifted her suitcase from where she had stacked it on an inverted chair.

Kate hauled another suitcase from a precarious position

on the top of the television. "Another Slice of Heaven shot should take care of anything out to get you."

He stacked her file folders on top and hooked the door open with his foot. "Good idea. You're buying."

The Sly Dog was indeed a slice of Heaven, even if Kate did stick with bottled beer having names she recognized. Sunday brought out a smaller crowd, but the band kept the place hopping. Trudy and Hyde sat with a couple Kate met the night before. Eyebrows lifted when she walked in with Butch. He wanted to keep it quiet that she would be staying with him. With his divorce proceedings starting, he expected the eye of public opinion to be watching him, and didn't want her dragged into it. Kate argued that paying him rent would keep everything above board, but Butch wouldn't have any of it. So they concocted the true story that Butch would be driving Kate to work in the morning where she would get a company truck.

None of his friends believed it. Kate saw it in their faces. They all thought she and Butch were sleeping together. She looked at the strong jaw and dusty blue eyes and didn't mind the rumor. It elevated her stock, the thought that she could have a man like Butch.

The talking faded when Angie joined the table. She dressed for attention in a fuzzy white sweater and paisley leggings. A bright pink scarf wrapped twice around her throat brought attention to her face.

"Butch," she said, making it three syllables. "Can I have a word with you?"

"No," Trudy said. "The word is no."

Butch sighed heavily but stood. "Trudy, stop it. Angie, there's nothing to talk about."

"Just a word," she asked again, leading him away from the table.

Kate couldn't hear the conversation, but she could read the body language. Butch started standing tall and proud, but minute by minute, he shrank until he looked like a boy facing his teacher. Whatever weight Angie had, she threw. Butch needed help. He needed three seconds of courage.

Kate moved behind Angie's shoulder where Butch could see her. She stood there, silently, repeatedly puffing her cheeks out like a bullfrog. Butch smiled and, in that moment, remembered himself. He struck a Superman pose.

Of course, Angie turned around and busted her. "You, you, you interfering little—"

"Enough, Angie." Butch stepped away from Angie, capturing Kate's wrist in passing. "I said no. How are you at darts, Katie?"

"Better than I am at cooking."

They threw a game, but Butch's heart wasn't in it. Kate saw him repeatedly looking over his shoulder like lightning might strike at any moment. He needed a distraction.

Kate pulled the darts from the board and held them. "What do you say we make this interesting? A friendly wager?"

Those dusty blues snapped to her. "I've seen your idea of a bet."

"Then you know I mean what I say. Let's make this interesting."

Butch rolled his eyes. "Twenty bucks?"

Kate snorted. "If I win, you get up on stage and sing 'I'm a Little Tea Pot.'"

Butch's eyes flashed wide, then that slow smiled she loved shone through. "If I win, you have to do the 'Hokey Pokey.'"

She winced. She had planned to throw the game to give his ego a stroke, but the "Hokey Pokey", alone, in the middle of a bar full of strangers? That was so far outside the comfort zone, it wasn't even in the same zip code.

"Chicken?"

"You're going down, big man."

They didn't talk. With stakes this high, they kept their focus where it needed to be. He led. She led. She gave him a good game, but in the end, she stood, sweaty palms and all, in front of the stage and the band.

B utch read the fear in her eyes. She looked at the door but didn't run. He wasn't sure he wouldn't have made a break for it if the darts had gone the other way. He'd do what he could to make this good for her.

Butch jumped up on the stage and spoke with the band. "Hey, boys, I need a favor. I'm going to call 'The Hokey Pokey.' Will ya back me?"

The band members grinned at one another, then back at Butch. The lead guitarist answered. "Sure, Butch. Anything you want."

Butch took the mic and called out loud and proud. "How y'all doin' tonight?" Cheers and clapping answered. "We're going to do a little throw back number. Back, like way back, to elementary school. Girls, grab your guys and get ready for a little Hokey Pokey."

The band played as a circle formed with Kate on the side where Butch could see her. Twenty women and a handful of men stood elbow to elbow when Butch began to call. "You put your right leg in, you put your right leg out—your other right, Cordell, that's it—you put your right leg in, now shake it like that leg hound of yours is on it. That's right. Do the Hokey Pokey, and you turn yourself around. That's what it's all about. Left leg, that's your other right, Cordell." The laughter grew as the rounds went on. Butch kept his eye on Kate. In the middle of mass humiliation, she hammed it up, getting as silly as everyone else. "You put your backside in, you put your backside out. You put your backside in, and you shake it all about. Come on, Katie. Shake that backside. Shake it like you mean it. Drop it like it's hot!"

Kate shook her tight little butt six inches from the floor to a round of applause. Then she blew him a kiss.

"That's my girl." Butch shook his head at her antics. "Come on, y'all, bring it home. That's what it's all about!"

The joint roared with approval. It wasn't every night you got old school funky with a performer of Butch's caliber. He shook hands with each member of the band. "Can I ask another favor? Play a slow one?"

"You got it, Butch," the lead guitarist said.

The audience engulfed Butch when he jumped off the stage. Kate had drifted to the back of the room, watching as couples met on the dance floor. It took several minutes for Butch to wade through the handshakes and hugs to reach her.

"That was some mighty fine Hokey Pokey-ing."

Kate bowed her head with mock graciousness. "Thank you. I was a champion Hokey Pokey-er in my preschool class. So tell me, did you enjoy your win?" Her eyes twinkled, and her hair hung in frizzed ringlets down her back.

The silly stunt filled the dark and cold corners of Butch's heart with laughter. "I did. It was more interesting than taking twenty off you. Come here." He pulled her to the center of the dance floor.

"Where are we going?"

"Here." He tugged until she fell into his arms and held her close when she stood awkwardly in his embrace. "You're supposed to relax when you dance."

She took three steps backward with Butch following. "I don't know how to dance."

"It's easy. The first thing to know is that the man leads. I step, you follow. Not vice versa." He took three steps backward, putting them back in the middle of the floor.

She pushed at his chest. "You're too close. I can't see my feet."

"You're not supposed to see your feet. You're supposed to look at me. Put your arms around me. Most women put their arms around a man's neck, but I'm willing to explore any more interesting ideas you might have."

Color crept into Kate's face, but she slid her hands up his chest until they reached the back of his neck.

"Now sway back and forth with me." He pressed his hips against her stomach, showing her which way he wanted to go.

She lifted her chin. "I'm going to step on your feet."

Butch dipped his head and captured her words. Her soft lips opened with a gasp. Butch made the brief kiss sweet, intimate. He didn't push her for more but cradled her to his chest, showing his growing affection. Her hands had tightened on his neck, her whole body stopped moving. He stroked the lines of her back, the curves of her waist and hips while humming the ballad in her ear, swaying in time. The closeness had other effects. His body hardened, wanting more, but Butch focused on Katie. By the time the bridge ended, she rewarded his patience by melting in his embrace. Her soft curves followed his hard lines. When the song ended, he tipped her chin up and kissed her forehead, her nose, and her lips.

"You taste as sweet as summer strawberries."

She stepped back and reached to smooth her hair.

Butch caught that nervous hand and brought it to his mouth. The contrast in Katie intrigued him, challenged him to discover the real woman. On the surface, she wore the skin of a quick-witted, exuberant woman. But beneath lived a shy woman who blushed at a compliment and looked on the verge of running.

"I…I don't think this is a good idea." She tugged at her captured hand.

Butch held that hand to his heart. "What, honey?"

"I'm your roommate. That makes this…"

Butch raised an eyebrow, challenging her to finish her thought. A shout of his name from across the room caught his attention. "Looks like you won a reprieve. Don't disappear on me. Remember, I'm your ride home." He kissed her knuckles before releasing her hand.

The second Butch's back turned, Kate ran to the only sanctuary a woman had: the ladies' room. She rushed into a stall and sat on the seat, fully clothed. *What happened?* She intended the whole Hokey Pokey thing to be a gag to pick up Butch's spirits. She'd overshot. By several states.

What was he thinking, kissing her? She really wanted to know, because her brain stopped working when she felt that soft weight on her lips. Then his hips started moving, and she felt a different kind of weight pressed into her belly.

This was a bad idea. A bad, bad, bad idea. He flirted with her! What was he thinking?

Not that she completely hated it. Butch did more than make her heart go pitter patter. She liked his mouth, liked his lips on her, liked his voice in her ear.

But that wasn't the point, was it? They had a...contract. An implied but firm contract. They were roommates with chores performed in exchange for room and board.

She liked his home. Doing the chores would be more like play than work. Maybe they would work together. If it was warm enough, he could do it with his shirt off.

No no no no no!

Yes!

She had to think what could happen if this went anywhere.

Kate jerked to her feet and pushed open the stall door. She needed to be outside. She needed space to think.

"You!" Venom poured out with the word. Angie Mc-Cormick stalked across the tile floor, her heels clicking with each step. The pretty pin-up face mutated into that of a bitter, lonely woman. The lines carved in the carefully applied makeup showed the years over thirty Angie tried to erase.

Her finger in Kate's chest, she spoke through a tight mask of hatred. "You have no right interfering in Butch McCormick's business."

Over Angie's shoulder, Kate saw Trudy come into the restroom.

Trudy stilled for a moment, looked at the scene, and frowned. "Neither do you." She yanked on Angie's arm, spinning her away from Kate.

Kate planted her feet, ready to defend herself. Angie stepped to the side, opening up room between the two of them. Standing three paces apart, Angie and Trudy had eyes only for each other.

Angie pitched forward, jabbing her index finger toward Trudy. "This is none of your business either, Trudy. You think you're something special? You are nothing but a cheap groupie. You've always been jealous of me."

Trudy looked at Angie's tightly stretched shirt. "The only thing cheap here is your boob job."

Angie's face flushed with color. She trembled with the insult but didn't respond, verbally or otherwise. Then the door pushed opened, and two denim-clad women entered, laughing about the Hokey Pokey. Angie darted behind the women, catching the door before it closed. She narrowed her eyes at Trudy. "One of these days, you're going to get yours."

Chapter Four

Kate knelt next to an iron-framed bed. She blew lightly across a cup of coffee, the steam teasing the hair that laid across Butch's cheek. His eyelashes fluttered. He inhaled deeply and exhaled a slow, satisfied sigh. Kate crept closer to the bed and blew again. Butch rolled toward her, and the elaborate quilt slid to his waist. His arm fell off the bed, landing heavily on her thigh.

Kate blew the steaming coffee a third time, and he inhaled again; this time his lashes lifted.

His hazy eyes, open to the narrowest of slits, roamed over her face. "What are you doing?"

"Waking you. I made coffee. Coffee worth waking up for."

"What time is it?" Butch asked, his voice thick with sleep.

"Six thirty."

Butch groaned and rolled away from her, draping his

arm over his eyes. "In the morning?"

"Of course in the morning. I thought farm boys were all about 'early to bed, early to rise.'" When he curled into the quilt, Kate sat on the edge of the bed and sipped the coffee. "Come on, lazy bones. You're driving me to work this morning, remember?"

Butch twisted to look at her. "It's still night. The damned rooster isn't even up yet." On cue, a rooster crowed from behind the house. Butch kicked at the quilt like a grumpy child, coming to stand in front of her as rumpled as the bed he'd left. "It's a conspiracy. A goddamned conspiracy. That better be a freaking great cup of coffee."

Kate stood, protecting the coffee as the blankets flew. She sipped as she appraised the twisted sleep pants, the mess of hair, the narrow eyes, and broad shoulders. Definitely not a morning person. She thought she might have to make a habit of waking him just to see that twist to his mouth. "I've been accused of a lot of things, but never conspiring with a cock." She handed him the appeasing cup, her gaze racing over the picture he made, so she could take another look when she had a few minutes to herself.

He sipped the coffee, groaning deep in his throat. "That's good. Aren't you full of surprises? What's in this?"

"It's a coveted family secret. How long until you'll be ready to go?"

He swallowed half the cup. "Ten minutes. Maybe less if you make me a cup to go."

"Consider it done."

Better than his word, Butch stumbled down the stairs five minutes later. A baseball hat with a stitched guitar on it contained his curly hair. He wore the shirt he'd worn the night before but inside out. Rumpled jeans and cowboy boots finished the package. "You ready?"

Kate nodded, handing over a silver travel mug. "Your shirt is inside out. How did you button it that way?"

He answered by stripping the button-down shirt over his head, which turned it right side out, and pulling it back on like a T-shirt.

"Interesting approach."

Butch sipped the hot coffee. "No point getting fancy. I'm going back to bed as soon as I get you off and running." He went into the kitchen and retrieved his keys and phone from the counter. He shoved his phone in his pocket and tossed the keys at Kate. "You're driving."

The rising sun painted a sky no camera could capture, but Kate missed it. Her sharp eyes focused on landmarks and crossroads to make sure she could find her way back again. She turned left where Butch's road teed into a state route. In the field at the intersection, a lone bull faced east, basking in the early morning sun.

"Have you ever ridden a live bull?" she asked.

Butch shook his head. "I've always thought riding the mechanical one was stupid enough. My brother Jeb did it once, though."

"Just once?"

Butch nodded and laughed. "He broke his arm."

Kate wondered at his sense of humor. "Why is that funny?"

"Jeb couldn't have been nineteen, trying to impress a girl. His legs went all wonky after he got thrown. A stick figure of a rodeo clown tried to get him out, but Jeb wouldn't cooperate. God knows what he was thinking. The clown finally got Jeb out of the ring and then cold cocked him. Jeb flipped over a pile of gear and came up with a broken arm. Then Mama got ahold of him. I told him riding a bull was a stupid way to impress girls. Better to go with flowers."

"Flowers are a classic for a reason. Speaking of bulls, I liked your bar, even if the bull was out of commission. You have good friends, but they don't think much of your ex, Angie."

Butch sighed. "She's never liked the Sly Dog. She only comes out to corner me. It's not a fun life, but it is predictable."

"Was she serious about wanting to vaccinate snakes?" Kate saw his reflection nod. "I support environmental efforts. This building will be LEED certified, which means it's being constructed in a sustainable manner. There is actually a big role in architecture for sustainable and environmental stewardship...but vaccinating snakes is a new one for me. Is that a Tennessee thing?"

"More like an Angie thing. We were high school sweethearts. I had just turned eighteen when she got pregnant. We married a week after graduating high school. She lost the baby before the end of that summer. At eighteen, we were just too damned young."

Kate couldn't imagine being married now, let alone at that age. "When I was eighteen, I was executing my great escape from my family."

"Where did you escape to?"

"New York City. Columbia University."

"So it worked?"

"I'm here, aren't I? Well, here we are. Work sweet work." Kate steered the pickup truck through the gate and across the uneven ground to an enclave of trailers in one corner of the site.

Butch had seen dozens of construction sites, many from the window of a car as his life raced by at thirty-five to seventy miles an hour. He'd never given more than a passing thought about what happened on the other side of the fence. Like Alice through the looking glass, he put one foot down on that gravel and dirt surface and found himself in another world. Through the fence, he saw the world he lived in, exactly two hundred feet and a world away. The world on this side of the fence towered ten times larger than life. Tires on machinery stood taller than a man. The earth had been torn open, and from her womb rose a steel frame that juxtaposed elegance with brute strength.

He whistled long and low as he came around to the back of his truck. He lowered the tailgate and pulled out the boxes that had been in Kate's trunk. "I never thought much about how you built a building."

Kate worked next to him, taking the boxes and stacking them against the trailer. "From the bottom up. Come on inside. I'll get you another cup of coffee and give you a tour."

Butch followed Kate up five steps and into the triple-wide, white trailer. He'd been in trailers before. Some of his best friends grew up in double-wides, but nothing like this. This trailer specialized in business. High-tech business. A desk with a flat screen computer monitor and a vase of dying flowers greeted visitors just inside the trailer door. Five folding chairs claimed space around a small conference table to the left, and across from it, four cubicles made a hallway to an office with a door.

Kate tugged on his sleeve and led him through the space. "That's my office." She entered the room at the end of the hall, tossed her bag onto the cluttered desktop, and gestured to the corner. "There she is."

A scale model of an expansive but graceful structure stood proudly on a round table under the window. Butch bent close, and his gaze followed his fingers over the elegant curves that reminded him of soft ripples in the stream on the farm. "It looks like water, the way it flows."

"That's exactly what I was going for. Exactly." She mirrored his pose, grinning ear to ear. "Do you want to see the real thing?"

Her broad smile, open and honest, told Butch what Kate hadn't said aloud. She took pride in her work, this work. He remembered the nerves that beset him when he played for her, sharing his passion, and wondered if she felt the same.

Kate handed Butch a hard hat and put her own on, threading her ponytail through until her hair fell down her back and her hat sat on her head. She pulled on a neon-yellow vest and handed him a matching one. "Ready?"

His hat stuffed into his back pocket and outfitted to match, Butch gave a sharp nod. "Lead on."

Kate gestured wildly as she led him through the acres of construction. Her energy and excitement for the work radiated out as she took the time to explain details of the art and science that would make this building stand for generations.

As they rounded the corner and returned to the trailer, Kate pointed to the names painted proudly on the side of the white trailer. "Tom and I started our own architecture

and engineering firm two years ago. The concept for the Cicada building is mine. Tom is the structural engineer. Now
I manage the construction from here and work with my father's crews while Tom manages the engineering in Michigan. Well, that's the tour. What do you think?"

Butch couldn't help being impressed, even if he had to
hear about Tom. As the day broke around them, men in denim and plaid with reflective vests and hard hats huddled in
groups near the trailer. Kate greeted them, many by name,
as she walked Butch back to his truck. The seasoned veter-
ans eyed the newcomer whose smooth soles of his favorite boots slid off the rocky surface, causing him to side step
more than once. Most didn't spare him a second thought, but
a few stared, as if trying to place him. Butch stripped off the
vest and handed it and the hard hat back to Kate. He quickly
pulled his hat from his pocket and put it back on his head.

"I thought I understood what was going on here. Now
I understand there's a lot more to understand. This is…
impressive." He reached for Kate's hand.

She beamed at his compliment but took a half-step
back, swatting his hand away. "No hand holding on the job."

In an instant, Kate had changed from open and warm to
closed and guarded. Butch crowded her, pushing that invisible line of hers. "Does that mean no kiss good-bye?"

She bit her lip as if considering it. "Will you take an
I.O.U?"

He looked to the bluing sky, pinching his chin in consid-
eration. "Well, now, if I do that, I'll have to charge you interest. Where's your marker?"

"You don't think I'm good for it?" Kate shook her head
at him then picked up a piece of gravel. She brushed most

of the dirt off on her vest and put the rock in Butch's hand. "How's that?"

Butch held the rock between two fingers and examined it. "You have twenty-four hours before interest starts accumulating. I'm going to get out of your way now. You do what you do best, and I'll do what I do best."

"I'm not going to ask what the interest rate is. What are you going to do today, Mr. Songwriter?"

"Go back to bed. No one in their right mind is up this time of day." Butch opened his truck door, and slid onto the seat. "Are you going to remember the way home?"

"You mean your house? Yes. It wasn't that hard. I'll call you if I get turned around."

"Kate. Kate." A short little woman in work boots and jeans shuffled across open ground to join Kate outside the truck door.

"Good morning, Paula," Kate said. "This is my friend, Butch. Butch, this is my administrative assistant, Paula."

Paula gave Butch a polite nod, dismissed him, then shot her wide, brown eyes back to his face.

Butch pulled his hat lower and acted normal. "It's nice to meet you, Paula. Katie, I'm going to get out of your way now. I'll see you later."

As soon as he backed away, people clustered around Kate, and her day started. She turned her back on him, quickly entrenched in the details of her project and crew, but Paula's gaze followed him until he turned onto the main road.

"Have mercy," Butch prayed out loud. "I know lying is one of the ten big ones, but this is a little lie. I told her I was a songwriter. Can't you play along for a little longer?"

Butch got his answer ten hours later when the door slammed shut with more bang than his .44 revolver.

Butch spun away from his work on his new piano and stopped cold. Kate stood in the doorway to the living room. She pointed a trembling finger at him. When she spoke, her voice cracked.

"Guess what I found out today? You are the King of Nashville. You've won Grammys and played in stadiums and have a number one song on the charts. Everyone got a big laugh that I didn't know it was *the* Butch McCormick I dragged across a dusty construction site. What I don't get is why you strung me along? You did your good deed. Why didn't you just take me to my motel and return to your superstar life?" A tear ran down her cheek. "Never mind. It doesn't matter."

Butch knew he risked anger, but he didn't anticipate the pain, the anguish displayed on her face. He'd humiliated her, and her running upstairs didn't hide it from him. Butch cursed himself as he ran up after her.

"Katie. It wasn't like that."

Kate had pulled the suitcase from under the bed and shoved her clothes in by the fistful.

"Katie, I swear to God, I didn't mean to hurt you."

Kate didn't wipe at the tears, letting them fall as she pulled the drawer full of socks and underwear from the dresser. She poured the contents into the suitcase. More landed out than in. "It doesn't matter." She picked up handful of socks and threw them at the open case.

Butch grabbed her arm and spun her to face him. "I'm sorry. I'm sorry I didn't tell you everything."

"You lied," Kate said, her teeth gnashed together. "Let

me go."

Butch refused to back away from the threat of temper. She wasn't mad, though he guessed she would have preferred that to the tears. "I didn't lie. I told you I was a songwriter. I just underplayed things a little. It's not a big deal."

"Not a big deal?" Her voice climbed up the register. She shoved his chest but didn't gain an inch. "You've got gold records…and awards…you're famous. Why would you do this? Why? What did you get out of lying to me?"

Butch let go of her arms and cradled her face in his palms. He wiped her tears with his thumbs. "I like you. I want you to like me. For me. Not because of the music thing."

Kate shook her head and stepped away. "I did like you for you. I liked you because you helped out a stranger, because you have a table full of high school friends, because you shared your mother's fried chicken, which was the best I've ever tasted. I may not have had a lot to give in return, but I did not deserve to be played like a fool."

"I didn't. I swear I didn't. Let me try to explain." Butch pulled her to him, needing to soothe away the pain he'd caused. "I love what I do. I have the best job in the world. But sometimes, people treat me differently. I came home because somewhere along the way, I lost myself. I just want to be me again. When you didn't recognize me, it was so damned liberating. You didn't have any expectations of me."

Some of the fight went out of her, softening her body against his.

"I know something about living under expectations. I wouldn't have treated you any differently. Butch? Why did you invite me to stay here?"

Butch snorted. "Like I said, that place was a hole."

Kate planted her hands on his chest and put distance between them. "I'm not a rebound girl. You're getting divorced, you're on the rebound. I'm stranded here. I'm alone."

Butch captured her hands. "I've been alone for over a year. Nothing has interested me except my music. Now here you are, and the world is full of color. You can't ask me to ignore it. I couldn't do it if I wanted to."

She tried pushing away again. "I don't think—"

"Shh, don't think," Butch gathered her close, whispered into her hair. "Nothing's going to happen that we don't both want. Just relax. Just relax against me."

Kate let her head rest on his chest. "You're still a bastard for lying to me."

"I maintain that I didn't lie and have the birth certificate to prove I'm not a bastard." Butch kissed her hair. "But I'm sorry I made you feel foolish. Let me make it up to you. What do you say?"

"How?"

Butch smiled at the wealth of suspicion in that single word.

Butch steered Kate past several tables of satisfied customers in the ice cream parlor that kept the town happy the whole hot, long summer.

"You think ice cream is going to get you out of trouble?"

"The best damned ice cream in the state of Tennessee. Maybe the country." Butch held out a chair at a table in the center of a window that looked out over the town square.

On the drive in, Kate sat quietly staring out the window

while her restless hands played with anything within reach. She held herself at a distance, not physically, but emotionally.

Butch tried to ease her into conversation "Did you have a good day?"

"Productive." Kate crossed her arms on the table. "I spoke with Cicada, and they're satisfied with the progress. There are always issues with construction, but all in all, things are moving along. They had concerns that some of your friends and neighbors are not taking to the project. They warned me to be on alert."

Butch nodded. It took sharing a ham sandwich with his father to figure out the unholy construction project his mother ranted about at dinner was Kate's dream building. The property had been farmed by the Parson family for three generations. There wouldn't be crops grown on the property again. Some people took exception to that. "Some folks around here want farmland to stay farmland."

The matronly proprietor walked toward their table, a mounded bowl of ice cream in each hand. Butch had noticed the interest Ms. Etta James took in Kate since they had walked in. Ms. Etta had a reputation as a love expert, taking credit for as many as twenty time-tested marriages.

"All right now children." Etta crossed the checkered-board floor. "Maple pecan for Butch and vanilla bean for his lady."

Kate smiled at the proprietor. "Kate. My name is Kate."

"It is good to meet you, Kate. I hope you'll bring Butch around a bit more."

"It's he who brought me around." Kate tasted the creamy, white treat flecked with vanilla bean. "This is wonderful."

"Try it with a bite of Butch's maple pecan." Etta turned

the full force of her person to Butch. "I knew those other girls weren't for you, Butch. Angie is rocky road. Rocky road and maple pecan don't go together. The second one, she was tutti fruity. The last one didn't eat ice cream. Said it would ruin her figure. As if," Etta huffed. "But this one. Well it's easy to see what's between you." She gave the pair her nod of approval and disappeared into the back room.

"She's a character." Kate ate her ice cream slowly, her gaze focusing on the small dish in front of her.

"She is. Most small towns are full of them." Butch watched Kate for a moment. "What are you thinking?"

Kate didn't look up. "She thinks we're, you know, together."

Butch could read little beyond that she wasn't happy with the implication. Why? He was a hell of a catch. All the tabloids agreed. Why did the idea of them being together bother her? "You don't like that?"

She shrugged, her eyes still down. "I'm beginning to see what you mean about people getting the wrong idea. I don't want to complicate your life."

She smoothed her hair and glanced around the room to see who might be watching. She was uncomfortable, and that was not the way Butch wanted her. He wanted her happy. It occurred to him that over the last few days, when she was happy, he was happy. Ms. Etta saw something between them. Maybe it was something as simple as happiness. Whatever this was, he hadn't gone looking for it, but he wasn't going to let it get away either.

"I think of you more as an enhancement to my life. What about you?"

She looked up finally. The doubt of self-consciousness

melted into a fragile smile. "I think of you as the ten dollars in a pair of jeans."

"What?" He laughed out loud. "Explain that one to me."

"You know, when you pulled on a pair of jeans and find ten dollars in the pocket you didn't know you had. It's a thrill."

"Okay, I think I like that, being the thrill in your life. Long as it's not a cheap thrill." Butch covered her hand with his, capturing her gaze. "We good?"

Kate set her spoon in the bowl and looked him in the eyes. "A question. How frequently do you plan on being a bastard? Because if we end up here night after night, I'm going to get as big as a cow." Kate let a slow smile warm her glacial-blue eyes.

"How about once a week, only on pretty nights made for holding hands and eating ice cream? When you finish yours, we can take a walk. Let me show you my town."

B utch took Kate's hand and tucked it into his arm. "It's a perfect evening for a walk."

"I don't think it's evening yet. We just had ice cream for dinner. What are we? Twelve?"

"It was a better dinner than I might have had."

Kate snickered. "Especially if I had cooked."

"That chicken of yours sure was…special."

She laughed. "I still don't know what went wrong."

"I do." Butch paused for dramatic effect. "Everything."

In companionable silence, they walked around the small town square. Kate's gaze absorbed the architecture of the town: the simple brick work, the framework, the gingerbread trim. If he hadn't held her hand, she would have tripped into the street a half dozen times.

"I love the gazebo," Kate said. "I don't recognize the style of the detail."

Butch steered them to the garden in the middle of the square and the ten-sided gazebo. "This dates back to the Civil War. It was first used to share news of the war. Later, wives and loved ones came here for news of soldiers. It was a tradition that carried through the world wars. Sometime after that, it became a place for lovers."

Kate climbed the three short steps onto the well-preserved wood. The posts, rails, and benches were covered in carvings. She fingered one particularly deep carving. DS+TR '68.

"My parents are over here." Butch pointed to a carving at his eye height.

"ED&JM 4Ever. How sweet."

"My father, the poet."

Kate's gazed roamed over the countless names and initials. "Are you in here?"

"Oh. No. I suppose that says something. In high school Angie and I were too busy, you know. Later, she wanted to, but things happened so fast, and then we weren't together any more. It's funny, we were together for two years of high school but didn't manage to stay married six months."

"What about the other Mrs. McCormicks?"

Butch never considered bringing Tessa, his second wife, or Fawn here. "No. They aren't here either. Tessa, ever the artist, wanted to put her initials only on her own work. And Fawn? Well, she would have laughed out loud at even the idea. She'd have called it tacky, so I never brought it up."

Kate reached out and laced her fingers through his. "I'm sorry."

The touch of her hand in his sent a jolt of awareness through Butch. Her shy little touches tied him in knots. Butch brought her fingers to his mouth. "For what?"

Her gaze focused on their joined hands. "Love lost, I guess."

"Do you have a lost love story?"

"I don't have a love story. I mean, I've spent my entire life around men. Most times I'm more comfortable around men than women, but I've never been *that* kind of girl. Usually I'm regaled to the role of the girl who is a friend, you know, the one the real girlfriend hates without reason. I had to grow a thick skin young, growing up with three rough-and-tumble boys. One time, the boys blew up my Barbie dolls with firecrackers and called me a baby when I cried. I tried to fit in. I played football and baseball and built buildings with Legos. When I was better than they were, they teased me again. I had a choice: stand up for myself or become a door mat. I chose to stand, and nearly every day since has felt like a fight. I've never had the time to write a love story."

"You don't date?" Butch nibbled at her knuckles, enjoying the way she fidgeted in reaction.

"Now and then. I had a 'girls gone wild' phase when I first went to New York. I dated some but nothing serious. I don't get asked out very often so…"

"But you're out now. With me."

She smiled up at him. "Well, look at us. Aren't we something?"

Butch had left California, had come back home, to

rediscover himself. The woman in his arms embodied beautiful, alluring. Fresh, natural, wild, she appealed to him on an elemental level. Serendipity played a role, he knew, leading Kate from Michigan to his driveway at precisely the moment he decided to join the world of the living. In the few days he'd known her, she dressed in jeans and plain shirts. Her face never had makeup, and her hair either flew wild or trailed into a ponytail. She wore simple diamond solitaires in her ears. She didn't try to impress him, and yet her every little movement held his undivided attention.

With his free hand, Butch dug into the pocket of his jeans. Kate tried to step back, but Butch kept her in place, pulling on the hand still laced with his.

She furrowed her brow. "What are you doing?"

With triumph, Butch held up the rock she'd given him that morning and he'd kept in his pocket all day. "I'm calling in your marker."

Kate leaned in to him, her gaze on his mouth. "Well, I wouldn't want to get a reputation as a welsher."

Butch lowered his head, letting her brush her lips over his. A touch more than a kiss. He intended to stand there, showing her he wouldn't ask for more than she gave, but his hands rose of their own accord to cradle her head, tipping up her chin. He pressed his lips to the corners of her mouth, her chin, her eyes, and the tip of her nose before returning to her mouth for more. The hunger in him demanded more. He nipped her lower lip, pulling her tightly against him. Kate gasped, and Butch took the opening, running his tongue along the inside of her lips. She made a small, helpless sound, like she was drowning in him. God, he hoped she was, because he was quickly becoming lost in her. She tasted even sweeter than she smelled. Oh, God, he needed more.

"This here is a family town. We got laws against this type of display."

Butch swore as Kate's body froze, pressed against his own. "I know you got something better to do than watch us, Sheriff." Butch held Kate still when she would have put space between them.

"Clyde, there is *nothing* better than busting your balls."

"Watch your language," Butch said. "There's a lady present. Katie, it looks like I have no choice but to introduce you to my brother, Jebediah. Jeb, this is Katie."

Jeb took a long, deep breath before nodding his head. "Ma'am."

"Nice to meet you, Jeb."

Butch rolled his eyes as Jeb stared Kate down. She held her own, not withering under the glare Butch had watched Jeb practice until he perfected intimidation. Jeb had the same gray eyes as Butch but had jet-black hair he wore military style. His expressionless face, more like a machine than a man, bore little resemblance to his younger brother.

Butch tucked Kate under his shoulder in a message to his brother. "You doing something besides disturbing my evening?"

Kate elbowed him and stepped away to stand on her own.

Jeb didn't take his gaze off the redhead. "Have you seen Angie around?"

"She was at the Sly Dog last night. Why?" Butch leaned against the post behind him, as Kate put a prim distance between them.

Jeb leaned against the gazebo frame, mirroring his brother's pose. "Her mother's looking for her. Angie was supposed to take her to see her sister today but never showed. She didn't call either."

"That's not like her," Butch said.

Kate inched closer to the steps. "Did you check where the snakes are?"

Jeb scowled at her. "What?"

"Her current crusade," Butch answered. "She's trying to save the Northern Pine Snake."

"Is that a real crusade?" Jeb asked.

"She thinks it is."

Jeb whacked his leg with his hat. "Oh, Christ, Butch. What did you do?"

Butch rolled his eyes. "Nothing. I did absolutely nothing."

Kate gestured in the direction of Butch's truck. "If you need to go look for her, I can find my way back to the house. I want to get started on—"

"I'll keep my eye out for Angie and tell her to call her mother if I see her. Good night, Jeb." Butch pulled Kate to his side and talked over her. He was not telling his brother Kate was living with him. He was going to get an earful as it was.

Jeb didn't change his expression, but he gave the slightest nod. "'Night, Butch. Ma'am."

"Sir," Kate said as Butch pulled her away.

Kate figured she still had about two hours of daylight left. She paced the living room as she ran down the list Butch had made. "Repair shutters. Clean gutters. Paint house. That'll take more than a few hours. Clear creek. Fix chicken coop fence. What part of the creek needs to be cleared?"

Butch sat at the piano, flexing his fingers as if to warm them up. "Back by the pond. Some trees fell in it and are blocking it. The land by it floods when it rains."

"By that big puddle we jumped over?"

"You mean wallowed in? Yes, right next to it."

"They are calling for rain later this week. I should be able to make some headway on that." Kate watched Butch's fingers play a tune she'd heard before. She wondered if he'd written it, wondered how many of his songs she knew. "The piano's new. It wasn't here yesterday."

"My manager, Landon Finch. I told him I needed a piano, and this was delivered today. I sat down, and the songs are just leaping off of the keys."

"I love days like that. It's like that old expression 'Find something you love to do, and you'll never work a day in your life.' Do you have a chainsaw and some rope?"

"Everything we need should be in the barn. Let me change, and I'll meet you out there." Butch stood but ran his fingers over the keys one more time. Obviously he wanted to be at his piano.

"Just point me in the right direction. You don't need to help."

Butch frowned. "Well, that doesn't seem right."

She cocked her head. "Do you want to go clear the stream?"

"Want to? No. But have you ever done it before?"

"Sure. I clear the horse trails on a non-profit park system every year. When it comes to this kind of work, I'm older than my years. Plus, I like it. I'll get to work off Miss Etta's ice cream while playing with power tools. What more could a girl want?"

Butch laughed. "I have so much I could teach you. But seriously, you might need help."

"I might, and if I do, I'll save it for another day. I'm proud of my 'smart girl' title. I'm not going to risk it by doing more than I know I can. I appreciate the offer, but let me do this for you. Okay?"

"Still doesn't seem right." Even as Butch said the words, he turned back to the piano. "I'll be right here if you need anything."

Kate stood behind him, listening to his music. His fingers rained up and down the keys, the notes tumbling joyously like children rolling down a hill. The tones washed over her, cleansing her. More than once, Kate had walked through construction sites when an April rain had chased everyone else indoors. Now, like then, she felt like she was the only person in a peaceful world. She swayed, mesmerized, feeling as though falling into a dream. This was his gift. This is where he needed to be.

Butch stopped playing, looking up at Kate. "Did you need something?"

"No, sorry. I'll get out of your way." She left him to his work and went to tackle her own. The big dog found Kate inside the barn and attached himself to her hip.

"If we are going to be friends, you need to give me some space. Sit." She gave his ears a good rub and went to work. Kate found the chainsaw and did a quick inspection. The chain was tight and oiled, and the fuel tank was full. Kate piled the chainsaw and coils of rope on the tractor. She retrieved her protective eyewear and ear plugs from her truck, along with the heavy leather gloves made to fit her smaller hands and the rubber boots that came up to her knees. "Are you ready to do this, Chubsy?"

The dog barked and trotted out of the barn. Kate followed in the tractor. The two rambled along the perimeter of the fields companionably until she met the small stream.

The juvenile trees cluttered the stream bank, the largest one less than half a foot in diameter. The heavy-duty chainsaw would cut through the wood like butter. Kate cut the fallen trees with practiced efficiency and used the tractor to pull the trunks up to the top of the bank to be trimmed and hauled another day. This would be enough to open the flow of the creek when the next rain came. Kate worked her way upstream toward the pond, cutting leaning trees and clearing brush. Something about the way a chainsaw made her arms hum gave her a feeling of accomplishment.

The sun hovered an inch above the horizon when Kate reached the pond. Fifteen minutes and she would be done for the night. She ran her arm across her forehead, clearing away the sheen of sweat. "I think we can do it, Chubsy. I think we can beat the sun."

Kate stepped down a steep section of slope. The rubber boots that kept her feet dry lacked the traction she needed on this section of the stream bank. Her gloved hands wrapped around branches as she lowered herself to the water's edge. A slender but tall tree had snapped and toppled across the creek. Kate secured the loose end of the rope to the ragged trunk then picked along the bank, looking for an easier climb up. Bright colors caught her eye. Something pink and stringy lay tangled in the fingers of a low branch. She took off her gloves and fingered the thick, finely woven material.

"Somebody had to be upset they lost this," Kate said aloud as she worked to unwind what became a long scarf. She stretched to her right, rising to her toes to unhitch the material when the muddy slope of the stream bank gave way under her feet. Kate scrambled for firm footing, but gravity pulled her downward. One heel caught on something, but the other didn't. Arms flailing, Kate found no hand holds and landed in the creek.

"Almost stayed dry." The cold, clean water quickly soaked into her jeans. The front of her legs were wet, the back coated in mud. Her wet hands and arms chilled in the evening air. Kate looked for her gloves, relieved to see them waiting for her on the soft mud of the bank. "Okay, enough of this." She imitated Bambi on ice, the wet stones of the creek and slick soles of her boots made getting upright downright impossible. Kate rolled to one side and ungracefully scooted to the muddy edge. First, she retrieved her gloves, shoving her fingers into the latent warmth. Then, she looked for the best route up.

Washout around a large drainage pipe created a clear path to the top. Small trees and exposed roots promised to make the climb doable. Kate picked her way along the back and stepped onto a small cluster of debris pushed aside by the washout. She picked her first foot position carefully, then placed her left foot next to the corrugated metal of the drain pipe. Kate checked the pipe, making sure some animal wasn't going to jump at her from its depths, and saw two thick trunks, half buried in mud. Kate stared at them, and the trunks became a pair of legs. Human legs.

Chapter Five

Kate rubbed her hand over her pounding heart to soothe it, to stop it from bursting out of her skin. She looked around while her mind raced. She was alone on unfamiliar ground. In minutes, it would be dark.

Her hands shook as she lowered herself down the few steps she had taken. She couldn't hear anything except her own breathing, fast and ragged.

It couldn't be a body. It couldn't. It probably was just two logs trapped in the washout and a healthy dose of an overactive imagination.

She shivered as though it were twenty degrees colder.

A hand on the lip of the drainage pipe, Kate stepped onto the fine, washed earth, her foot sinking an inch. She planned to lean down, brush the mud away and prove to herself it was nothing but wood.

She planted her other foot inches from the log, closed her eyes, and turned her head away as she reached blindly with her gloved hand.

Stiff, woven material moved under her touch.

Fear burst from her in a piercing shout. Kate staggered back, her feet sliding on the mud. She tumbled to the water, falling to her hands and knees, and she violently emptied her stomach. The sound of movement came from nearby.

"Help! Help me!"

The shadows had taken the lead as the sun continued to fade. In that moment, Kate realized she was alone with a body. Would someone who killed once hesitate to kill again?

Shallow breaths tortured her lungs, her body, as she ran as much as her boots, the night, and the earth allowed. Back to the downed tree, to the rope that led up to the tractor.

Night had claimed the creek. Though Kate couldn't see, she knew something followed her.

Faster. Faster, faster. She needed to be faster.

"Wooof!"

"No!" Kate shrieked into the darkness, tripped, and fell hard to the earth. With another thunderous bark, Chubsy leapt to her side.

"Oh my God. Oh my God." As she repeated the litany, Kate clung to the massive dog.

He seemed to understand her distress and pressed his strong body to hers.

"I don't know what to do. I don't know what to do. We should get help. Absolutely. We should do that. Okay." Rational thought slowly emerged. "The first thing they are going to ask us is if the person is alive."

Kate jerked her head up. "You don't think they would be alive, do you?"

Chubsy looked straight at her, his eyes beacons in the

night. His breath turned her stomach again.

Kate pulled back and climbed to her feet. "Come on. We have to look. We have to try."

With her hand on Chubsy's thick neck, Kate walked back to the drain. She found the legs, but the light had faded. She could tell the body lay face down. She found the feet—small bare feet—but couldn't break the grip of the earth.

She needed a flashlight.

She remembered her phone, sealed up tight in a pocket. "Stupid. Stupid. Stupid." Kate dug it out and dialed the number Butch had programmed. The screen said "connecting," but the call never did. "Stupid service."

The flashlight app still worked. She and Chubsy winced as a thousand points of white LED light assaulted their eyes. Kate shone the light on the body. The legs lay in the washout, but the torso was in the forty-eight inch pipe. Kate looked at Chubsy, who calmly sniffed at the legs. His silent confidence steadied her. She bent low and walked into the pipe, straddling the body. Fine silt made for a soft bed. Clear water ran over that bed but only a few inches deep. The last of the rain from the days before. The body, unable to sink in the pipe the way the legs had in the ground, wore a wet and matted sweater, the face pitched to one side, blond hair cast in all directions. With a steadying breath, Kate used a gloved finger to rake the hair from the face.

She closed her eyes and hung her head. "Dear God. Angie."

Butch closed the door after his brother left around four in the morning. Kate curled in the corner of the couch beneath a thick blanket, Chubsy stretched across the floor below her. The dog usually slept at the big house with the other dogs his parents kept. This one made an exception tonight.

Butch squatted down and ran his fingers along Kate's jaw. She hadn't said a word in hours. "Time to go to bed, Katie."

Kate shook her head and whispered in a rusty voice. "There's no point. I have to be up in two hours anyway."

Butch kept his touch light. "Take the day off."

"I can't. I have things to do. Meetings."

"You can't do them on no sleep."

"I don't think I would sleep even if I closed my eyes."

Butch understood. He had gone to watch, to help pull Angie from the stream. Jeb wouldn't let him down into the water, but Butch had seen her. He had seen Angie when they put her on the stretcher, before they zipped the black bag over her head. She hadn't been in the water long, but neither the water nor the animals had been kind.

Kate looked into his eyes with an eloquent misery on her face. Dark smudges dulled her bright eyes. Her brows pressed together and up in an unanswerable query.

Butch read the exhaustion and suspected she was afraid of nightmares. Hell, he was, too. Butch left her to pull a pillow from his bed. Then he considered doing something he had never done in this house: locking the doors. He punched his bed, angry that somebody made him feel threatened in his own home, in his own town. "Screw that. If somebody wants a piece of me, let them try to take it." He pulled the revolver from his bedside table.

His air of righteousness lasted until he stepped into the living room. The strong woman he'd come to admire looked beaten. He didn't care what happened to him, but he wasn't alone anymore. He locked the front door then the back door before going to her.

"What are you doing?" she asked.

"Lying down." Butch put the pillow against the arm of the couch. He tucked the gun under the couch, the butt within easy reach. He took the blanket from around her shoulders and then stretched out, taking her body with his. He draped the blanket over them, tucked her in, wrapped his arm around her waist, and buried his nose in her hair.

Kate squirmed away from the edge of the couch. "We don't fit."

"We fit just fine." Butch locked his arm down, trapping her against him. He felt the tension that racked her body and drew little circles on her back to ease it.

"I'm afraid." She whispered the confession against his throat.

"I have you. Just rest, Katie. We'll get to the bottom of it in the light of day."

B utch woke to the bright light of day and the dark scowl of his brother. He propped himself up on one elbow and looked for Kate.

"She's not here," Jeb said in that cold, emotionless tone of his.

Butch fell back on the couch. "What time is it?"

"Eight-thirty, you dumb son-of-a-bitch. How long has she been living here?" Jeb paced in front of the couch with fisted hands. His teeth clenched tight enough to make the muscles of his jaw twitch.

Butch stared at the ceiling. "Who said she was living here?"

Jeb pulled the pillow from the floor and brought it down on his brother's gut. "Don't. Just don't. I saw her stuff in my room."

Butch rolled off the couch and looked up at his brother. "Your old room. You don't live here. Why are you snooping around my house?"

"How long?" Jeb asked quietly.

"Since Sunday night. She was staying in one of those flea bags on 31. I couldn't leave her there. I just couldn't."

Jeb kicked the couch making it up jump back three inches. "Goddamn it, Butch. You have a freaking hero complex. You don't have to save every woman with a sad story and a pretty face."

"This is different—"

"Different? Of course this is different. Every damned one of them is different, except they're all the same! What the hell is wrong with you?!" Jeb stalked away from Butch as he ranted.

Butch sat up straighter, narrowing his eyes at his brother. Jeb had been gone a long while. What did he know about Butch's life, the choices he'd made? It had been a long time since he'd needed his big brother around, a longer time since he'd had him. "It's none of your business what I do and who I do it with."

"She's fucking living here." Jeb spoke quietly again and

narrowed his gaze. "What does she do?"

Butch didn't know which was harder to take: the yelling or that damned cold, superior tone. He dropped an arm over his eyes wanting to ignore both. "She's an architect. That Cicada building is hers."

Jeb kicked his brother's leg, his tone softening with disbelief. "Shit. You really are the biggest idiot on the planet. Does Mom know?"

Something in that little kick was the Jeb he grew up with, the one he missed. "No. And no one knows she's staying here."

Jeb laughed sardonically. "Clyde, after last night, everyone knows she's living here."

"Son of a bitch. Sometimes I hate small towns. This is going to be one hell of a long day."

"Tell me about it. I'm meeting the boys back out here this morning. I'm hoping the daylight will tell us more than the night did. Do you have any coffee?"

Butch rolled and came to his feet. "If we're lucky." He hoped Katie had left him a pot of her special brew. Maybe after a cup or ten, he'd feel human again. Mostly full, the pot of coffee felt warm to the touch. Butch poured two cups and heated them to scalding in the microwave.

Jeb sipped, nodded. "This is good coffee. Better than you ever made. That's what? Nutmeg?"

"No idea." Butch settled against the counter and nursed his own. Jeb looked so tall and sure standing in the kitchen of their childhood home. He'd been up later than the rest of them, yet here he was, back at it without a word of complaint. "How do you do this job, Jeb? How can you look at that… this…what people do to each other day in and day out?"

Jeb shrugged it off. "If I didn't do it, somebody's going to think it's all right to come into our town and hurt our family, our friends. Somebody has to draw the line. Somebody has to say, 'Not on my watch.'"

"What are you going to do for Angie?"

Jeb's face changed, hardening again into that familiar stranger. "I'm going to do my job. I'm going to find the son-of-a-bitch who hurt her and lock them away in a small room where the sun doesn't shine for a hell of a long time."

Butch noted the set in Jeb's jaw, and his admiration for his brother grew.

"I need to ask you some questions. You want to do this now?"

Butch's eyes widened, and he had to force his hands to relax. "Yeah, let's get this done."

"Sit down." Jeb pulled a notebook from his pocket and sat at the kitchen table. "When was the last time you saw her?"

Butch took the chair across from Jeb. "I told you that last night."

"I know, but tell it to me again, and don't leave anything out."

Butch nodded and gulped the coffee. "Sunday night, Katie and I went up to the Sly Dog again after we moved her things into *her* room. Trudy, Hyde, and a few of the others were there, Angie included." Butch walked Jeb through the night, focusing on Angie.

"What time did you leave?"

"We didn't stay long, maybe a little before nine. Katie had to work yesterday. Do you know that woman woke me up at half past six *in the morning*? Who gets up that time of day?"

Jeb rolled his eyes. "Was Angie still at the bar when you left?"

"Yeah. She was. I'm certain."

"Did you give her money?"

Butch shook his head, his gaze on his coffee. "Not much. I gave her a little and told her it was the last. I did it, Jeb. I told her I was cutting her off."

"What did she do?"

"Nothing. She didn't get a chance. I saw Katie ready to leave, so I made my excuses."

"Were you serious? About cutting her off?"

Butch pressed his lips together tightly. He had been serious about ending the support, but he hadn't told Finch when he talked to him after the piano delivery. He didn't want to look at the 'why' too hard, afraid of what he might see. "Yes. I was going to cut the amount of the checks over a few months."

"You didn't see her after the Sly Dog? Yesterday?"

"No. I didn't see her, talk to her, or think about her until last night in the town square when you asked whether I'd seen her."

Jeb fell back into his chair. "When was the last time you were back by the pond?"

"Sunday afternoon. I took Katie for a ride on the tractor. We went to the pond, but we weren't over by the drain pipe. Before then, it was about a week. I'd been making the rounds to see what needs to be done."

Jeb leaned forward. "You planning on staying?"

"I can't say I really have plans. Right now, I'm not planning to leave."

"Dad and Mama like having you close. I like having you around where I can keep my eye on you."

Butch gave him a weak smile. "Do you ever feel like you don't belong anywhere? When I'm here, as comfortable as it is with you and Dad and Mama, I'm not part of this anymore. I don't know the stories, I'm not part of the memories, and I feel like I'm missing out on the rest of the world. When I'm out there and playing, I feel alive. But then I go home to a cold hotel room, and I'm alone. I still don't know the stories, I'm still not part of the memories."

Jeb took in a deep breath and released it slowly. "Everything I've ever believed in is right here. I want you to stay. I miss my brother."

There was a loud rap on the back door. "You in there, Sheriff?"

Jeb climbed to his feet. "I'm here, Duncan. Go on back, I'll be right behind you," he called out. "What are you doing today, Butch?"

"Working. The music's pulling at me. I'll also go see Angie's mother, I expect."

Kate leaned over her foreman's shoulder, checking the line on the concrete form as he worked. "It's off. It can't be off."

"The line is fine. You're off. Don't you have something better to do than annoy me?" Dave Waters was as much her uncle as he was her foreman, but that only went so far during the working day.

Kate's phone rang. Paula had better not be calling about

somebody else crying on her shoulder. Some days it felt like she ran a daycare instead of a construction site. "What?" Kate barked loudly.

"Sheriff McCormick is here to see you."

"Who?"

A baritone came through the phone. "Katie, it's Jeb. I need to talk to you."

Her voice pitched up an octave. "Does it have to be now? I'm in the middle of something." She scowled as the men began to frame a critical wall.

"Yeah, it has to be now."

"Five minutes," she said and then spoke again to Waters. "Measure it again. If it's not right, I'm gonna plant my boot squarely on your ass."

"Three minutes," Jeb said in her ear.

"I said five. Give me back to Paula. Paula? Give the sheriff some coffee, and make him comfortable. If he starts touching things, use the wooden spoon."

"Four minutes." Kate thundered into her office. "We split the difference."

Jeb crouched at the scale model, staring into the little windows.

"Impressed?"

Jeb wore his emotionless mask, but Kate heard the kid-like wonder in his voice. "Hell yeah. I can even see into the rooms. There are little people in there."

"If you like that, you're going to love it when we're done." She waited quietly while Paula brought her a fresh cup of coffee.

Jeb took a sip from his own cup. "You make damned good coffee. I believe this is the same brand you have at my brother's house."

"Family recipe. It's a feature on all Riley projects." Kate gestured to an empty chair. "I think we're about done with the requisite small talk. I hope you've had a more productive day than I've had."

Jeb sighed. "Between the tractor and the clearing you did, any physical evidence is gone."

Kate stilled. She'd had a hard morning on the job. Two hours of haunted sleep made focusing a Herculean effort. She'd been worn down when she walked in to talk to Jeb, and now any remaining blood quickly drained from her face. "I didn't know. I swear I didn't."

Jeb pulled his notebook out. "The sign on the trailer says Riley. Architects and Engineers. That you?"

"I'm one of the architects. The lead one."

"What about the other name on the trailer. Riley Brothers General Contractors?"

"The family business. It's run by my father and uncle, supports my cousins. I'm wearing both hats right now."

"How long have you been in our neck of the woods?"

"Three months. My foreman, Dave Waters, and I came down after the New Year. We hired men, set things up, and broke ground a few weeks later."

Jeb didn't react as he made notes. "You took the tractor out yesterday?"

"To clear the trees. Butch wouldn't take any money for letting me stay at his house, so I insisted on working off my room and board in chores."

Jeb leaned back, rocking the chair on two legs. "How did you meet Butch?" Jeb let the chair fall back to four legs. He seemed to relax a degree, taking notes as she told her story. "Did you do any other chores?"

"Butch was working by the road to hang your grandfather's sign. I stopped for directions. Things didn't work out, and I ended up back where I started but with a shredded tire. Butch let me stay. I wouldn't call it a chore, but as a thank you, I fixed the tractor. A big-assed wrench was gumming up the works. After that, I snatched Butch's to-do list. The stream was the first thing I tackled."

"Tell me about Sunday night at the Sly Dog."

Kate told Jeb how Angie cornered Butch and how she had distracted him by making faces. "A while later, she followed me into the ladies' room."

Jeb held his hand up. "How do you know she followed you?"

"She didn't use the bathroom. She didn't have her purse, fix her makeup, or brush her hair. I came out of a stall, and she came at me. She surprised the hell out of me. I've hung out in some rough places but never had anyone put their hands on me the way she did. Trudy came in as Angie poked me in the tit while saying I should stay out of the way. Trudy stepped in before I could do anything. I thought there was going to be a fight, but Angie used the first excuse to leave."

"Did you know Butch gave Angie money?"

Kate's phone rang. She silenced it without looking at it. "No. When I came out of the bathroom with Trudy, I went outside for some fresh air. Butch came out a few minutes later. I'd had enough, and he brought me back to the house."

"You didn't tell Butch what happened. Why?"

Kate leaned forward, her blue eyes honest and open. "It was just so weird. I had only known Butch for two days. I'd already pushed my luck by letting him know what I thought about foster care for snakes. I know it's none of my business, but stupid is stupid. There're plenty of legit environmental causes if he really wants to get involved."

Jeb pursed his lips and closed his eyes. "So you went back to the house, and…?"

"I organized my things, and I was in bed by ten."

"And my brother?"

"I heard him playing the guitar in his studio room. He was still playing when I fell asleep."

Jeb nodded. "All right, then. Tell me about last night." He held up his hand when she started to protest. "Tell me again. Everything. Details, like did you notice any fresh tracks?"

It took Kate another half hour to walk through those two hours before the previous night's sunset. "I don't know what caught my attention. Dusk can play tricks on your eyes, you know? I was so afraid, I didn't think clearly."

A fist pounded on the door, and Kate jumped and knocked over her coffee cup. She was grateful to see she had drunk every last drop, although she didn't remember it.

"What the hell? A closed door means I'm busy," Kate yelled.

Paula's voice filtered through the thin door. "Waters called. Those boys did it again. He needs you out there. Now."

She tossed Jeb a hard hat. "Come on. Maybe I can make use of you."

Jeb caught the hat and followed her out to the site. After a few minutes' walk, Waters stalked toward them, his fists clenched tight.

"Sheriff Jeb McCormick, my foreman, Dave Waters. What's the problem, Dave?"

Dave shook Jeb's hand, then cut Kate a look. "One of those kids dumped again."

"Damn it. Those lazy dumbasses. The stream that cuts through here is a big fishing stream."

Jeb scowled at her. "I've fished in it all my life."

"Cicada made it very clear that they have no interest in impacting the stream. I support their approach, philosophically and ethically, and made it a feature of the campus. If that weren't enough, it's illegal to dump, but some people don't buy into pollution and the problems it causes. We're fighting hundreds of years of bad habits."

They quickly covered the quarter mile to the stream. Jeb pulled up short when he saw the five "kids," as Waters called them. Those kids were young men from the county, each barely twenty years old, sitting on a downed tree looking guilty as charged.

One of the men recognized Jeb and bounded up. "Sheriff—"

"Shut up," Kate snapped. "This is my job site, and you will address me, do you understand?" She paused long enough for the "yes ma'ams" to be muttered. "What about Waters's direction that there would be no dumping from this job into the water didn't you understand? Look at that mess. What's downstream of here?"

"Painted Rock," one of them answered.

"You fish there?" Kate demanded.

They all nodded.

"Do you want to eat a fish that swam through and breathed that milky crap you dumped?"

"No ma'am," they muttered.

"Goddamn it. I've had it."

"Kate," Waters interrupted. "They've all got good hands and strong backs—"

"But rocks in their heads," she finished for him.

"Still, I can get a lot more done with them than without them."

Kate wanted to boot them all off the job, not just for what they did, but because she hadn't slept, and her stomach kept rolling when she thought about what happened last night.

But Waters wanted them. He'd taught Kate everything she knew about being on-site. He had pushed her until there were no soft curves left; he had to, or she would have gotten eaten alive. For that, and so much more, she respected him. So he would have his way.

Kate stood in a broad stance with her hands on her hips and looked down at the men. "You want them, fine; you can have them. But get that stream cleaned up, now. And the next time you pull something like this on my job, I'm personally hauling your sorry asses over to the EPA. Got it?"

"Yes ma'am," they muttered and looked to Jeb.

"Don't look at me. I fish out of this stream, too. I'll haul you in and let the EPA make the drive over. And I don't even want to think about what your mamas will do to you."

The men cringed again. Kate turned to leave, hopeful she wouldn't have this problem again. As she walked away, Waters walked with her.

"You were right," Waters said. "It was off by two inches. Always said you had the best eye I'd ever seen."

"I don't know why you doubted me. I learned from the

best." Kate glanced over Waters's shoulder. "I'm serious about the dumping, Dave. I can get you new men."

"I know you can, grasshopper, but I'll take the devil I know. They'll stay in line. I'll have to remember to call their mothers. Never used that one before."

"You're going to keep them on?" Jeb asked, keeping pace.

"What Waters wants, Waters gets. He's the best there is for a reason. Do you have any more questions?"

Jeb caught her arm to bring her to a stop. "Where were you yesterday until you met up with my brother?"

"Butch dropped me here just before seven in the morning. I didn't get a chance to breathe before the middle of the afternoon. I left around four-thirty, determined to move back out of his house."

Jeb's head jerked up. "Why?"

"I didn't know who he was." She shrugged off the embarrassment she had told herself she was over. "He didn't tell me the whole story. Paula recognized him along with a few of the guys. Makes sense now. I felt foolish. They're all asking me questions about him, and I'm blabbering on about how he helped me out and how I hoped he made it big someday, because he was really good."

"Why did you stay?"

Kate slapped her hands on her dusty jeans and frowned. "Because I like his house. Because I hated the motel. Because he bought me ice cream. Because I like him. Because he asked me to stay."

Jeb studied her face.

Kate firmed her mouth. "You don't trust me."

"No, ma'am, I don't. Butch has done a good thing with

his music, but it brings out all kinds. People relate to his music, and think they know him. He's soft hearted, too soft for his own good."

"And you're going to protect him."

Jeb nodded. "He is my little brother."

Kate lifted her chin defiantly. "I don't want anything from him. I don't need anything from him."

"He's not staying, you know. He's just visiting before his tour starts. He lives in California." Jeb removed the hard hat and put his own back in place. "Let me know if you have any more trouble with those 'kids.'"

Kate nodded and turned her back on him, leaving him to find his own way out as she climbed into the trailer. She still had hours of work ahead of her and a splitting headache. "I need more coffee, Paula."

"Is everything all right?"

"God only knows. I need to get through some of this paperwork. Only let the important calls through, please."

"Butch McCormick?" Paula asked with a grin.

"Sure." Why not? Jeb told her Butch wasn't staying to run her off. What Jeb didn't think about was she wasn't staying either. In less than a year, this project would be done, and she would be off to the next. That would be then. This was now.

"Your father?"

"Tell him I'm on-site." Kate took the fresh cup from Paula and went to her office, closing the door behind her. She woke her computer and set to work approving invoices, reviewing shop drawings, and updating the schedule. Hours later, she drove her work truck to the house blurry-eyed and parked on the wide gravel drive.

B utch had spent the day at Angie's mother's house, as had most of the town. With Angie's mother, Margie, being a widow, Butch was the closest thing to family she had in town. He did what he could. He helped with the arrangements, called Angie's friends, the few who hadn't already heard, and found the snake people and called them, too. Just when he thought he had things under control, he received a phone call from Fawn that took the drama to a new level. The day had been long and emotionally draining. He turned into his drive and felt a punch of excitement at seeing Kate's truck parked at the front walk.

He wondered if she'd made dinner, then cringed and hoped she didn't. He'd scrape together something for them. Wine would be nice. Something to warm them.

Butch parked in the garage and walked into the dark house. He knew immediately she wasn't there. He checked her bedroom and the living room anyway. The house felt alive when she was in it. Now, it felt like it was hibernating, waiting for her to come home so life would continue again.

Butch came down the steps and walked straight out the back door to the barn. The dog Kate had come to call Chubsy wandered through the yard, looking around like he'd lost something, before he went back out the way he'd come. Butch told himself he was overreacting. Likely, Kate was working on the chore list and would be back when she finished or the sun set. Hungry himself, he hunted through the kitchen and settled on a container of soup his mother put in his freezer. He set a pot on the stove and started to heat dinner, watching through the window as the light faded.

When the sun set, worry took center stage. Butch rubbed his sweaty palms against his thighs while he looked around for clues. The tractor was parked in its usual spot. She wasn't fixing shutters or painting walls. He didn't think she would have walked off into the fields. Not for work, anyway. He ran to his truck and drove back to the place where Angie had been found.

He banged his head a time or two as he drove too fast over the uneven ground. He slowed down, realizing if she were out here, she walked in the dark. He crept along, keeping his eyes sweeping from left to right across the windshield. He reached the pond without seeing her. Nearing panic, he pulled out his phone.

"Jeb, I can't find Katie."

"What do you mean you can't find her?"

"Her work truck is here, but I can't find her. She's not in the house or the barn. I'm back by the pond. It's as dark as midnight, Jeb."

"Okay. Stay calm. I'll be right over. Check her truck. See if anything is missing."

Butch buckled his seat belt and made it back to the house in half the time. The truck skidded to a halt across the gravel driveway. In the moonlight, Butch could see her truck wasn't empty. "Katie!"

The world moved in a viscous slow motion. The harder Butch pushed, the faster he ran, the slower he moved. Tears filled his eyes as he wrenched the door open and pulled her rag doll body into his arms.

Chapter Six

With hard, demanding hands, Butch yanked Kate from where she lay draped over the steering wheel. She came up, swimming for the surface from a deep sleep. Legs kicked and hands clawed, catching Butch in the shoulder. He pinned her to the truck, his mind still doubting that she lived and breathed.

Small fists thumped his back. "Get off of me. Get. Off. Me. Can't. Breathe."

Butch loosened the steel bands of his arms but didn't let go. His heart still pounded, his stomach still lodged in his throat. In light of what happened to Angie, he just couldn't let go. "Thank God. I thought you were dead." He buried his face in her neck and inhaled her sweet scent.

Kate relaxed, wrapping her arms around his neck. She stroked his hair as if willing both of their hearts to downshift to first gear. "I'm not dead. I'm just really tired. Tired and hungry."

Taking her face in his hands, Butch brushed his lips over her tired eyes and her downturned lips. "I have just the thing for that. Chicken soup and a soft bed."

"Add in a shower, and it sounds like heaven to me."

The lights from Jeb's sheriff's truck cut through the night like a beacon. Kate closed her eyes and pulled her face from Butch's hands to bury against his neck. The engine cut, and boots shuffled across the gravel.

"You found her," Jeb said.

"Asleep in her truck," Butch answered, his arms wrapped protectively around Kate's head.

"Just like you after a show." Jeb walked past Butch toward the house. "You got anything to eat? I missed dinner."

Butch set the small table for three and served the soup his mother made and a box of saltines. He and Jeb talked about meaningless topics over the thick and fragrant soup. Kate ate two bites before pitching forward, all but falling asleep in her bowl. Jeb saved the bowl while Butch caught her up in his arms.

Katie's head snapped up, her wild gaze sweeping the room as her hands grasped the collar of Butch's shirt. "What's going on? What are you doing?"

"Easy, Tiger. I'm just putting you to bed."

"My bed." Her head fell heavily into the niche in his shoulder.

Butch tickled her ribs. "I like to think of it as our bed."

"I'm not sleeping with you." Kate's eyes were already closed again.

Butch ignored Jeb's snicker. "You slept with me last night, and we did just fine." He carried her up the stairs and tucked her in his bed.

"I'm not easy," she mumbled, more asleep than awake.

Butch brushed her hair from her face. "Now there's a surprise. Get some sleep. I'll seduce you in the morning."

She snuggled into the blanket, a smile growing across her lips. "Maybe I'll seduce you."

"Maybe you will, but not before dawn. We're sleeping in tomorrow."

B utch woke to the sound of the water running in the shower. Seven-thirty. "It's better than six," he muttered, rolling over. Right behind the wall, Kate stood naked in a fall of hot water. Her long red hair, her stubborn chin, her creamy skin. She always wore jeans and a cotton shirt. He'd gotten his hands on her enough to know she hid shapely muscle under all that material. Did she wear sexy panties? He'd have to buy her some. Midnight blue. With lace. Lots of lace.

Butch climbed out of bed and into a worn pair of jeans. He fastened the button over his cock, made raging by an active imagination. He limped down the stairs to make coffee and wait for her. He wanted to see her, be there for her, before her day started. "God, I'm pathetic."

Kate landed in the kitchen fifteen minutes later, her hair in a wet ponytail trailing down her back. "I didn't expect to see you up this early."

"Me neither." Butch shoved the cup into her hand, frustrated by his own behavior. He should be in bed, but instead he leaned against the counter and crossed his ankles. "Feeling better?"

Kate smiled radiantly. "I feel fantastic. See what twelve hours of sleep can do for you?"

Butch surveyed the wiggle in her step and the twinkle in her eyes. She fired on all cylinders this morning. "I'm a big proponent of sleep. I'm going right back there after you leave."

Kate sashayed over to Butch. He raised an eyebrow, trying to read that look in her eyes. Trouble brewed there with a little something else. He didn't move as she wrapped her arms around his neck and pressed her soft lips to his.

"Good morning." She kissed him a second time. "Thank you for getting up." She kissed him again. "Thank you for making coffee."

He leaned into Katie, his breath fast and ragged, his fingers itching to touch her skin. "Are you seducing me?"

She nipped his lower lip. "I'm thanking you. How could that ever be mixed up with seducing?" While her words disavowed seduction, her tone embodied it. She dropped her voice to the lowest register, a whiskey whisper that invited him to long, hot nights…and mornings. Her fingers knotted in his hair, holding him captive as she closed the scant inches between them.

Butch tugged at her shirt until his fingers found her bare skin. He brushed his tips along the waist band, stroking the skin as soft as silk. When she pulled away, Butch rested his forehead on hers. "Damn it. Now I'm going to have to get up every morning."

Kate's eyes shined as she laughed. She planted a hard kiss on his mouth and stepped away. "What are you doing today after you're done sleeping?"

"Fawn, my newest ex-to-be, called yesterday. She wants

to meet me tomorrow to discuss things. I'll have to go out to California."

"I heard you live there. I guess it doesn't make sense that this is your home."

"Why doesn't it make sense?" Unexpectedly offended, Butch's brows furrowed. Had he fallen so low he wasn't good enough to call this place home?

"You're, like, rich and famous, and this house, as great as it is, is empty. I don't know why it didn't occur to me before. Too much going on, I guess. So if you're going home — "

"She lives there," he said hastily. "I live here. At least now I do." Well, that felt right. He lived here.

Kate unzipped the top of her jeans and re-tucked her shirt. "Then why go to California?"

"What?" Butch's eyes were on her hands, his mind in the gutter.

"Why fly out to California?" Kate sat on a chair and pulled on a boot.

"Because that's where she is."

Kate rolled her eyes. "So? You're here. And you filed the papers here. Tell her planes go both ways and to get her butt out here. Where are you going to meet her?"

"Here?" He looked at the little table with four mismatched chairs.

Kate shook her head. "You know nothing about negotiating, do you? Because that's what this is. You need someone on your side. A shark. Never negotiate alone."

Butch smiled. "You?"

Kate laced up her other boot. "No, I'm too impatient. Tom does all our contracts. Who handles your contracts?"

"Finch."

Kate stood tall, a woman ready to take on the day. "Call him." A challenge.

Butch rolled his eyes but picked up his phone from the counter and called Finch, pressing the speakerphone button before it rang.

The man answered the first ring. "Butch? You know it's before ten in the morning?"

Kate muffled a laugh. "You have a reputation."

"Who's with you?" Finch asked.

"Landon Finch, my agent, manager, and handler, meet Kate Riley, my roommate, handyman, and soon-to-be lover."

Kate blushed, which Butch found intriguing given the depth with which she kissed him moments ago. Importantly, though, she hadn't discouraged him, and she hadn't denied it.

Kate leaned against the counter next to Butch. "Nice to meet you, Finch."

"Likewise. What's going on, Butch?" Clicking in the background said the voice that talked to them multitasked. Standard for Finch. The man seldom did one thing at a time.

"Fawn called and wants to meet. She wants me to come out to California—"

"And you said, 'Hell no?'" The clicking stopped, the voice at full attention.

"See?" Kate poked him in the ribs. "I told you that was the right answer. Finch, Butch needs a shark in his corner. Do you know any?"

"Baby, who do you think they used as a stand in for *Jaws*?" Finch's teeth snapped. "Let me make some calls. Rosencrantz, Bloom, and Cromwell have offices in Nashville. We'll meet there. There's nothing like high-powered litigators to scare people into settling. You make a list of all joint assets and what you want."

Butch rubbed his hair. "I don't want anything except my equipment and Tessa's art."

"You don't want the house?" Finch asked.

"She painted the entire thing pink. I didn't take a healthy crap the entire year I lived there."

Kate wrinkled her nose. "Too much information, Butch. Now that I know you're in good hands, I'm going to work. Don't agree to anything without Finch's okay."

Butch rolled his eyes again. "For Heaven's sake. I'm not a child."

"No, you're just too nice for your own good. Fortunately for you, you have me. I've never been accused of being nice."

Finch laughed. "I've been telling him that for years. Do like Kate says, and don't agree to anything without me."

Kate stepped into her office, turned her computer on, and called Tom. She knew without looking that the three missed calls were from him. They always started their day with a quick call, and she had missed their normal time.

"Something wrong, Kate?"

She fell into her chair and rocked back, looking at the ceiling. "Good morning to you, too."

He grunted. "Good morning. You're late. What happened?"

Kate hated that Tom had a sixth sense about her and trouble. Denying it made it worse. Tom always found out. Going the long route of denial only made it louder. "Not with the job. I decided to move to that inn I told you about, Elderberry Farm—you know how I hated that motel—anyway, I was helping the owner clear some brush, and I found a body."

"You found a body? Jesus, Kate. When?" Disbelief unseated annoyance.

"Monday night."

"And you didn't say anything yesterday?" Tom's voice climbed up a few decibels. Irritation took hold, knocking disbelief to the ground.

Why hadn't she told him? She didn't try to hide it from him. If anything, she didn't tell him to avoid thinking about it, because then the remnants of fear she'd felt on the water's edge crept in. She shook herself like a wet dog. "I think I was in shock. I didn't get much sleep Monday night, with the cops and all. I really crashed last night."

"I bet. Do they know who it was?"

Kate inhaled. "Yep. The innkeeper's ex-wife."

"What?" Tom roared. "The old man's ex-wife?"

"Yeah, well, he's not as old as I made him out to be. And, he's famous in some circles. His name is Butch McCormick."

"The country music star?" Now Tom shouted at the top of his lungs.

Kate rolled her eyes. "Has everyone heard of him but me?"

"Isn't he married to some actress?"

"Fawn would be his soon-to-be third ex-wife. Angie was his first."

Tom got really quiet. "Are you sleeping with him?"

Kate pursed her lips. "That's none of your business."

"Let me get this straight," Tom said softly. "You're living

in a house with Butch McCormick when you discover the body of his first ex-wife, while he's still married to his ex-wife to be, while we are building the highest-profile project of our careers, and you don't think it's any of my business?"

"I haven't slept with him." Kate knew Tom heard the implied "yet." "There's nothing to be done. The sheriff, Butch's brother, is investigating. Can we talk about work?"

"Yeah, sure." He said the words slowly then paused. "We have a web conference call set up at eleven to coordinate the HVAC. I emailed you the drawings this morning."

Kate leaned on her desk, grateful Tom had dropped the topic so readily. She opened her email and waited while the files loaded. He usually was a bulldog once he sank his teeth in something. He must have been worried about the drawings. She'd make a point of being ready for the meeting. "Got it. I'll review them before the call."

Construction sites had plenty of days filled with drama, which made days like this worth appreciating. The call with HVAC worked out needed details. The forms came off the concrete pours and looked perfect. Nobody acted like a moron. An afternoon rain rewarded a productive morning with an excuse to head out a few hours early. She drove to Butch's house looking forward to a quiet evening with him. She didn't date much and, while she played it up this morning, didn't have a lot of experience with seducing a man. She thought she'd done okay except it worried her that he didn't move. If he really liked what she did, wouldn't he have touched her more? All he did was run his fingers along her waistband. True, the electricity that charged through her system nearly gave her a coronary. She wondered if it felt like that for him. She should do something, she decided, to say she was interested in a little something more, even if it was just a short-lived affair while they were both in town. The timing sucked. Starting the divorce process had to be the worst time to start any kind of new relationship.

Relationship. Now there's a word. Did she want a relationship with Butch? She'd be crazy not to want a relationship with a man like him. He appealed to her on so many levels. She admired his creative side—it took an amazingly smart and talented person to play and write music. She loved his casual manner. Kate knew she was high strung and she was worse when she worried or stressed. Around Butch, she laughed more, had fun more, liked herself better. Yeah, she'd be crazy not to want to be with him.

Except…she wasn't staying.

For the first time she could remember, the idea of moving to the next project saddened her instead of excited. Kate turned into Butch's driveway, resolve taking hold. She was here, now. She didn't have a year to give him, but she would offer him what she had.

Kate parked her truck on the edge of the gravel driveway, next to a sheriff's truck. She told herself not to read into it. Jeb stopping by didn't have to mean he'd solved Angie's murder. He could just be saying hello to Butch, or, more likely, warning him off a certain redhead. Kate stomped onto the porch ready for an argument with Butch's older brother.

She faced an unexpected sight—Butch and Jeb standing in the living room, arms crossed and glaring at each other.

"What's happened now?" she asked.

"The preliminary time of death is between nine and noon on Monday," Jeb said.

"I was on the jobsite." Kate pictured her day with an

odd curiosity of wondering where she had been at the fatal moment. "I had a phone call at nine, then inspected an excavation."

Butch glared at his brother. "I was in bed asleep."

The gears kicked into place, and Kate's thermometer went from room temperature to are-you-fucking-kidding-me hot. "You think your brother did this?" Your family watched your back, not stabbed you in it. If Jeb wouldn't defend Butch, then she would. Kate stepped toe-to-toe with Jeb. "I've known him for a few days, and I know he's too good of a man to do anything like this. You should be ashamed of yourself."

Jeb lowered that steel gaze to Kate. "Don't act like you know my brother. You're just his latest fancy. Butch is just like Baskin-Robbins: thirty-one flavors, one for each day of the month."

Butch pulled Kate behind him. "What the hell, Jeb? I told you, it's not like that."

Kate clawed her way around the buffer Butch created to yell at Jeb. "You narrow-minded asshole." The insult stung. How had she let herself fantasize that a man like Butch could have any real interest in someone like her? She may not know how to be a girl, but a woman in a world of contractors, she knew how to stand up for herself and for Butch. "Get your mind out of his bed and out there looking for who did this. He's being set up. You'd see that if you pulled your head out of your ass."

Butch pulled her by the shoulders and stepped between the two again. "Kate, stop. Jeb doesn't—"

"Who do you think you're talking to? A night in lock up would teach you respect for the badge." Jeb strained to see around Butch, lips tight as he spoke.

Kate grabbed onto Butch's hips and leaned until she saw those stormy eyes. "I have respect for the badge, it's the man behind it that I think is incompetent. You don't have to arrest me to prove it."

Distracted by the fight in front of her, Kate missed the storm that brewed behind.

"What the hell is going on?"

Tom Riley filled the doorway. Her cousin always did love a good entrance. A looming six foot four with dark features, broad shoulders, and hands like ham hocks, Tom demanded attention. His long, dark brown hair matched the color of his menacing eyes. A scowl tightened his face with outrage.

Kate turned to face her cousin as her mind raced. She should have known he gave in too easily. Grateful he didn't put up a fight, Kate missed it as early warning of a bigger storm. "Tom. What hell are you doing here?"

"Of course, this would be Tom," Butch said.

Tom looked down at Kate, ready to jump into the middle of her fight. "I've come to pull you out of this mess you've gotten yourself into."

"I'm not in a mess."

"Yes, you are," Jeb said.

"Shut up," Kate snapped at Jeb and struck a composed stance for her cousin. "Tom, I'm in the middle of something here."

Tom glared at Jeb, though he spoke to Kate. "I heard what you're in the middle of, and we're going."

"She's not going anywhere." Butch tucked Kate under his shoulder. "Jeb, do what you have to do. I know you don't believe I did that to Angie. Find who did. It wasn't me."

Jeb slapped his hands on his thighs and then flung them in the air. "Take off those goddamned rose-colored glasses. You think it's just a coincidence that she shows up here, moves into your house and—poof—your ex-wife is dead after confronting her in the bathroom?"

Butch pushed Kate firmly behind him. "You think Katie did that to Angie?"

Tom stalked across the floor. "I've heard enough. Let's go, Kate. Next time you want to talk to her, do it through our lawyer."

Kate jumped back and avoided Tom's hand. "I'm not going with you." Kate scrambled to put the couch between her and Tom. She knew she was faster, but if Tom got his hands on her, she was toast.

"The hell you are." Tom took off after her.

Butch and Jeb shouted at the circling pair. Kate dashed around the room. Tom jumped on the couch, tipped it, and caught Kate by the waist. He flung her over his shoulder and ran toward the door. Kate pounded on his back to no effect, arching her back to overbalance him. There was a sharp crack and a high-pitched yelp.

Kate squeezed her eyes shut, but still the world spun. A heavy thud sounded, and then something soft cushioned her.

"Kate? Kate? Come on, Kate. Open your eyes. You're scaring me." A hand pressed into her shoulder.

"Tom?"

Tom let out a breath. "That's right, Kate. It's Tom."

"Tom," Kate repeated. Then she led with her left, intending to dislodge the arm that trapped her. "Jerk." She missed his arm but found his jaw.

Tom fell to his knees on the floor while Kate scrambled to her feet.

"You can't make me leave." The world spun. There was three of everything and too much noise.

Tom reached out for Kate with arms twice as long as they should have been. Kate dodged him again. Her legs were too long, her knees too knobby, but she refused to fall. Solid hands wrapped around her waist and pulled her against a hard body, and she threw elbows, kicking out in random directions.

Butch's voice reached through the chaos. "Enough. Stop it. Everyone. Katie, let me look at you."

She stood in Butch's arms, watching her cousin sit on the ceiling.

"Shit. You really got me that time." Tom rubbed his jaw as the floor swung left then right, left then right.

Jeb stood over Tom with his practiced glare. "Do you want to press charges for assault, Kate?"

"She can't," Tom said. "I'm family. She'd just have to bail me out. I'm Tom Riley, Kate's cousin and partner."

Silence weighed heavily with the energy of the chaos drained. Jeb had left after his radio squawked about a problem elsewhere in the county but not before he warned he'd be back after work. Kate turned down an offer of a redlight escort to the emergency room, which left Tom tending to her sore head. Tom finished the chore and went to the job site, after accepting Butch's offer of a bed and a meal. Kate washed off the day with a hot shower, after which, she went in search of company to break the silence.

She found Butch in the living room with sheets of legal paper scattered across a folding table. With one elbow planted on the table, Butch supported his head with his hand while his other arm pinned the legal pad to the surface. His hair stood on end, pointing in all directions. As she watched, he lifted his head and ran his supporting hand through his hair. Agitated fingers sent the strands even more askew. He tore the sheet of paper from the pad, wadded it up, and started again.

"Music is hard work, huh?"

Butch stared out of the top of his eyes, looking as if someone pulled out his fingernails with a pair of pliers. "This ain't work. It's torture. As directed by Mr. Finch, I am making a list my marital assets by the end of the day. That man does love his deadlines."

Kate smiled wryly. "Deadlines make things happen."

Butch's scowl deepened. "You even sound like him. Are you going to help me or what?"

Kate climbed over the arm of the couch, threading her legs under the table. "What can I do?"

"I don't know. Fawn and I were only married for two years, but she went on a spending spree the day after we said 'I do.' We have two houses—not counting this one, which is my parents'—four cars, art, my instruments and equipment, and four bank accounts."

Kate read the legal document as he ranted about the most recent years of his life. "Well, it's a good thing you knew Finch before you met Fawn. Just glancing over this, I'll say it looks like as tight a contract as I've ever read."

Butch took a drag from his latest bottle of beer. Two empties already sat on a corner. Butch had an edge to him. One he deserved to have.

The way Kate read it, Butch was a little angry, a little frustrated, a little overwhelmed, and a little lost. She took his hand, kissed his palm, and cradled it to her cheek. "I'm sorry. I wish I could take it all away for you."

Butch leaned forward and, with a long sigh, rested his head on her shoulder. She snuggled against him. He stayed quiet, still, and she wondered once again what he was thinking.

As if he heard her unspoken question, he turned his head and whispered softly to her, "What do you see in me?"

Chapter Seven

Kate's mouth went dry, and she forgot every word she'd ever learned. "Um, huh?"

Butch burrowed into the den of red hair at the base of her neck. "Humor me. I'm wallowing in self-pity. Tell me something good about me."

Kate wrapped her arms around him and held him to her heart. "I look at you, and I see everything a man should be. Wickedly smart, incredibly talented, and hot as hell." She pressed her lips to his hair when she felt his smile against her skin. "You're strong without being overbearing. You're kind. Don't dismiss that. There isn't enough kindness in the world. Strength and kindness can change the world. I've never met a man as passionate as you. Your passion comes through in your music. It's like you can reach into my soul and heal the wounds."

"You have wounds?" His husky voice, audible only in the silence of the house, bared the depth of his unhappiness.

Kate closed her eyes tightly and answered softly. "Doesn't everyone?"

"Tell me more about the hot as hell part."

Kate chuckled, glad for his attempt to lighten the mood. "Well, you are. There's this spot I just love. Right here." She caressed the intriguing little dip between his shoulder and his neck. "I know this must hurt like hell, but you had the courage to love. That's not a little thing either. Too many people can't trust, can't give themselves freely. Having the capacity to love and the courage to love makes you an incredible man."

"Have you ever been in love?"

"I told you, I don't have a love story. There have been men I've cared about, certainly men I've been attracted to, but I'm not sure I've ever been in love. I don't know." She paused. "I don't think they were in love with me either."

"Why would you say that?"

Kate rested her cheek against his hair. Closing her eyes, she told him her biggest fear. "I'm just not that lovable. I'm not very good at being a girl."

Butch sat up, lifting her chin to look at him when she tried to hide. "I think you're very good at being a girl, Katie."

Kate hated how every emotion painted her cheeks. She treasured Butch's compliment, would hold it close to her heart, but didn't know what to say next. "I, uh, like that you call me Katie. No one has ever called me that."

B utch rubbed his lips over hers, soothing her and, in turn, soothing his own ache. "Katie. My Katie."

Had he ever been in love before? He'd never had this easy kind of happy. Angie had been his first love. They figured it all out together. They'd both made their share of mistakes, but they always had each other to fall back on. His second wife, Tessa, had been his spiritual mate. As driven about her art as Butch was about his music, Tessa ignited something in him that had never been touched before. But when his path veered from hers, she walked away. She chose her uncompromising art over her husband.

So why had he fallen for Fawn? He didn't like the answer. She needed him. Maybe he had a hero complex like Jeb had said. Young, talented, and beautiful, Fawn had looked at him as though he could walk on water. She was everything his ego needed until her own career began. Overnight he became old, out of step, unsupportive.

"What are you thinking about?" Kate asked in a quiet voice.

He settled her onto the couch next to him, lacing their fingers together. "My ex-wives. I don't think I made good choices."

One side of Kate's mouth curled upward. "Well, hindsight is always twenty-twenty. Next time, just ask your brother. He'll tell you if you're making a mistake. You haven't said anything about the second ex-Mrs. McCormick. Where is she?"

"Tessa? She died a few years ago. She was a ceramic artist and did beautiful work. There was a fire in her studio, and she didn't survive. You'll appreciate this bit of irony. I signed with Finch mid-marriage. He had us file a bunch of papers making us partners in each other's work. After the divorce, we kept the partnership. After she died, the value of her art skyrocketed. Between the sales and the insurance, she made me a rich man as much as I earned it. I started an art endowment in her name at her college with part of the money."

"See how good you are? Who else would have thought to use the money to help kids? You're a good man, Butch McCormick. Don't let anyone tell you differently. That includes you, muscles."

Butch pressed her hand to his lips, his eyes nearly burning with tears.

"I am glad for the twisted fate that brought me here. I'll even take the shredded tire and banged up wheel well, because I know when I look back on my time in Tennessee, you're going to be the best part."

He loved the idea of being her best part of Tennessee. He wanted to do something for both of them, something to write a story that would remind them both of this unexpected time together.

"Katie, I'm going to play at the Grand Ole Opry on Saturday."

She looked up him with confused eyes. "Okay. Where is that?"

Butch frowned at her clear lack of education. "In Nashville. You've never heard of the Grand Ole Opry?"

Kate pressed her lips together tightly. "Should I have?"

"Hell, yes. You're coming with me. Trudy and Hyde usually come with me. We'll drag Jeb and make a weekend of it."

"Can Tom come, too?"

"Sure. The ladies will adore him." Butch waved at the spread of papers on the table. "I need a break from this. I'm going to go upstairs and play for a bit. Call me when Jeb and

Tom are back, please." He stood from the couch, walking away from the remnants of his life. Then he stopped, went back to Kate and kissed her deeply. Sweetly. A word floated in his mind: love.

K ate sat on a folding chair in the middle of the front yard. Chubsy sat on her feet. Both of them looked at Butch's house. The classic farmhouse had an off-set front door, with tall windows and a low porch that ran the width of the house. The house sat atop a small hill overlooking the road. It wasn't imposing, but cozy. She smiled, imagining Butch and Jeb as children, running around the yard causing all sorts of trouble. She imagined their children would do the same.

"Children?" Had she actually thought about children? Kate looked at the little hillside that would make a perfect sledding hill, if it ever snowed enough to sled.

Tom pulled up the driveway and blocked Butch's truck in the garage.

Kate made a note on the edge of the paper. "Going to need a better way to park."

A door slammed closed and Tom's voice called across the yard. "You know you look like a crazy lady sitting on that chair facing the wrong way and talking to yourself. Maybe you hit your head harder than we thought."

"Ha ha. I'm working on something. If you're not going to be helpful, go away." Kate twisted, hiding her work from him.

"Ok. You have my curiosity up. What are you working

on?"

"Butch's house. You won't believe how much crap he has at his house in California. He's going to need twice the square footage to handle even half of it. I thought the old farmhouse could be spruced up a bit. Look here." Kate held out her sketch pad. "It needs new bedrooms—ones with closets—and the one bathroom thing has to go. I thought if we got rid of the second floor altogether, just opened it up like a vaulted ceiling, and salvaged the wood, we could add wings here and here." She pointed to the east and west sides of the house. "We'll have to move the garage, but he needs more parking anyway."

"At this rate he will. Where did you find that chair?"

"Garage." Kate smiled when he returned and planted his chair next to hers. "He needs a studio, a big one. I think an office would make sense, too. He can't work on card tables and boxes."

Tom pulled a pen from his pocket and drew on the nearest corner. "Maybe three wings would be better. Make it into a square, like this, with a courtyard. We could separate the living quarters, his work space, and visitor rooms."

Kate nodded. "Unless we soundproof the studio, you wouldn't want bedrooms near it. He's a night owl."

"The west wing will be the bedrooms. First floor will have four bedrooms and two baths. The upstairs will be the master suite with a sitting room and office."

"Unconventional. I like it. Plus the sun won't wake him."

"Exactly, and he'll have good light in the evening."

"The east wing will be his performance wing with easy access from the central house. There." Kate showed Tom the sketch pad. "By the way, Butch wants us to go to the Grand

Old Opera with him on Saturday."

"Opera? Seriously?"

"I guess. It's in Nashville. I didn't have a chance to look it up on the Internet. He said the ladies would love you."

"Well, naturally. Count me in. Look at this." Tom steered them back to the house. "I can do a lot with the roofline."

"We could do two floors on the studio. The second floor can have a balcony."

Tom grinned. "Excellent. Let's take a look at her bones."

The pair of bone diggers invaded the house, tapping on the walls and crawling on the floor. "This wall isn't a bearing wall."

Butch stopped playing and looked up from the piano. "What's a bearing wall?"

"A wall that holds the house up," Tom answered. "We can't cut one."

Butch frowned. "Why would you be cutting my walls?"

Kate stood up, pointing to the closed door off the living room. "To make room for all your shit. What's behind this door?"

"My grandparents' bedroom." Butch slid off the bench and opened the door. The forgotten bedroom held a treasure trove of goods.

Katie stepped around a pair of stacked chairs. "Huh. There's more furniture in here than in the whole house."

"What do we do with this?" Tom asked.

"We'll cut the wall and build the studio out from here. We can build the stairs up to the second floor."

"Studio?" Butch nearly ran into Kate, he followed so closely. "A studio with a second floor?"

Kate elbowed his ribs teasingly. "And a balcony."

"I like balconies."

"Who doesn't?" Tom considered the walls, the ceiling. "The plaster will come down easily enough. I like the idea of salvaging the wood for the bedrooms, but I think we need to go high tech in here. Do you want a recording studio or just a practice studio?"

Butch blinked once then again. "I don't know. Both?"

Tom smiled. "Good answer. Can we get into the attic?"

"He needs to look at her bones," Kate explained.

Butch led the way up the stairs to a panel in the hallway ceiling. Tom pulled a chair from Butch's studio room. With the low ceilings, the small boost gave Tom enough to poke his head in.

"She looks healthy, Kate. Definitely looks good." Tom reset the covering panel in place and jumped down to the floor. "The exposed wood is gorgeous, but there's no insulation. If we don't want to burn all of Butch's money heating this place, we need to insulate."

Butch moved the chair out of the way. "Cooling is harder. We hardly use the heat."

"Huh. Makes sense, though." Kate bit her lip. "Is the roof original?"

"No. My dad replaced it about ten years ago. It nearly killed him to have the original slate removed."

Possibilities filled her mind. "Make my day, Butch. Please tell me he saved it."

"Every last stone."

The trio traipsed down the stairs lost in their plans for the great farm revival. Butch flipped through Katie's crude sketches, but he could see it. His home. It was everything he never knew he wanted. The screen door closed.

"Mama. Dad." Butch shoved the pad back at Kate and glared at Jeb. "What are y'all doing here?"

"Having dinner." His mother pointed to her cheek.

Butch obediently kissed her cheek. "Mama and Dad, this is Katie and Tom Riley. These are my parents, John and Emily."

Butch favored his father with his light hair and sharp features, but he had his mother's easy smile. Jeb had his mother's darker features, but his mouth was set in the same stoic position as his father's.

"Jeb tells me you are living with Butch," Emily said to Kate.

"It's more like rooming with instead of living with."

"For now," Butch said just to watch her blush. He dragged her under his shoulder. Kate pushed away, but Butch held strong.

"How's your head, Katie?" Jeb asked.

"Tender."

Emily looked at Kate, her brows pressed together in question. "What happened to your head?"

Kate unconsciously touched the knot on the back of her head. "Bumped it wrestling with my cousin. Not a big deal."

Emily felt the knot. "You need ice. Good Lord, John, it's like a house full of teenagers again. We best stock up on the first aid. I suppose none of you cook either." Emily sighed. "Butch, Jeb, clear that junk off the table and set it properly. Tom and John, fetch the chairs. Katie, you're with me in the kitchen."

Kate looked up at Butch with panic in her eyes.

"Mama, cooking really isn't Katie's thing. I'll help you in the kitchen, and Katie can help Jeb." Butch pushed Kate to his brother and swept his mother into the kitchen before she could protest.

Kate stacked Butch's papers and took them up to his room. Her gaze swept through the living room while they moved the table, looking for an escape. Jeb laughed quietly.

"What?"

"You're scared."

Kate wrinkled her nose. "I am not."

"Sure you are. Your hands are sweaty, and you're fidgety. You didn't flinch fighting with Tom and me yesterday, but here you are, shaking in your boots in front of my parents."

"You know what, Jeb? Fuc-functional table. Works as a desk and a table." Katie patted the table as Emily walked in.

"Oh yeah, it's a really unique piece. It's what we locals call a 'card table.'" Jeb laughed at Kate behind his mother's back.

Kate followed his lead and flipped him off when Emily turned her back to pin Jeb with a steely look. "When are you going to bring home a nice girl?" Emily asked her oldest son.

"When I find one as good as you," he said smoothly.

Kate coughed into her hand. "Kiss ass."

Jeb flicked the table cloth at Kate, and a tug of war broke out. Jeb yanked and pulled Kate halfway across the table as they both laughed.

"Take it easy, Clyde," Butch reprimanded. "She's half cracked as it is."

"The hell I am," Katie denied.

Tom slapped her hip. "He meant your head."

Kate pulled Butch aside, and Jeb and Tom followed. "I can't be here. I'm going to say something stupid, and they're going to hate me."

Butch ran his hands up and down her arms. "You're not going to say anything stupid, Katie."

"She usually does," Tom said. "She opens her mouth and shoves her whole foot in it."

Kate pulled down on Butch's shirt, bringing his face to hers. "You see? I'm a fucking disaster."

Jeb flinched. "Don't say 'fuck.' Goddamn it, Jesus Christ, and holy shit are also no-nos with Mama."

"Are you kids hungry?" Emily called. "Soup's on."

Kate managed to get the shirts of all three men in her grip. "If I go down, we all go down."

They walked like a gaggle of geese to the table. Jeb sat at the head with Kate next to him and Butch on her other side. Tom sat across from Kate, within kicking distance. John sat at the other end of the table, and Emily settled in between her husband and Tom.

"Well, this is nice." Emily reached out her hands to her husband and Tom. Her sons followed suit.

Tom jumped when Emily grasped his hand. Kate slapped at Jeb when he did the same. Jeb locked his fingers with hers. Kate looked at Tom who shrugged his shoulders at the circle that was made.

"Dear Lord," Emily began. "We thank you for the new friends you have brought to our table this evening. In these trying times, we rely on you, dear Lord, to help us find our way. We ask for your blessing for our meal here this evening. Amen."

"Amen," Jeb, Butch, and John answered in unison.

"Amen," Katie and Tom muttered a half-second behind.

Katie raised an eyebrow at Tom. He shrugged his shoulders again. He didn't know what they were supposed to do any more than she did. Emily took charge of Tom's plate and loaded it heavily with ham, creamy potatoes, and buttered peas. Butch served Kate a much smaller portion, for which she was grateful.

"So," Emily began as she served her husband. "Where are y'all from?"

"Michigan," Tom answered. "Detroit."

Emily shimmied in her seat. "The motor city. What was that like? Growing up there?"

Katie's brows pressed down. "Just normal?"

Tom kicked her and glared.

"What do y'all do?"

"Tom is a structural engineer," Kate said with pride.

"Katie is an architect. A damned good one," Tom said and got three kicks in the shin.

Kate smiled at her cousin. He called her Katie.

Emily's eyebrows disappeared above her bangs. "Oh, well. That's very interesting. What are y'all doing down here?"

Butch shook his head. Katie and Tom shut their mouths tight, leaving Jeb to answer. "Now, Mama, you need to keep an open mind."

Emily tapped her fork on her plate one, two…five times. "About what?"

Jeb sighed. "It's their building going up on the Parsons farm."

Emily picked up her napkin and touched it daintily to her thin lips. She closed her eyes and just held the napkin in place. The room became very quiet, the tension stretching out until it was as tight as a drum. Butch and John kept their eyes on their plates and filled their mouths with dinner. Tom glanced at Kate, looking as clueless as a man can when a woman is upset. Katie shifted in her seat; she never could stand an elephant in the room. If it stood there, she poked it.

"You object to the Cicada project?" Katie asked carefully but got kicked anyway.

"I do." Emily replaced the napkin in her lap. "I object to our farmland being bought up cheaply, raked over, and turned into a fresh pile of concrete."

Kate put her silverware down, set her elbows on the table, and linked her fingers to cradle her chin. She looked at Emily, giving her full attention. "I can see why you would object to that. But that isn't what happened."

Emily crossed her arms over her chest and leaned away from the table. "Just how would you know what happened?"

"Katie and I negotiated the deal." Tom turned toward Emily.

Tom never let Kate take the heat alone for a decision they made together. The resolute commitment they built as children had grown as they became adults, professionals, and partners. Where Kate was, Tom stood behind her as her second and vice versa. Individually, they were impressive. Together, they dominated and succeeded.

"All right," Emily said. "Explain to me how that monstrosity you are building is not destroying our way of life."

Katie took her time, selecting her words carefully. She'd heard too many smart people say really stupid things because they weren't thinking. "Tom and I have been working with Cicada for over a year on the type of building they wanted for their world headquarters. They wanted a place that reflected their principles and their priorities. They've had a presence in central Tennessee for over fifty years. They started in Chicago, but they found a home with the people here in Tennessee, and it was their first choice for where to invest in their future. When we found Mr. Parsons, his farm had been on the market for over a year."

"You lowballed him," Emily accused, her narrow gaze darting between the cousins.

"We did," Tom agreed. "And he countered with a figure that was overpriced. That's part of negotiating. In the end, the price was fair to both parties."

Emily huffed. "Four hundred acres of farmland are gone."

Kate nodded. "How much did you offer Mr. Parsons for it?"

Emily's chin jerked up. "Us? We have all we can handle already."

"How about your neighbors? The ones that like to yell when they drive by. How much did they offer Mr. Parsons? Why did he turn them down?"

"They don't want his farm," Emily admitted uncomfortably.

Tom leaned forward, speaking in a gentle voice. "Do you know why Mr. Parsons wanted to sell his farm?"

Emily nodded. "His wife passed on, and his arthritis is bad. His kids didn't want the farm." Her voice was only a shade above a whisper.

Kate lifted her head and held out her right palm. "So on one hand, we have a man who wanted to retire but couldn't afford to. His children didn't want his farm. His neighbors didn't want his farm." Kate flipped her over left palm. "On the other hand, we have a company who felt a deep connection to central Tennessee and wanted to make it a showpiece for the world." She clasped her hands. "Together we have a good fit. We'll employ over two dozen local laborers for nearly a year and then two hundred people will work there. That doesn't count the local subcontractors and suppliers we're using. All of that tax money stays right here. Yes, the farmland is gone, but there are good things, too. Mr. Parsons can retire and nurse his knees, the buildings won't become dilapidated and the land overgrown. In terms of jobs and money for the community, the land is going to be more productive under Cicada than it ever was producing soybeans. I'm not saying every project is a win-win or it isn't important to protect a way of life that has helped you raise such a wonderful family. I'm just saying this isn't one of those projects where the land is being raped to dump a pile of concrete."

Emily looked around the table at the averted eyes.

Eventually Jeb cleared his throat. "It's true, Mama. They've hired county boys. They're doing good work."

Emily stood with her plate in hand. "Well, it seems you've given me something to think about." Then she silently slipped into the kitchen and out the back door.

Morning had yet to break when Kate stumbled into the kitchen in stockinged feet.

Tom sat at the kitchen table sipping coffee while playing on the computer. "How's your head? I worried you might have a concussion."

"Please. My head is harder than that. And it is better today, so don't lecture me." Kate poured herself a cup of coffee but knew in the silence her cousin gave her one of his "bullshit" looks. With an exaggerated sigh, she conceded. "I'll keep it light. I won't swear at anyone." When Tom chuckled, Kate amended her statement. "Well, I won't yell."

"Completely reasonable."

Kate ran her fingers through her hair and twisted the mane into a braid. "Did you see my hair brush? I thought I left it in the bathroom, but I can't find it."

Tom turned the laptop toward Kate. "Haven't seen it. Maybe it's in Butch's room. Look, I found it."

"Found what?" She bent over to see the screen without the glare.

"The Grand Ole Opry. It's a live radio show with different acts. Every Friday and Saturday night."

The webpage contained images of happy people with guitars and cowboy hats. "What kind of music? Opera? He hasn't played any opera since I've been here. When did cowboy hats become an opera thing?"

"Not opera. Country music." Tom clicked a link and a tinny, twangy song rang out.

"Oh. Okay. That makes more sense." Kate straightened up. "Do you think we have to wear something? You know, like cowboy hats or boots?"

Tom stopped the sample and gaped up at her. "God, I hope not. Look at all these sparkly things they're wearing—and those are the guys."

"What are y'all looking at?"

At the sound of Jeb's voice, Kate stepped in front of the computer. She heard the click behind her back as Tom hastily closed it. "Progress schedule. Work. Nothing interesting."

Tom poked her in the back, and Kate shut up.

Jeb poured a cup of coffee and leaned against the counter. "Are you working today?"

Kate nodded. "Light duty. Nothing too heavy or too loud."

"And no driving, just to be safe"

"Yes, Sheriff. No driving."

Kate kept her day light. She would have lied to anyone who asked and said it was because she promised to take it easy. The truth was she wasn't one hundred percent. She knew it when she didn't mind sitting at her desk and catching up on paperwork. Paperwork was a necessary evil—emphasis on the evil. Kate poured through the daily reports, submittals, invoices, and emails, and by early afternoon could see the top of her desk.

Paula rapped twice on the doorway as she poked her head in. "Kate, the sheriff is here to see you."

Kate met Jeb in the middle of the trailer. "What happened? Did you find something?"

His face an iron mask, Jeb gave no indication of his agenda. "Is there somewhere we could talk?"

"Hold my calls, Paula. All of them." Kate led Jeb into her office where she shut the door and both the windows.

Jeb paced back and forth in the small space, like a rat caught in the maze. Kate stood behind her desk, facing him with crossed arms. The anxiety he radiated tripped her own radar. She shifted her weight between her feet, waiting for Jeb to talk.

"I found her cell phone. The last call came from Butch's house."

All the color drained from Kate's face. "You don't think that… No, of course you don't."

"Someone is setting my brother up. That's what I think, and I'm so…I'm not thinking straight. I needed to talk to someone. I'm getting in my own way, and I know it."

"You can't talk to your staff, can you? Sheriff McCormick, brother of the leading suspect."

"I have to preserve some semblance of objectivity if I'm going to stay on the case, but I'm not in the least bit objective."

Katie took a step back at the fierce look in his eye. Something dangerous lived inside Jebediah McCormick, something he did a damned good job of keeping under wraps. A man like Jeb didn't ask for help lightly. Butch needed Jeb to survive his ex-wife's death, and it looked like Jeb needed Katie to beat back his own monster.

"What's bothering you the most? Let's just get it out in the open."

Chapter Eight

Those cold, gray eyes settled on her face. "Someone went into that goddamned house while he was asleep. Asleep! When I think about what they could have done." Jeb struck at the desk that stood between them.

Angry men didn't faze Kate. Twenty-nine years of living with it desensitized her to the raw emotion that was a symptom, not a cause. She ratcheted down her own response, leaning casually against the file cabinet behind her. "It's a Steelcase desk. It's been kicked more than a few times and has never dented. Have at it."

His mouth curled into an ugly sneer, his eyes focusing on the desk as though it was his mortal enemy. Jeb reeled back and kicked the desk again. Thunder roared in the small room, giving voice to Jeb's hostility.

"Is it helping?"

Jeb didn't look at her but kicked the desk again. "No. Damn it, no."

Despite bragging about her desk, Kate wasn't sure it could take this kind of punishment. Fortunately, a construction site offered options. "Come with me."

Outfitted with a hard hat and safety glasses, a bewildered Jeb followed Kate out into the yard a short distance away from the productive construction. She stopped at an equipment trailer and selected a twelve-pound sledgehammer before continuing to a pile of excavated rock.

"Take off your shirt, you don't want to get it sweaty."

Jeb scowled and crossed his arms. "This isn't going to help."

"It will if you do it right. Do you know how to swing a sledge? I've been doing it since I was fifteen. Do you need a lesson?"

Jeb stripped his shirt, muttering under his breath. "I don't need a lesson in swinging a sledge."

Kate swallowed a smile when he ripped the buttons open on his uniform and stood in his T-shirt. Men were so easy.

She set the hammer on the ground at his feet and stepped a safe distance away. Jeb picked up the hammer and brought it down on a thick slab of concrete. He adjusted his grip. He adjusted his stance, looking for a rhythm.

Each stroke of the hammer was a shot to her head but Kate pushed it away. Pain was temporary. "Smooth, easy, downward. There ya go." She eased him into conversation to help focus his thoughts. "How come you and Butch call each other Clyde? Was Clyde a favorite uncle or something?"

Jeb found a rhythm that suited him and started talking in small bursts between each fall of the hammer. "Trudy's family owns the farm next to ours. Her old man had an ass,

Clyde, which was as mean and stubborn as he was. If you came to close to him, he'd bite and kick."

"Her father or the ass?"

"Both, but I was talking about the ass."

"I only have experience with the two-legged kind of ass. Is that normal for the four-legged kind?"

"Clyde was the most unreasonable animal I've ever met." Jeb fell into a steady rhythm. "Mama hated it. She would chase it away from her garden. Sometimes with a shotgun."

"She shot it?" Kate asked in both surprise and admiration. She noticed Jeb start to sweat, and the knot between his brows loosened, the set of his mouth eased.

"No. Wanted to, no doubt. One day, Butch and I were arguing, the way brothers do. She got a hold of us and said if we were going to act like Clyde, she was going to treat us like Clyde, and she tossed us out of the house. We started calling each other Clyde while we rolled on the ground, fighting over whose fault the whole thing was."

Kate wanted to crawl into a bottle of codeine, close her eyes, and just float. Instead, she kept her gaze on Jeb. "That's it, Clyde. You found the rhythm. You got it. Now talk to me."

Jeb heaved and smashed. "Angie's car was spotted in an abandoned lot outside of town." Heave, smash. "It was unlocked, no damage." Heave, smash. "Her phone was wedged between the driver's seat and the center console." Heave, smash.

"Her purse?"

Heave, smash. "Haven't found it." Heave, smash. "Yet."

Kate watched the weight of blinding fury that came with hostility fade as the confident, hard-ass she knew to be Jebediah McCormick re-emerged. She saw it in his eyes, heard it in the challenge of the word "yet."

Heave, smash. "She called Butch's house Sunday night. Nine forty-eight. The call lasted two minutes and six seconds."

Kate shook her head. "That's not right, Jeb. The phone didn't ring. I didn't go to bed until ten. I was with Butch, listening to him play until then. The phone didn't ring."

Heave, smash. "Are you sure you just didn't hear it?"

"That's possible, but I absolutely know neither of us answered it, even if it did ring."

Heave, smash. "Butch called her at eight thirty-three Monday morning. This time the call was shorter. Just a minute and a half."

"Somebody called her Monday morning. I wouldn't assume it was Butch. All he wanted to do was go back to bed after dropping me at work."

Heave, smash. "Somebody called her."

"That somebody wasn't there when he got home from dropping me off at the job site. He would have told you."

Heave, smash. "Somebody came in after he was home."

Kate furrowed her brow. "That's scary. He's upstairs asleep, and someone is creeping through his house. Maybe they didn't know he was home."

Heave, smash. "His truck was in the garage."

"What if he woke up?"

Heave, smash. "Either they would have hurt him, or—"

"He knows them," they said in unison.

Jeb dropped the hammer and picked up his shirt. "Damn it. Damn it. I need to get into the house."

"Come back to the trailer, I'll get you a towel. Butch is in Nashville today, so the house is empty."

Jeb quickly lifted the hammer to his shoulder when Kate would have picked it up. He put it back in the tool shed and walked with her back to her office. There, she dug into a black gym bag and tossed him a thick towel. He wiped the sweat from his face and neck. "I have to think this through. I have to do it right, or I'll make it worse."

"I want to help but don't know the rules. Tell me what to do…or what not to do." As she stood from bending over, her office spun in time with the pounding of her head.

"I'm going to need to go through the house and figure out who's been there." Jeb shrugged on his shirt, quickly buttoning it.

"Besides you, me, Tom, and your parents?"

"Yeah." Jeb pulled his shirt back on. "It's been Grand Central Station lately. You all right?"

"My head is killing me. Is it okay if I go back to the house with you? I need to lie down. I won't touch anything."

"I'm glad you're taking care of yourself." Jeb handed her the safety glasses. "I was going say you look like shit, but I didn't think you'd take too kindly to it."

Kate tossed the glasses on her desk, powered down her computer, and texted Tom her plans. A nap, just an hour, and she'd be back on her feet. "I take great care of myself whenever the men in my life stay out of the way."

Butch took the back roads out of Nashville. His stomach had turned through the entire meeting. He'd sat opposite Fawn, faced off against a woman he once thought he loved. The dispassion with which they discussed the

details—sometimes intimate details—of their short life together sickened him. Butch said little throughout the meeting, letting Finch do the talking. Fawn, on the other hand,
alternately spewed venom and nonsense while her attorney,
present on speakerphone, failed to contain the damage.
Finch made mincemeat out of Fawn Jordan. Being right,
having the moral upper hand, should have made Butch feel
good. But it didn't.

Butch saw shadows of the girl he married in the woman
sitting across from him in her designer dress and camera-
ready hair. She wasn't as innocent as she had been, but she
was still in over her head. Butch didn't want blood. He just
wanted out.

The powerful engine of the truck vibrated under his feet
as Butch raced through the back roads. He'd taken the long
way home, needing the quiet and the sweet country air just
to be able to breathe. How had he been able to breathe in
Los Angeles for those few years? Well, he hadn't really. He
spent more time in his cabin in the mountains than he had at
their home. He could breathe there. He needed more than
concrete and steel.

Butch turned onto his road. Jeb waited at the stop sign,
and Butch pulled up next to his brother. "What are you
doing out this way?"

"Driving your Kate around. That is one helluva woman
you've got there. I wouldn't do anything stupid when you
get home."

Butch noticed a change in Jeb's attitude toward Kate.
The chronic distrust in his voice had changed to something
that sounded like respect. When had that happened? Why
was Jeb driving Kate anywhere? "What's going on?"

"I'm going to get Mama and Dad. We'll be back with dinner shortly."

Butch drove the quarter mile to the house, puzzling out what happened while he'd been in Nashville. With a half-smile teasing his mouth, he realized anything could have happened. Damn near anything. "What're you up to, Katie?" He never wondered what any of his wives were doing when he was away from home. He always knew. Angie was about her crusades, Tessa "created," and Fawn spent money and networked. Katie? Lord only knew what she was doing.

Well, maybe not the Lord.

Butch pulled up the drive and watched the redhead pace the length of the porch in long, thundering strides. She pushed at the flaming hair that swirled around her in matted disarray. Everything about her stance, everything about her movement, said if she came after you, she was bringing the fires of hell with her.

Butch left the truck in the driveway and walked toward her. He didn't notice his stomach had stopped turning. He didn't notice he felt like he was home. He only noticed the woman with the clear blue eyes locked on his.

Kate threw her hands in the air and shouted to him. "The world is full of idiots."

Butch stood at the base of the porch, putting his eyes on level with her chest. "I believe I can agree with you on that."

She planted her boots squarely in front of him. "You have your stupid idiots, your dumb-ass idiots, and your gar-den-variety idiots. I just got a call from Tom that a stupid idiot decided the site was a NASCAR test track and tried to lay down some rubber. The stupid idiot lost control and nearly put the car in a twenty-foot pit. That's one less stupid idiot I have to pay. Before that, a dumb-ass idiot nearly fried himself by not cutting the power to the circuit he was tapping. Let workman's comp pay for that one. And then we have your garden-variety idiots."

Butch scratched his head, hiding his grin. "I'm not your garden-variety idiot, am I?"

She narrowed her eyes challengingly. "Did you agree to anything today without your shark?"

He laid his right hand over his heart. "No, ma'am. My shark did all the talking."

Kate nodded sharply and then restarted the rant. "Then you're not a garden-variety idiot, or at least you're a smart enough idiot not to admit it. The thing about idiocy? You can't do anything about it. You can't beat it out of a man. You can't cure it. There's no shot for it, no pills to pop, no surgery to take that part out. Oh, sure, once in a while you can get lucky and vote it out of office, but usually you're just hosed until it dies."

Butch barked out a belly full of laughter, mounted the two steps to the porch, and wrapped his arms around her.

She leaned away from him, a stern look in her eyes. "Glad you find this so amusing. I was gone thirty minutes, just thirty minutes, and a plague of idiocy breaks out on my site." With a long sigh, she leaned her weight against him. "Screw it. Tom and Waters can deal with it."

Butch loved the feeling of her revved body going soft against his. There was so much strength in this little package, so much fire and passion. He would never tire of coming home to her adventures.

Kate drew circles on his back. "How did your thing go?"

"Don't want to talk about it," he said in her hair.

"That bad?"

"I just want that part of the day to be over. I want the good part to start." He swayed gently. "You're home early."

"My head hurt. It was getting better until—" She stiffened. "What are you doing?"

Butch pulled her hair back, kissed her neck. "Dancing with you."

Kate pushed against his chest. "Well stop. I don't know how to dance."

The order made him smile. He tightened his arms, in case she decided to make a break for it. "Sure you do. You danced with me at the Sly Dog."

"No, I didn't. I just stood there. You danced." She pushed at his arms, but he didn't let her retreat.

"All you have to do is relax, like you were." Butch began singing in her ear. It was an old standard, one even she knew.

"Love me tender, love me sweet, never let me go. You have made my life complete and I love you so." He hummed a little, feeling those words resonating in his soul. He wanted to tell her but feared his feelings would scare her. Still, he wanted her to know what she meant to him, hoped she felt the same. He tightened his arms around her.

Kate held on to him and followed his lead. The man had a way of taking her off her game like no other. Here she was, ready to take a broadsword to the idiots of the world, and he had her dancing on the porch. Then his words touched her. Like little threads of magic, the words he sang wound through her head and her heart and her soul, making her feel alive in a way she never had. She closed her eyes, holding those words to her heart. Words spoken by a man of her dreams. Could he ever really mean them for her? Did she want him to? A man like Butch would change her life. Did she want that?

He chased the last rational thought from her head when he bent down and kissed her. Instinct and need rose and Kate met his kiss with equaled passion. At that moment, the world fell away. Sensation painted her world in scarlet red. Against that back drop, she saw only Butch. Her body heated, consumed by the flames he fanned in her. Butch ended the kiss and looked into her eyes. She saw his worry there, reminding her of the day he'd had. Tonight, he wouldn't worry about a thing. "Come inside. Let me take care of you. I'll make some dinner, and we can spend the evening pretending the idiots of the world don't exist."

Butch kissed the tip of her nose. "Making dinner is not taking care of me. That's adding insult to injury."

Kate tickled him, and he jumped away. "I meant I would heat up leftovers, not actually cook. Jeez. Have a little faith." She took his hand and led him into the house.

"Jeb said he was coming back with my folks and dinner."

Kate stopped abruptly just inside the door. She had forgotten. Butch had kissed away her good sense. When Jeb came back, Butch would have a new mess to deal with.

"You're not afraid of my mama, are you?" Butch asked, misunderstanding her reluctance.

"Hmm? No. I'm impressed she's willing to come back after last night. I don't think I'm ever going to be on her favorite list, but I'm not afraid of her. Why don't you play piano until they get here? I could probably make a salad or something to go with whatever they bring."

Kate steered Butch to his piano, and once she got him to sit, his hands moved of their own accord. She stood behind him and watched. His fingers swept strong and sure across the keys with remarkable speed. Quick, powerful music. The sharp movement of the white keys reminded her of watching a hail storm and ice hitting the ground with enough energy to bounce up and strike again.

Gradually, his head bowed as if weary. The tone changed, the rhythm slowed, the pitch raised, and he cried. Not from his eyes; that would have been easier to take. But from his heart, from his soul. He wept, and it broke her heart.

Kate brushed away her own real tears. "Enough." She stomped her foot hard enough to make Butch jump. "We are not going to let them do this to you." She climbed on the bench and straddled his lap while the piano bellowed in dissonance. "This is not who you are." She said the words that came from her heart. "You are not going to let your ex and her lawyers make you feel you are anything less than extraordinary. Let them take their money and their pound of flesh, but don't you dare let them touch your heart and soul. I've been around a lot of people, a lot of good people, and you're one of the best. Look through my eyes, and see what I see."

Kate pulled his head to hers and opened herself to him. She kissed him as she had never kissed another man. For keeps.

After a moment of surprise, Butch kissed her back. "Be with me. Make me feel alive." He bent her over the piano keys and while the strings rang out, he loved her. His hands tugged her black shirt from her jeans and found the soft, hot skin beneath. While she clung to his shoulders, his hands raced up and down her ribs, feeling every line of her tucked-in waist and firm muscles. With each touch, her heart raced. Her breasts heaved against his chest, begging for his attention. Her back arched, inviting him to taste.

He worked his way from her mouth to her chin to her sensitive throat. His hands spanned her waist, his thumbs tracing the arch of her ribs. Her stomach fluttered beneath his hands. She rocked her hips against his. Closer. She wanted to be closer.

A muffled cough broke through the heat. "Clyde, I've heard of piano for four hands, but that's an unusual style you two have."

Kate jumped, her elbows crashing down on the piano. Running was her first instinct, but Butch held her in place. His forehead to hers. Their breath mutually ragged.

Butch's fingers dug into her hips, holding her as he looked over his shoulder to his brother. "Clyde, can you just get lost for a few more minutes?"

Jeb stood in the doorway, the screen door closed tight against his back. "Clyde, I could, but I don't think Mama's gonna accommodate you, and I'm sure whatever you could do in a few minutes would not impress your lady."

The screen door opened with a sharp *tsk* from Emily McCormick. "This chicken needs to go in the oven. John, did you bring the applesauce? Jebediah, why are you blocking the door?"

Kate jumped from Butch's lap, trading grace for speed. Facing the wall, she tugged down her shirt and re-tucked it. Presentable, she turned and faced the parents of the man she had come to realize she was falling for. "Hi, Emily, John."

"Hello, dear. Is that cousin of yours home? I made fried chicken. He's not going to want to miss out on it." Emily walked through to the kitchen, her voice trailing behind her.

Butch called after his mother. "You just made me fried chicken last weekend. Are you trying to make me fat? You know I pay a trainer a lot of money to keep me lean."

Emily's voice carried to the living room. "I don't know why you pay them all that money. You look fine just the way you are."

Jeb leaned against the doorway, looking between the kitchen and his brother, the devil in his eyes. "I keep telling him honest work would do more for his body and his soul than some high-priced trainer."

Emily poked her head out of the kitchen. "When was the last time you went to church, Butch?"

"My soul's just fine, Mama." Butch narrowed his eyes at Jeb's silent laughter. "Stop trying to get me in trouble."

"You and I are going to have a talk," Emily said to Butch, then she turned to Kate. "Is Tom on his way home?"

"Calling now." Kate pulled her phone from her pocket and dialed. "Emily wants you to come home for dinner. I'm pretty sure no one's eating until you're here."

Butch bent close to the phone. "Family rules, Tom. Get home now."

Emily came into the living room, wiping her hands on a towel. She took the phone out of Kate's hand. "Tom, it's Emily. It's well past time you were done working. Clean up, and get on home. I made my famous fried chicken." She paused to listen. "Fifteen minutes is just fine."

Emily patted Kate's arm when she returned the phone. "Now, let's get to work. Jeb, Butch, set the table. John, you have chairs. Katie, you're with me."

Kate grasped Butch's hand. His mother was making a real effort to be friendly, and Kate wanted to avoid causing another scene. Butch took a step forward, but Kate stilled him with a tug on his hand. She needed to do this.

"Emily, I know we didn't get off on the best foot last night, but I want us to be friends."

Emily cocked her head in a kind, motherly manner. "Good. I want that, too."

Kate's hand squeezed Butch's to the bone. "And friends are honest with each other, so I'm going to be honest with you. I can't cook. I can't make toast without burning it. Even boiling water puts up a fight."

Butch stepped closed to Kate. "I can attest to that, Mama. Katie is a woman of many talents but none in the kitchen."

A knowing smile grew on his mother's kind face. "All new homemakers are like that. It just takes time, practice, and patience. Unpack my bags while I make gravy for the potatoes."

Kate looked up at Butch. "Did your mother just imply…?"

Jeb's heavy hand fell on Butch's shoulder. "Yep. I could get used to you as a sister-in-law."

The smell of home cooking filled the farmhouse. With so many hands, preparing for dinner was light work. Tom walked in, covered in dirt and smelling like a productive day. "Am I late?"

Butch set the last plate on the table. "You are officially on time, but go wash up, or Mama won't let you near the table.

In minutes, everyone sat at the table in the same seats

as the night before. Tom set the tone for the meal telling of the NASCAR idiot who nearly put his Camaro into the basement of an elevator shaft. Jeb topped that with a topless dancer who stopped a would-be robber using only her G-string. Then Butch jumped in with the woman in Dallas who tattooed his face on her breast.

Kate's jaw fell open. "Are you so famous you have psycho, obsessed fans?"

Butch puckered his lips. "Psycho and obsessed might be a bit harsh. Enthusiastic. I have enthusiastic fans. That sounds much better."

Jeb cleared his throat and played with his mashed pota-toes. "Speaking of psycho and obsessed, I need to talk to you about something. We found Angie's car and her cell phone."

Emily pressed her hand to her heart. "Such a sweet thing. I still can't believe what happened, and right here. It's good news you found them, right, Jeb?"

Butch set his fork down. "I hear a 'but' coming."

Jeb let his own fork fall to his plate. "The last call to her was Monday morning at eight thirty-three from a phone in this house."

Butch shook his head back and forth slowly. "No. There's some mistake. I was asleep. I was here by eight and went back to bed. It was too damned early to be up."

Jeb angled his chair to face Butch directly. "Did Angie call you Sunday night? A little before ten?"

"No. No one called after Katie and I came home from the Sly Dog. The phone never rang. I don't think it rang all day."

Jeb sat quietly, his jaw flexing as he ground his teeth, a sign he was thinking. "When was the last time you used the house phone?"

Butch dropped his elbows to the table and buried his hands in his hair. "I don't know, Jeb. I usually use my cell phone. I'm not sure I've used it since I've been back."

Jeb pulled out his phone, thumbed through his contacts, pressed a button, and waited.

Chapter Nine

The phone didn't ring. Butch jumped up, his chair falling to the floor with a crash. He ran for the phone, intending to find out why, but Jeb leaped up, cutting him off.

Butch shoved at his brother. "What the hell is going on?"

"Don't touch it, Butch. Don't touch anything. I want to call some people in. Do I have your permission to search the house? Dad? You, too?"

Butch stalked away to stand in the picture window. "Goddamn it, Jeb, you sound like the law."

"I am the law, and I've got to do this legally, or anything I find could be thrown out in court."

Butch raised his chin. "And if you do it legally, and someone's planted something on me, you could use it to hang me."

Emily stepped between her sons. "John Michael McCormick, Jr., don't speak to your brother that way."

"It's all right, Mama." Jeb rested his hands on his

mother's shoulders. "He's right. If I found evidence about Angie, it could be used against him." Jeb looked into his brother's eyes. "I'm asking you to trust me, Butch. I know I'm just a local sheriff now, but I'm good at this. Let me search the house. I ran through it before, unofficially, but let me do this right."

Butch let his hands drop with a heavy slap. This couldn't be real. But if it was, there was no one Butch wanted on his side more than his brother. He nodded his consent.

Jeb stood, phone in hand. "Finish your dinner. It'll take the boys a little while to get here."

"I'm not hungry."

"Go eat anyway. This is going to take a while." Jeb crossed to Butch and stood shoulder to shoulder with him. "Who has access to the house?"

"Is that a serious question? This house hasn't been locked since the day it was built, just like every other farmhouse in this county." Butch sighed. That was the problem with good people living in a good place. People shared what they had and borrowed what they needed to get by. Deals were done on a handshake. A thing like murder could change all that.

Jeb herded Butch back to the table. "Have you noticed anything missing? Out of place?"

Butch sat, shook his head hard enough to send his long hair flying.

"Yes you did," Kate said. "The wrench. The big-assed wrench."

Emily cleared her throat. "Language, please."

Butch focused on his brother, who looked right back with raised eyebrows.

"Granddad's biggest wrench was missing from the

workbench. I thought it was there the first weekend I was back, but I can't be sure. I wasn't taking inventory, just looking around, but I don't remember anything being out of place."

Jeb pulled his notebook from his shirt pocket and made a note. "Did you ever find it?"

"Katie did. Inside the tractor." Butch turned to his father. "That's why it wouldn't move that day I tried to use it. Kate had to nearly take the whole tractor apart to find it."

John looked at Kate. "How would it get in there?"

"With help, that's for sure. The gears were stuck on it. It's a good thing you guys stopped when you did. I imagine it could have really damaged the machine."

Jeb looked between Butch and Kate. "Anything else missing or out of place?"

Butch ran his hands through his hair. "I don't have much. I thought I set that picture of all of us on the shelf." He pointed to a small framed photo of him with his parents and brother. "Mama gave it to me my first night back. I laid it there, but I didn't set it up."

"All right. What else?"

"I don't know, Jeb. I don't. I've been messed up since I've been back. I keep losing things and forgetting what I'm doing."

Kate leaned close to Butch, resting her hand on his knee. "I've been around you for nearly a week. You aren't absent-minded. You haven't lost anything. Somebody's doing this to you, and we're going to figure out who."

With a chirpy rap on the door, Trudy walked in carrying a bag in each hand. "Anyone in the mood for ice cream?"

Butch paced the long porch, his hands shoved so deep in his pockets he could scratch his ankles. The State boys arrived in short order and picked through the house. His house. That's what it was.

"Damn it all. What are they doing in there?" Butch looked through the window to see a pair of armed men going into his grandparents' bedroom. He paced to the end of the porch, kicking sharply at the post that held the roof.

Kate came to stand next to him, staring into the rainy night. "Add that to the list."

"Add what?" Butch looked down into scheming eyes that sparkled in the ambient light.

A smile grew to match. "The porch."

Tom stepped to Butch's left side, a big hand thumping his shoulder. "A kick-ass porch. It's on the list." Tom hopped to the ground despite the rain.

Kate winked and followed him. "The kick-ass goes without saying. It'll be one of ours, after all."

His mother and father broke off from a conversation with Trudy and Hyde, distracted by the pair squatting on the soft ground. His mother looked at Butch in a silent question then put it directly to the cousins. "What are you two talking about?"

Kate stood and flashed Emily a pure, fun-loving grin. "Ideas."

John slipped out of his light jacket to drape it across his wife's shoulders. "Come to the big house. Standing out in the rain isn't helping anyone."

At his own dining room table, John sat huddled with Kate and Tom. "I never liked the bedrooms myself. Too danged small and no closets. Of course, when I was growing up in that house, we didn't have a lot of stuff to put into closets."

Kate bounced in her seat. "It sounds like your son has a lot of stuff—"

"I don't need it," Butch snapped from a corner of the room. The position let him keep an eye on the front door for his brother and on the conspiracy developing at the dining room table but didn't invite conversation. He abandoned his position, crossed into the living room, and stared out the front window. In the dark, wet night, the window reflected back the tight face of an angry man. He didn't recognize himself in that face. He looked at Kate in the reflection, already regretting the way he snapped at her.

She met his gaze and gave him a private smile. She hid her mouth from prying eyes and blew him a kiss. Butch reveled in the intimacy of being close to her.

"Of course you're fine." Trudy sat curled up in an armchair, content as a cat. "You never needed anything California had to offer."

Butch snorted. He turned around, leaning against the window frame and looking at Trudy. He didn't waste his breath on an argument.

"I'm serious, Butchy. You can travel around the world fifty times, and you aren't going to find any place as good as home."

Hyde saved Butch from the fruitless conversation when he finished his second bowl of ice cream and changed the topic. "I should finish your Shelby tomorrow, Little Red.

That's a sweet ride you got."

"No shit." Kate jumped to her feet and did a quick shuffle. "Really? You wouldn't be messing with me, would you?"

"I've messed with many a pretty lady, but never you. I'll bring her over when she's done."

Trudy wrinkled her nose. "It's going to rain. It's supposed to rain all night and all day tomorrow, too."

Hyde shrugged dismissively. "Won't slow us down much."

Katie danced and spun to face Tom. "What do you want to do?"

Tom tilted his head back, gaze to the ceiling. "I need things. I was planning to come down here, slap you around a bit, and go back up to Michigan. I didn't pack enough to stay."

Katie grabbed two fists of her cousin's shirt and shook him, although he didn't move. "A mall? You want to go to a mall? We finally have a day off. Let's do something fun."

Hyde scraped his empty bowl, licked his spoon again. "Aren't you two just a little too happy about a rainy day?"

Tom unwrapped Kate's fingers from his shirt. "Our fathers worked every day it didn't rain. Sun, clouds, wind, cold, heat. But not when it rained. Those were our holidays."

Kate crossed her arms and pouted at her cousin. "And you want to spend this one at the mall."

Trudy unwound her long legs and rose from the chair like royalty. "I'll go with you, Tom. We'll shop, and I'll show you all my favorite places. You'll see why this is the best county in the state." She tossed her hair back and graced Tom with her homecoming queen smile.

The corner of Tom's mouth twitched. "Any day with a

beautiful woman is a sunny day to me."

Trudy beamed at Tom while behind his back, Katie gagged.

Hyde took the truly empty bowl to the kitchen. "We'll get the Shelby on her feet in the morning. By then, Butch will have his sorry ass out of bed. He'll keep you company, won't you?"

Headlights wound up the long drive, cutting through the veil of rain. Butch grabbed the curtains. "He's here."

Jeb stepped into the light spilling from the big house. His head hung low, and rain bounced off his hood. The sagging shoulders and slow strides made Butch swallow hard. Good news did not come from body language like that.

Jeb stepped onto the porch, shook off the water, and entered the house. He raised his hood, showing his blank face. "Hyde, take Trudy home."

Trudy ran to Butch, her hands on his forearm. "I want to stay."

"Go on home, Trudy." Butch looked over Trudy's head, his gaze on his brother's face. He knew they found something. "Go."

Trudy tossed her hair with a small *hmph*. "Are they staying?"

Hyde slid his hat on. "Come on, Trudy. You heard the sheriff. Little Red, I'll see you in the morning." Hyde swept his arm around Trudy's waist and ushered her into the rain.

"I'll come by tomorrow, Tom," Trudy shouted as Jeb shut the door behind them.

"Tell me," Butch demanded.

Jeb sank heavily into a living room chair. John came into the living room, as did Kate and Tom, but no one came between the brothers.

"Was someone in my house?"

"I think so. We got a partial. Did any of you touch the family picture on the shelf or the phone in Granddad's room?"

Tom held up his hands in innocence. "I didn't touch any phone or any photo in any room."

Kate crossed her heart. "Me neither."

Butch closed his eyes and pinched the bridge of his nose. "I handled the picture, but I didn't remember there was a phone in Granddad's room. I took some chairs and a table out of the room, but there wasn't a phone on them."

"I need prints for you, Kate, and Tom. To eliminate you."

His brother wanted to eliminate him. Butch felt like doing a little "eliminating" himself. Instead, he simply said, "Fine."

When Kate started to nod, Tom rested his hand on her forearm. "I want to help, Jeb, I do. But I don't understand what's going on. I'm not so sure Kate and I should be giving our fingerprints without talking to someone."

"Tom—"

Jeb rose to his feet, and his movement interrupted Kate's argument. His hands ran over his buzz cut. "It's all right. Call your attorney. He can come down with you if you like. Butch, call Finch. I hope to God you don't need a lawyer, but you're going to need your agent. Your ex-wife getting murdered in the field behind your house isn't going to stay a small-town secret much longer."

Emily had come down the stairs, a knit blanket draped over her arm. "Do y'all want to sleep here tonight? Kate can take the guest room and—"

"No. I'm not getting chased out of my house." Butch

held his chin high, making sure everyone in that room heard what he said. "I'm sleeping in my own bed."

Kate threaded her arm through Butch's. "Then let's go. I've had enough intrigue for one night."

"If you're going, I'm going." Tom held out his hand to John. "Thank you, sir."

John shook the strong hand, the muscles in his forearms straining. "We'll talk more about that little project for Butch's house. Jeb, you staying or going?"

Butch stood defiant, Kate and Tom on his flanks.

Jeb rolled his eyes and almost smiled. "Going. Somebody has to keep an eye on the boy and the two city slickers."

K ate woke to soft light and a muted percussion. The hushed sound of the soft, spring rain tugged at her to get up to play. Kate stretched, but a heavy weight across her waist held her in place. Sprawled beside her, Butch held on like a possessive child with his teddy bear. Kate slowly turned to face him. Butch was a handsome man, and in his sleep he looked like a model for a Greek statue. He could model for Apollo, with his long, sun-bleached curls. Kate drew her fingers across his full lips, unable to resist touching him. His dusty-blue eyes fluttered, opening to hers. He smiled dozily, snuggled into her, and soon snored lightly.

Kate lay there staring at the ceiling while the rain played on. She turned her head to kiss his cheek. Why did she feel so comfortable with him? She should be freaked out with Angie's murder, but she knew Butch had nothing to do with it. She trusted him innately.

All the men she knew were either loud, crude, over educated, or brilliant, or in the case of her family, all of the above. It was a refreshing change to be with a man who did his own thing on his own time table, without all the noise. He may sleep away perfectly good mornings, but he didn't just follow in someone else's footsteps. He made his own way.

Kate savored the intimacy of sharing Butch's bed. She never shared a man's bed without sex being first and foremost. It was exquisite torture having his body this close. Together, yet apart. Her body ached. Her breasts, the junction of her thighs, the muscles of her stomach craved him. And yet, there was something perfect about this. Kate closed her eyes and breathed him in. She willed herself back to sleep. It was, after all, her day off.

Crap, she was awake.

K ate bounced into the kitchen. The cold shower had taken the edge off just enough that she could think without imagining Butch au natural.

Jeb laughed from his seat next to the kitchen window, an empty plate in front of him. "Don't you two know what sleeping in means?"

"It's nearly eight-thirty. I slept in over two hours." She poured a cup of coffee.

Tom sat with his elbows on the table, his forearms curled around a plate of eggs and toast. "Ignore him, Kate. He's just grumpy because he's sore. There are eggs in the skillet."

Kate walked over to Jeb and pushed her index finger into his shoulder blade. "Here?"

Jeb jumped. "Ouch! Goddamn it." He threw an elbow toward Kate then winced, swearing all over again. "Don't touch me."

Tom sipped his coffee. "Waters told me you were swinging the hammer. He said you didn't do too badly for a cop." Tom winked at Kate. "Let us know if you're up for some demolition work. We pay cash."

Jeb looked at Kate, then Tom with cop eyes. He pursed his lips as if to say something then, with a heavy sigh, shook his head. "I'll take a pass, but thanks for the offer. Did you think any more about the fingerprints?"

"I called our attorney." Tom leaned back in his chair, crossing his thick arms over his chest. "We don't have to, Kate. He's not arresting us, and we have no obligation."

Kate used a small dessert plate for a scoop of eggs. She ate a few bites before answering, using the time to reason it through. Her prints were in this house. She'd been living here for almost a week. Her prints were supposed to be here. "I don't see how Jeb can prove someone is setting Butch up if he can't show someone else has been in the house. I want to do this, because it will show there's another person in play here."

"I knew you'd say that." Tom turned to Jeb. "Do you mind if we get this done early? I'm going shopping later with Trudy."

"We can go now. You'll be back in a half hour. No point waking Butch, he can come down later." Jeb stood slowly and shuffled to the door.

Kate set her half-full cup of coffee on the counter. She snickered when Jeb caused a traffic jam at the back door.

"I'd forgotten how much work swinging a sledge is.

Couldn't I have kicked your desk a few more times?"

"Venting demons takes work. Sometimes painful work." She poked his shoulder again and snickered when Jeb swore at her.

B utch woke to the sound of his own voice coming through his window. "Here, boy" told the stories of the adventures he'd had with his favorite dog, a black Lab named Max. He'd sung the song a thousand times, and it still made him smile. That's how he knew it was a good song. It never got old.

"Damn it, I know what I'm doing." Hyde used the same voice when he lost at poker.

"If that's what you look like when you know what you're doing, I'm afraid to see you when you're clueless. Let me do it."

"Watch your fingers. Dang it. Will you just let me…"

Butch huffed out a laugh. "Not your normal sound of spring."

"That's right," Hyde said, his voice suddenly smooth, coaxing. "Easy does it, girl. That's right. Let Hyde do the work. We're almost there. That feels good, doesn't it?"

Kate giggled, and a switch flipped inside Butch. What the hell was Hyde doing? Butch kicked at the sheet and nearly fell out of bed scrambling to the window. Below, Hyde and Katie laid on a sheet of plastic, their legs poking out from under the Shelby. Separately. Of course separately. What did he think they were doing?

"It feels good to have everything in the right place,

doesn't it? I know it does. Hyde knows."

Butch curled his fingers into the wood of the windowsill, pressing his head against the screen in the window to see better. What were they doing? Hyde should have fixed the car before he brought it over.

Kate said something. Hyde laughed. Butch's brows pressed down. Hyde crawled out from under the car, Kate mirroring him.

"She's perfect." Kate patted the car affectionately, running her fingers over the curves. "Want to take her for a spin?"

"Hell yeah. Just let me clean up."

"I'm going to tell Butch we're going out for a test drive. What do I owe you?"

He handed her a bill. "Just the cost of the parts."

"And your time?" Kate read the paper.

Hyde shook his head. "Any friend of Butch's is a friend of mine."

"No, Hyde. I earn my way. Your time's as valuable as mine. I'm paying you."

Hyde cocked his head and softened his tone to a saintly patience. "Little Red, you and I are going to have a long talk about being gentlemanly."

Kate crossed her arms over her stomach, shifted her weight to one foot, and tapped the other. "You're not being gentlemanly. You're being pigheaded. This isn't over." She stalked toward the house. The screen door slammed.

Butch chuckled as he slid back into bed to wait for her. After a minute of waiting, he went downstairs to find her. "Katie?"

Kate came out of the kitchen into the entryway biting

her lip. "Did you go into the kitchen?"

"No, not yet. Why?"

She wrung her hands. "I set a coffee cup on the counter, and it's not in the same place. I'm sure it's not."

Butch went to her. "Where's Jeb? Tom?"

"Jeb's at work. Tom and I went with him this morning to get our fingerprints taken. Tom left with Trudy a little while ago." Her voice climbed. "Are you sure you didn't do it?"

"Of course I'm sure, but there are plenty of us around here. Aren't you getting upset over nothing?"

"You don't think someone was in the house again?"

He pulled her close to ease the stress that had crept in. "Because a coffee cup isn't where you remembered? No, honey. It's your day off. Enjoy it. Take Hyde for a ride in that pretty car of yours. When you get back, I'll take you on a picnic."

Kate shook her head. "I should stay."

He caught her chin with his fingers. "Don't argue with me." He kissed her nose. "I have work to do, and you and Hyde bickering like cats and dogs won't do much for my creativity. Go have fun with Hyde. Don't worry about anything."

Four hours later, Butch wanted her home. It wasn't that he was lonely. He'd been alone for the last year with no problem. It wasn't that he was bored. He had a piano, his guitars, and more material in his head than he could manage. It wasn't that he was jealous. Hyde had been his friend nearly as long as Jeb had been his brother.

He simply wanted Katie home. He called her cell but didn't leave a message. He called back an hour later, checking on the car, letting her know he finished working.

He couldn't sit still any longer.

For the first time in weeks, Butch felt like doing something physical. He didn't have his gym, but he had a barn full of straw that had to be stacked. He pulled a pair of heavy-duty gloves from the workbench and went about re-arranging the bales. One. Two. Three.

Fifty. Fifty-one. Fifty-two.

One hundred six. One hundred seven.

Instead of calming him down, it revved Butch up.

K ate let Hyde drive back to the garage. Under his direction, she had driven through miles of rolling county roads. Now it was his turn for a little fun. Hyde had done more than replace the tire and repair the wheel well. He'd tuned her Shelby until she purred down the road. The man did appreciate a fine piece of machinery. Kate imagined he would do the same for the right lady. "How come you aren't married with children, Hyde?"

Hyde's shoulders jerked back. "Me? Aw, hell, I don't know. I'm not very good around women."

"I noticed that." Kate smiled when Hyde blushed. "You're all tongue and thumbs around women. But around a car, you're smooth as silk."

"I don't want to be smooth as silk. I want to be as smooth as cream. Cream tastes good."

Kate rolled her eyes. "Fine, be smooth as cream. The point is, you should be, and you're not."

"I don't know what to say to a woman." Hyde fingered the bill on his ball cap.

"That's bullshit. You don't have any trouble talking to

me."

Hyde pushed the hat off his head, pulled it right back on, and glanced at her. "You're not a woman."

Kate winced, and Hyde saw it.

He took his foot off the gas, letting the speedometer fall as he apologized. "Oh, I didn't mean it like that. I just meant that you're more like one of the guys than a girl."

He'd hit a sore spot. Just one of the guys. Sometimes, all she wanted to be was one of the girls. Then it occurred to her she had hit one of Hyde's sore spots. And with her usual tact, she'd jammed her finger in the spot just like she had done to Jeb's shoulder that morning. No wonder men didn't see her as feminine. An elephant in a tutu had more charm that she did.

"I'm sorry, Hyde. I just mean I think you're a great guy, and I'm surprised some woman hasn't swept you off your feet yet."

Hyde downshifted to in-town speeds and soon turned into the parking lot of his shop. As the engine idled contently, Hyde struggled for words. "Well, jeez."

"You're a good friend." When Hyde blushed, Kate leaned over and kissed his cheek, her hand on his coat.

Hyde got out of the car, then bent down to look at her. "I appreciate what you said. So, friend to friend, you and Butch got a thing, right?"

"Something. I think. Maybe." A tingle of excitement zipped through Kate at the idea of her and Butch "having a thing." They'd danced. They'd kissed. That was definitely a thing. A thing she wanted more of right then. She got out, went around to the driver's side, and got back into the car. After she closed the door, she rolled down the window and adjusted her seat and mirrors. "You have any interest in servicing the site trucks? A few are due for maintenance."

Hyde took a step back from the door. "I'd appreciate the work. I'll give you a discount."

"The hell you will. I'm paying going rates, or I'm giving the work to your competition."

Hyde pressed his lips tight. "Little Red, you're not winning on this one."

Kate threw the Shelby into gear and drove around him. "The hell I'm not. By the way, I paid my bill. Check your pocket." She beat it to the driveway, watching in the side view mirror as Hyde shook a fist full of money at her.

She kept the driver's window down, despite the light rain that fell. Freedom was a cool, spring day and miles of pretty, open road. With the after-market radio blaring, Kate sang loud and out of tune all the way to Elderberry Farm.

The gravel popped under her tires as she rolled up the long drive and parked in front of the garage.

Butch walked out of the barn wearing jeans, boots, and a good, healthy sweat. His bare chest heaved as he pulled the gloves off his hands.

Kate moved toward him, liking the look in his eyes. "What has you all hot and bothered?"

Chapter Ten

Butch walked right up to Kate, invading her personal space to capture that smart aleck mouth. His hands, flushed with the power of hard work, curled around her waist and pinned her to him.

She pulled back, gasping for air. "Wow. What have you been up to?"

"I've been thinking about you. All damned day." Butch bent forward, forcing Kate back until only his arms kept her upright. Her hands clutched at his shoulders, drawing him closer. "Do you know what it does to me? Sleeping next to you? Feeling your body against mine? Smelling your sweet scent calling to me? Do you have any idea what it does?"

Kate didn't retreat from his need but looked him in the eye and met him with her own. "Yeah, I do. What are you going to do about it?" With a wicked grin, she broke his hold on her and ran for the house.

Butch caught her in the kitchen, sweeping her off her

feet. Kate shifted in his arms, wrapping her legs around his narrow hips. "Hurry," she said, finding his earlobe with her tongue.

The steps creaked as Butch carried her up the stairs. Kate used her hands, her mouth on his exposed body. Her frenzied exploration drove his need, drove his legs until then they were finally in the bedroom they shared. Butch lifted her hips, tossing her on the bed. She laughed as she landed, welcoming him as he covered her body with his own. His hands caught hers, and he held them above her head, taking her mouth. All his. The way her passion matched his, Butch hoped it meant she saw him as all hers.

Kate spread her legs wide, cradling him in the place he most wanted to be. Her body quivered in anticipation.

Butch pushed himself higher until he was over her, blocking everything else. His tongue captured her mouth, taking her prisoner. She followed his demanding lead, enticing him to take more.

He held her wrists with one hand, using the other to push her T-shirt up until he cupped her breast.

"More. I want more," she said, brazen about her needs.

"I'll give you all you can take." There were too many clothes and not enough room. He rolled, and they fell off the bed. Butch managed to land first, then he rolled her beneath him again.

She cried out in frustration. "Let me touch you."

Butch rolled until she sat astride him. Her hands stroked across his chest and arms while he tore the clothing from her body. He needed to feel her soft, hot skin under his hands. He flung her bra across the room and, rising up, locked his mouth onto her breast. She arched back. Her hands clenched in his hair, holding him to her breast. Passion overwhelmed him. The urge to have her, to possess her, to consume her drove him into a frenzy. He took her other breast into his mouth, suckling hard and teasing her nipple, while his hand slid around the curve of her waist to the rivet.

Kate guided his head back, fastening her mouth to his. She pushed him to the floor, sliding down as she explored every plane of his body. She licked his nipple. When his body jolted, she flicked it with the tip of her tongue and then sucked hard.

"That's it," Butch said as warning an instant before he rolled her beneath him. His breath was fast and ragged as he peeled the jeans from her body.

She lay in front of him, a hungry look in her eyes as her hands ran across his stomach. Her body undulated against the painted wood, her red hair spilling across the floor, wearing only delicate black panties against her creamy skin. Her skin was flushed and her mouth swollen, her chest heaved with peaked nipples. "You see what you do to me?"

Butch had never seen anyone so beautiful in his life. Need surged through him again, hard. The need to claim her, to have her. Butch bent his head and nipped at her mound through the thin material. She pushed against his mouth, her scent calling to him. The harder he nipped, the deeper he nuzzled, the more ragged her breathing became, and the faster she pushed at him.

"Butch, please."

Butch tore the panties from her hips. "Sweet heaven."

From the fiery nest of curls rose a tattoo of a scarlet red phoenix with outstretched wings. Butch pinned her hips to the floor and bathed the mythical creature with his tongue.

Her fingers pulled at his hair, urging him on. His hands moved between her legs to her core. He slid a finger into her moist heat and was bathed in her need for him.

Butch knelt up, kicked his shoes off, and took her mouth again. He undid his jeans and slid them down far enough to free himself. He was so hard, he was going to embarrass himself soon if he didn't do something about it. Then he froze. "I don't have any protection. I mean I wasn't planning…I didn't intend…this wasn't why…I'm clean. I just had an exam for new insurance. I have papers I can show you." What was he babbling? He knew he needed to shut up before he ruined the moment.

Kate placed a finger on his lips, silencing him. "It's okay. I'm on the pill, and per my last checkup, I'm clean, too." She spread her legs wide, inviting him into her body, a seductive smile stealing across her face.

Butch slid into her without preamble. Kate came off the ground, and Butch belted his arms around her. She was so hot and so tight, he couldn't remember how to breathe. Her fingers buried deep into his back, openly demanding his attention. His hips took on a rhythm of their own, finding a stride that had Kate mewing like a cat. Her helpless little sounds burned him up. Harder and harder he drove into her until she opened her mouth to scream, and he captured it. He swallowed the sound of her first climax with him, taking her into him for always. For always, he thought as he thrust deep into her. His own climax shattered him, challenging everything he thought he knew sex to be. Aftershocks rippled through her, and he pressed on her most sensitive spot, adding to her pleasure until his strength gave out, and he collapsed onto her.

Butch lay in the heady haze of good, hard sex. When he could breathe again, he propped himself up on his elbows and looked down at Kate. Her wide eyes stared up at him. Big and blue and wide. He lowered his head and kissed her lovingly, reverently.

"Did I hurt you?" he whispered.

She stared at him with those eyes too wide and shook her head.

He didn't want to move, but knew he had to be crushing her against the hard floor. Butch let their bodies separate but, feeling a little desolate, held her head to kiss her again. He rolled to his feet, pulled his jeans back over his hips. He picked her from the floor and lay on the bed with her. Kate's head found the niche in his shoulder, her naked body forming against his. She fit perfectly. Her head was right under his chin, and her soft breasts nestled against his chest. He didn't try to fight the impulse to run his hands over the curves of her back and hips.

After a moment, Butch began to worry. Kate laid so quiet, so still.

"Are you going to talk to me?"

Kate looked at him with wide eyes. "I think you swept me off my feet."

Butch buried his hands in her hair and took her mouth again. "It's about damned time. You've had me ever since you held that damned wrench above your head like it was a NASCAR cup."

"That would be the Stanley Cup, where I come from." Kate smiled contently. Her fingertips traced the contours of his rounded pec and flat stomach.

"Yeah, we like that one, too." Butch shifted toward her,

improving her access. He wanted her to touch him. "You're so beautiful."

Kate's chin came up, and she blushed. "You think I'm beautiful?"

"No. I know you're beautiful." The gravel popped on the driveway below, warning of impending and unwelcome company. Butch kissed her upturned mouth and pulled her up to sit. "Come on, we'd better get you dressed before our roommates come back."

Kate slid off the bed slowly, as though she didn't want to go. She fished her bra off the chair and picked up her panties by a frayed end. "You tore these!"

Butch grinned at her proudly. "You drive me crazy. I was in a hurry."

"Wait until you see what I do to you tonight." She took a new pair of panties from her dresser drawer and put them on slowly as Butch watched. Then she shimmied back into her jeans.

Her teasing words and the quick shake of her hips had Butch stirring again. "I think I discovered something today." He found her shirt and pulled it over her head, pausing to stroke the soft skin of her breasts.

Kate dropped her head back as he touched. "A bed is softer than the floor?"

"Yes, but no. I have a soft spot for you. I didn't like being here without you today. I know I told you to go," he said when she lifted her head and started to interrupt. "I won't pretend it makes sense. This has never happened to me before, so you're just going to have to be a good little woman and not press me on this."

Kate laughed like he had hoped she would and flashed

him a wicked little grin. "Right, because I am the model for a good little woman. I hate to be the one to tell you this, but you're in for a world of trouble if a good little woman is what you need."

Butch tugged her hair back and kissed her hard. "A good little woman and a lot of really hot sex." Butch relished the ability to touch her and, if he read her reaction right, she enjoyed touching him just as much. "Did you eat lunch?"

Kate shook her head. "You promised me a picnic. Rain or not, I'm holding you to it." She found his shirt, turned it right side out, and held it out for him. Butch let her dress him, encouraging her to put her hands on him.

Butch had planned the picnic while he moved the bales. He'd planned to charm her, maybe sweet talk her into a little kissing. It was a good plan then. It was a good plan now. "Let's go to the kitchen and see what we can find."

"Maybe we can order pizza."

He stopped at the bottom of the stairs, holding her there. "Who has pizza on a picnic?"

"Who says you can't have pizza on a picnic?" With a satisfied smile, Kate fell into him.

Butch took her hips and lifted until her legs wrapped around him. With her hair falling around them, Kate pressed her lips to his.

"Clyde, I've told you about that kind of behavior." The screen door squeaked in protest when Jeb pulled it open.

Butch held Kate's hips against his when she would have jumped back. His gaze roamed over her face with warm eyes, and a cocky smile curved his lips. "I'm in the privacy of my own house, Sheriff." The smile was only for her. "What I do with a pretty girl here is between her and me."

Jeb grinned at his brother. "Nice to see you kids are getting along. What do we have to eat? I missed lunch."

Getting all six of them to Nashville had been a feat. Tom and Hyde climbed in with Jeb while Butch took Trudy and Kate. Kate was ready in five minutes with one small, half-empty duffle bag. Trudy hauled two roller bags and spent ten minutes picking out driving shoes before racing ahead of Kate for the front passenger seat. Trudy manned the radio and the climate controls with authority, complaining that Butch's songs weren't played enough and the wind was ruining her hair.

Butch had wanted Kate with him, but she just smiled and slid into the back seat. Sunglasses on, she sat right in the middle, where Butch saw her with a glance in the rearview mirror. The entire drive, she had a smile on her face and her head on a swivel taking in everything. That was Kate.

Trudy walked into the Hermitage in downtown Nashville like she owned the place. This was one of Butch's favorite hotels, and he had treated her to the classic decadence before. She barely glanced at the suited valets and bellmen as she dove into the eclectic little shop inside, leaving others to deal with her bags and debris.

Kate followed Butch in and goggled as if she'd walked into a cathedral. The marble floor and vaulted ceiling captured the little architect's attention so much so that Butch had to take her arm to save her from tripping up the stairs and walking into furniture. While Butch checked in, Kate begged paper from the front desk and sat on one of the plush couches to sketch. Butch watched her while the others checked in. Something in her eyes—a light, a twinkle that came with a pure joy of life—showed the way she appreciated the beauty around her. An older couple with that same twinkle in their eyes looked over Kate's shoulder, and she talked to them for several minutes about the features of the architecture.

Butch left the bags to the bellman and swept Kate off of her feet to get her out of the lobby. Kate kicked and squirmed but couldn't break his hold.

"Put me down." She pushed at his arm. "We're in public."

"In this beautiful place, with a sexy woman, it's a man's prerogative to be romantic. Stop fussing."

She kicked her legs for freedom. "Someone might see us."

"I just don't care." Wasn't that something? He didn't care who saw him with this woman in his arms. In fact, he wanted everyone to see him, see them together. His Katie.

When her frown subsided into a shy smile, he leaned in and rewarded her with a kiss.

Her head rested on his shoulder as they rode the elevator up, butterfly kisses tickling his neck. The bellman opened the door, and Butch carried Katie inside, putting her on her feet so he could tip the bellman on his way out. As soon as the door had closed, he tackled her onto the oversized bed. They tumbled and laughed and tickled until neither of them could breathe, then he kissed her and loved her with all his heart. Completely relaxed and thoroughly satisfied, she turned her head into the pile of pillows with a happy little sigh.

As Butch came out of the shower with a decadently thick towel tucked around his waist and another drying his hair,

Katie lay sprawled, naked as a jaybird on the bed, exactly as he had left her. With her arms above her head, her ripe breasts, draped in a mess of her red hair, called invitingly to him. He couldn't resist stroking the little phoenix winking up at him.

In her light sleep, the fingers drawing over her sensitive skin raised goose bumps on her skin and tightened her nipples. She shifted her hips to stroke, to soothe. She opened her eyes to find him staring down at her.

She smiled up sexily. "You look good wet."

Butch smiled. He didn't say anything. He just ran his calloused fingertips over the peek-a-boo tattoo.

She licked her lips, rolling her head in the pillow. "What are you doing?"

"Taking a picture."

Her eyes flashed, and she snatched the sheet over her in a move that was sheer speed. "No, you aren't, you pervert."

Butch roared out and fell on to her, hugging her sheet-wrapped body. "Not with a camera, you prude. With my mind. I want to remember forever what you looked like here, sexually tamed by yours truly."

Kate laughed and narrowed her eyes. "Sexually tamed? Ha! You didn't tame me."

Butch readied to pounce on her again when his phone rang. "Trudy," he said to Kate before he answered the phone. "I know we said thirty minutes. No, I didn't know that was forty-five minutes ago. Yes, we're on our way." With a sigh, Butch cast aside the towel and pulled on underwear and jeans. "We're late for an afternoon of good food and better music."

Kate slid out of the bed and purposely brushed Butch as

she went for her jeans. "Hmm. Food sounds good. Something has my appetite up." In under five minutes, Kate wore jeans and a pale green blouse, had her hair in a twisted, sexy flip, and stood waiting at the door.

"Well, little woman, you'd better eat up, because you are going to need all that energy for what I have planned for you tonight."

Kate and Tom walked along Broadway like the tourists they were. It was the middle of the afternoon, but music spilled into the street like prime-time Friday night. People milled around everywhere, shopping with street vendors, taking pictures of famous bars. Tom and Kate elbowed each other and pointed and giggled at the sights while their four friends walked around like they were back in their old neighborhood.

Butch held the door open at Jack's Barbecue and treated them all to one of the finest meals in town. Trudy delicately nibbled. Kate devoured some of the best ribs she had ever tasted. Butch wore a ball cap low on his head, but that didn't stop people from staring or coming up to him. Butch was polite, too polite, Kate thought as his lunch got cold while everyone else ate.

"I would weigh two hundred pounds if I lived here." Kate pushed the rest of her ribs away and licked the sauce off her fingers.

Tom snagged Kate's plate of leftovers as though they were at home. "I would want this every day. Do they deliver?"

Trudy pushed her food aside and wiped her fingers with

the lemon-scented wet wipe. "I feel like dancing tonight and need a new pair of boots to do it in."

Jeb winked at Hyde. "You need to get yourself a pair of cowboy boots, Tom. The women around here, well, they know a colt from a stallion by what's on a man's feet. You want a warm bed tonight? You got to trade in those boats on your feet for some real boots."

Kate chuckled softly, as a large portion of the female population they had passed on the street had already noticed Tom. With his dark features and the black shirt stretched across his sculpted chest, women tripped over their feet to get a good look. Kate didn't think he'd have too hard of a time finding a dancing partner, but when in Rome.

Tom smiled. "Boots, huh? I could wear boots."

With lunch finished, Trudy led the way, trotting a half step in front of everyone the short distance to Second Street and into Nashville Cowboy. The big, open store was all hardwood and new leather. Shelves of cowboy boots from the simple to the ornate lined the walls, while a sign over a doorway at the back advertised "buy one, get two free." Trudy sprinted to the back room, looking for the deal of the century, while Kate perused the size seven selections in the front room. Jeb and Hyde steered Tom toward the men's side of the store. Kate watched them with an eagle eye. Those two were up to something. She just wasn't sure what it was.

Butch, recognized again, stood in a conversation with a mother and her two teenaged daughters, who petted him like he was a golden retriever. Kate split her attention, watching him sign autographs and keeping an eye on her cousin. She picked up a boot to look like she was interested in being there.

"Five hundred dollars?" she gagged.

"And worth every penny," a striking salesman said. A few years younger than her, he had a pretty-boy face that would always look younger than his years. "These are all leather and handmade to last a lifetime."

"For that kind of money, they'd better do more than last."

"Try a pair on, and you'll see the difference. Cowboy boots fit different than other boots, and it's a difference that matters."

Kate rolled her eyes and let him have his way. They weren't leaving anytime soon, so she might as well do something to pass the time. While the salesman went to get the pair of boots, Kate looked through a rack of dresses. She didn't own any. She had a few skirts, black ones she wore for formal meetings and presentations. Mostly, she wore pants. Denim, khaki, linen, pleated, flat front, and fitted waist filled her closet. Though pretty, these dresses would be out of place. They were light and fresh as a spring field blooming with wild flowers.

She pulled out one in her size and held it up to the mirror. In the reflection, she saw Butch had said his good-byes to his fans and tried on a pair of boots. Kate caught his eye, and he flashed an appreciative grin.

"The changing room is right there," the salesman said. "Try it on, and we'll see how it looks with the boots."

Kate rolled her eyes at him again, letting him know she knew he was working her. Then, she swallowed hard. The girl in her wanted to be indulged. Impulse took over, and she practically dove into the changing room, where she tore off her jeans and slid into the pretty dress before she could talk herself out of it.

"That is an amazing dress on you." The salesman waited at a bench with a pair of brown leather boots with intricate stitching. "Try these on."

Kate slid her feet into boots that hugged her feet without binding. She stood, her hands compulsively smoothed the soft cotton over her flat stomach. "I don't think this is me. There's more of me out of it than in. For this kind of money, you would think it would cover something."

Kate stared at herself in the mirror and frowned, disappointed. She wanted to look like a country princess. She wanted to look like a swan, elegant and beautiful. Instead, all she saw was an ugly duckling with too much shape and muscle to be pretty.

Butch came up behind her, wrapped his arm around her waist, and drew his lips across her nearly bare shoulder. "I told you, you were beautiful."

Kate shook her head in denial. "I'm all…yuck."

"There isn't one spot of you that's yuck. I've been over every inch of you. I know what I'm talking about. I like the dress…and the boots." Jeb called Butch away and left Kate looking at herself in the mirror.

She touched the spot where his lips had been. "I'll take them," she told the salesman. "And I'll pay for his boots, too."

Butch spoke with two young women who bounced with every word. Kate butted in long enough to get Butch to take off the boots he wore. The girls were ecstatic to have their photo taken with a shoeless Butch McCormick and swore their undying allegiance to him, like, forever.

The salesman cut the tags off the boots, and Kate handed

them to Butch. He put them on while he listened to them list
their favorite songs. Kate watched him, gentle and generous
with his time with strangers, while she folded her old clothes
into the store bag.

Tom walked up to the cash register to pay for his boots,
looking at Kate as though she'd grown two heads.

"Those look good on you." Kate used her arms to cover
bare skin.

Tom swung a leg back and forth. "They're lighter than
my work boots."

"No steel in the toes would make them lighter. The sole
isn't as thick. And they look better."

"Let's wait outside. I want to look around."

Kate leaned against the building while Tom stood under
a tree, blatantly grinning at every single female that walked
by, age, race, shape, and size be damned. Nearly all of them
grinned back. When he chose to use it, Tom had an animal
magnetism that rivaled an African lion.

Hyde came out of the store empty-handed.

"Not buying today?" Kate asked.

"Nope. The ones I have are just fine. What's he doing?"
Hyde pointed to Tom with his chin.

"Flirting."

His beefy arms crossed and an easy going smile on his
face, Tom said something to every man-less woman that
walked by. And it worked. They smiled at him, giggled,
stopped, and talked.

When there was a lull, Hyde crossed the sidewalk. "How
do you do that?"

Tom grinned. "The secret is to make every woman feel
like she's special."

"Every woman *is* special," Kate scoffed.

"Exactly my point," Tom said. "Blondes, brunettes, hell, even redheads are beautiful. Tall, short, trim, curvy. How many are actually made to feel special? Appreciated? That's what I do, I appreciate. Try it."

"What if she ain't my type?"

"You aren't going to marry her. Just appreciate her."

A thirty-something woman with business on her mind walked toward them with long strides. Hyde leaned against the tree and appreciated the way her heels clicked in a quick rapport. "Afternoon, ma'am. I hope you have a beautiful day."

The woman snapped startled, green eyes to Hyde, and her face warmed into a friendly smile. "Thank you. I hope you do, too." That smile stayed on her face while she walked past him and was still there when she glanced back over her shoulder.

Hyde scratched the back of his neck. "Well I'll be damned."

Trudy fell out of the store carrying a stuffed bag that nearly dragged on the ground. You would have thought she had netted the big game on a safari by the smile on her face. Jeb followed her out, glaring between Trudy and Butch. Butch came out last, shoving his wallet back into his pocket. He wrapped his arm around Kate's waist and held her back from the others.

"Why did you do that?" He glowered down at her. "I was going to buy you the boots. And the dress."

Kate withdrew subtly under the unexpected reprimand. "I buy my own clothes. I don't need you to buy me stuff."

Butch blinked at her. "I'm with a woman, I pay. That was

the way I was raised. A man takes care of his woman. Not the other way around. You shouldn't have bought me the boots."

"What's the big deal? You bought lunch."

"A barbecue lunch is not the same as a new pair of boots."

Kate pulled away, uncomfortable with his reaction, self-conscious about her gift. "You won't take any money for the room, and you've been feeding Tom and me for a week."

Butch's voice stayed quiet but dropped an octave. "So this is some kind of payback?"

Kate walked faster, trying to escape his disapproval. "No. No, not like that at all. I like the way they look on you. You like them. You were busy, I have money. I wanted to do something nice for you. It's not a big deal."

"What are you two doing back there?" Trudy called. "I need to change before we leave for the Opry. Get a move on."

Butch grew silent. Kate put some space between them as they worked their way up the hill to the Hermitage. She felt foolish, clomping up the hill in boots and a dress. She couldn't wait to get to the room and put her jeans on. And a bra. She felt naked without a bra.

The others crossed the street, disappearing through the doors held open by the gloved doormen. She stopped at the curb, waited for a car to pass, and shuffled across the road.

"Katie. Wait."

She stopped only because Butch took her arm, but she couldn't look at him.

"You bought that dress for me, didn't you? And the boots." He lifted her chin until he held her gaze.

"I, uh, wanted to do something to, um, show you how you make me feel."

He took her mouth with his, bending her back until her arms wrapped around his neck. He held her to him, assaulting her mouth until her full lips were swollen and body breathless. "Thank you," he said against her throat. "This is one of the best presents I've ever gotten."

The crowd went wild when Butch McCormick stepped out from the wings to host his portion of the Grand Ole Opry that night. Kate sat wide-eyed while little old ladies from as far away as Kansas swarmed into the aisles to snap pictures of the stars on stage. Butch wore his favorite faded jeans, the trendy button-down shirt Trudy had insisted upon, and the boots Kate gave him. "Y'all like my new boots? Fancy, aren't they? I don't think I'll be bringing in the hay in these, but they sure are nice for dancing."

Kate laughed as Butch did a quick shuffle, remembering what they had done just a few hours ago with their boots on. Save a horse, ride a cowboy.

Butch danced over to his acoustic guitar and played a dreamy melody that quieted the audience right down. He sang of hot summer days and slow summer nights, of girls that tasted like sweet lemons and honeysuckle, of old friends and lost loves. The ladies adored him. Kate saw more than a few draw fingers over tear-filled eyes as they came to their feet.

Butch made a few jokes to dry the tears and traded the acoustic for electric. "It must be these boots. I just can't stop dancing."

He tore into a fast, upbeat tune. Some were on their feet, others in a seat, but everyone in the house moved.

Near the end of Butch's set, Kate saw Jeb jerk to attention. He whispered to Tom and Hyde, and the three men slunk out of their seats. Kate watched them disappear through a door and reappear in the wings. Jeb approached a tall woman with a Barbie-doll figure and a yard of thick, blond hair.

Kate leaned in toward Trudy. "Who is Jeb talking to?"

Trudy looked past Jeb, her breath catching. When she spoke, she practically growled. "Fawn."

Chapter Eleven

"Are those real?" Kate asked.

"The diamonds are, the tits aren't," Trudy said. "She made him give them to her as a wedding present. She said they went with the dress."

"The diamonds or the tits?"

"Both."

Butch introduced the next performer—a little, old man of great renown whose last record was released a decade before Kate was born—and went off stage the opposite direction of his ex. Security joined Jeb, and Kate lost sight of them as they stepped deep into the wings. When the curtain fell on the second intermission, Kate and Trudy sprinted from their chairs to get backstage. A big man with a flat face, who looked as dense as he was thick, blocked the doorway.

"Do you know who I am?" Trudy demanded. "I am Butch McCormick's best friend. I demand to see him."

When that didn't work, Trudy pouted, then begged, and

finally cursed before lifting her chin in the air and walking to the bar. Two Jack and Diet Cokes later, she sat stewing about the fact that the security guards didn't have her name and face committed to memory. The intermission ended, and they returned to their seats.

Kate watched the last portion of the show anxiously. She wanted to be with Butch but had no idea where he was or how to get to him. Each minute lasted an hour. She just sat with nothing to do but wait.

"We are going," Butch insisted. "Everywhere." Butch wanted to share Nashville with Kate and wasn't going to let his ex-wife spoil it. He had brought Fawn here only a few years earlier, wanting to share his past with her, but she wasn't interested in his past, only her future. He expected Kate to be different, and she didn't disappoint. Kate stayed close to Butch, absorbing the scene. She asked about the old times, laughed at Butch's audacity, made friends with every bartender, and left as a favored guest. Butch loved the way she jumped in with both feet and accepted the sometimes odd assortment of characters without reservation. Exuding a natural sexuality that captured and held people's interest, she paid attention to each and every one of them, drawing out details, rewarding the far-fetched storytelling with hearty laughter. He had no idea why she didn't previously have a man wrapped around her day and night.

While Kate explored new territory, Trudy hung on Butch's arm as they bar hopped around the music district. Butch expected Kate to be a little jealous that Trudy kept coming between them. Maybe he wanted her to be a little jealous and hang on him herself, but when Katie smiled at him, they shared a private moment, one that lovers shared, one that transcended charming strangers and clingy friends. Butch gave a lock of her hair a tug, laughing together at the fish story that had grown six inches since he'd heard it last.

In one of his favorite little bars, Steel Strings, Trudy pushed Butch to the stage when the band took a break. He chuckled when Trudy pulled Kate off the bar stool at the back of the long room and raced ahead of the crowd to a pair of empty chairs at the front of the stage.

Butch sat on a stool, cradling a borrowed guitar. "Y'all don't mind if I play around?" he asked the crowd.

The crowd cheered, and the owner, Donny Dowd, the man who had given him a start not so long ago, loved it when the patrons ordered another round instead of walking down the street. Flashes from cameras, phones, and tablets lit up the room like the Fourth of July.

"Let's have a round of applause for the boys."

Cheers rose from the crowd and bounced off the ceiling.

"I've been working on some new songs, and y'all are going to be my guinea pigs."

The crowd clapped and whistled, egging Butch on. "This one doesn't have a name yet. It's about my parents and the way my mother looks when my father walks into the room." A romantic, hopeful song spun from the guitar as Butch sang about the light in her eyes, the spring in her step, and the reason she laughed. How he was the one she reached out for, the one she held on to.

Butch finished the song, and the ladies went wild. They bounded to their feet in a standing ovation and elbowed the men they were with until they stood, too.

A tall blonde with huge rocks stepped onto the stage, a full plastic cup in hand. "Looks like you have another hit, Butch."

"Fawn." Butch steeled himself. He had hoped the conversation Jeb had with Fawn at the Opry would settle things for the night. A flair for drama enhanced Fawn's talent as an actress. She could make a scene like the best of them. With the divorce now public, that's the way she would view this, him—as a scene to be made. He had a choice: the high road or the low road. "Everyone, you know Fawn Jordan. Fawn, this is everyone."

Fawn stalked across the small stage. Butch knew from the look in her eye that trouble came with her. With a quick flick of the wrist, her cup emptied. Butch pushed the borrowed guitar out of the splash zone in the nick of time. The well-aimed drink soaked his hair. Ice fell to the floor, bouncing across the worn stage.

Butch took a deep breath and thought he should have seen that coming. At the back of the room, Jeb and security rushed to their feet, but the going was rough as the audience clogged the aisle to watch celebrity lives crash and burn. On his own for a few more minutes, Butch ignored Fawn and talked to the audience.

"I don't think she liked my song. I thought it was pretty good, myself."

Fawn pitched forward at the hips. "Don't you dare pull that bullshit, Butch McCormick. You sit up here, painting a picture of a good man, a family man, when you are nothing but a selfish, egotistical, backstabbing son-of-a-bitch. You think you can just toss me out? I'm not one of your bitches, bouncing across the stage to kiss your feet just to be thrown out in the morning. The minute you're not the most famous person under the roof you toss me out. I'm your wife. You have responsibilities to me."

Butch knew he shouldn't say anything. You didn't win the battle by sticking your head out in a gun fight. He knew that. But you didn't win by keeping your head down and never firing a shot, either. "Likewise."

Fawn's eyes flashed, and Butch knew she understood the deeply layered accusation. She never wanted a husband, she wanted an agent. She insulted everything he believed in when she used their marriage as a career booster. With the flatness in his voice and the resignation in his eyes, he told her.

Fawn arched her back, outrage and alcohol straining her made up face. "You no good son-of-a-bitch."

Fawn raised her hand to slap him. Butch saw it, expected it, but Kate leapt onto the stage to stand squarely in front of Butch. Trudy clamored up onto the stage to run to Butch's side.

"It's time for you to go," Kate said, in a controlled, neutral voice.

"Katie." Butch calmly set the guitar back on the stand. "Go on and sit down. Don't get in the middle of this."

Fawn glared at Kate. "You're protecting his little whore?"

Security approached rapidly. Jeb stopped being polite and physically moved people out of his way.

Kate spoke softly. "This isn't the kind of publicity you want, Fawn."

"How the hell do you know what I want?" Fawn screamed and swung out at Kate, drawing dagger-like fingernails across Kate's throat. Pushing Kate to the ground,

Fawn launched herself at Trudy.

"You backwoods whore," Fawn screamed, this time slapping Trudy, pulling her hair.

Butch couldn't move fast enough. He tried to separate the two women, but Fawn kept coming, and Trudy fought back. Kate set her brow, lifted Fawn by the waist and tossed her away from Trudy. Butch tied Trudy up, stopping certain retaliation. But it wasn't over. With fire in her eyes, Fawn charged Kate. Kate set her feet wide and steady.

Butch winced. This wasn't what he wanted. "Katie, no."

Kate never flinched. She simply stepped out of the way at the last minute. Thick electric cords that snaked across the stage caught Fawn's fuck-me heels, sending her careening into the set-up of guitars.

Fawn screamed as she covered her nose. "You bitch! I want you arrested. I'm going to sue you for every cent you have!"

Trudy clung to Butch, keeping him from getting to Kate. "Trudy, let me go."

"I think my nose is broken." Trudy wrapped her arms around Butch's waist, preventing him from walking.

Kate pressed a hand to the scratches on her neck, muttering words not fit for prime time. She stepped over the two guitars that were collateral damage.

Butch saw the storm front brewing. He didn't want Kate involved in the mess of his life. He refused to have her dragged through the mud. Frustrated, Butch pulled at the arms Trudy had locked around him. "Trudy, let go! Kate. Don't. Damn it. Jeb! Get up here."

The muscles in Kate's bare arms flexed as she took the bleached hair by the roots. "Try that again, and I don't care who you are, you'll find yourself at the dark end of a deep hole."

Security reached the stage, pulling Kate away and lifting Fawn to her feet.

"You assholes! Get your hands off of me. I'm going to sue you, too. You…Edward. And you, too, José," she said, reading the tags on their shirts.

Flashes from the audience made it look like Steel Strings had installed a disco ball. Butch knew where those pictures were headed. Where they already were. What picture had she painted of him? A petty husband, jealous of her success. He wanted to tell the world how she turned him out of their house, out of their bed the minute she didn't need him.

But he didn't.

Even with adrenaline coursing through his veins, he wouldn't air dirty laundry in a public shouting match. He followed security until he reached Kate, dropping his voice low enough that no one would hear but her. "I said no. What part of that didn't you get?"

Kate tugged the now strapless dress upward. "But she — "

"Butch?" Trudy's voice trembled from behind him.

K ate's heart sunk when Butch turned away from her. She lived with the cold shoulder her entire life, yet the bite stung when she thought herself immune. Tom leaped onto the stage, and she let him lead her to the edge.

"I'm impressed, Katie. I would have laid her out."

Hyde took the last drag of his beer and held his hand out, helping Kate jump from the short stage. "She didn't need to. The ex-Mrs. McCormick did the work for her."

Butch jumped from the stage and scowled at Kate as he went swiftly past to talk to Donny, the owner.

Good, Kate thought, be pissed. He should be pissed with the way the fake-titted Fawn Jordan treated him.

Jeb elbowed Tom. "Get her out of here before Fawn presses charges. We'll meet you back at the hotel."

Kate gawked for an instant before she found her voice. "Her press charges? Are you fucking kidding me? She tripped."

Tom followed Jeb's advice and pulled his cousin out the back door and into the alley.

"This is bullshit, Tom. She comes in and *assaults* Butch *twice*, and she gets escorted out the front door. I protected Trudy, and I get dragged out the back like yesterday's trash. I didn't even hit her."

"I'm not dragging you out like yesterday's trash." But he was. Tom had both hands firmly around her arms and pulled Kate in the opposite direction of Fawn Jordan.

In the skinny alley with brick walks and a sour smell, Kate shouted in a voice too high and too loud. "How could he just sit there and take it?"

"He lives in a different world, Kate." Tom used the deliberately calm tone Kate hated as he maneuvered her out of the firestorm. "People watch what celebrities do. They take pictures and tell stories. It doesn't matter if it's real or fair. It looked to me like Fawn came off as the insane one."

"Don't talk to me like I'm not quite bright." Kate shook off her cousin's hands and fell into step next to him. She still glowered, but her temperature crawled back down the thermometer.

"How's your neck?"

"It stings like hell. I bet she dipped those things in poison. Watch, I'm going to get tetanus or rabies or some fucked up STD." Kate walked to a small park near the Hermitage. "I don't want to go in yet. Let's sit for a few minutes, maybe they'll come by." Sitting in the cool night, the sounds of a vibrant nightlife in the distance, the adrenalin wore off, and she began to see other points of view. "Where were you and Jeb that whole time?"

Tom sat on the bench, draping an arm across the back. "Trapped behind a wall of people."

She sighed heavily. "What do you think I should have done?"

Tom puckered his lips as he thought. After a long moment, he answered. "Nothing. It was his fight."

Kate dropped her head back and looked at the stars. "But—"

"I know. I couldn't have done it either. But think it through. If you hadn't jumped on stage, what would have happened?"

"She would have hit him," she said definitively.

"She would have tried," Tom corrected. "Didn't you see his face? She wasn't going to succeed."

"I was watching her. Did you see her face? She hated him. She wanted to hurt him."

"Yeah, I got that. That's why I get what you did."

All of the venom had drained away. Kate didn't want to fight or argue, but she worried Butch wouldn't be in the same mind. "He's going to be mad. Think he's a yeller? I hope so. I know how to deal with loud mad. Quiet mad rips my guts out."

Tom pushed to his feet. "Looks like we're about to find out."

Kate stood, watching the four friends file out of a cab. Trudy walked sandwiched between Butch and Hyde, hunched over and covering her face. Jeb paid the cab, then followed behind, his glare threatening anyone approaching.

Tom called out. "Jeb. Butch."

Butch turned and abandoned Trudy to Hyde, stalking down the street until he stood in front of Kate. "What the hell did you think you were doing coming up on the stage?" Butch managed to yell without raising his voice. A honed, steel edge came into it as sharp as any knife.

Though she didn't feel physically threatened, he definitely invaded her space. "I was helping you. She was—"

"Helping me?" Butch looked miserable. His long hair poked out in all directions, matted with drying beer. His shirt clung to his chest, the crumpled tails out of his jeans. His eyes were flat, hard, angry. "That was helping me? Brawling with my not-quite-ex-wife in no way helped me. This isn't your world where you can bark orders and people jump. This is my world."

Kate spoke calmly, hoping he couldn't sense the pounding of her heart and the bile rising up the back of her throat. "It wasn't a brawl. Not on my end. I just pulled her off of Trudy. I specifically did not get into a brawl. You wouldn't be yelling like this if Jeb did the same thing."

Butch inhaled sharply, and his teeth dug into his lip. He wanted to deny it. She read it on his face. "The difference," he said, his voice now barely above a whisper, "is you and I have a relationship. What happened tonight isn't going to make it easier to divorce her. Tomorrow the story and pictures will be all over the internet. Hell, they're probably there already." Butch ran a hand through his hair, disgust showed on his face when it didn't comb through. "Your face will be all over the internet. Shit. I have to call Finch." Butch took three deep breaths while Katie held hers, expecting him to tell her good-bye. Instead, he held out his hand. "Let's go."

For nearly an hour, Butch had Finch on speaker phone. Jeb, Hyde, and Tom played on smartphones, monitoring postings about Butch like election night results. Trudy sat curled on a chair, the ice pack on her nose doing little to abate the bloom of blue and purple around her eyes.

Kate needed some space. Too many big bodies, too much emotion, too little square footage. Pulling comfortable clothes from the dresser, she found space in the oversized bathroom. She showered, taking her time to wash the hairspray and knots from her hair. Her neck stung when the water touched the scratches.

It all went to hell so fast. Tempers could run high on a construction site but nothing like Fawn's. Kate decided she preferred physical catastrophes to emotional ones. The physical ones were, more or less, predictable. Shit fell down. Things blew up. The only edge emotional catastrophes had was people didn't die from them. They might feel like it at the time, but they survived.

Except Angie.

Kate scrubbed her face again and shut the water off. She dried off slowly and indulged in smoothing her skin with the creamy lotion provided by the hotel. She dressed in her favorite clothes and went into the bedroom to rejoin the fray. Quiet had overtaken the room. "Where is everyone?"

Butch sat on the chair, his eyes closed, his head back. "Sent them on." He lifted his head to look at her. "A shower sounds good. Care to join me?"

"I just finished, but you go ahead. Take your time." When the bathroom door closed, Kate called room service. "What do you have that's fast?"

When the food arrived, Kate dragged the bedspread to the floor and filled it with the silver topped dishes that piqued both curiosity and appetite. Room service delivered faster than she thought possible — but then it was Butch Mc-Cormick's room. She began to understand what his name meant. She set the last plate as Butch came out of the bathroom wearing only a pair of sleep pants. His towel-dried hair flopped across his eyes, which looked tired and worn. The lines around his mouth pulled his face down...until he saw what waited for him.

"A picnic? Is there pizza?" Years faded from his face, and light reached his eyes.

"It's an adventure picnic. I have no idea what's under here. Sit down. Pick one."

Kate crawled across the eclectic spread and lifted the lids of his selections. They fed each other, drank, laughed.

"What's under that one?" Butch pointed to the one nearest Kate.

She lifted the lid. "Yum. Cheesecake with raspberry sauce. That makes three desserts. Add in two appetizers and a side dish, and we have a lot of food but nothing that constitutes a meal."

Butch reached for the smart phone he had avoided since coming out of the shower. The closer his hand got, the more anxiety showed in the lines of his face.

Kate covered his hand with hers, wanting to give him a bit more of a reprieve. "Don't."

His gaze moved from the technology to her eyes. "You don't understand."

"I know. For a little while, let's pretend you don't understand either." She crawled over the array of plates and lids and rolled Butch to his back. It pleased her that his hands went to her hips, lifting her to straddle him. She stripped her shirt off. Butch bowed up, his mouth going to her breast. She arched back, holding his head to her.

In a husky voice, he whispered against her creamy skin. "You're a gift. You're a goddamned gift."

Butch woke in a tangle of sheets alone. The sun fought valiantly through the darkening drapes, brightening the room. An empty bed was the downside of sleeping with a woman who rose with the sun.

The handle of the hallway door jiggled, then the artificial light from the hall peeked in as Kate entered. She'd opened the door only wide enough to slide her body through then pushed her back against the closed door. Dressed in shorts and a clingy top, her hair poked out from the band that held it. "Holy shit."

Butch propped himself up on his elbows as the tension in her body set off his own warning system. "Something happen?"

"You have to get out of here. Now." Kate went to the closet, pulled out Butch's bag, and started packing his clothes. "There must be a back door. We can get a cab and then—"

"Stop." Butch slid from the bed wearing nothing but a frown and stilled her sweaty body. "What were you doing?"

"Running. I couldn't just sit here in the dark while you slept." She pulled a pair of jeans from the floor and shoved them into his belly. "You need to get dressed."

He covered her hands and used his winning smile to calm her. "Why? I look good naked. You know it."

"There are a bunch of people down there waiting to jump on your carcass and strip the meat from your bones."

Butch winced. "Katie. That's disgusting."

"I know, so you need to sneak out the back door." She went into the bathroom and raked his toiletries into his bag with one swoop of her arm.

"Stop. Stop and talk to me." He took the bag from her and led her into the main room.

"Okay, but you need to get dressed. You're...distracting."

"Fine." He sat her on the chair, kissed her nose, and disappeared around the corner. "Talk. Are they reporters?"

"Fans. Reporters. Bloggers. Nut cases. Is there a difference?" She sounded worried on his behalf. A mother tiger, Kate protected what she cared about.

He had no doubt he had achieved that status as he stepped into the jeans Kate had shoved at him. "Absolutely. Did you talk to them? Did they recognize you?"

"No one noticed me." Her voice floated around the corner. "A hive of them hovered around the front doors, buzzing about the Fawn incident last night."

Butch took a soft T-shirt in burgundy red from the bag. He pulled it over his head and smoothed the wrinkles as he stretched it down his chest. "What was the buzz?"

Kate appeared in the doorway. "You name it. Fawn's a

bitch. You're a cheat. She's so sweet and innocent. You're a hometown hero. They wanted to know about Trudy. Some tagged her as being with you before Fawn, wondered if you slept with her before and during your marriage."

That didn't surprise him. The way Trudy clung generated those types of questions. "What about you?"

Kate pursed her lips. "What about me?"

"Did they pick up on you?" He dug out his toothbrush and paste and made use of them.

"No. I told you. No one noticed me. Why?"

Barefoot, Butch walked across the room and gathered Kate into his arms. "We need to talk."

Kate pushed away. "You sound serious."

Butch led her into the main room, sat on the chair, and pulled her into his lap. "You remember when we were standing on the sidewalk last night? I told you we had a relationship."

"I remember."

He smiled at the wealth of suspicion in those two words. "Well, do you agree we have a relationship?"

Kate rolled her eyes. "We have sex, a lot of sex. You don't do that without a relationship. I don't do that without a relationship. But…"

Butch held her in place when she squirmed. "But?"

She slapped her thighs, her voice strained. "What does the word 'relationship' mean? Does it mean having warm feelings for each other? Does it mean being exclusive? Does it mean calling each other boyfriend and girlfriend?"

"Yes. For me it's all of those and more."

Kate shook her head. "Not for me. Not this fast. Not ever. Look, I don't come from a nice quiet upbringing on a farm that's been in the family for more generations than I can count. I come from a world where nothing is permanent. You do a job, then you move on. You work with people, then you move on. Do I have feelings for you? Yes, absolutely. I told you I do. How that's possible in this short time, I'm not sure, but yeah, they are there. But what does that mean in the long run? I just don't know."

Butch laced his fingers through hers, and she instantly tightened. They were opposites: he willing to leap for the opportunity to love, she thinking, hesitating, and not knowing what he saw so simply in her eyes. "We're exclusive. We agree on that. It's me for you, and you for me. Has been almost since you broke down in my driveway."

She shifted again, trying to put space between them. "That's ridiculous. Love at first sight."

A smile curled the edge of his lips. What she did to him was ridiculous all right. "Sight. Sound. Scent. Touch. Taste. You invaded all of my senses." He placed his fingers under her chin and drew her around to face him. "And I touch yours. Admit it."

He felt her breath catch. When her hands fisted in his T-shirt, he kissed her deeply. Butch held her there, making sure he flooded all of her senses. "Admit it."

She kneaded his shoulder, giving back what she got. "God. You do. Yeah, you do."

When it came to the bedroom, his Katie had no inhibitions, but when it came to affairs of her heart, she acted like a skittish colt.

"Butch, it doesn't change my story. When this building is done, I'll be off to the next project. What happens then?"

Definitely skittish. "How long? How long 'til the

project's done?"

"End of the year."

"That gives me eight months to show you what commitment means." He pressed his lips to her forehead. "But first, we have to face a reality of my life."

To Butch's mind, Kate was a civilian, a professional woman used to coming and going with no one to answer to except her family. Overnight, she became the girlfriend of an entertainer, a public figure with little privacy. They had an advantage in that the press, the media, had little interest in non-public relations. In short, Kate wouldn't sell newspapers or advertisements. Thank heaven for small favors. She listened intently as he instructed her on living a public life.

"But, they haven't put us together." Kate sat up taller, her fingers playing with his shirt. "If anything, they think you and Trudy are an item. I can just leave. Walk right out the door, the way I came in. Then you can come out, shaking hands, flashing that little boy smile of yours, kissing babies, and we're both good."

"Little boy smile of mine?"

"You know, the one that gets you out of trouble. Think about it."

Butch did and liked the idea. He called Jeb, Tom, Trudy, and Hyde up. "The media is outside waiting for me."

Trudy sported dual black eyes. "Look what that bitch did to me. I can't be photographed, Butch. Not like this."

Jeb stepped next to his brother. "I'll go out with Butch. Hyde, you take everyone else out thirty minutes after we leave. Butch? You ready to go?"

"One minute. Katie, can I have a word?" Butch led her into the bathroom, the only private space in the crowded room. He closed the door behind them and kissed her until every nerve in his body fired in triplicate.

Kate's dreamy eyes looked into his. "That's a word? Someday, you'll have to give me a whole sentence."

"I'll give you a whole paragraph later tonight." Satisfied he would be on her mind, Butch left the bathroom and picked up his bag. "Ready, Jeb."

The elevator to the lobby crawled down the shaft. Butch's heart raced as he stepped into the swarm of professional and amateur media as much as when he stepped on stage. Just another show.

Chapter Twelve

"Morning, y'all. Well, I guess it's afternoon."

"Butch, what happened between you and Fawn?"

"Butch, who is the blonde you were with?"

"Butch, were you sleeping with her while married?"

The questions ranged from common to rude to crude.

"Fawn always has put on one hell of a show. Last night was no exception. As you all surmised, we are splitting after two years of marriage. Fawn is an exceptional actress. I wish her nothing but personal happiness and professional success."

"What happened, Butch?"

Butch rubbed his hand over his heart. "Whatever happens between two people?"

"She accused you of cheating."

"She did. I'm not going to drag our personal life out for y'all except to say I don't cheat. I don't believe in it."

"Are you ready for the tour?"

A flood of relief went through Butch. The quick change of topic told him he was riding on top of the wave. "Details are being finalized. Y'all can check my website for the tour dates. Rehearsals start soon, and we'll kick it off right here in Nashville."

"You played new music last night. Are you going to play new music on tour?"

Butch rubbed his chin. "Now, that's an idea. I'll have to give it some thought. I'll play the favorites, of course, and music from my recent album, but it could be fun to play new music."

The valet pulled Butch's truck to the curb, a finite end to the impromptu press conference. Butch moved to the passenger door while Jeb took care of the valet. "Y'all, that's my ride. I appreciate your time. See you next time around."

Sunday evening, Tom shared a specialty of his—chicken parmesan. The house smelled of garlic and cheese and a pungent sauce—in a word: delicious. Kate set the table, tossed the salad, and otherwise stayed out of Tom's way. With the high drama of the previous night, everyone had gone their own way, searching for a bit of peace and quiet. Tom ended that with two words.

"Dinner's on!"

Jeb set his book on the couch and wandered to the table, staring at Tom's T-shirt as he sat. "'Will cook for sex.' Does that work for you?"

Tom flashed his killer smile. "Don't need it to, but it's a

nice perk for the ladies."

"Don't get him started, Jeb." Kate looked to the stairs. "I'll go get Butch."

Music coming from the second floor ended, and Butch ran down the stairs. "Something smells great." But Butch's face fell when he saw the dish waiting for him. He poked the meat with a fork.

Tom pressed his brows together. "Don't you like Italian?"

Butch flashed a glance at Kate and raised an eyebrow to Tom. "You cooked, right?"

Tom caught the glance and broke into a belly laugh. "You didn't eat anything she cooked, did you? Rule number one: do not eat Kate's cooking."

Kate and Tom had joked for years about Kate's inability in the kitchen. If she couldn't beat them, she'd bluff like she could, so she lifted her chin haughtily. "It was your recipe."

"Honey, it takes more to make a good meal than just a recipe."

"Oh, yeah, hot shot? What does it take?"

Tom's cell phone rang. "I don't know. But you don't have it. Excuse me. I need to take this."

At the other end of the table, Jeb ate like a starving man. He twirled the pasta and shoved golf ball sized forkfuls into his mouth. With each bite, his eyes rolled to the back of his head.

"Easy there, Clyde, or you and that pasta will need to get a room." Butch cut a piece of the succulent chicken. "Speaking of which, are you staying here again?"

Jeb used bread to mop sauce from the plate, his face intent on his task. "Yep. Someone has to keep an eye on y'all."

Kate knew Jeb had an apartment in town, but he liked to stay here. The hot meals had something to do with it, but Kate suspected there was more.

"This is some good eating," Jeb said. "You care if I take some for my lunch tomorrow?"

Butch grinned at Kate. "My mother spoiled him. No PB&J for her Jebediah. She packed him 'big boy' lunches. Sandwiches, potato salad, fruit, pies. That's what he's used to. It also explains why he's packed on the pounds since he's been home."

Jeb pointed his fork at his brother. "That's easy for you to say, Clyde. You have a personal trainer. Try working for a living, and see how easy it is to keep the pounds at bay."

"I work damned hard, and you know it."

Tom poked his head around the corner. "Kate, your father wants to talk to you."

Kate rolled her eyes but followed Tom into the kitchen. She would take the high road. This time, she wouldn't sink to her father's levels. Kate accepted Tom's phone. "Hi, Dad. How is your weekend?"

"It would have been a hell of a lot better if Cicada would pay their bills." Thirty years of yelling over heavy machinery polished her father's gravelly voice. The lack of edge didn't soften the effect. It intensified it, like Marlon Brando's in *The Godfather*.

She had missed an argument with her father, thanks to a concrete pour. She'd hoped he'd forget about it, but that was like hoping an elephant forgot his trunk. "Dad, the invoice went in exactly when it was supposed to. You can't expect Cicada to pay in a week. By contract, they have thirty days." Kate picked at her ragged nails, chipped and rough from days on the construction site, irritated that her hands looked so bad. She paced while she listened to her father rant on about credit and unpaid bills. "Dad, you aren't listening to me. There isn't a credit problem. There aren't unpaid bills. I send you the spreadsheet every week. The accounts are up-to-date."

Tom leaned against the counter. She knew he stood in silent support for Kate's non-stop battles with her father.

She stopped short. "You can't expect me to drive all the way to Detroit to show you how to read a spreadsheet. Get Tony to do it. I've got work to do here. We need to make these pours this week to stay on schedule."

Her father's voice pumped out of the miniature speaker. "This might be your goddamned project, Kate, but it's *my* goddamned company. I'm not cutting one more check, not one more, little girl, until I'm convinced we're on solid ground."

Kate closed her eyes as resolve set in. She did a good job. A damned good job. If he was too stubborn to see it, he could find someone else as a project manager, as a daughter. "I'm not doing it. I have a full schedule here, where the work is."

"You are my daughter, and you work for me. If I say come home, the only thing you say is 'yes, sir.' Understood?"

A tear rolled down Kate's cheek. "Half of this company is mine. I'm not coming. Yell, scream, swear, cut me off, but get it through your head that I'm running this job." She lowered a trembling hand, swept her thumb over the "end" button and handed the phone back to Tom. "We may not be related anymore."

"Not likely." Tom caught her neck in the crux of his arm

and mussed her hair. "Come on. Let's finish dinner."

Kate ducked under his arm and stepped toward the back door. Each little battle with her father cost her psychologically and emotionally until she was an empty shell. She needed time to recharge her internal battery. "I'm done. I'll be out in the barn."

Kate stood in short sleeves gazing in wide wonder at the pastel chalk drawing sky. The blurred lines between blue, pink, purple, and orange showed how opposites could be good together. One didn't yield to the other but complimented, making the whole much more vivid than either could be alone.

She wanted to be that pink, that orange, full of life, vitality.

Instead, she had cultivated a role as an outsider in life. One that didn't warrant a place in the sky. She was beige, and beige didn't belong in sunsets.

In the barn, Kate turned the light on over the work bench and took the to-do list from where it hung on the peg board. She had crossed most of the items off. Two had been added in Tom's handwriting. One sat on the workbench, a chair with as much wobble as a rocking chair. "You just need a little TLC. Then you'll be good as new."

Working with her hands usually soothed her, giving her a feeling of accomplishment, but not today.

When are you going to learn, Kate? Some things are meant to be done by a man's hands.

"My hands are just as capable as any man's." She looked at the hands that worked for a living. She didn't wear nail polish. She didn't have nails to polish. Those fingers worked a loose joint, and the leg came off in her hand. "Shit."

What are you doing? Look first. How many times do I have to tell you to use your brain first?

"I know. I know, I know, I know."

The fuck you do. Look at the mess you made.

The chair, in three pieces, spread across the bench. The wood of one leg split along the grain.

Nice job. You just made bad worse.

"Leave me alone. God. Just leave me alone." She raged into the big space, but her hands shook, and another tear threatened to fall.

"It's times like this when you shouldn't be alone."

Kate jumped and spun in mid-air at the sound of Butch's voice. "Wh-what are you doing here?"

He sauntered across the floor, a casual confidence that projected calm. "It is my barn."

"Yes, I know, I mean—"

"You takin' the chair apart?" He pointed with his chin to the skeleton.

Kate turned her back to Butch. "I was trying to fix it, but it gave up."

Butch's arm wrapped around her shoulders, pinning her back to his chest. "What happened?"

"The leg joints had loosened. I thought a few pins would—"

"Not the chair. In the kitchen." His soft voice held sympathy and understanding.

But how could he understand? Everyone loved Butch.

"Oh. It doesn't matter."

Butch nipped at her shoulder, the bite stinging through her light shirt before his mouth followed the curve of her neck, creating a jolt of electricity that outpaced the sting.

He spoke against her ear. "It does. Whatever it is, it does to you. I want to be a part of it. I've given you thirty minutes to yourself. Now it's time to talk to me."

Thirty minutes? She glanced to the barn door where night waited on the other side. The curve of Butch's shoulder cradled her weary head, lending strength to a body drained of energy. His arms tightened, a physical reminder she was not alone. Not wanting to be alone, she pushed through the heartache and spoke. "It's the same old story. My father and me. We're like flint and steel. Gasoline and fire. Electricity and water." Kate told him what happened, her voice flat and soft. "He wanted a son. He got me. I know he'll never be proud of me. It doesn't matter how hard I work or what I do, I'll never be good enough."

Butch flipped her around so fast her head caught up two minutes later. Anger brought color to his cheeks. She knew what came next, but he didn't yell. He just stared with clenched teeth.

Kate's chin fell to her chest, resigned. "You're mad at me."

He bent over until they stood eye to eye. A storm brewed in those gray eyes. "You don't honestly believe that, do you?"

She tried to step back, but he pinned her to the workbench. He left her nowhere to hide, physically or emotionally. "That I'm not good enough? No. Not most of the time."

"If you believe it, even for a minute, your father is one hell of an SOB. Is this why you can't believe we can love each other? Has your father fucked you up that bad?"

"He has nothing to do with us." Trapped, without enough air to breathe, Kate slid to the right. "Look at my life. How would we make something work?"

Butch locked his arms onto the workbench. "You're not running. I'm getting down to the root of what has you so screwed up. Maybe I should be grateful. If you were any less nuts you'd be married with two point five kids and a minivan."

Kate gasped loudly, offended to the core. "How dare you! I would never drive a minivan."

Butch rubbed his chin. "Maybe a station wagon."

Her lips pursed about to snap back, and then her face crumbled. She would never have a minivan or a station wagon, because there wouldn't be kids to put in one. Her head dropped, and her shoulders sagged. "What's so wrong with me?"

Butch gathered her against his chest, his fingers burying deep in her long hair. "Let's be clear on this. Nothing is wrong with you. You're the woman I've been looking for my whole life."

She rolled her head against him, his words conflicting with her history as an adult. "You don't know me. I'm loud and impetuous. I never do what's expected. I'm trouble. It just finds me."

"Hell, yes, you're trouble. Exactly the kind of trouble I want, the kind of trouble I need."

Kate lifted her head and wiped tears with the back of her hand. "I hate him, Butch."

Butch brought her back to his chest, wrapping her up to protect her from words that cut deeper than any knife could. "No, honey. If you hated him, this wouldn't be an issue. He's your father, and you love him."

"It would be easier if I hated him. I hate myself for

wanting him to be proud of me. I can do all of these…remarkable things. I can stand up to stubborn boards and pissed off subcontractors and community activists, but I can't cut the cord when it comes to my father." She whispered the confession.

Butch took her face in his hands. "Why, Katie? No lies, here. Tell me, tell yourself, why don't you walk away from your father?"

Kate focused on his eyes and asked herself the one question she never thought to ask. Why? "I don't want to be alone. If I walk away from him, I'll have to walk away from them all. If I fail, my father will take me back. He would never let me forget I failed, but he wouldn't turn me out. Ever. He'd clean up any mess I made."

"Because he loves you."

An emotion she couldn't name seized her throat. She ran through scenario after scenario and in all of them, no matter how ridiculous, her father would be there for her. Only one explanation made sense.

"He loves me." Overwhelmed, she wrapped her arms around Butch. "God, he has a rotten way of showing it."

"It would seem. How about you? What have you done to show him?"

K ate had never had weeks as good as the two that followed. The project proceeded with the normal hiccups and starts, which meant it went smoothly. She spent as much time out on the site as she could, watching her imagination take shape in concrete and steel, enjoying the warm spring temperatures. Her admin, Paula, planted a few flowers out-side the trailer. They should have been pathetically lonely in the field of washed aggregate and stone, but instead they were sweet.

Life with her father improved. She scoured the internet looking for something to give her father. The search ended with the "Jelly of the Month Club." Kate and her father shared a love of the National Lampoon's *Christmas Vacation* movie, making the gift a perfect inside joke. The call after the first delivery started with "What the hell is this?" but ended with a fifteen minute debate on whether apple butter qualified as a jelly. He said yes, Kate said no, just for the debate. The near daily arguments continued, but Kate bifurcated them into separate work and entertainment categories.

Speaking of sweet, coming home each night was the cherry on her sundae. Butch met her on the porch every night, no matter what time she rolled in. He bought her flow-ers, a first for her, and a new dress, complete with matching underwear. She started seeing herself through his eyes. Un-comfortable at first, she grew to like thinking of herself as sexy as well as smart.

Kate returned Butch's attention, his affection. For him, the weeks had been hard. Angie's body had been released. He spent much of his time with Angie's mother, planning and then attending the funeral. The investigation into her death continued. Butch hadn't been charged, but questions were still being asked.

As if that weren't hard enough, he had to go into Nash-ville twice to meet with his divorce attorneys. Fawn went in and out of town, living in a hotel and setting up a not-for-profit "Butch McCormick Sucks" club. Maybe she hadn't done that literally, but she had been generously giving her time to tabloids and been very loose lipped about their relationship.

Butch juggled all that with the planning and rehearsals for his tour. Eight weeks until he hit the road in a bus decked out like a McMansion.

The strain dragged Butch down. The constant stories and the parade of pictures stripped away his pride. He tried to hide it from her, but she was getting to know him well, too. Kate worked at making the little moments of his life the ones he remembered. She loved being silly, spontaneous for him. One clear night, she took him up to the garage roof to count the stars. By twenty, the lead fog around him lifted, and he laughed again.

For all her questions, all her doubts about a relationship, being in one with Butch proved easy. Was she falling in love? Maybe. While she had been careful not to talk about a long-term future together, it became easy to see what life could be.

A full house added to the chaotic happiness. Tom stayed in the largest bedroom, sleeping across the bed that belonged in the room and the one Butch had pushed in to make his studio. With his help, Kate had crossed off most of the items on the fix-it list.

Jeb stayed most nights. Still quiet, Kate had caught him smiling when he thought no one watched. Trudy and Hyde were frequent guests. John and Emily enjoyed dinner with a full house at least twice a week.

As April gave way to May, a routine evolved. Tom made breakfast, always setting a full plate, covered with a clean dishcloth, in the microwave for Butch. Butch came down each morning, stumbling blindly into the kitchen to sit with Kate then going back to bed after she, Tom, and Jeb went to work. They took turns making dinner, Kate ordering take-out on her days.

Any spare time Kate found, she devoted to designing the sprawling, two-story house to fit Butch's lifestyle and all his California shit. Tom offered his unsolicited two cents, and Jeb tended to hover. He gave only one opinion. "Those bathrooms in the Hermitage are nice."

The Sly Dog had also become part of their routine. Tom and Kate had been welcomed to the point where walking into the bar was meeting up with extended family. Sunday night, they shared a long table with Butch, Trudy, Hyde, and two couples.

Butch finished his second beer, pushing the empty away from him. "Y'all want to come into Nashville for a rehearsal? Tuesday? Maybe Wednesday?"

"I can't do Tuesday," Kate said, squeezing Butch's hand for his attention. "I'm going to Louisville for a trade show. I won't be back until late."

"Are you taking the Shelby?" Hyde asked.

She pulled out her phone and brought up the weather app. "Oh, yeah. It'll be a nice day to stretch her legs."

"How about you drop your work truck off tomorrow? I'll do the oil service while you're gone."

Tom nudged Kate's elbow. "I'll follow you over in the morning."

"Perfect. Does Wednesday work for watching Butch?" When everyone around the table nodded, Kate turned to Butch. "Looks like you have your audience."

"I'll send y'all the address last minute. This is a closed

show." His cell phone rang. Butch read the screen, his shoulders sagging. "Fawn." He watched it ring. On the third, he dismissed the call and shoved the phone in his pocket.

Butch took Kate's hand and pulled her from her chair. "Come on, Katie. Let's play a game of darts. We'll make it interesting. If I win, you have to go up to the mic and yodel."

"You have to sing 'It's a Small World' in a munchkin voice."

"Damn. All right. But just so you know, I'm not going to let you win just to be gentlemanly. The stakes are too steep."

Her eyes flashed, and she snatched her hand from his. "Ha. Let me win. You better tune up your pipes, muscles. You have five minutes. I have to make a ladies' run."

B utch admired the way she moved through the crowd. The tight jeans gave him a lot to admire. He had his hands on her butt each night and knew full well it wasn't the jeans that gave her that shape. Tonight. Tonight he would give it the attention it deserved.

Trudy drummed her blue-raspberry-polished fingers over Butch's forearm. "Where is Kate going to stay when you're on tour?"

Butch did a double take from where Kate disappeared into the crowd to Trudy's concerned gaze. "The house, of course. Where else?"

"Don't you think it's about time she found a place of her own? She's been living off you for four weeks, Butch." Trudy held her hands up, palms out. "I'm saying this for your own good. I wouldn't forgive myself if another city woman took advantage of your good nature."

Butch snatched his arm from under Trudy's hand. "Nobody is taking advantage of me. Katie and Tom do more around the house than I do. Tom's welcome to stay as long as he wants. And Katie, well, I'm thinking about keeping her."

Butch had finished thinking about it and decided to keep Kate. He'd fallen in love, and he'd fallen hard. Everything about her drew him. The look in her eye, her intelligence and determination, the sweet things she did to make him smile, not to mention the feel of her revved body beneath his hands and her sweet little sigh before she fell asleep in his arms. Butch was biding his time, waiting for Kate to realize she loved him. She was getting closer. Every day, she was getting closer, whether she knew it or not.

Kate was staying but Butch knew better than to say that to Trudy. His friend was within her rights to question his judgement, but that wouldn't change his mind.

"'Scuse me. Looks like my game's about to start." Butch met Kate halfway across the dance floor. "We can save us both time if you just hop up on the stage now. Band looks about ready for a break."

"You're welcome to hop up there. I see my seat is open." She pointed to an empty table closest to the band.

Butch collected two sets of darts from the small shelf where they were kept. "There's no need to make things hard on yourself."

Kate slid in front of him, her hand discretely stroking over the zipper of his jeans. "I like when you make things hard on me."

Butch forgot his name for that instant before she walked away. His body, seeing the green light, raced off the block.

"Damned woman, giving me a false start."

She flipped her flaming mane over her shoulders, smoldering eyes laughing at him. "You ready to do this?"

"You are trouble, honey. Every ounce of you."

"Y'all just starting?" Hyde came over with another buddy, four bottles of beer between them. "Can we play?"

"Sure," Butch said. "Let's make it interesting."

A match played for a million dollars couldn't have been tenser. After all, a man could live without a million dollars, but he couldn't live without his dignity. Kate zeroed out first, hitting her double on her third try. Butch closed from behind, zeroing out while Hyde and his buddy cursed the board that kept moving on them.

"Clear the way. Move it," Hyde said, swinging his arms to part the Dead Sea. He looked over his shoulder at Kate. "You're dead to me, Little Red."

Kate laughed, climbed up on a chair, and draped herself over Butch's shoulders. "I love you, Hyde. You're just like a cousin to me. On your mark, get set, GO!"

With a string of curses, Hyde and his buddy leap frogged the length of the bar. Butch hitched Kate's leg over his hips and followed the pair out of the game room. Confused looks and snickers grew into belly laughs from the crowd when Hyde tripped over his buddy and they ended up in a pile on the floor. An elderly lady who couldn't see farther than the end of her hand stepped on Hyde's foot and spilled ginger ale that smelled like rye over the pair.

Hyde leapt to his feet, shaking like a dog. "Damn it to hell, that's cold."

The woman looked over the top of her glasses. "Language, Mr. Spence."

"Yes ma'am," he said respectfully to his fourth grade teacher. Hyde looked over Butch's shoulder, his brows knit together. The understanding pushed them into his hairline. "Vulture, Butch. Out the back." As Butch turned to look, his friend pulled him forward. "Abbey McNeil. Go. I'll stall her."

Butch hitched Kate up on his back and made a beeline for the kitchen doors.

Kate tightened her grip on Butch. "Who is Abbey McNeil and why are we running from her?"

"We aren't running, we're walking. She is a reporter for Nashville's version of *The Hollywood Reporter*. We've been able to keep you out of the headlines so far. It wouldn't last if she caught me wearing you like a coat."

"I'm not afraid of her."

"Neither am I. Keep your head down."

K ate stood in the darkened room, wondering how a man could fall asleep so darned quick. It was a talent, to be vitally alive one minute and sawing logs a few minutes later. Kate decided she'd take it as a compliment. She drained his virile butt. No time to gloat, she heard movement through the wall. Kate snatched her robe from the bed post and darted out the door to beat Jeb to the bathroom.

They definitely needed more bathrooms. Four adults and one bathroom was a frat house, not the way adults lived. Sharing a bathroom with three men and no counter space bordered on inhumane.

A fist pounded on the door. "Time's up. Out." The three

words Jeb used every morning. Kate wasn't sure he was capable of more without coffee.

With her hair in a towel turban and her body wrapped in her robe, she relinquished the bathroom to Jeb and ran to Butch's room.

Kate opened her drawers and rooted through her clothes, selecting them by feel. Each morning, she wondered why she didn't pick out her clothes the night before. Too elementary school.

Her phone rang. She grabbed it up without looking to keep it from waking Butch.

"Did you see the OSHA inspection certificate?"

"No, Dad. They sent it straight to you. How did we do?"

"How did we do?" And so the first rant of the day started. He read the report out loud. Kate took it at first, employing her water-off-a-duck strategy. Then he got personal. "If you think I'm going to have my name on a project that's a hazard—"

"Hazard? Your dementia is showing again. You just read the entire report to me, and there was no hazard—"

"Don't argue with me, little girl—"

"Likewise, old man—"

"Have Tom call me. He'll get to the bottom of this."

They hung up at the same time.

Butch rolled on his side, propping his head on his arm. "I don't know how I feel about you bringing your father into our bedroom."

Kate slam dunked the phone onto the end of the bed. "I am not in the mood for cute." She stormed the two steps to the nightstand and her watch.

Butch grabbed her wrist, gave a twist and had her

sprawled across the bed. The towel fell off her head, and the robe gapped open, the morning air chilling her still-wet skin.

"I. Am. Not—"

Butch's mouth closed around one tight nipple while his hand teased the other. A musician made his living with his hands, talented hands, a singer with his silver tongue. Butch showed Kate exactly how talented he was. He slid down her body, his teeth leaving a trail of sensation across her ribs. He stopped at her belly button, pinning her hips to the mattress with his shoulders. Kate knew where he headed and an urgent need took hold. She pushed at his shoulders, encouraging him to continue his journey south.

Down he slid, his hands caressing her curves. His tongue attended to her tattoo as his hand followed the line of her butt, placing her leg over his shoulder.

Kate dug her other heel into the mattress, moving higher, drawing him lower.

He laughed softly as he moved to where she wanted him. She opened, but he kept her at bay, blowing softly over her enflamed body.

"Butch," she begged as she fought his hold, her body unable to be still.

He kissed the little nub that brought her so much pleasure. "I'm right here." He used his tongue ruthlessly, bringing her to the blinding edge of passion again and again.

Her heels dug into his back, her stubby nails into the arms that held her. He nipped her, just a little sting to trigger her pleasure center.

Her legs locked like vice grips, holding him as she pulsed with waves of ecstasy. He pushed his tongue into her, stroking her clenching body from the inside.

Kate lifted off the bed, unable to restrain herself. "Oh. God. You're killing me. You have to stop."

His tongue stroked her swollen center. "No, I don't."

Kate cried out as his teeth sent her into overdrive. She was beyond anything rational. Every little sensation he caused created a firestorm in her feminine core. Desperate for a reprieve but not an end, Kate pushed Butch's shoulder away with her foot. She followed, rolling up and pushing him down. His head bumped the foot of the bed.

"Sorry," she muttered, guiding his hips closer to her.

He was full again and needing her, and Kate settled between his legs and licked him like a lollipop.

"Have mercy."

She licked him again. "Is that what you want? Mercy?"

"Hell no."

Kate returned his attention with a slow, patient, deliberate love that had him covering his face with a pillow and moaning out loud. Her tongue bathed the head of his cock and teased the spot just below that, for him, was magic. His body responded beautifully to her touch. His hard-earned muscles trembling, begging for her caress. She took him fully into her mouth, humming as she savored his size and texture.

The world spun, and in that instant she was under him, with him buried deep inside her. She cried out as he triggered turbulent sensations that brought her aroused body off the bed. He moved in a slow, languid motion that tortured them both. His arms shook with the effort of holding up his chest. Her heels dug into buttocks, drawing him deeper. He withdrew nearly fully and then thrust deeply, setting off a cascade of spasms, first in Kate, then his own.

As his last drop released, his arms gave out. Ungracefully,

he collapsed onto Kate.

"I think I'm blind." Kate wrapped her arms around Butch, not ready to let go. He'd taken her over the edge many times since that first desperate union, but this one was for the record books. "I'm boneless, too."

"Likewise." The mattress muffled his voice. He turned his head and pressed his lips to her temple. "I may never move."

Kate snuggled into the hollow of his neck. "You're gonna have to. You weigh a lot."

Butch shifted his weight so she could see his face. He looked different. There was something in his eyes, something she couldn't quite define.

"Katie, I—"

"Kate!" Tom yelled, the steps creaking under his weight. "We need to get going. Concrete's coming at nine, and we need to drop your truck off. I'm leaving in ten. Get a move on!"

Kate looked up at Butch, willing him to finish his thought. Whatever was on his mind was important to him. She could see that in his face, and she more than wanted to know what he was thinking. She needed to know. "Tell me."

For a moment she thought he would.

Instead, he briefly rested his forehead against hers. "Come on, sexy." Butch rolled off of her and out of bed. "Let's get you going before he breaks down our door."

Butch stood barefoot on the gravel driveway, watching as Kate turned the truck around and raced down the drive after her cousin, a cloud of dust in her wake. Her brake lights flashed at the end of the driveway, she turned onto the street, and with a wave out the window, she was gone. Butch stayed put, watching until she drove over the crest of a hill and out of sight, already anticipating her return.

He'd hit a double this morning. He thought the chances for a triple were in his favor. Maybe he'd go for a Grand Slam.

Butch walked to the house, telling his feet to toughen up, and found Trudy sitting at the kitchen table sipping coffee. "Good morning, Trudy. I didn't see you come in."

"I didn't want to interrupt you sending Kate and Tom off to work." She rose and poured another cup of coffee, setting it down for Butch opposite her. "Sit down. I'll make you breakfast."

"Got it right here." Butch took the plate he knew waited in the microwave and divided it in two. He set one in front of Trudy. "Tom makes breakfast. He's a good cook. It's handy to have a man who can fix dinner and gutters, don't you think?"

Trudy deserved a good man, one who knew how to treat a lady. She had a rough childhood. Her father dying had been an odd sort of blessing, and the insurance policy had kept her family's farm afloat. Butch didn't know much about Trudy's finances today, but he knew payments had to have run out years ago. He hoped she'd find a man to settle down with and enjoy life a bit. He wanted to see his friend happy.

"He'll make a good husband for the right woman." Butch dug into the three-inch-thick breakfast casserole.

Trudy giggled. "Haven't you been paying attention? Tom isn't husband material. He doesn't want to settle down any more than you want to get up at six in the morning." She forked a dainty bite.

"The right woman would change his mind. You spent the day with him. What did you think?"

Her brows shot up. She dropped the bite. "You mean me? And Tom? No, Butch."

"Why not, Trud? He owns his own firm, has manners as good as a boy from Michigan could have, and is a good looking guy." Butch ticked off Tom's attributes on his fingers. "He's a catch."

Trudy stood, shaking her head emphatically. "No, Butch. He's not who I'm interested in."

Butch cocked a brow, thinking as he ate. Trudy had never so much as hinted at a man in the past weeks. "What's his name? I'll call him up and lasso him in for you. You deserve to be happy, Trudy."

"I deserve to be loved. He needs to come to me on his own. It's not real if he doesn't come on his own."

Butch understood and knew her to be right but still wanted her to be happy. If he found out who her beau was, maybe he could nudge him in the right direction. His mother always said nudging and interfering were two different things. "His name?"

Trudy pursed her lips, turned an invisible key, and threw it over her shoulder.

"Well, whoever the son-of-a-bitch is, he's the luckiest man in the world."

Trudy blushed, and even her ears turned rosy. "That's the sweetest thing to say. Maybe my luck will change."

"I hope so." Butch set the still-full coffee on the counter next to the stack of breakfast plates—his chore. "I have to get to rehearsal. One of the guys has a gig this evening, so we had to rearrange the schedule to be done by mid-afternoon. I'll take care of these dishes later, I guess."

"Go on. I'll tidy up for you." Trudy waved him off.

Butch laid a peck on her cheek. "You're the best."

He took his time in the shower, singing because he enjoyed the sound. Maybe he'd record in the shower sometime. Tunes for the wet and naked. He laughed at his own joke.

Towels hung everywhere in the bathroom. Two off the hooks on the back of the door, one on the door knob, one on the stingy towel rack. Every towel a different color. Katie's shampoo and conditioner balanced precariously in the corner of the tub-shower. Jeb and Tom shared a more manly scented shampoo. Butch carried his own in after Kate complained she couldn't sleep with a man who smelled like her cousin.

Five songs and a thorough scrubbing later, Butch returned to his bedroom to find the bed made and clothes laid out for him. The jeans he put on. The button-down he put back in the closet in favor of a soft, cotton shirt.

Neat as a pin, the kitchen showed no signs of inhabitants. The table even gleamed in the sunlight. Butch texted Trudy.

U r the best. Thx. B.

Monday's practice session polished the concert set until it shone so brightly he needed sunglasses. Butch had put the band together using musicians he'd worked with before. Half played on the album the tour promoted, half were friends and friends of friends. Butch tweaked the play list, adding in a slot for new music. He liked mixing it up. Playing the same thing every night could get old. When it did, the audience could tell. He wasn't a rookie anymore. He'd earned his artistic license and intended to use it.

With a job well done, Butch called it a day. He stepped out of an unmarked door and squinted at the afternoon sun.

"Butch McCormick. I missed you last night at your bar. Who would have thought I'd run into you here?" The shapely blonde in a tight dress the color of a fire engine and screaming high heels painted with the American flag sat on the bumper of his truck.

"Abbey McNeil. You're sitting on my truck."

She tossed her teased, blond tresses over her shoulder and pressed a hand over the diamond-accent *A* pendant that was her signature piece. "Am I? That's just fate, don't you think? I just sat for a little rest. It's been a very busy day."

"Likewise. If you'll excuse me—"

"I interviewed Fawn Jordan today. She had quite a story to tell." Abbey crossed her legs, bouncing the stars and stripes in a quick little rhythm. "Care to share your side?"

Butch unlocked the truck and carefully moved his guitar from his back to the rear seat. "I don't, Abbey. I truly don't. It doesn't matter what's truth and what's fiction, you have papers to sell."

"You're getting facts and truth mixed. Facts are for court. Truth sells papers. Once people believe something, it's truth, regardless of the facts." She stood then, nearly eye to eye in the stilts on her feet. "You and I have worked the same block for a while now. I like you, Butch. I want to be your friend." She ran her fingers up his arm. "Right now, you need all the friends you can find. Get me?"

Butch didn't want to imagine the stories Fawn would spin. He'd left the social stalking to Finch for sanity's sake, but it wouldn't be smart to shut it out altogether. Finch taught him that attention and media were tools to be used, because as Abbey said, facts didn't matter. Truth did. Butch checked his watch. He had two hours before he needed to meet Katie at Hyde's garage. "How about I buy you a sweet tea?"

"How lovely." She laced her arm in his. "I know a little place."

Abbey McNeil earned her reputation as ruthless, using whatever it took for a story. Right then, she used her thigh, pressed tight against Butch's in this little bar, to show her interest. The touch made Butch feel like cockroaches ran over his skin. He only wanted one woman pressed against him, but he stayed where he was. There was nothing personal about this.

Butch smiled, inviting the conversation. "Where do we begin?"

Chapter Thirteen

Kate opened her eyes, listening to birds already busy with their day. Her alarm went off, reminding her she had a busy day, too. Her fingertips just reached the button that silenced the noise. She awoke wrapped around Butch, her body well-loved and tantalizingly sore. He had come to her the night before like a starving man and she was a buffet. Again and again he came back, hungry for still more. She stretched to ease those aches, and Butch rubbed against her in his sleep. She lifted her chin and nibbled at his jaw while her hands slid across his naked hips. Butch groaned softly, breathlessly, still asleep. Kate swirled her fingers over his ass, exploring his body, watching every small reaction. She knew he woke when he inhaled deeply. She moved swiftly, rolling him to his back and covering his body with hers. Butch moved beneath her, his hands groped blindly for a hold. Kate slid down him, trailing kisses along the hair on his chest to his flat stomach to the niche in his hips that she loved to nibble.

Kate took Butch in her hand and drew her tongue up the length of him. Butch gasped and went rigid. Kate dipped her head and licked him again, taking time to swirl her tongue around his engorged head.

"Oh, God," Butch gasped and lifted her until she straddled him.

Kate planted her hands on his chest and let her weight slide his length. "You have no patience."

"I don't want patience. I want you. Only you." His fingers pressed into her hips, moving her to the rhythm he wanted. He pried his eyes open and smiled slowly, as if he enjoyed the view.

Kate dropped her head back, spilling her hair down his arms, across her back. She ground against him until she flew over the edge. While her body convulsed, she swirled her hips and did something with her muscles that yanked him over that edge the like a fifteen-year-old with his father's *Playboy*. His hands clenched in her hair, and he pulled her down to his chest where he kept her pinned.

She snuggled into him, content as a cat. "Good morning."

"G'night," he mumbled and turned his face into her hair.

Kate laughed, kissed his gruff jaw, and moved to separate their bodies. "I need to get up. I'm going to Louisville today."

With a deep inhale, Butch opened his arms, setting her free. He looked at the clock and grinned. "It's nearly a decent time of day. You starting to see things my way?"

Kate brushed the curls from his eyes. "Absolutely not. I thought I'd indulge you since I don't have to be in Louisville until nine."

"Hmmm. Nine. What would happen if you were late?"

He dipped his head, nibbling her neck.

She turned her head, improving his access. "Thinking of setting a record for recovery?"

Butch caught her hands and lifted his head to look at her face. "Mmmm. Wondering if in your calculations you considered that Louisville is in the Eastern Time zone?"

Her entire body jolted, the haze of cosmic sex cleared. "Lemme up."

"Slow down. Racing isn't going to make up an hour." Butch held her as she struggled. "Simmer down, and I'll let you up."

The panic that came with the realization of tardiness passed. This wasn't a meeting, it was a trade show. If she missed a session, no blood, no foul. "Okay. I won't race. Promise. But I need to get going." Kate climbed out of bed and made quick work of her morning routine.

Butch sat up in bed as she tossed clothes left and right. "Did you find your cell phone?"

"No. Hyde didn't find it in my truck, it's not in my office."

Butch arranged the pillows behind his back. "Where did you have it last?"

She'd been asking herself that since she realized she didn't have it. "I don't remember having it at all yesterday."

"You talked to your father in the morning. Something about a report."

"How could I forget?" Kate flipped the light on.

Butch threw his arm over his eyes. "Son of a bitch. A little warning."

"Come out, come out where ever you are." Kate crawled across the floor of their bedroom, searching by the light of a single lamp. She found the shoes from the night before, a bra, and one of Butch's T-shirts. "It has to be here. Butch, call it."

Sitting up in bed, Butch used his cell phone and dialed her number. Within minutes, the connection went through, and Kate's phone rang.

"Ha!" Kate dug between the tucked-in cover and the mattress beneath. "Whew. Lucky the battery didn't die." Kate sat on the edge of the bed, leaning into Butch. "Have a good day today. I'll miss you." She pressed her lips to his.

Butch caught the back of her head in his palm, taking the good-bye kiss to something that invited her to return quickly. "Come back soon."

"Fast as I can."

B utch finished a piano version of his current chart topper at half the tempo he'd recorded it. Tom set a magazine on the wooden surface and a beer wet with condensate on top of it. "Thanks. Good day?"

"Hell no. I always have to work twice as hard when Kate's not there. She keeps everyone and everything in line and my world is better for it, and if you ever tell her I said that, I'll call you out as the lying bastard you are. I could use a drink."

Jeb shoved a pile of potato chips into his mouth and curled the top of the bag down, munching then swallowing as he put the bag away. "I know just the place for a drink and a bite. You in, Clyde?"

"Might as well," Butch said, knowing if he didn't go out he'd watch the clock until Kate returned. "You buy and we'll even count it as your turn cooking. You wanna join us, Trudy?"

Trudy had called on her way home and stopped in. "I'm going to pass in favor of a bubble bath and a home-style pedicure. Why don't you give Hyde a call? Save him from working late."

Butch texted Hyde. *Heading to SD. You in?*

The response was as fast as technology allowed. *Yup. On my way.*

"He's in," Butch said. "Sure we can't talk you into it, Trud?"

Trudy cleared the coffee table. "Not tonight, Butchy."

Tom dropped to the floor and pounded out pushups.

"What are you doing?" Jeb stood, brushing any lingering crumbs from his shirt.

"Prepping. Appreciating the ladies doesn't happen by accident." Tom did ten push-ups with clapping between. "Practice." *Clap.* "Makes." *Clap.* "Perfect." *Clap*.

The Sly Dog was scant on patrons, but what it lacked in people, it made up for with gusto. The waitress kept the four men playing pool well supplied with good beer and cheap nachos. While Hyde lined up his shot, Tom leaned on his cue, watching the way she flowed around the obstacles with the full tray balanced on one hand.

"Are you a dancer?"

The cute blonde with short hair and shorter shorts eyed him up and down before answering. "I've always danced. I was on the dance squad in high school."

"Doesn't surprise me one bit. You are a thing of beauty and so graceful when you walk around. I can't keep my eyes off you."

"Then how are you up three balls?" Jeb asked.

She raised an eyebrow. "Three balls? That's impressive. Most men have trouble managing two. You need anything else, Jeb? Butch? Hyde?"

"I'm done," Jeb said. "I'm driving."

"I'll have one more," Butch said.

Hyde lifted his empty. "Me, too."

"And you?" she asked.

"I'm Tom. Do you have any sweet tea?"

"Well, that would be me. Tiffany."

"Just bring Butch's beer, sweet T." Jeb rolled his eyes and sent her on her way. He looked at Tom before lining up his shot. "What is with you and women?"

"I like the ladies."

Butch's phone rang. He read the screen and immediately answered it. "What's the good word, Finch?"

Finch had been earning his keep managing the fallout from the Fawn incident. So far, most of the Internet play had been in his favor, painting Fawn as a bitter ex. The meet with Abbey McNeil helped. Abbey didn't play fair, she played favorites, and Butch had made the cut. Butch denied flirting with Abbey, he just talked. Either way, Finch approved.

"Abbey post another blog on Fawn's breasts?"

"Fawn is missing."

Butch frowned, waving Jeb, Tom, and Hyde to silence. "Missing? What do you mean missing? I'm putting you on speaker. Jeb's here."

"Hold on. Let's get someplace I can hear myself think." Jeb signaled to the owner, received a nod, and led the way to the office. The four men squeezed in. A glorified closet, the office had the two things they needed: quiet and a closed door. "All right. What do we have?"

Butch set the phone on the cluttered desk. A tinny version of Finch's voice filled the space. "Fawn left her hotel this morning and hasn't been seen since. She told her personal assistant, an Arturo Youngblood, that she was going to see you about the divorce."

"I haven't seen her, Finch. I've been tied up all day. Even saw the lawyers."

"Did you call her?" Jeb asked, frowning.

"No," Butch denied vehemently.

Finch cleared his throat. "Her flavor of the month claimed you asked to meet her to discuss the divorce privately."

Butch denied it hotly. "I didn't, Jeb. Finch, you know I was leaving all of that to you."

Jeb edged toward the phone. "Finch, do you know what time she left the hotel?"

"Nine-thirty. The concierge made note because of the fuss she made on her way out."

"I'll make a few calls," Jeb said. "If she was coming this way, maybe my boys know something. We shouldn't jump to conclusions. We have enough of our own problems. The State Police are taking over the investigation into Angie's death due to the conflict of interest." Jeb looked at Butch. "I was going to tell you when we were alone."

Butch folded his arms and glared at his brother. "What conflict of interest?"

"My ex-sister-in-law was found strangled on my parents' property, and my brother is their strongest suspect."

Finch jumped in. "I'm going to call in the morning and set up a meeting. I want to be ahead of them on this. Let me get to work. Call me back if you need me."

Butch slapped his palms on his thighs. "What is there to be ahead of? I didn't do this. What motivation did I have to kill Angie? Lots of people have exes. That can't be a reason to kill."

Jeb squeezed Butch's shoulder. "No. No, it's not. The case they'll build will be based on her repeatedly asking for money. You gave it to her, but it wasn't enough for Angie. You told her no, cut her off, but she kept after you. Monday morning, you invited her over, maybe took her for a walk by the creek. You'd had enough."

Butch's stomach revolted. He swallowed hard to keep the bile in place. "Jesus, Jeb. It's not true. You gotta know it's not true."

"I do. I also know you didn't cut Angie off. I know you threatened to, but you didn't. There was no obligation to pay her a cent, yet you did. Even though opportunity existed, the motive isn't there. The State Police are good people. They'll see there's no evidence." Jeb ran his hands through his short hair, his only nervous habit. "We did find something of a more personal nature, though. I need to tell you before they do. Let's go back to the old house."

Butch didn't care if Tom and Hyde were there. "Just say it, Jeb."

Jeb narrowed his eyes then nodded. "You weren't the baby's father. It was there, in Angie's diary."

Butch chewed on the information, but it didn't fit with his understanding of reality. Like looking at a map where north pointed down, it didn't quite make sense. "No. She was pregnant. That's why we got married."

Jeb looked Butch square in the eye. "I know, but it wasn't yours."

The party broke up then. Jeb drove back to the old house where Butch sought the refuge of wood and steel. Night pressed against the single pane windows, listening to the story Butch wove. He played the songs of his life, from seventeen through today. How would his life be different today if he hadn't married Angie? Would he have tried college? Would he have hit the road sooner? Without a doubt, his path would have been different. Butch believed every decision created a unique path. Would he have ever met Tessa? Fawn? Would he have traded one bad choice for another?

Butch picked a simple twelve-bar blues tune. "Every path has joy. Every path has pain. For a tree to grow, takes sunshine and rain. I don't know which way to go. I only know from which I came."

Floor boards groaned in the hallway. The house agreed, he thought, then movement caught his eye.

"I'm touched. Just one day apart, and you're singing the blues." Kate stood in the doorway with a teasing smile, her hair three hundred sixty degrees of red froth.

She looked…perfect. "Did you drive all the way with the windows down?"

"Hell, yes. What's the point of driving if you can't feel it? Besides, my day was weird."

"Betcha mine was weirder." Butch set the guitar in the stand and held his arms wide until Kate filled them.

She kissed his neck. "Care to make it interesting?"

"You go first."

"I spent most of the day in mind-numbing sessions about interesting topics presented by middle-aged white guys who were as entertaining as toast. I got to lunch late, so all the seats were taken, and got to have my own private picnic on a square of sidewalk. In the exhibition hall, vendors ignored me to kiss up to zit-faced twenty-somethings with business cards. That wasn't really bad, because if they realized the kind of capital I could swing, they'd have been on me like flies on shit. Day ended with being stood up by the one vendor I wanted to see. We were supposed to have dinner but he never showed. No call. No email. Nada. I ate dinner pathetically alone. Your turn."

"I started the day visiting Angie's mother. Her living room is filled with the wilting flowers from the funeral. From there I went to see the divorce attorneys. I know I over pay them because of how many teeth they show when they see me. They're just way too happy. Then I went to rehearsal, where I played like I was in a middle school band. Went to the bar with Jeb, Tom, and Hyde, where I found out my first wife lied about the baby being mine, and my brother has been removed from the case."

"Shit. You win."

"I'm not done. Finch called to say Fawn is missing."

"I suppose it's too much to hope she went back to California. Well, you definitely win." She stripped off her shirt. "Ready for your prize?"

"Oh, I love your idea of interesting," he said, taking her to the floor.

Kate ran down the stairs, the steps thundering and squeaking under her feet. Due to a hard rain, she'd taken Wednesday off to spend with Butch, and she was itching to get back to work. She landed in the kitchen, disappointment saddening her face. "Crap. It's only you."

Butch raised an eyebrow. "That's not what you were saying last night."

"Damn it. Tom's left. I wanted to get a ride. I don't like taking the Shelby on site. Too much debris." She sat on a chair and pulled socks onto her bare feet.

"Wasn't Hyde supposed to have your truck back yesterday?"

"Yeah but there was some wreck and he had to bump me. He's supposed to be done today and I hope he is. We're pouring one of the partially exposed walls, and I'd like to get around in my own truck." She sighed heavily.

That bad boy smile grew across Butch's face. "I could be persuaded to drive you."

Kate loved that expression of his. Good things always followed. "Persuade, huh. I suppose you have ideas."

He wiggled his eyebrows. "Many ideas. Make sure you eat today, you're going to need your energy."

She tied her boots, her body tingling with anticipation. "Rest up, muscles. You're going to need *your* energy."

Minutes later, Kate checked out the sky from Butch's passenger seat. Above the rolling green hills, gray clouds thickened. They were set to pour a critical wall today. It had been scheduled for yesterday, but an all-day rain nixed that plan. Today the forecast called for overcast skies. The sky above them looked like it planned to do more than just be cloudy. "Just a few hours, then you can do your worst."

"If it rains again, come on home, and I'll teach you a game. It's called 'Hay Rollin.'" Butch turned into the entrance.

"How do you play?"

Butch kept his eyes on the road and his face straight.

"We find a stack of hay and roll around. First one to get naked wins. There's Hyde."

Butch parked next to the white truck Kate used day-in, day-out. Pick-up trucks and the occasional sedan pulled on site as workers reported for the day. Hyde stood behind Kate's truck, watching the comings and goings.

Kate slammed her door and rounded the back of the truck. "Hey, Hyde. Thanks for bringing her home. Anything I should know about?"

Hyde hooked his thumbs in his pockets. "Not mechanically. She's tip top."

Butch put a foot on the truck's bumper, resting his forearm on his knee. "What about non-mechanically?"

Hyde squirmed, shuffling his thick paws on the dirt. "It's gonna sound crazy, but I think someone moved your truck. I put her in an empty bay to lock it up 'cause of all the small tools you keep in it. No point inviting foolishness. When I pulled her out this morning, she was nose in. I swear I backed her in."

Kate rounded on the truck and threw the door open. "Is anything missing?"

Hyde followed her around, Butch with him. "Not that I can see. You keep a neat truck, so I thought you might be able to tell."

She climbed in, searching the center storage area, glove box, and rear seat. Everything she could think of, she found where it should be. "Huh. That is weird."

Hyde pulled his ball cap off and ran a hand through his hair. "Maybe I'm just imaginin'."

Butch tipped his own hat as another worker waved in greeting. "Nothing wrong with imagining. I make good money at it. Need a ride back to the garage?"

"Yep. Little Red, I did a standard service for your, Tom's, and Waters's trucks. Tom's will need brakes next go around. Otherwise, you're good to go. Here's your bill."

Kate gave him a warning glare as she took the paper. If he undercharged her, she would have to get creative. She read over the parts costs, the labor hours, and the rate. "Looks fair. We'll get it processed. Thanks."

An hour and a half later, Kate got the call she'd been waiting for. Waters and Tom were ready to pour the concrete wall. Her truck bounced across the yard, racing against dark gray clouds.

Kate parked a truck length from the edge of the dig. This end of the building would be the crowning glory. The Cicada Headquarters would house the corporate staff, but it would also be a center for manufacturing and shipping. Much of the square footage was exactly that—square. Not here. A dramatic, double-story, open space with nearly a third of it receded into the earth, this part of the building looked like a super-sized version of a walkout basement. However, the skylights and glass-beaded concrete would make it a museum-quality gallery.

Today her crew poured the second level of the outer wall. The form work had been set for days, waiting for the weather to cooperate. Kate could have been pressing her luck pouring today, but waiting for perfect condition would kill a schedule.

Kate slid out of the truck and balanced three cups of coffee as she shut the door. Waters stood at the near end, watching over the progress. Over three feet wide, the form work started ten feet below ground and ended two feet above. Work today would be done from top-side. That's where the party was. Large beige tarps had been draped over the forms as protection from prior rains. The last section of the wall sat open to the sky, waiting on concrete from the truck that maneuvered into position.

Kate handed Waters the steamy cup of coffee. "Here you go, chief. It'll put a spring in your step." Kate rocked back and forth on her heels, curbing anticipation as she watched the men mill about. "You double checked the line, right? I thought you were ready to pour."

"You have no patience, Kate. You never have. Concrete is an art. You don't rush art."

Kate wrinkled her nose with faux disdain. "You're slow. You're so slow, you'd get trampled in a turtle stampede."

Waters raised an eyebrow to her. "I can still pull you over my knee."

"Why don't you pour the concrete instead? At least you have a chance of coming out on the winning end of that job."

Waters rubbed his weathered hand over his shadowed jaw. "You always did have a fast mouth." He raised his voice to be heard down the length of the wall. "All right, boys. The boss lady wants us to get going."

Kate kicked mud at Waters. "I hate when you call me that."

"I know." Waters grinned like a bear with a fish. "Why are you in such a good mood anyway?"

"I love this part. It's the point where my imagination becomes real. I worked hard on this. You, Tom, the crew. I couldn't ask for a better team. Look at the columns. They're beautiful. The wall's going to be the same. I know it."

"The mix is a pain in the ass to work with. It sets instantly.

There's no time for second chances. Let me get over there."
Waters took charge of the crew, directing laborers and driv-
ers into final position. The turning drum on the concrete
truck kicked into another gear and, moments later, a crys-
talline concoction slid down the chute and into the form.
Three pairs of hands worked fast to move the quick-setting
concrete into position. Tom personally vibrated down the
concrete so no air pockets would mar the sparkling wall.

Waters shouted for the tarp to be stripped from the next
section as the wind kicked up. He looked to the sky and then
over his shoulder at Kate. He shook his head.

"Come on. Hold off." Kate measured the darkness in
the clouds. "You're not even supposed to be here." Her crew
worked fast, moving down the line, closer to where she waited at the starting point of the wall.

A few taunting drops fell, so few Kate could count them.
Under Waters's orchestration, the crew moved as a single
unit. They had taken that rain cloud as a personal challenge,
determined to beat Mother Nature at her own game.

Kate stepped back, giving the crew the room it needed to remove the last section of tarp. She saw it, thirty seconds after the men peeling the tarp did. She fumbled for
her phone, shouting at her crew while the call went through.
"Jeb. We need you here. Bring an ambulance."

Chapter Fourteen

Lightning cracked, whipping across the boiling sky. Thunder like a herd of elephants announced the opening of the heavens. Cold, heavy rain fell to the earth. First as a drop here and there, then in sheets so thick Kate lost sight of the men working next to her.

All hands scurried in the rain, draping the enormous tarps back over the forms to keep the rain off of the work. Sirens competed for air space as four vehicles sped to the site. Jeb led the pack in his sheriff's truck. Butch brought up the rear. A gust of wind pillowed the tarp and pulled Kate toward the hole. Her legs dug in uselessly as the earth turned to mud and gave way under her weight.

Butch jumped from the truck and fought to her side. Self-preservation kicked in, and Kate let go of the tarp. She flailed her arms, trying to gain her balance as the mud under her feet moved. Butch pulled her against him, turning as the tarp lashed his back.

"We have to get the form covered," Kate shouted over the wind.

Jeb, Butch, and the deputies worked with Kate's crew to pin the tarp and weigh it down. Not soon enough, the storm lessened, passing on. It slowed to a steady rain but left everyone covered in mud, the sheriff's men included.

Jeb left two men at the scene and shepherded everyone else into the trailer conference area. There hadn't been time for questions when they arrived. With things now under some semblance of control, Jeb took the lead. "What the hell is going on?"

Waters drew a muddy towel down his face. "There's a body in the wall. A woman. We found her when we pulled the tarp off."

Jeb took a deep breath. "Did you recognize her?"

Waters shook his head. "She's head down. Can't see her face. She has blond hair. A lot of it."

Kate rested her hand on Waters's shoulder. "We didn't know what to do when it started pouring. We tried to cover everything with the tarps to keep it dry."

With the rain down to a drizzle, Jeb walked out to the site with his men, Kate, Tom, Butch, and Waters. Tom and Waters pulled back the tarp, sheeting any trapped water into the hole behind it. A woman had been stuffed into the wall. She was stuck sideways between the pale green rods that lined the front and back of the form. Somebody went to some effort to get her in there, as she wouldn't have gotten down that far on her own.

"We didn't see her until we pulled back the tarp." Waters explained about the rain and the process. "The concrete flowed ahead of where we worked. It looks like part of her is in, part of her is out of it."

Jeb stood on the forms, shining a flashlight below. "When did you cover it?"

"Originally? Tuesday morning. We just opened it up today as we went along."

Jeb looked at his deputy. "Get the kit. Everyone out. Now. Back to the trailer."

Kate did as Jeb said when she would rather have been out with his men. Out there, she could have been useful. Here, she paced like a caged animal, running from questions she didn't have the answers to. "Just let me think," she barked at the voices in her head. She clapped her hands sharply, pulling all eyes to her. "This is what we're going to do. First, everyone give the sheriff full access. I know no one on this site had anything to do with that woman's death, so we have nothing to be worried about. Second, everyone will receive full pay for today. Tomorrow, we'll shift work around to other areas. Tom and I will deal with the investigators and inspections. We've had a good safety record so far, but we're going to have to be perfect now. No short cuts. You see any, you tell Waters, Tom, or me."

Tom curled around a cup of coffee. "Kate, Jeb could shut the site down for a while."

"We'll deal with that if and when it happens. This is a Riley project. We take care of ours. Hell, we can send them to Butch's to start on the house."

The men and women around the table, many wet to the bone, had been still since they sat. Paula played hostess, scavenged supplies of towels and rags, coffee and water, hugs and pats. Kate noticed some stirred as shock wore off. Thinking, planning, talking helped everyone's sanity.

"Who could it be?" a laborer asked. "How could she have gotten in there?"

"How are we going to get her out?" Waters asked. "She's half embedded in concrete. We take those forms down now, and we'll have her and hundreds of pounds of concrete in the basement. It might be fast setting concrete, but not that fast. I'm thinking we'll have to wait until it hardens and jackhammer her out."

"I've never jackhammered a body out of concrete," the laborer said. "This is Tennessee, not New Jersey."

"I'm going to do it," Tom said. "We'll see if Jeb will let us out there. We can drive some sort of dam in at the joints and take apart just the last panel of the form. From there, we'll take it in layers. Everything stays tied off. Belt and suspenders. Nobody else gets hurt. Butch, is there a doctor in town who could work with me?"

Butch leaned against the outer wall of Kate's office, his arms crossed over his chest. "Doc Johnson. He retired three years ago but passes the time teaching at the university and stands in for the coroner."

Kate sighed heavily, leaning next to, but not touching, Butch. "I need to call Cicada…and my father."

"Can I talk to you a minute?" Butch pulled Kate into the privacy of her office. "I hate to do this, but I need to go for a few hours. Are you going to be okay here?"

She brushed the tips of her fingers over the hair on his arm. She didn't actually feel skin, so it didn't count as touching. "I was so glad to see you, I didn't think to ask why you're here."

"I stopped to talk to Jeb after dropping Hyde at the garage. I heard Tom's call come in." Butch pressed her hand to his arm, holding when she pulled back.

"No intimate touching on the job. Can I ask where you're going?"

"No one can see us so it doesn't count. Finch and I are meeting the state investigators in Nashville. I'll be back as quickly as I can."

"Good. I'm glad he'll be with you. Don't worry about us." She forced an encouraging smile to her face. "Give them hell."

"That's what I pay Finch for." He leaned in to kiss her, but she ducked under him.

"No kissing either."

Butch sweated the meeting during the wet drive to Nashville. He didn't kill Angie but he knew his word didn't mean a whole lot to law enforcement. The media circus that set up tent around his and Fawn's divorce hadn't noticed Angie. As Butch believed in counting his blessing instead of questioning them, he didn't care why. Jeb didn't attend the meeting but sent a deputy with a two-inch-thick folder. After two hours, they were on their fifth trip around the mulberry bush.

"Anything else, Mr. McCormick?" The investigator had hazel eyes that could scare a spring straight.

"I didn't kill Angie. She wasn't my wife, but she was part of my life. I wanted her to have a long, happy life. I'd hoped she'd find a good man, settle down. She wasn't perfect, and neither was I, but isn't that normal? She was trying to save snakes, for gosh sakes. How is that a reason to kill someone?"

"How much money did you say you gave her that night at the bar?"

Butch shook his head. "Whatever was in my pocket. I had already paid the bar tab. It couldn't have been more than seventy, eighty dollars."

"You didn't count it?"

"No. Kate was walking out. I shoved the money at Angie and followed Kate. She looked upset, so I followed her."

An eyebrow raised. "Was she upset?"

"No. More…overwhelmed. A country bar can be a lot for a stranger from Michigan to handle all at once. I took her home, that is, to the house. She was staying with me."

"Kate Riley is your lover."

"She is now. Then, she was my tractor mechanic." Butch re-explained the chores-for-room-and-board agreement.

"Back to Angie, I understand y'all married because of a baby. You know it wasn't yours?" The investigator said it with the cold knife of truth.

"Not until my brother told me yesterday."

"How did that make you feel?"

"Not murderous, if that's what you're asking. It was fourteen years ago. Finding out made me feel…introspective. You know, how would my life have been different if it weren't for that day she came to me, tears running down her face, saying she was pregnant? Maybe I would've gone to college. I was considering it, loosely. Maybe I'd have gotten a job and never chased the dream. Losing the baby and then my wife gave me motivation to do something with my life."

The investigator closed the file on his desk and read the sign off to the recording device. "We'll be in touch if we have any more questions." The investigator offered a hand, and

Butch took it.

Finch extended his. "Any idea when you'll make a decision?"

The investigator shook it. "When I'm done considering."

On the drive back home, the wind pulled at the clouds like greedy fingers on cotton candy. Fingers of sunlight shone through, lighting rain-drenched fields. Butch took it as a sign. The investigator shook his hand, which had to be a good sign, too.

Butch raced to the construction site, determined to support Kate as she'd been doing for him. Finding a body on the project site was going to create a lot of headaches for Kate. Somebody associated with the project had to have done it. Who else would think to bury a body into a concrete wall?

By late afternoon, the rain made a soggy, muddy mess of the site. Butch drove back to the work area, unwilling to walk through the mud in his suit. The rain had stopped, letting the tarp be removed and the work of freeing the body begin.

Kate sat in Butch's truck in stockinged feet while Tom and Waters worked with Doc Johnson and Jeb to free the trapped woman.

Butch rested his hand on Kate's knee, content when she didn't pull away. Kate glued her gaze to Tom's back. Jeb had kicked her out as Butch pulled up, dragging her to the truck and into the passenger seat, delivering her into Butch's keeping.

"This is my crime scene. Stay," Jeb had said and walked away.

Butch had taken one look at the boots coated in thick mud and demanded she take them off.

She sat in the truck quietly, mud splattered on her pants,

her brows pressed between her eyes. "My mind just keeps spinning. Who is she? How did she get here? Here, of all places. You can't just walk around the site and not be noticed. How did she get inside the form work? Does someone hate the idea of the Cicada headquarters here so much that they were willing to kill to sabotage the project?"

"I don't know, Katie. I just don't know. Maybe once we know who she is, some of this will make some sense."

"Maybe." She changed the subject. "How did it go with the State Investigator?"

Butch took a deep breath and thought about it. "I think he wants to suspect me. I'm perfect, right? The ex-husband who she was hounding for money to save snakes. She was called from my house, found in my backyard. His biggest problem is…I'm too perfect, and I have Jeb and Finch. Finch gave him a run for his money."

"Are you worried they'll charge you?"

"Yes and no. If they do charge me, I'm in a world of hurt. I was in bed asleep and can't do a damned thing to prove it. So yes, I'm worried about it. But on the other hand, I know I didn't kill Angie, and everyone who knows me knows I couldn't have killed Angie. So what's there to worry about?"

"I wish I could be as relaxed about life as you are. I can't seem to downshift. These past weeks have been a…a…I can't think of a word."

Butch gave her a cocky grin. "I can think of a word, but if you won't let me kiss you on the site, I doubt you'd want me to say the word."

Jeb climbed out of the hole and stomped over to the truck. Mud splattered with every heavy step. Butch opened the door but stayed out of the mud.

"It's her, Butch. It's Fawn."

Butch blinked once. Twice. "What do you mean it's Fawn?" He frowned and blinked again. He looked down, noticed he held Kate's hand, and squeezed it.

"Doc says she was dead before she was dumped in the wall. Someone hit her with something heavy in the back of the head. Butch, when was the last time you spoke to her?"

Butch forgot about the mud and stepped out of the truck. He ran his hand through his thick hair as he started to pace. "Last Friday at the attorneys, Jeb. She called Sunday, but I didn't answer. I swear it."

Jeb patted his brother's arm but looked into the truck. "Go back to the house and stay there. It's going to take us a while to finish up. Then I need to talk to both of you."

Kate looked up from the bench where she sat brushing rust off a lawn mower blade in the old barn. Time stopped mattering hours before, but the sky that had brightened after the rain had darkened again. In the open barn door, a rumpled figure stood. "You look like crap. Why don't you go shower and change?"

"This is official," Jeb said.

"I know, but I'm not going anywhere, and neither is Fawn. Take a few minutes."

Kate figured Jeb hadn't eaten, so she left the barn and went to the house. She waited for Jeb in the living room with a plate of hot food and a cold beer on a TV tray. She left the couch to him and sat in the armchair with her chin raised and her legs crossed. "You look better."

"Long day." Jeb shuffled in and took a seat on the couch.

Kate huffed. "That's an understatement."

They sat in companionable silence while he ate, neither in a hurry to face what came next. They listened to Butch playing in the studio.

"He's been writing some good stuff," Jeb said.

Kate nodded. "I didn't know musicians worked that hard. It's easy to buy the up-all-night, sleep-all-day mystic."

"Butch has always had a way with words. Me? I've always been better with my hands."

"Likewise. The words used in my family tend to be short and loud. I'm very proud of what he can do."

"You can tell me it's none of my business if you want, but what are your intentions with my brother?"

Kate looked at Jeb for a long minute, her heart in her throat. "I think I'm in love with him."

Jeb chewed a bite of a roll slowly. "You think?"

Kate looked at her empty hands, uncomfortable saying it out loud. "I've never been in love before. I've never felt this way about anyone before."

"I hear a 'but' coming."

Kate smiled shyly, wondering which shade of red her face currently matched. Pomegranate, maybe. "*But* I've only known him for a few weeks. Can you fall in love that fast? *But* he's been married three times. My longest relationship lasted six months. *But* he's a high-profile celebrity, and I'm usually covered in mud. He's so far out of my league, I can't even afford the price of a ticket."

Jeb swallowed his bite, his gaze back on his plate. "You're wrong there."

The steps creaked, warning that Butch was about to

join them. Kate sat quietly while Jeb finished the last of the mashed potatoes and gravy. She kept her gaze on the stairs, waiting for Butch. Then she saw his sweet smile and his broad shoulders, and the world became a better place.

His emotional tank empty, Butch lumbered down the creaking stairs to face his brother, his lover, and his dead wife. A song for Angie tugged at him but stalled when he heard Jeb go down stairs after his shower. He'd played with the words, but they wouldn't come, not while he worried about what Jeb had to say.

Butch had considered calling Finch. When should he start thinking about lawyers? If it was anyone but Jeb, it would be now. But it was Jeb, and Butch trusted his brother.

He came down the steps into the living room of his childhood, and that's when he saw it. Katie's eyes lit up. It was as if she had been staring at the empty staircase, waiting for him. Her face relaxed, looking younger as she smiled. And that smile was most evident in the depths of her liquid, blue eyes.

Butch winked at her, broadening her smile. Then he looked to Jeb. "You ready for this?"

Jeb nodded and cleared his mostly finished plate to the kitchen. He returned to the living room with a file folder and ushered Kate from the armchair to the couch where his brother sat. Butch pulled Kate in close while Jeb took her previous place in the chair, sitting with his legs wide and his elbows on his knees.

"The last time you both saw Fawn was when?"

"Friday," Butch said.

"That Saturday in Nashville," Kate answered.

"Butch, did you call her to talk about the divorce terms?"

"I didn't call her. Period. Not to talk about the divorce or anything else."

Jeb spread the folder open on the floor and passed a cell phone statement to Butch. "Her assistant sent me her cell phone record. Do any of these numbers look familiar?"

"That can't be right." Kate pointed to a 313 area code. "That's my phone number. Monday at four-thirty. What were we doing?"

Butch had been in that bar with Abbey McNeil, which he was smart enough to tell Jeb in private. "I was in Nashville. Rehearsals."

"I was at work. I didn't have my phone that whole day."

Jeb took the phone record back. "Do you have it now?"

Kate pulled it from her pocket. "I found it the next morning stuck between the mattress and covers."

Jeb pulled on a pair of latex gloves, took the phone, and searched Kate's call record. There it was. An outgoing call to Fawn.

Kate looked back and forth between the brothers. "I didn't call her." She'd lost the color in her face, and her eyes went wide.

Butch squeezed her hand as she held on to his like a talisman. "I know you didn't, honey."

"Can anyone vouch for you at four-thirty?" Jeb asked.

Kate didn't blink as she stared at Jeb. "I don't know."

"We'll need to ask." Jeb tilted the phone in the light. "I want to see if I can get any prints off of this."

Kate waved her hand at the phone. "Fine. I didn't do

this, Jeb."

Jeb caught her eyes and held them.

"What?" Kate asked. "If you have something to say, Jeb, say it."

"The scene was compromised. Between the rain and everyone working to get the site covered, the area is one big mud puddle."

"I ordered them to cover the forms. To help, Jeb, with the storm." Kate closed her eyes and swallowed. "I compromised the site. Again. Just like I did with Angie."

Jeb nodded. "Somebody saw you, Kate."

Tom filled the doorway. "Somebody saw Kate do what?" He stood with his arm hanging heavy, looking wet and muddy, exhausted and mean. Dark bags circled his eyes, and concrete dust frosted his hair. "What exactly did somebody see?"

Jeb stood to face Tom. "Somebody saw her driving on the site."

Kate huffed out a laugh. "Oooo, somebody saw me driving around my own site. Let's see, I only do that about ten times a day."

"This was Tuesday, after dark," Jeb said. "One of the men spotted you driving your truck. You had someone with you."

"It wasn't me! I was in Louisville all day. I came home around ten thirty. All of you were here!"

Jeb jotted down notes. "You took your truck to Louisville?"

"No. I dropped it off with Hyde Monday before work. I took the Shelby to Louisville. Hyde brought the truck back this morning."

Butch laced his fingers with Kate's, facing this as a team. "Jeb, Hyde thought the truck had been moved. He thought he backed the truck into an empty bay, but this morning it was turned around."

Jeb's lips tightened until they didn't exist. "I'll talk to him." He looked at Kate. "Do I have your permission to search the truck? I need to take a look."

"Yes, but I went through it this morning after Hyde talked to us. I didn't notice anything out of place."

Will power. Butch knew that alone kept Kate in the house with him instead of out in the driveway with Jeb and Tom. Her right foot tapped a quick little beat. The fingers of her hand, wrapped under her chest, drummed on her rib cage.

"I'm trying not to be freaked out at the idea that someone took a joy ride in my truck. It's like someone rummaging through my underwear without my permission. The idea that someone used my truck to dump Fawn's body is going to make me puke. I'll never drive it again."

Butch wrapped his arms across her shoulders. "I wish I had a clue as to what is going on."

"What's going on is someone is fucking with us. Setting you up for Angie; me up for Fawn. My phone is ringing." Kate snatched the phone off the piano bench.

"Don't touch it," Butch said, catching her by the arm. "Jeb is going to check it for prints."

"Well I can touch it. He expects to find my prints," Kate reasoned. "It's the Cicada CEO. I need to take it. Chuck. I'm glad you called me back. You heard about the trouble?"

Butch quietly stepped outside, leaving Kate to her call and curious himself as to what progress Jeb made. The doors of the truck stood open, light spilling across the gravel drive. Butch couldn't see Jeb but knew he stood on the driver's side, bent into the truck. Tom stood in the open passenger door, looking at Jeb, his back to Butch. He answered questions Jeb asked. Neither noticed him standing in the shadows behind Tom.

"Are these gloves Kate's?" Jeb spoke, his voice muffled by the truck, but Butch heard him clearly.

"They look like the pair she wears, and they're in her truck," Tom answered.

"So you're saying they are hers?"

Silence hung a moment. "Are you asking as Jeb my drinking buddy or Jeb the sheriff?"

"All right. I'm going to take her truck in."

"She's not going to be happy."

"Tom, I'm worried about your cousin."

"You don't think she killed Fawn, do you?"

"I haven't always been a county sheriff. I've seen things that would give grown men nightmares. I've seen evil at work, Tom. So I know what I'm talking about when I say something evil is at work, right here in my hometown. It's taken me too long to see it, and now three women are dead."

"Three?" Tom shifted, letting more light spill out toward Butch.

"Butch has three dead wives." Jeb crossed his arms.

Tom clenched his fists. "And now you think someone is targeting Kate."

Jeb sighed. "Setting her up? Definitely. Let's just hope

she doesn't end up as number four."

Tom spoke, his voice a dangerous growl. "She's not going to be here for it to happen."

Jeb spoke gently. "She can't leave, Tom. She's a person of interest in Fawn's death."

Butch gritted his teeth and stepped into the light. "How long have you suspected something is going on?"

Tom jumped at the sound of Butch's voice, planting his shoulder into the edge of the door. "Shit! How long have you been standing there?"

"Long enough. Why didn't you tell me, Jeb?"

Quiet and stern, Jeb spoke through his teeth. "It's just a suspicion. I don't know anything. Yet."

"I have three dead ex-wives, the last of which was kind enough to die and save me a definitely ugly, potentially expensive divorce. Has someone been cleaning up after me? Has someone been taking care of my 'problems?'"

Jeb shook his head. "I don't know, but I'm going to have Tessa's case re-evaluated. At this point, I have a hard time believing the fire was an accident."

Tom shoved his way past Butch. "Shit. I'm getting Kate out of here. Screw your person of interest. Where is she?"

"On the phone," Butch said. "Is that all right, Jeb? It rang, and she answered it. It was Cicada."

Kate leaped off the porch, her feet landing on the ground before the screen door slapped shut. "Tom!" Kate screamed as she tore down the walkway. "Tom!"

The three men jumped in conditioned response to a

panicked woman. Butch ran across the gravel drive and caught Kate as she flew across the yard. Kate pushed his arms away. "Don't touch me. Not now. You can't be nice to me."

Butch held her around the waist. "What happened, Kate?"

Kate tried to spin out of Butch's grip. "Chuck Allen called. He wants to cancel the contract. I need to meet him tomorrow in Chicago. Tom, you need to take care of the site—"

"Bullshit, Kate. Bullshit. This is our business, our project. I'm going with you." Tom stormed across the driveway, challenging her orders.

Kate hung on Butch's arms, shaking her head emphatically.

Tom shouted, losing the cool facade he maintained. "Don't argue with me about this. Jeb has the site shut down, no one is working tomorrow. Waters can take care of things here."

"Butch, let go of me. I need to think." Kate pushed out of Butch's arms and stalked around the yard.

Butch turned to Tom as Kate paced from him. "Could they really cancel the contract?"

"Cicada can cancel the contract at their convenience, which would mean Riley Architects and Engineers wouldn't be able to make payroll, which would mean Riley Architects and Engineers would cease to exist, which would mean—"

"We go home," Kate said, her eyes glassy with tears.

Butch grabbed her arms in an unbreakable grip. "Over my dead body."

Chapter Fifteen

Butch dragged Kate behind as he stomped from the yard. The cold light of the moon lit the way, matching his mood. He moved quickly, not slowing when Kate slipped and shuffled on the gravel. She raked her fingers down Butch's arm when she stumbled, catching on his waistband.

"Stop. Butch. What are you doing?"

"Taking you out behind the barn. It's the place we take people around here when they're being stupid." They rounded the barn, and Butch swung Kate so her back came up hard against the rough wood. Something dominant pumped through his body, beating as if it had a pulse of its own. "You are being downright stupid if you think you're going to walk away."

Kate looked up at Butch, her voice cracking. "You don't understand. I'm losing the contract of a lifetime. I'm losing my project. I'm losing my company. I'm going to Chicago to try to stop it. And if I can't…"

Butch's hands cupped her face. Tears ran from her baby-doll-blue eyes, across his fingers. "And if you can't, you're just going to quit? I'm disappointed in you, Katie. I never thought you were a quitter."

Kate thumped her hands against his chest. "I'm not quitting." She pushed ineffectually at him. "I'm not quitting. I'm planning."

"You're planning to run. You talk a good game, but things get a little rough, and Little Katie goes running to Daddy."

She pressed her lips firmly. Fire kindled and burned away the panic but created an opening for a coldness that worried Butch more. She stood stock still, her palms flat on his chest, and spoke slowly, distinctly enunciating each carefully selected word. "The *last* thing I want to do is go back to Detroit and listen to him tell me 'I told you so' for the next twenty years. But Detroit is our base. There we have a chance at surviving. Tom can—"

"Surviving isn't the same as living. You deserve better than surviving." Butch wrapped his arms around her, hoping to thaw that cold, calculating facade with body heat.

Her rigid body didn't yield. "Butch."

He felt her take a deep breath, as though she were preparing herself for something difficult. He told himself not to react, whatever she said.

Butch felt more than heard her reedy voice. "I don't know if I can do this."

He didn't know which "this" she meant. It didn't matter. "You can. And won't be doing it alone. Remember the first day we met? You helped me hang Granddad's sign. What would have happened if I'd have done that alone?"

"You would have pulled something. Maybe broken your foot when you dropped the sign on it."

"But together, we made everything right. I know, for myself, it's easier to think that I'm better on my own. But it's not true. Not for me. Not for you. You have me. You have Tom, Waters, Jeb, Hyde, Trudy, your family. Even your father. All of us are on your side. We'll do what needs to be done, one day at a time."

Silent for a moment, she slid her hands around his waist, as if letting him be the strength that held her up. "It's not as scary when you put it that way." She rose on her toes, brushing her lips against his. "Thank you."

Wild strawberries filled his senses. His gut clenched. He hungered for her. He nipped at her lip until she opened. His fingers crawled up her stomach, gripped the edge of her shirt, and pulled it over her head.

The dim light made every creamy curve a hidden valley to explore. Lace the color of her hair cupped breasts high and firm. He bent down and took her nipple into his mouth, teasing the tender skin through the rough lace. Kate gasped, clutching at Butch's shoulder, pulling at his hair.

Butch lifted his face, and she fell into him, locking her mouth to his. Butch brought himself to full height, bending Kate back into his arms while he devoured her. His desire for his woman intensified, driving him forward, forcing her to take a step to stay on her feet. He took a step and then another, into the darkened barn, across the open space. Butch spun her around, and she caught herself on a thick wooden ladder.

"Climb up," Butch said.

"What are we doing?"

Butch ran his hands over the firm globes of her buttocks and urged her up the ladder. "Finishing what we started in the hay loft."

"I've never been in a hay loft."

Butch bit her earlobe, his hands guiding her in the direction he needed. She resisted, teasing him by arching her back, pushing her butt into the cradle of his hips. She ground against him until he panted in ragged breaths, then she raced up the ladder.

Butch tore up after her. At the top, he stripped off his shirt and laid it out on the wooden floor. Kate stood just out of his reach, running her hands up and down her body.

Butch pointed to the spot in front of him. "Come here."

Half of Kate's mouth curled into a devilish smile. "You. Come. Here." Kate cupped her breasts in offering.

Butch took the bait and leaped over the splayed shirt. With a flick of his fingers, the bra fell away, and those delicious breasts were in his mouth. He attacked the waist of her jeans and stripped her of the denim and panties beneath. Kate kicked her way free and launched her own campaign, popping open the button on his jeans and sliding her hand inside.

Butch sucked air in sharply, releasing it in a low, guttural rumble. His hips thrust against the palm of her hand. She pushed the jeans down his hips until they fell into a pool at his ankles. Kate caressed him, stroked him as she sank to her knees.

He flexed his hands, needing something to do with them. He found the thick of her hair, and knotted them together. She wouldn't be leaving him anytime soon. The sight of her overpowered rational thought. Kate ran her tongue up the length of him, and all thought abandoned him. He leaned over her, blissfully helpless as she had her way. Her hair brushed against his overheated body, and his gut tightened. He forced himself to inhale, struggling for control. She knew he teetered on the edge, he was sure she knew. She toyed with him, driving him hard only to pull back at the last instant. She took him again to the precipice of ecstasy, her throaty laugh the last straw.

Butch rolled Kate to the floor and buried his body to the hilt. He raged against her on the hay-covered floor, shedding the guise of the smooth, graceful lover. Through the haze of lust, a thought came into his mind. This could be the last time he ever had her. She considered leaving him. She said it simply. Just run home.

Vexation gained a foothold. How could she? He had seen the light in her eyes. Warm. Radiant. All for him.

Butch locked his elbows and stared down in to her eyes. "Goddamn you. I'm your home. Tell me you know that." He crushed his mouth to hers, thrusting relentlessly until she convulsed around him. In the moment of her surrender, he soared.

Sweat covered their heaving bodies. As sanity returned, Butch realized he had to be crushing her. He rolled until she laid sprawled across him, where she belonged.

Residual fear speared hotly. He slapped her ass. "If you think you're leaving, you're a goddamned idiot."

Kate jumped at the swat, then snuggled closer. "Stop swearing at me. I'm not a goddamned idiot. I just have to think. I'll figure something out."

"Together." Satisfied with the determination he heard, Butch stroked her back, starting at her butt and moving up the line of her back and down again. "As soon as I can get the feeling back below my waist, we'll figure this out together."

Kate paced the kitchen wearing the only pair of dress pants she had brought. She epitomized the successful professional in the black pants, white blouse, and black and white silk scarf. Beneath that controlled veneer buzzed a bundle of nerves that wore a rut in the kitchen floor.

Tom, by comparison, looked like he stepped off the set of *The Godfather*. The dark suit made his shoulders look as wide as a prize bull. Stern and menacing dark brown eyes didn't blink. He leaned against the counter, saying nothing as Kate paced.

Butch walked into the kitchen on long, confident strides in faded jeans, his lucky shirt, and the boots Kate had bought for him.

Kate stopped at the top of route. "When did you say the car was going to be here?"

"I cancelled it," Butch said. "I'm taking you myself. Let me pour a cup of coffee, and we'll go."

Tom silently asked Kate for an explanation, but she could only shrug her shoulders. As far as she knew, Butch had arranged a chartered plane into Chicago and a car service to and from the airport. Given the urgency, neither Kate nor Tom could argue with the amount of time they would save avoiding a commercial flight.

They rode to the county airport in silence. Kate mentally rehearsed her response to every argument. The hardest were the emotional ones, like believing the building would be cursed. She didn't know Chuck Allen to be an emotional man, but there weren't any rational reasons to pull the contract. Yes, she was a suspect. Kate fought hard to adopt Butch's philosophy. She knew she didn't kill Fawn. Butch, Jeb, and Tom knew she didn't do it, so she wasn't going to worry about the investigation. She trusted Jeb to catch the bad guy, because that was what a sheriff did.

Butch parked the truck in the lot and led Kate and Tom into the small building that served as the terminal. Butch used the charter service often enough that he knew everyone, and quickly they moved to the plane. When Kate started up the portable staircase, Butch followed her.

Kate stopped and looked down at him. "What are you doing?"

"Going with you. Get on up there."

"You can't go with us."

"Yes, I can." Butch took her hand in his. "Now we can either stand here and argue for ten minutes and then get on the plane together, or we can hold hands and go now, saving us time and aggravation."

The Cicada CEO worked out of an overcrowded office in a three-floor warehouse where everyone still knew everyone by sight. In the last fifteen years, the business had grown, thanks to quality-made machinery and a shrewd eye for finance packaging. The core of Cicada's business had shifted, moving farther south and reaching across the border. The company had a reputation for innovative thinking and craftsmanship and wanted a headquarters that matched.

The young assistant escorted the trio through a hallway stacked shoulder high with banker's boxes. A bark of laughter rolled out the conference room door as they approached. Kate held her head high as she led the parade inside.

Chuck Allen, a remarkably unremarkable man of average height with black hair, brown eyes, and a slender build, sat at a conference table as old as the company. What Chuck lacked in stature, he made up for in grit and nerve. "The Riley twins." Chuck rose to greet them. Polite but without a sign of the humor that sounded moments before. "Tom, Kate. Thank you for coming."

"Good to see you, Chuck." Kate eyed the man who rose with Chuck, slick with a trendy haircut and a fast smile. Not big and thick like Tom, he stood a bit over six feet with broad shoulders and an athletic build, more like a cyclist than a weight lifter, and carried himself with an air of confidence. Highlights streaked his sandy-brown hair, and his hazel eyes dared her to trust him. Kate dropped her lashes, declining the invitation, and turned her attention back to Allen. "This is Butch McCormick—"

"Their musician." Butch offered a hand to the stern faced CEO.

Chuck shook the hand. "Ah, yes. I've heard a lot about you, Mr. McCormick."

"Butch," he corrected. "Finch. Good to see you found your way."

Landon Finch took Butch's hand and clapped his back. Kate nearly choked on her tongue. Butch brought his shark for her.

"Chuck and I were just getting acquainted. This must be Kate Riley." Finch extended his hand. "Talented architect, shrewd contractor. You have quite a reputation."

Kate accepted the hand and smiled in acceptance of the compliment. "Taking a page from the legendary Mae West, 'When I'm good, I'm very good. But when I'm bad, I'm better.'"

Tom offered his hand. "I know the voice, nice to see the face. Tom Riley."

"You have a reputation all your own, don't you? Ah, that's a subject for another day." Finch motioned the players into position. "Let's play ball. How to move forward with the headquarters given the current situation?"

Chuck surveyed the outfield before stepping into the box. He didn't ease into the game but swung at the first pitch. "The entire situation with Ms. Jordan is deplorable."

Chuck nipped the top of the ball, Finch maneuvered into position to field the weakly hit grounder. "Absolutely, not least of all for Butch and for Fawn." Finch tossed it to Butch.

"Fawn and I had been apart for over a year, but there was no animosity, at least on my part. Our careers took us in separate directions. Fawn was a good person, she just wasn't the woman I married. I'm sure she thought the same of me."

Chuck raised his eyebrows and nodded. Kate had done her research before starting work for Cicada. Chuck Allen was on this third wife, one nearly half his age. He was quoted in a magazine as saying all of his wives loved his money but were shocked he actually worked long, hard hours for it.

"My condolences." With a quick flick of his wrist, he popped one alone the baseline. "But I can't dismiss the fact that she was killed on Cicada property."

Finch sprinted to the left to get under the ball.

"Absolutely. The sheriff, Butch's brother, believes the suspect dumped her body there because of the project. Specifically to implicate Kate in the death. As brutal as it was, it was also poorly planned and sloppily executed. Kate had been hours away at a trade show in Kentucky at the time poor Fawn was killed. The facts will come out, in due time."

Chuck stepped out of the box and adjusted his gloves. With a tug on his hat, he stepped in, ready for the next pitch, determination carved in the lines of his face. "This isn't the kind of publicity I want for Cicada."

Finch dove to the right, snatching the line drive from the air. "There's a saying in show business—there's no such thing as bad publicity. Look at this." Finch pulled a manila folder from his case and slid it to Allen.

Chuck opened the folder and picked up a glossy spread featuring iconic images of Maya Angelo, Ruby Dee, Amelia Earhart, and Fawn Jordan. Gone but not forgotten. Other images painted Cicada as a champion for women, challenging the status quo, investing in young and disadvantaged women.

Chuck raised a brow. "You think this will work?"

"I know this will work. Branding is all about telling your story, selling the image you want the public to see. You say nothing, pull the project, and hide, and you sell the image of a guilty coward. You stand behind the project, behind Fawn, and you stand for the American ideals of hard work and fair play."

"We'll build a memorial," Kate said. "One of the pillars in the gallery will be steel and glass. Simple, elegant, beautiful."

"Like Fawn." Finch smiled and patted Kate's hand. "That is a wonderful thought. The morbid fact is people are intrigued by the death of a celebrity, especially if it is layered in mystery. I'll bet there are dozens of people outside your site now, scrambling to get a look inside. Canceling the project won't make the curious and the fanatical disappear, but going forward with it creates the opportunity for you to elevate Cicada's visibility on a national and international stage. Think about it, Chuck. We don't get to choose our fifteen minutes of fame, just what we do with it."

Chuck stepped out of the box and ran his handkerchief across a sweaty brow. Down to his last out. He stepped back in the box, brought the bat to his shoulder and pulled it short at the last moment, working the bunt. "I can't handle that kind of exposure."

Finch leaned in, snagged the ball, and beat Chuck to first base. "I can. First, a press conference. We need you front and center. The man in charge. I'll make the calls. You need a black suit."

While Chuck and Finch coordinated the details, Kate excused herself and found a narrow spot in a crowded cubicle where she could breathe. She realized she hadn't been able to function since she talked to Chuck the night before. She hadn't eaten, hadn't slept, and hadn't thought a coherent thought for over fourteen hours. All at once, clarity burned away the fog. Adrenaline beat at her weary body, pooling tears of relief in her eyes. Her hands shook when she lifted them, and her heart pounded.

Hands slid around her waist. She inhaled the scent of her own personal hero. Her hands clasped around those that held her.

Butch pressed against her back. "Are you okay? You looked a little pale when you left."

She let her head fall back onto his shoulder, angling her

face toward his. "I don't know what I did to deserve you, but I wish I could do it a thousand times. Thank you." Kate turned in his arms, rose on her toes and wrapped her arms around his head. She pressed her lips to his, pouring in emotions she didn't have the words to express. Then, she found that she did. "I love you."

Butch crushed her against him. "Thank God. I've wanted to tell you for weeks. I love you with everything I am."

Finch poked his head around the corner. "You two want to get back in here and finish the job?"

"We're coming, Finch." When they were alone again, Butch pressed a kiss to Kate's temple. "I planned on our first 'I love you' being romantic, maybe with candlelight and wine. Not in a cramped corner stacked with boxes."

"This is perfect." Kate pressed a kiss to his chest. "This is just perfect."

Kate paced off sixty feet, dropped a spot of neon pink spray paint, turned left, paced another sixty feet, and dropped a spot of paint.

John kicked the stones with his goatskin boots. "So this is the big plan?"

Kate smiled at John and goose walked to connect the dots with the bright paint. "Well, it's an idea. We were looking at different wings but wanted something that went with the farmhouse. This would be the courtyard here. That wing," she said pointing west, "would be Butch's wing. No morning sun to disturb his beauty sleep. Then the east wing would be for Jeb. The first floor will be shared space with bedrooms upstairs. I thought we could use breezeways to connect the wings, do them like covered bridges."

"Are you really going to build this? For Butch?"

"Oh, I don't know. I'm just doing this to keep my mind busy. It's Monday. Jeb let Tom open most of the site back up but wants me to stay away until things settle down. I can only do so much paperwork before I get antsy."

"Are those people still outside the fence?"

"Yep." Kate rolled her eyes. "I guess it's down to less than a dozen people. A few photographers, mostly fans with nothing better to do with their lives. Honestly, tell me who has time to stand outside a construction site and wave a lighter in the middle of the day. Don't these people work?"

"Makes you wonder, doesn't it? Have you heard from Butch?"

"He's called ten times since he left on Friday." Kate giggled as she drew lines on the grass. "I know I shouldn't laugh, but your son is in over his head. It's a good thing Trudy went with him. She'll get that house in shape lickety-split. It sounds like they will be bringing a ton of crap back. He'll need a bigger house one way or another."

"Build the house," John said.

Kate stopped mid-spray. "The cost—"

"I want my boys to stay," John interrupted. "They were gone for too long. Jeb joined the Marines. He never would tell me what he did for them but three years ago, he went on a mission. For six months, we didn't know if he was dead or alive. Emily prayed and cried and prayed some more. Year and a half ago, he came home, nearly a stranger. He doesn't laugh anymore."

"He laughs. I've seen him. He and Butch tease."

John nodded. "He's better around Butch. While Jeb was off saving the world, Butch was out there, seeing the country, making his mark, falling for the wrong women. He came back a lost man. It's only been these last few weeks that he's acted like his old self."

Her face hot, did John know she was the next wrong woman? Kate studied the ground and kicked a rock. "He loves me." After a moment she added, "And I love him."

John took her hand and squeezed it. "Build the house. I have some money saved. Bring my boys home."

Kate flashed him a mischievous grin. "It's going to be amazing. Listen to what Tom came up with." Kate moved across the back of the house painting a picture of a country villa, her hands moving across the scene to draw the picture for John. "It's going to be a dichotomy. Old and new. Traditional and modern. Large and intimate."

Jeb came out the kitchen door as Kate painted her picture, and she quickly enveloped him into the tale. "Jeb's wing will have four bedrooms, a sitting room, and the crowned prince of bathrooms, just like in the Hermitage, right, Jeb?"

The first prick of trouble came when he wouldn't meet her eyes. Jeb stood in the future courtyard, his hands hanging stiffly at his sides, looking at the worn patch of dirt.

"What's the matter, Jeb?" Kate invaded his space, panic injected a flutter in her voice. "Did something happen to Butch?"

"No, Katie. Butch is fine."

Kate let out the breath she held. "Oh, you scared me. With all of the bad luck going around, I was afraid something happened."

Jeb lifted his eyes to her. "Something did happen, Katie."

His calm voice lacked expression. "The County Prosecutor is getting a lot of pressure on Fawn's case. Those people outside the site, her agent, the press are demanding he do something."

The can of spray paint fell from Kate's hand. "Oh, God. You're arresting me."

Chapter Sixteen

"How could you think I did that to her?" Kate's throat tightened, choking her voice. "I was in Kentucky."

"I'm not arresting you."

Kate stumbled back, hearing the implied "yet."

"But I have to take you in for questioning."

"W-why?"

Jeb swallowed hard, spoke quietly. "The gloves retrieved from your truck were stained with Fawn's blood. There were splatters on the seat. Fawn's rental car was found abandoned near the construction site. We collected red hairs from the driver's seat. The call came from your cell and you were placed at the scene—"

"It wasn't me, Jeb. It wasn't me." Kate's voice rose to a squeak.

"And with the witness statement…" He shook his head. "I'll have you back here before dinner."

Kate trembled. She truly hadn't thought she would be

considered a suspect. Everything about going with Jeb terrified her. She had no experience with the law. What if they didn't believe her? Would they put her in a cell? Would they take her fingerprints and mug shot? What would happen to her career? To her business? No one would hire an architect with a record. Petrified, she couldn't move.

John's supporting arm came across her shoulders. She leaned into him as tears rolled unchecked from her eyes.

"Don't be afraid, I won't let anything happen to you. Trust me, Kate. I know what I'm asking, but trust me to get to the bottom of this."

Think. Think. Think.

She couldn't. She felt like the gum on the bottom of society's shoe. People she passed either wouldn't look at her or looked with a repulsive sneer on their faces. She wasn't sure which was worse. Humiliated, degraded, she followed where they led, into a small room with a stark, steel table and heavy duty chairs. There she sat. And sat. And sat.

She wanted to go home.

Now she wasn't alone anymore, which scared her more.

"Where were you on Tuesday between ten a.m. and eight p.m.?"

Kate looked at the investigator with the crooked tie.

Jeb had contacted Garrison Leeds, an attorney friend of his, and requested he help Kate.

Leeds spoke. "As Ms. Riley's statement says, she was in Louisville, Kentucky."

"Can she prove it? Who saw her? Who could vouch for

her?" The investigator looked at Kate. "Did you meet with anyone?"

Think. Think. Think.

"I...I was stood up. Supposed to meet a guy, but he stood me up. I ate at a bar. Alone."

A hand rested on her forearm. "Did you pay with a credit card?"

Kate looked at the hand, wishing it was Butch's. She closed her eyes and wished for him.

Leeds squeezed her arm. "Kate, did you pay with a credit card?"

Think. Think. Think.

She cleared her throat. "I used my company card." Tears flowed unabated. "I also bought lunch earlier and then gas, too. Before I left Louisville, I filled up. And they should have record of where I signed in that morning and got my guest pass."

The small plane landed, and the door opened as the stairs locked in place. Butch ran down the steps faster than was smart and strode across the pavement, his hands fisted and his jaw set.

Jeb stepped out of the terminal, his hat in his hand. "Clyde, I'm glad your—"

Butch lunged at his brother, taking him down to the pavement. The two men rolled, cursing at each other. Trapped on the small plane for hours, Butch thought only of kicking the living hell out of his brother. With his training, Jeb got the upper hand and quickly pinned Butch to the tarmac.

"Goddamn it, calm down," Jeb shouted.

Trudy flounced down the stairs in a floor-length fur, sunglasses, a wide-brimmed, pink hat, and matching three-inch heels. She danced over to the men in small, fluttering steps that made the coat swirl around her ankles. "Boys, you're embarrassing me." With the admonishment, she turned up her nose and walked into the terminal.

Jeb tasted the blood in the corner of his mouth and glared down into his brother's face. "You done?"

Butch struggled uselessly against Jeb's grip, shouted in frustration, then counted to ten. "For now. Let me up."

Jeb rose nimbly to his feet and held his hand out to his brother. "Don't hit me again. You got a freebie. You hit me again, I'm hitting back."

Butch nodded curtly. "How is she?"

Jeb pulled Butch to his feet. "Not good. She hasn't said a word since I brought her home. The lawyers were good... and fast. Butch, I swear to you, I'll figure this out."

Butch put his hand on Jeb's shoulder. "I know you will. Sorry about your mouth."

Jeb shrugged. "I'd have done the same."

As Butch and Jeb pulled up the driveway, Tom came out the door, moving like a boxer with quick, agitated motions and his face set in agony as though he were slowly being tortured.

"Butch, you need to take care of her. Now. She won't talk to me. She won't even look at me."

"Where is she?"

"In the barn." Tom looked up the drive as though he'd made that walk several times and considered doing it again. He shook his head and turned back to Butch. "You have to help her."

Butch rubbed his sweaty hands on his jeans as he went around the house to the barn. The door gaped wide, but light didn't shine from it. In early evening, Butch squinted under the brilliant spring sun, but the barn would be dark. It always was.

Kate sat cross-legged on the floor with a rusty sheet of metal stretched across her lap. She brushed the steel wool in her hand absently across the pitted blade, her stroke devoid of energy. She didn't look at her work but stared at an infinite spot on the old tractor. Her usually sparkling blue eyes were flat, and her mouth hung slightly open as if it took too much strength to close her lips.

She didn't move when Butch walked in. Her eyes didn't flash, she didn't turn her head, she didn't acknowledge him in any way. She just continued to run the steel wool listlessly over the hunk of steel.

"Katie? Katie, honey?" Butch took slow, quiet steps to her side, not sure whether she knew he was with her. He touched her shoulder with his fingertips, needing the contact. She jumped at his touch, drawing the flat of her hand along the sharpest edge of the blade.

Kate lifted her hand and watched as the rich blood welled in the cut and ran down her arm.

Butch cursed and tore the shirt from his back to wrap around her hand. "Come on, Katie. We need to get this cleaned up before you get an infection."

Kate sat on the ground, looking past him. "I need to

think."

Butch swore again. He kicked the blade from her lap, pulled her up from the ground and into his arms. Halfway out of the barn, her arms locked around his neck. He cradled her head against his shoulder and held her close as he strode into the kitchen.

"I have you, Katie. That's right, just hold on to me. I love you and won't let you go," Butch whispered gently into her ear when she had buried her face in his neck.

She seemed so small in his arms, so dramatically different than the larger-than-life woman who stomped and cursed her way into his world. He set her on the counter and unwrapped the blood-stained shirt from her hand.

"What the hell happened?" Tom walked into the kitchen, shouting as he saw Kate.

"She cut herself on a rusty piece of metal. It isn't deep for all the blood." Butch rigorously cleaned the cut with soap and water. Kate's shoulders flinched now and then, but she didn't make a sound, she didn't try to pull away. "There's a first aid kit in the upstairs bathroom. Can you get it for me?"

Tom ran for the kit while Butch held a clean cloth to the cut.

Butch cupped her face with his free hand, stroking her cheek. He lifted her chin. "Look at me." Butch looked into her eyes as they became glossy and spilled silent tears. He dropped his head and caught them on his lips, kissing her cheeks.

"I wished for you," Kate said, her voice rough and thick.

Butch pulled her into his arms, locking her against his chest. "I'm home, honey." Wild strawberries filled his head, this time triggering something protective in him. He wanted to sweep her away from all of this, hide her in his cabin in the Californian hills so nothing could hurt her. Then he would spend days loving that vacant look off of her face. "We're home."

Butch stayed by Kate's side. She existed in a nearly catatonic state, eating what she was fed, walking where she was led. She said only that she needed to think. Butch had made love to Kate, sweetly, gently, telling her everything he found so wonderful about her, showing her how he loved her. She had accepted him, she had moved with him and then curled around him, but she was still lost somewhere inside of her mind that he couldn't quite get to.

Tuesday, Kate sat curled on the couch while Butch pounded on the piano. A small recording device took in the heavy, angry bellows that raged from the instrument and resounded through the too empty room. Tom stalked in, dusty from a morning on the job site, his brows pressed low as though he felt the frustration and impotence that seethed from the abused keys.

Tom crossed the room to Kate and brushed her hair from her face. "What do we do?" he asked Butch.

Butch dropped heavy hands onto the piano, sending up a boom of dissonance. "I'm out of ideas. Should we call someone?" He expected Doc Johnson had to know a shrink or two.

Tom's eyes flashed. He pulled his cell phone out and waited until a deep, gruff voice answered. "It's Tom. I have Butch McCormick with me. The country music star? Yeah, that's him. He's sleeping with Kate." With that courteous introduction, Tom shoved the phone into Butch's hand.

Butch held the phone to his ear out of habit. "Hello?"

He jerked the phone away as two minutes of some of the most creative swearing he had ever heard roared out of the phone. He had a growing understanding of why Kate kept their relationship a secret. Butch looked at Tom who stood there with his arms crossed and mouth clenched in determination.

Ed Riley roared. "Let me talk to my daughter, you son of a bitch."

At Tom's nod of encouragement, Butch carried the phone to Kate. "Your father wants to talk to you."

Kate looked like a porcelain doll with eyes too wide. Butch pulled the phone back, instinctively protecting her, but Tom took it from his hand and pressed the speaker button.

"She's here, Uncle Ed." Tom held the phone near Kate's chin.

When she spoke, it was the voice of a little girl. "Daddy?"

"Is that the way I raised you?" The old man bellowed so loud Butch easily heard every word he said.

Kate closed her eyes, her heavy head resting wearily on a battered pillow. "I don't understand."

"Who was the son of a bitch? Who was I just talking to?"

Kate pressed her hand to the phone, holding it herself as she spoke in a slow, quiet voice. "Butch, Daddy. His name is Butch McCormick."

"You're sleeping with him?"

Kate frowned, her voice hardening. "I'm not answering that."

"You don't have to. Tom told me. I didn't raise you to be some asshole's whore."

Kate sat up, defiance strengthening her body. "Butch

isn't an asshole. Sleeping with a man doesn't make me a whore."

"Well it's not going to find you a husband. Men like easy women in their beds, not in their houses."

Kate sprang to her feet in a burst of energy that made Tom jump back. "What makes you think I want a goddamned husband? God himself knows I don't need another man in my life. And if I want a house, I'll buy one myself!"

"Don't raise your voice to me, young lady. Marriage is a sacred institution."

"Ha! Tell that to that woman you married. Fucking Butch may not be a sacred institution, but the man knows the way to Heaven."

Butch cringed at Kate's graphic description of him to her father. *Her father.* He cut his gaze to Tom who was doubled over in silent laughter.

"Butch?" the old man continued. "What kind of fucking name is Butch? He isn't good enough for you. I know those musician types. Woman in every town, kid in every other."

Kate circled the couch with powerful strides. "You don't know Butch, Dad. You don't know a thing about him. He loves me."

Ed Riley laughed like a hyena. "Son of a bitch, you're gullible. For a smart woman, Kate, you're stupid as hell. He's not going to buy the cow when you're giving him the milk for free."

Kate growled into the phone. "Thirty-seven. Dad. That's how many guys I've been with. Thirty-seven. And you know what? I'm not on the giving end—I'm on the getting end."

"I'm going to come down there and break that man's neck—"

She stopped pacing and held the phone at face level as though he were in the room. "No, you're not. You're not going to touch him. He's mine. From now on, I'm the only one who can break his neck. You don't touch him. You don't talk to him. You don't think about him."

"The hell I will—"

"Enough," Kate screamed. "I love him. End of story. I'm going. I have things to do." Kate whipped the phone at her cousin.

Tom reached for the phone, grimacing when he caught it.

"Couldn't keep your mouth shut, could you? Idiot." Kate stormed out of the house.

"She's back." Tom grinned up at Butch. "Nobody gets her going like her father."

Kate opened the screen door and leaned in. "Are you two coming?"

"Gimme your keys," Kate snapped, not caring whose keys she got. "I'm not taking my Mustang out to the site. With my luck, a piece of rebar will pierce my gas tank and cause an inferno."

Tom tossed his keys. "Wait. I'll drive."

Kate snatched them out of mid-air. "Get in. Are you coming, Butch?"

"I'll follow you."

Kate slammed the door of Tom's work truck and peeled out. She barreled down the road with a full head of steam, blowing a stop sign and scaring the hell out of a field of horses. Tom hung on to the Jesus bar and screamed a prayer at the top of his lungs.

"I want that wall taken apart. Whoever killed that woman left something behind, and I want it."

"What do you want me to do?" Tom asked. "Jeb took everything that was buried with her."

"Jeb took everything he could see. I want that wall reduced to beach sand. If someone spit in that concrete I want it. And we are going over everything, from scratch. Waters will do it. The old goat doesn't miss a trick." Kate took the entrance to the site on two wheels and parked the truck outside the trailer in her usual spot.

"We can't do it alone, Kate. If the police aren't here, they'll just accuse us of planting the evidence."

"Then get them here. I don't care how."

Kate found Waters and pulled him from his work to comb the scene. "And don't just look in that area they taped off. None of those cops had ever set foot on a job site. They didn't know what they were looking at. You do. Nobody knows this shit like you do. The killer left something behind."

Waters's sharp eyes were game. "How do you know?"

"Because nobody's perfect. Find me proof someone else was here. I want to talk to the man who claims to have seen me."

"Thompson. I'll send him over. Be nice, Kate."

Kate rolled her eyes and crossed her arms. "You know what they say about nice guys." Kate tapped her foot as she watched Waters walk across the yard.

A voice behind her cleared his throat.

Kate turned her ice blue eyes on him. "You have something to say?"

Butch smiled wickedly and pulled her against him so their hips crashed. "It's nice to have you back." He bent his head and caught her snarling mouth.

She gave a hard push at his chest. "This is a construction site. No kissing. Period. And move your hands."

Butch tempted fate by moving his hands south and cupping her butt.

A throat cleared. "You wanted to see me?"

Kate spun to face Joel Thompson. The full face, ten years older than his age, hung slack. This man didn't want trouble with the boss.

"You told the sheriff you saw me last Tuesday."

"I didn't have a choice." Thompson held his hands up in surrender. "Look. I was laid off for a year. You run a good site, and I'm glad for the work. I just told the sheriff what I saw."

Kate rethought her approach. It took nerve to come to work after fingering the boss for murder. That told her a lot. "It wasn't me. I was in Kentucky. But someone went through a lot of effort to make it look like it was me. I want to know what you saw."

Thompson buried his hands in his jeans and studied the rocks. "It was just like I told the sheriff. Waters needed a few men to put in extra hours to be ready for the next day. I volunteered. I could use the money. I went to my car to call my wife. I just hung up when you pulled into the site in your company truck. You waved to me, and you drove off to the left."

Kate began to pace. "Did you see my face?"

"No. It was dark. The light over the parking area reflected off the windshield but I could tell there was someone in the truck with you."

"With me? Who?" When Thompson shrugged, she pressed on with her questions. "Did you see my hair?"

Thompson shook his head. "Your arm. You were driving with the windows down and your arm out."

"Did I have on a short sleeved shirt?"

Thompson shook his head. "The kind that ends around your elbow. It was a really bright pink. The fingernails matched."

Kate stopped pacing. "What do you mean the fingernails matched?"

"There were pink and long. Shiny."

"Thompson, sit." Kate whirled on Butch. "Call your dumbass brother. When he gets here, teach him how to interview a witness."

B utch placed the call. "Jeb, I need you at Kate's project."

"What's happened? Is Kate with you?"

Butch looked to where Tom, Waters, and Kate stood twenty feet away. Kate gestured wildly as she spoke. "Yeah, she woke up, so to speak. We're at the site."

A second call came in. Hyde. Butch let it go to voicemail.

"Fuck me to hell and back. What is she doing?"

"She wants Waters and Tom to take another look at things—"

"Stop them. Right this minute. Anything they find is useless. I'm on my way."

"Katie!" Butch shoved his phone in his pocket, yelling across the lot. "Kate. Waters. Wait for Jeb."

Butch paced on sentry duty, keeping the three accounted for until Jeb could get there. The party huddled around the hood of Tom's truck, looking at the plans. Butch listened as they speculated how the killer had gotten the body into the wall form. The snap of gravel pulled Butch's attention away from the group. He met his brother when he parked away from the others. "You don't show up that fast for anything but dinner, Clyde. What gives?"

Jeb spoke to Butch but looked at the three conspirators. "I was taking another look where the rental car was found. What's going on?"

"Your witness seemed to remember something new. Kate wants Waters to take a look at the crime scene. She thinks he'll be able to tell if there is something out of place."

Jeb snorted as they crossed the parking area. "She thinks she knows more than crime scene investigators?"

Caught between your brother and your lover, there were no good options. "How many construction sites have they worked?"

"Shit. That woman of yours is something else. Glad to see she's snapped out of it. Thought we might have to bring in electroshock."

"That's what Tom did, in some respects."

"All right, Kate. I'm here. What do you have?"

Jeb listened and then called his crime scene team back out. Butch didn't know if Jeb did that because he thought something had been missed or as a favor. Either way, all involved took the job seriously. Jeb watched closely as Waters searched. A deputy used cones and bright yellow tape to rope off areas Waters indicated.

Butch waited out of the way with Kate. Per Jeb, Kate's

job was to let the others work. Butch's was to make sure Kate did hers. Tom and a laborer worked from ladders in the pit on the set wall. They used a magnifying glass to inspect the white dust while a deputy photographed the grains of sand that had been the wall.

"Here, Sheriff." Waters waved Jeb to the edge of cleared land. He pointed to a cone sitting on short scrubby grass. "That plumber's wrench isn't ours. It's an old one. Could be one of the local crew brought their own, but there was no need."

Kate did a quick dance and pointed her index finger up at Jeb. "I told you there was more. There had to be. See what Tom's found."

Jeb crossed his arms, a gesture Butch knew meant he wasn't moving. "I have a man with him. I'm going to talk to Thompson. You, go sit in your truck."

"I can't. You confiscated it. I guess you're stuck with me."

Jeb looked over Kate's head at Butch. "If you want to help, do something with her."

"Hyde called. His message sounded like nothing but heavy breathing. Let's run into town and see what he wants."

"He probably just butt dialed you, and he's thirty minutes away. If something happens, I want to be here."

"If you stay here, something will happen. Not in a good way." Butch took her by the elbow and steered toward the parking area. "Jeb will call. Tom's here. He'd call, too. Pissing Jeb off is only going to cause more problems."

"Fine. Gimme your keys."

"Not a chance." When Kate's stubborn chin came up, Butch couldn't resist pinching it between his fingers and kissing it.

"No. Kissing," Kate growled.

Butch laced his fingers with hers and pulled her behind him as he walked to his truck.

"And no holding hands. Sheesh. Are you trying to ruin my reputation?"

Butch looked over her head at the busy construction site. "I don't think you have to worry about that. Judging by how high everyone's jumped, I'd say your reputation is intact."

Kate climbed into the truck and buckled her seat belt. "It better be."

Butch drove out of the site and down the road a few miles, glancing at Kate as he drove. Back to her old self, her head swung left to right taking everything in. "So, my sweet Katie, have you really had thirty-seven lovers?"

"Thirty-seven?" Kate snorted a laugh. "Where did you get that from?"

"You said it to your father. By the way, I can't believe you said that to your father."

She wrinkled her nose. "I don't listen to half the stuff I tell my father. You shouldn't either."

"How many?" While no virgin, Butch thought Kate to be the kind of woman that was selective of her lovers.

She angled herself against the door, her bright eyes on him. "I may have exaggerated a little."

"What's exaggerating a little? Thirty? Twenty-five?"

"You aren't going to let this go, are you?" Kate's crooked smile dared him. "How many women have you had?"

While married, Butch had been devoutly faithful. But in between, there were no rules. Butch used the flat, commanding voice Jeb always used when he'd been trapped. "Enough to know it's time to change the subject."

Kate laughed happily, her hair flying around in the wind. "You were a man slut, weren't you?"

"I was not." His hot denial only fed her entertainment.

"Trophy man slut. A big time musician. I bet women across the country lost their panties to you. Should I check? Hashtag RocktheButch? You blushing?"

The hell he was. "Don't matter what was. Only what is." No truer words, he thought.

Butch parked in a customer space outside the old three-bay garage that proudly read HYDE'S SHOP. The tow truck Butch loaned him the money to buy sat at the ready next to the shop. Two bay doors stood open, welcoming friends and customers.

"Hyde. It's Butch and Little Red." Butch walked between the lifts, calling out again. The only sounds came from the street behind them.

"I don't think anyone's here."

Butch walked around the small garage but found no sign of Hyde. "This isn't right. When Hyde goes out, he closes the door and puts out his sign."

Kate walked around the lift that held a white sedan at chest height. "I'm surprised he locks up. I figured around here, he would leave everything open in case someone dropped by and needed to borrow something."

Butch heard the teasing and tossed it back. "I didn't say he locked the door. Just that he closed it. *Tsk. Tsk.* City folk."

Kate knelt to tie her shoe.

"Oh my God. Butch. Call an ambulance."

Chapter Seventeen

Kate found the controls and raised the rack on the empty bay. Butch jumped down as he dialed 9-1-1. "This is Butch McCormick. We need an ambulance at Hyde's Shop."

Butch had known Silvy Jones, the 9-1-1 operator, since he was a tot, just like everyone else in town. Butch heard her expert fingers flying over the keyboard as she began to question him in that cool and collected voice of hers.

"What's the problem, Butch?"

"Hyde's hurt. He's lying unconscious in one of his pits."

Hyde lay like a pile of rotten trash in the corner of the pit. His head lay against the concrete at an awkward angle, his arms and legs tangled. Kate had followed Butch down, racing around him to Hyde's side.

"I feel a pulse. I don't know how you can breathe like that, but I'm afraid to move you, big man." Kate held up her bloodied hand. "He's bleeding, Butch. From his head."

Even as Butch relayed the information, he could hear

the sirens in the background. It was a blessing that the fire station was only two blocks away. The ambulance crowded the small parking lot.

"They're here, Silvy. Thanks." Butch climbed halfway out of the pit and waved an arm. "Over here, boys. He's down here."

K ate paced the length of the pit, watching the paramedics work and feeling useless. Butch had gone into Hyde's office to call Hyde's mother. Through the office window, Kate saw he paced also. Another siren wailed its approach and abruptly stopped. Moments later, Jeb walked through the wide door.

"How is he?" Jeb squatted at the edge of the shallow pit.

"He hit his head hard, Sheriff. We're checking for other injuries before we move him."

Kate went to her knees next to Jeb. "He's going to be okay, right?"

Jeb patted her knee. "Hyde's got a thick head. That plays in his favor."

"Hyde's mother is going to meet them at the hospital." Butch jogged from the office. "What are you doing here?"

"I was one my way back from the construction site when I heard the call. Thank the Lord you came to check on him. I hate to think how long he could have been there."

In a silent vigil, the three watched the paramedics work. A stiff board was lowered into the pit. Careful hands wrapped Hyde's neck in a brace then uncurled his body, stretching him to full length and rolling him enough to slide the board beneath him. Jeb and Butch jumped up and went to the end of the pit, ready and willing to help their friend. Kate stayed out of the way, saying prayers for the man who'd become her friend. Then she spotted something.

"Guys? There's something under him."

The paramedics searched around Hyde. "It's just keys," one said. "Rental car," the other said.

Jeb squatted back down. "Why do you think it's for a rental car?"

"The key chain is for a rental company. You want them?"

"Leave them. Get Hyde out of there, I'll take a look at the keys myself."

"Right, Sheriff. There's a cell phone down here, too." The paramedics moved Hyde as smoothly as they could. Jeb jumped into the pit and lent his hands to moving Hyde after he'd been secured. Butch crouched on the floor and took one end of the board, waiting while the paramedics climbed out. Together, they pulled Hyde from the concrete vault.

Blood coated half his face, warping his features into something out of a zombie movie. One eye and ear were indistinguishable from the matted hair.

"Oh. Hyde." Kate pressed her hand to her heart, looking away, hoping it was just a bad dream. The concrete below held a pool of his blood that snaked in a thin strip across the floor to a center drain. The blood flow had welled up against a cell phone before flowing around.

Jeb focused on the scene. "Kate, run to my truck." He told her what he needed. "Tell Butch to call Silvy back and get my crew over here."

Kate ran out of the garage, looking for Jeb's truck. She found it on the side of the building, unlocked. She opened the small back door and collected the materials Jeb asked for before running to the ambulance where Butch helped settle Hyde on the stretcher. "Jeb wants you to call Silvy back, he needs his crew."

Butch's brows pressed down and reached for his phone. He kept the call short, running back into the garage. "What the hell, Jeb?"

Jeb stood at the edge of the pit, waiting to accept the items from Kate. "These keys match the rental company and model of the car Fawn rented. While y'all were outside, I took a quick look around, and that particular model car isn't here."

Kate asked the obvious. "How did Hyde get them?"

Jeb shook his head as he activated the screen on the phone. "Y'all happen to know his password? No? All right, I'm labeling this a suspicious scene. Nobody touch any-thing." He looked Kate in the eyes. "Don't touch a thing. I'm serious, Katie."

The warning in his voice amused her. "Sheesh. You destroy a crime scene or two and people start thinking they have to talk to you in little words."

Jeb gave her a rare teasing grin before focusing back on Hyde. "I know how fond you are of little words." He nodded toward the parking lot. "Looks like they're about ready to go."

Butch's gaze stayed on the ambulance as the doors closed and it pulled away. "I'm going with him to the hospital."

"Then I'm going, too." Kate held out her hand. "Give me your keys."

"Honey, I'm not giving you my keys. Not now. Not later."

"This is ridiculous. I drive faster."

"Drive the speed limit," Jeb said, sharply.

Kate rolled her eyes at Jeb. "Why can't you be one of those renegade sheriffs?"

The crow's feet at the corners of Jeb's eyes tightened, hinting at laughter that didn't reach his mouth. "Why can't you be one of those compliant women?"

"Why can't you—" Kate's phone rang. "Hold that thought. It's Tom. I'm putting him on speaker. What do you have for me, Tom?"

"Fingernails. Two pink fingernails. They were embedded deeper in the wall. Jeb, your deputy gave me the okay to call you while she finished working."

Vindication a palpable thing, Kate bounced around, off her feet more than on. "You can't still think it was me, Jeb."

Jeb tracked her path with his whole head, his features softened. "I never thought it was you, Katie. Let's be patient. They could be Fawn's fingernails."

Kate crouched down to look at Jeb's face. "Can you run DNA tests or something to catch the bitch?"

"It doesn't work that way," Jeb explained. "If we have two samples, we can tell if they match."

Butch rubbed his thumb over his jawline. "So if you have a sample of Katie's DNA, you can tell the nail-less bitch isn't her?"

"Yes, but—"

"Sign me up, Jeb." Kate leaped into Butch's arms. "I want this to end. The faster, the better."

Saturday morning looked like any other day. Fawn Jordan's death had temporarily shut work down but the project was recovering. The site had opened again, and the men on the crews were as eager to work the make-up hours as Kate was to have them made up. After all, no work, no pay. Kate and Tom modified their schedule and approach to leave the gallery until Jeb cleared it. The Cicada campaign to empower women changed opinions about the project. The Chicago office had received a hundred applications for work at the new place from local women. Interest in Fawn's death waned. The number of reporters, fans, and fanatics had fallen off dramatically. Photos had surfaced of Fawn partying it up with a couple of surfers that were not her husband, and most of the people who had jumped on the bandwagon, jumped right back off. Kate agreed with Tom that Landon Finch likely had something to do with those photos...or at least the timing. Regardless of the how, Kate no longer had to create a monument for Fawn. She would always be part of this place, but she would be far from the best part.

Kate had left the door to her office open, not so much wanting to invite human interaction as needing to see her escape route. She had started with the door closed but squirmed under the pressure of confinement. She needed the door open and the light background noise that came with Tom and Waters going in and out to concentrate on her work.

Samples for the interior and exterior walls had come in. Kate sat at her desk and pored through the color palettes, finish, and texture options. Selecting the tactile elements of the spaces attracted Kate to architecture. She had explored the wonderful collection of spaces that New York City had to offer and, as she much as she could, had explored other cities, soaking up the way each building made her feel. For the ones she liked, and maybe more importantly, for the ones she didn't like, she broke down the elements that created the feel. Her fingers ran over the samples, looking for the ones that said "Cicada."

The trailer door smashed open. Kate jumped behind her desk and sent the collection of samples exploding across the small room. "What the fuck!"

Jeb stalked across the trailer with fire in his eyes.

Kate retreated until her back was pressed against the cold hard steel of the filing cabinet. "What's happened now?"

"The lab results came back. He's dismissing you as a suspect, Kate." Jeb slapped the desk in triumph. "The prosecutor is looking at other possibilities."

Kate stared at Jeb. She blinked twice waiting for the "but." It never came. She let out the breath she held and turned her back on him when tears swamped her eyes. "I was so scared," she admitted in a whisper.

"I know." Jeb turned her into his arms. "I know you were. But you stood, straight and strong. You stood."

"Clyde, you better have a damned fine reason for having your hands on my woman."

Kate turned and jumped unabashedly into Butch's arms. "Jeb got me off. They don't think I did it anymore."

The arms around Kate tightened until she could barely breathe. She pulled back and saw Butch looking at his brother with gratitude in his eyes.

The corner of Jeb's mouth curled in a half smile, which was the equivalent of a big toothy grin on anyone else. "The facts stood for themselves. I just called in a few markers to help expedite the lab testing. The fingernails didn't belong to you or Fawn. We got statements from people at the tradeshow and the restaurant bartender, and video from the gas station puts you out of the state at the time of the body drop."

"I owe you one, Jeb," Butch said.

Kate twisted her head to look at Jeb. "No, I owe you, Jeb. Thank you for believing me and believing in me. And you." Kate looked back at Butch. "Thank you for putting up with me." She kissed him, brushing her lips softly over his. "Thank you for taking care of me when I didn't want it." She kissed the corners of his smiling mouth. "Thank you for loving me."

"What the hell? There's no kissing on a construction site." The surprise in Tom's voice made it an octave too high.

Kate burst into a fit of laughter. "I'm not a suspect!"

Tom punched the door. "Hot damn!" He celebrated by kicking the desk, tossing a pile of papers in the air, punching Butch's shoulder, spinning Kate in a quick circle, and heading for Jeb.

Jeb held out his hand, but Tom pushed past it.

"That's not going to do it, Clyde. I could kiss you, man."

Jeb shook off the hug. "I had a feeling there was more to that cooking-for-sex shirt than you let on."

Tom laughed. "We need to celebrate."

"There's only one place to go to celebrate," Butch said.

Tonight, Butch thought, they were going to drink until they couldn't see straight, but first things first. Kate,

Tom, and Jeb crowded into Hyde's small hospital room. Jeb propped a hip on a low windowsill. Butch and Tom swiped chairs from empty rooms after Katie pulled the only chair in Hyde's room close to the bed.

"So have you checked out your nurse?" Kate drummed her fingers over Hyde's forearm.

He was in a coma. Half of his hair had been shaved off and replaced with a white, gauzy bandage. His cheeks were expressionless, making him look childlike in his sleep, as long, thick lashes lay in a dark crescent.

Kate tapped his arm as if waking him from an afternoon nap. "You are going to want to see her. Long legs, pretty face, nice tits. I know you're a tit man."

It warmed Butch to watch Kate try to bait Hyde into waking. "How do you know he's a tit man?"

"Every man is a tit man," she said. "And Nurse Betty has enough for three women."

True enough, Butch thought. He didn't know a man who would turn down a nice pair. He poked her with his foot, egging her on. "Her name isn't Betty. It's Elizabeth."

Kate swatted blindly at him. "She looks at you, Hyde, when she's taking care of you. She likes what she sees, I can tell."

Butch poked at her again, grinning. "How can you tell?"

"I'm a woman. I can read the signs." Kate swatted blindly behind her back, missing him by a mile. "You're going to want to open your eyes, Hyde, and check her out. Oh, here she comes. Act natural." She patted his hand.

Butch shook in quiet laughter when the statuesque brunette strode easily into the group of friends and made small talk while she checked on Hyde. She ended her routine by stroking back the remaining hair from Hyde's forehead.

The minute the nurse left, Kate leaned in close again to Hyde. "Did you see that? Nurses don't just run their fingers through all their patients' hair. She's got the hots for you. Open your eyes before Tom decides to nibble." She paused. "Maybe if she kissed you?"

Kate lifted her gaze to Jeb. "Do you think this was an accident? Did Hyde just fall?"

Jeb straightened his shoulders. "Nothing says he didn't. His injuries are consistent with the fall." Jeb's frown deepened.

"There's a 'but.'" Butch stood, stretching out legs that were suddenly restless. "Say what you're not saying."

"But he had Fawn's car keys. Without a doubt, the keys that were found under Hyde are to Fawn's rental car."

Kate looked back at Hyde. "I wish you could tell us what happened. How did you get down there? There shouldn't have been room with the rack down."

"We noticed that, too," Jeb said. "It couldn't have been down when he fell. Somebody else was in that garage, even if he did fall."

"Wait," Tom said. "If they were after the keys, why didn't they go down and get them?"

Kate fussed with Hyde's blanket. "They wouldn't if they didn't know he had them or if they thought he'd put them somewhere else."

"What if he found something else they did know about, and that's what they took?" Tom jumped from the chair and paced. "I need paper. I can't think without a pencil in my hand. What else could he have found? And where could he have found any of this stuff?"

Butch watched as Kate and Tom sank into the mystery of a puzzle. They attacked the question of Hyde with the same leap-frog approach they'd used on the concept for his house. Butch felt oddly proud of himself when he could contribute to the fast thinking. "Best guess at where is in a car. He is a mechanic."

Kate narrowed her eyes at Jeb. "It wasn't *my* car."

Jeb didn't change his expression. "We have his appointments for the day and are interviewing everyone. If it was anyone but y'all, I wouldn't say this out loud, but we have to consider that we might have a serial killer on the loose."

The thought of a killer being that close to Hyde filled Butch with a cold and sudden dread. Angie. Fawn. Who was next? He began to pace, moving because he couldn't be still. "Jeb, what's going on?"

Jeb inhaled deeply. "It centers on you. That's clear enough. Somebody wants your ex-wives dead. Who in your life would want that? Ex-girlfriends, lovers?"

"Christ, Jeb. I was single longer than I was married to Angie or Fawn. I've had, uh…" Butch stalled, looking at Kate.

"A healthy sex life." Kate said it without judgment, with full acceptance of his life. Then she frowned, furrowing her brows. "Maybe it's somebody who wanted to be more than a girlfriend, more than a former lover."

"Why kill them after he's divorced?" Tom asked. "If it was somebody with designs on being the next Mrs. McCormick, why kill the ex-wives?"

"That's a question, isn't it?" Jeb stood. "I've drawn this out every way I can think of. Angie and Fawn. Tessa. Kate."

"Me?" Kate said in a squeaky echo.

Butch stopped pacing to face his brother, fists curled tightly. "What do Tessa and Kate have to do with this?"

Jeb faced Butch. "Somebody planted Fawn's body on Kate's job site, timed when she was out of the area. Then your friend Hyde ends up with a cracked skull while holding a set of keys that matched Fawn's rental car."

Silence hung, broken when Jeb continued. "Let's start at the beginning. Tessa died nearly six months after the divorce. When was the last time you'd spoken to her?"

Butch sighed heavily. "The day before she died."

"How did I not know that?" Jeb ran a hand through his hair, growling the next question. "What did you talk to her about?"

Butch backed away from Jeb. He sat in a chair, pulling Kate into his lap and holding her as protection against an ugly conversation. "She had called me about a week before. She was building a new workshop, and the costs were going to be higher than she expected."

Tom leaned forward, his elbows braced on his knees. "She wanted money."

Butch felt the judgement. It was theirs, it was his own. "I was still a partner in her art business. It made sense she'd call me."

"Did you give her any?" Jeb asked.

"I didn't have a lot to give. Finch had negotiated the record deal just after we split. The album hadn't come out yet, but between gigging and help from Mom and Dad, I made ends meet. I told her I could spare a few hundred, but that was it. She had her heart set on this kiln. The day before she died, she called. I put a check in the mail. She never cashed it."

"Who knew all this was going on?"

"That was a long time ago. Let me think. I was back here, living in my old bedroom when I wasn't on the road. Mom and Dad knew. Finch knew. You were off somewhere, Jeb. Hyde and I hung together still. Trudy was around a lot; she probably knew. I'm sure Mom told people, you know how she is when they play bridge."

"When did you find out about Tessa?"

"Her mother called me that afternoon. I met her parents at Tessa's studio. I'll tell you, Jeb, I've never seen anything like that. There was nothing left but cinders."

"Jesus." Tom sat at the edge of his chair, his head swinging between Butch and Jeb as though he watched a tennis match. Butch could only imagine what Tom thought of him. "How did the fire start? Weren't there smoke detectors?"

After living these past weeks with the intellectual engineer, Butch should have expected his head was in the details. "She'd been working with the kiln open. The investigator suspected her clothes caught fire and, well, it was an accident. Sloppy and preventable but an accident."

Jeb cut to the chase. "Did you profit from her death?"

"Jesus, Jeb."

"Just answer the question, Butch."

"Yeah. Finch had us take out insurance policies on each other, so there was money. It came in handy, too. Like I said, I borrowed from Mom and Dad to go on a tour Finch set up to coincide with the record coming out. That was where I was getting the money to send Tessa. I was going to come up short and didn't know what I was going to do about it. With the insurance, I had enough money that I didn't have to sleep on anyone's couch."

"Do you have an alibi for the time of the fire?"

"Alibi? It was an accident, and it was years ago, Jeb. How am I supposed to remember?" Butch snapped at his brother. He hated being dragged back into his sins. Why hadn't he insisted Tessa install a sprinkler system? Smoke alarms weren't enough when you worked with fire.

Kate rubbed her thumb in a circle in Butch's palm. He dropped his head to her shoulder, curling around her.

"I worked that night. In Nashville. I remember because I had to borrow gas money from Trudy, and she pissed me off, lecturing me about sending Tessa money. I went home after the gig, too broke to go out drinking. I was asleep when Mom woke me with the phone call."

Jeb took notes furiously, pausing to ask Butch for details on particular topics. Butch didn't have any animosity toward Tessa. Tessa had left him because of indifference. The spark that drew her to him like a fly to a flame had faded. She wanted a new flame and Butch just accepted it. Jeb rubbed a hand through his hair when Butch admitted it didn't bother him that Tessa called him for money.

"I don't understand how you couldn't at least be annoyed that a woman who walked out on you would call you when she needed money."

"It wasn't like that, Jeb."

"It was exactly like that, Butch. Why can't you see that?" When Butch didn't respond, Jeb forced himself to sit back down. "Let's talk about Angie." They covered old ground again, looking for new dirt.

Jeb turned to a new page in his notebook. "Based on what Margie Russell told me, Angie really had gotten involved with a preservation society that had a project to protect Northern Pine Snakes and their habitat. I did some research on the organization and contacted the lead staff member. He had his doubts about her. She seemed more interested in what they could do for her than vice versa. She wanted to be front and center. Their fundraising chair had recently left, so he gave Angie a chance. The organization is legitimate, as far as I can tell. What money they raised went to remediation and protection projects, including buying land through a trust. The part about finding foster homes seemed to be an interpretation of a project to develop a temporary habitat while permanent projects were constructed. Thanks to the scene at the Sly Dog, everyone in town knew Angie was hitting Butch up for money, and most all of them knew it wasn't the first time."

"Angie was Angie, Jeb. She wasn't devious, not the way everyone is making her out to be."

Jeb glared at his brother. "She lied to you about her pregnancy. She let you pay, out of the goodness of your heart, for her to live a carefree life. How are you not pissed off about that?"

Kate turned to look at Butch. Her fingers ran soothingly across his arm.

He kissed her lips, smiling when she blushed. "It was only money. It doesn't matter now."

Jeb swatted Butch's knee with his notebook. "What about Fawn? According to her assistant, she was going after everything you two had."

Comfortable in his own skin again, Butch looked at his brother's tightly drawn face. "She pretty much laid that out at our meeting. Fawn always thought she was entitled to more than she earned. What she didn't do was listen. Finch drew up the pre-nup. She was entitled to what she came in with, plus half of what we gained during our marriage. She started working at the soap a few months after we were married and spent nearly everything she made that first year. Then she said she needed some time to decide if she wanted a husband. I moved into my cabin, I wrote the new album, did some studio work but laid pretty low. There weren't a lot of gains to be split."

"Did she know that?"

"One of the great things about Fawn was she didn't let reality get in her way. She was good at fantasy and had a way of drawing people into it. She was an excellent stage actress."

Kate squeezed his hand. "I've been so caught up in my own drama, I didn't stop to think what this must be like for you. You loved these women."

Butch closed his eyes. "I thought I did. At one time, in my own way. The divorces were expensive and inconvenient, but shouldn't they be? And for the record, I didn't marry any of them expecting to divorce later. I certainly didn't want any of them dead."

Jeb brought them back on topic. "So Mom, Dad, Finch, Hyde, Trudy, and anybody Mom told, which by the time the gossip circuit was done could have been half the town, knew Tessa was shaking you down."

Butch scowled at Jeb's choice of words, but Jeb rolled right along.

"The entire town knew about Angie and the snakes, and thanks to the internet and media, the entire world knew about the bar fight with Fawn in Nashville."

"Doesn't exactly narrow the field, does it?" Tom walked

to the bright window and looked out.

Kate shifted across Butch's lap. "What if someone was trying to protect Butch?"

"Go on," Jeb said. "What are you thinking?"

She looked up at Butch. "If a woman was making calls for money to Tom, like the ones you were getting, I'd get in her face."

Tom turned around, leaning against the wide window frame. "Aw, you do love me."

"I wouldn't actually do anything to her. If I was going to hurt anyone, it would be Tom for being stupid enough to get involved in the first place and being stupider for not walking away."

Tom cringed. "Ouch. Not feeling the love now."

"So, Butch," Jeb said. "Who loves you enough to go after someone they think is threatening your financial security?"

"I swear I don't know. There's only you, Mom, and Dad. You were out of the country when Tessa died."

Jeb winced. "Lucky me. Dad would have been more likely to kick your ass, and Mom would have done it differently."

Butch nodded. "She would have used the gossip circuit to drive them to insanity and eventually suicide."

Kate's eyes grew huge. "Wow."

"Don't worry, honey. She likes you."

Jeb closed his notebook and stood looking down at Hyde. "Whoever it is, is here. My gut tells me there is more to Kate's involvement than convenience or coincidence. Same for what happened to Hyde."

Kate popped out of Butch's lap and paced the length of the room. "I'm not shaking Butch down for money. I don't want his money. I have plenty of my own with the project back on course."

Butch blew her a kiss. "You just use me for kinky sex. It's all right. I'm good with that."

Tom gagged. "Maybe the game is changing. Maybe it did start out as protecting Butch from money-grabbing ex-wives. But Kate's different. She has her own career, her own company, her own money. Maybe now it's not about protecting Butch from Kate but protecting Butch from himself."

Butch came to his feet, staring Tom down. "I don't need protecting from myself."

"Says you." Jeb leaned back in the chair. "Let's follow this through. Kate lives with Butch, and maybe the killer feels she's taking advantage of him as much as the ex-wives were."

"Then wouldn't the killer feel the same way about me?" Tom shook his head. "I haven't been threatened or implicated in any of this. It can't be just that." Tom's brows lowered, and he pursed his lips.

Jeb pressed him. "Is there something you're not saying?"

Tom rubbed the back of his neck. "I don't want turn attention toward someone with no real proof, like what happened to Katie."

"We're running out of ideas," Jeb said. "If you've got one, share it. You should know by now I'm not going to run off and arrest someone just because we're talking."

Tom took a deep breath. "To an outsider, there are some funny things. Maybe they're normal to you, but…"

Jeb pinned him with a glare. "But?"

"The way Trudy treats Butch isn't normal." Tom blurted it quickly, like a boy admitting to breaking his mother's favorite dish.

"No," Butch said, the denial instant and complete.

Jeb held his hand palm out to silence his brother. "Go on."

"Friends don't walk into friends' houses and make dinner. Friends who want to be girlfriends do. In Nashville, she hung on Butch constantly. She maneuvered Butch into buying her things."

Butch frowned. "She didn't maneuver me."

"Yes she did," Jeb said flatly. "She always does, and you always let her."

Tom shrugged his shoulders apologetically. "Butch, even Fawn thought she was your lover."

Butch shook his head. "We're friends. Trudy and Hyde and I have been friends since the second grade. Wherever we went, she went."

"Wherever you went, she followed," Jeb corrected.

Butch's head was going to explode. Were they really having this conversation? Was his flesh-and-blood brother really turning on the woman that had been a sister to them? "You want it to be her, Jeb?"

"I don't. I love Trudy, too. But I have to look at this differently. Impartially. And this makes some sense. She's always been a little too interested in you."

"Bullshit, Jeb. You can just cross Trudy off the list. I don't believe it, and I won't believe it until you bring me some proof. Did you talk to Trudy about Angie?"

"Of course I interviewed her. She had an altercation with the deceased, but at the time of Angie's death, Trudy worked in the fields." Jeb flipped back through the pages of his notebook. "She finished late afternoon. I checked the fields, and they had been turned." Jeb blew out a hard breath. "I want you to think long and hard about the people you know, Butch. Local girls you've dated, girls you've flirted with, girls who have given you long, adoring looks."

Butch slapped his palms against denim clad legs. "Adoring looks? You can't be serious."

"Maybe their fathers. Brothers, too." Tom pointed at Kate with his chin. "Family gets their own ideas of what should be."

Jeb's brows pressed together for a moment before he shook his head, scattering the expression. "That might work for framing Kate and murdering Fawn, but not necessarily for murdering women he'd already divorced. No. For now, we focus on who has their sights on Butch. Which brings us back to the start. I think Katie is in the most immediate danger. But, there's every reason to think through some warped sense of logic that any of us may be perceived as a threat. We all need to have our eyes and ears open at all times."

Chapter Eighteen

Keeping eyes and ears open was one thing; hiding in the house another. After dinner, they went to the Sly Dog to relax and feel alive. Jeb didn't approve, but outvoted three-to-one, he went along. Saturday nights, the Sly Dog always rocked. Tonight, the band whipped the crowd of construction workers and cowboys into a frenzy. Butch worked his way up to the bar, made an opening in the crowd, and snagged the bartender's attention.

"Looks like a good night tonight." Butch looked over the packed house.

"Better with you here. You class up the joint. Interested in playing later?"

"We'll see. Right now I just want a beer."

Tom and Jeb echoed the order.

"Speaking of classing up the place, what can I get you, sweetheart?" the bartender asked Kate.

Kate flashed a grin a mile wide and full of fun. Butch

had surprised her with a cute, blue dress cut low in the back and short on the leg. Kate had been pawing through her half of the meager closet when Butch tossed a white box on the bed. She accepted the gift quietly, hugging the cloth to her chest and spent twenty minutes putting on makeup and pinning her hair up on the sides so a red waterfall cascaded down the back.

"I want something tall and strong."

The man next to Kate signaled the bartender. "I got what the lady ordered." The man flexed his muscles.

Kate laughed at his antics.

Butch did not. "She'll have what I'm having." He wrapped a proprietary arm around her waist.

The woman was a trouble magnet, twice as much in a dress. Butch didn't let go of Kate until they were at the table Trudy guarded for them with the fierceness of a bulldog. Trudy dove for Butch's hand and led him to the chair next to hers. Butch dragged Kate along with him, pulled a chair out, and tugged until she sat.

Tom sat next to Kate, keeping his eyes on the crowd. "I like this place. The night is long, the shots are strong, the short skirts are just right."

"Ain't that the truth?" The words turned in Butch's head. He took out his phone and made a note.

The night is long, the shots are strong, the short skirts are just right.

Butch considered the picture Tom had painted, looking over the dance floor like a lion selecting a gazelle. He wore cowboy boots, a battered pair of jeans, and a cotton shirt that showed off the pump from the hundred pushups he did before leaving Butch's house.

Tom swallowed half his beer in one long gulp and let the bottle smack on the table. "Don't wait up for me." He threaded through the crowd, his gaze on the two girls dancing without a man between them. Both had long legs, long hair, and excellent credentials north and south of the border. Tom slid in between the girls like the crème filling between Oreo cookies and moved like he belonged there.

"How does he do it?" Jeb asked.

Kate laughed as Tom had both women by the hand, turning them in sexy circles. "You look up the word 'confidence' in the dictionary, and there's a picture of Tom."

Jeb spun his bottle on the table, gulped down a swallow, spun it again. "Does he ever get turned down?"

"Well, that depends who you ask. Tom is a firm believer that when one door closes, another opens up. Go join him. He'll share. Probably."

Jeb looked at Kate as if considering. He finished off his beer and swaggered over to the trio. Tom shook his hand, introduced the ladies, and delivered the blonde into Jeb's keeping for the next song.

Loud and animated chatter made the table lively. Trudy and her best girlfriends sat with Kate and Butch. Trudy told their Nashville adventure again, the size of that fish story growing.

"And so I said 'Do you know who I am? I'm Butch McCormick's best girl,' and I threw my drink in his face." Trudy's arms wrapped Butch's bicep while she told the tale of the security guard at the Opry.

Trudy touched him. Sure. But it didn't mean anything. She'd done that as long as he could remember.

Kate leaned over to him. "Dance with me."

Butch tipped his beer down his throat. "Not in the mood." It irritated him that Tom tried to throw Trudy under the bus and pissed him off that Jeb listened, but what really had him in a foul mood was the fact that he now questioned his friend's motives.

Kate stood and smoothed the dress he had bought her. "Please."

Butch shook his head, trying to remember why he wanted to go out. He wasn't fit for company and he knew it.

"All right." Kate turned to walk away.

"Where are you going?" Butch captured her hand.

"Dancing."

"I said I don't want to dance."

Kate patted his arm and pulled her hand free from his. "I heard you. I'm going to dance with Tom and Jeb." Kate joined them in the center of the dance floor. She put her hands in the air and copied the women dancing. In a place like the Sly Dog, a pretty woman in a short dress never danced alone for long. In minutes, Kate had two partners. She danced and spun on flat shoes that showed off every sassy feature. The tall man with a neat beard spun her until she fell laughing against a broad shouldered blond.

He wasn't chasing after her. She knew where he was. She could come to him. Butch cursed under his breath and drained his beer. "Does anyone want anything from the bar?"

"Oh," Trudy cooed, patting his arm. "Another margarita. They make the best margaritas here."

"No, they don't," Butch groused as he extracted his arm from her hold. "Anyone else? No?"

Butch fought his way up to the bar with the order for another round. So Trudy touched his arm. A touch on the hand here, a touch on the shoulder there. She was an affectionate person. Hell, he thought, it wasn't like she crawled in his lap. He looked over his shoulder, and she winked at him. "Christ."

While the bartender filled the order, the band had the crowd rocking. Butch couldn't see Kate in the throng of bodies, but he saw Tom and Jeb. They wouldn't let her go far. He made it back to the table and sat back down when Trudy automatically linked her arm in Butch's. Butch drew his arm out, shaking her off.

"What's the matter, honey? You're in a mood this evening."

"I'm fine." He took a long swallow.

Trudy moved behind him and began massaging his shoulders. She leaned down and kissed his cheek, making him jump. "Where's Kate?"

"Dancing," Butch snapped.

"No, she's not. Looks like you're on your own tonight."

Butch's head snapped up. The band took a break, and the dancers left the floor when the music from the CDs filled the joint. Butch found Jeb and Tom settling at a table in a corner with their partners, but there was no sign of Kate.

"Looks like she found some entertainment of her own," Trudy said. She bent to whisper against his ear. "I guess you're stuck with me."

Butch looked at Trudy, looked into her eyes to see what she kept in there. "We're friends, Trudy. Right?"

Trudy smiled, wide and warm. "The best kind of friends."

Butch looked hard and long into her face. All he saw was the girl next door who deserved better than the cards life dealt her. Tom was wrong. He unlocked her hands and stood, forcing Trudy a few steps back. "You should find someone to dance with, Trudy. You look too pretty to sit back here. I'm going to see where Kate ran off to." With his eyes scanning the crowd, Butch walked over to Tom and Jeb.

"Butch!" Tom greeted him. "Have you met Allison and Amazing, I mean Amanda?" The brunette in his lap giggled and slapped playfully at Tom's chest.

"It's a pleasure, ladies. Did you see where Kate went?"

Jeb had an arm around the blonde, Allison, looking relaxed, happy. "Nope. Don't worry, though. She can take care of herself."

Butch moved through the room with a new kind of urgency. No one found trouble like Kate. And in a room full of drunk and hot cowboys, he didn't want to think about the kind of trouble she could get into in that little, blue dress. What had he been thinking, buying her that dress? He found her in the game room, stretched out over a pool table with the three ball lined up for the corner pocket. She lifted her shapely left leg and with it the heads of every man in the room. Her dance partners stood behind her, admiring her...style.

With a quick, light stroke that bespoke of hours of time on a pool table, Kate sunk the three ball and left the four lined up with the side pocket. She went around the table and leaned over, giving the men a great view straight down her dress.

"What the hell are you doing?" Butch snapped at Kate.

His bark didn't faze her. "Working. I already took a hundred off of them."

"Best money I've spent in a long time." One flashed a grin.

Kate kept her eye on the ball. "Now I'm running the

table on them. They just don't know it yet." Kate sank the four ball but left the five in a difficult position with the seven between it and the corner pocket. The short skirt crept up her legs as she moved, hinting at the heaven beneath.

"Lord have mercy," the second one muttered.

"That's it." Butch heard the lust in the voice and snapped. He took Kate by the waist and dragged her from the table. The five ball shot to the left, banked off the bumper, and rolled to a slow and pathetic stop in the middle of the table.

Kate threw the stick down at the missed shot and planted her hands on Butch's chest. "What the hell? You ruined my shot."

Butch wrapped his hand around her upper arm and pulled her so she had to walk on her toes. "You're done. Let's go."

"I'm not done. I'm in the middle of a game."

Her two opponents stepped in front of Butch. "You heard her. She's in the middle of a game."

Butch brushed Kate behind him and planted his feet. "Game's over. You got a problem with that?"

The broad-shouldered one swung at Butch, but Butch caught the punch in one hand and returned it with the other. Butch hit the man high on the jaw and dropped him to the ground. His tall friend stepped back, hands up in surrender. "We didn't come out to fight."

Kate looked between Butch and the man on the floor. "What the hell was that?"

"The end of the evening. We're going home." Butch wrapped his hand around her wrist and left the bar, giving her no option whether to stay or go.

"Will you slow down and talk to me? What is the

problem?"

"You were all over them. Did you think I didn't see you?"

"I wasn't all over them. I never touched either of them. I just danced." She dug in at his truck, forcing him to face her.

"Then you should have been dancing with me." He spit out each word, hating the idea that she was with another man.

Kate threw it right back in his face. "That's what I said, but you didn't want to."

"Well, I want to dance now." Butch pinned her arms over her head and crushed his mouth to hers, intending to take away her choice. To his surprise, she went willingly into his arms, embracing the monster that raged within him, and by doing so, taming it.

She bit his lip, taking the kiss deeper, claiming it and him as her own. Neither spoke, locked together with a heat that steamed the night. Out of breath, they stood with their foreheads touching, panting for air.

"Until tonight, you're the only man I've ever danced with. Did you know that? I didn't even know how to dance before I met you." She whispered it on the night.

Butch looked into her blue eyes, shining in the light from the parking lot, made brighter by the dark fringe of mascara. Silky strands of hair escaped their pins and curled around her face. He brushed them back, her satiny skin smooth beneath his calloused fingers. "I really didn't like you dancing or shooting pool with anyone else."

She smiled as though it pleased her that he'd gone insane. "You're my first choice, every time for everything, Butch. But you have to know, I'm not going to sit on my hands when you say no. That just isn't me. I can't sit there, watching life go by because you're busy with something else. I don't expect you to put your life on hold for me. And if it looks like I'm moving on, well, you have to know that all I'm doing is passing time until you come back to me. I love you. I'm not going anywhere."

"I know." And he did. He felt the love she had for him every time she looked at him. "I love you, too. I lost it for a minute, but I'm here. I'm back."

"I think that qualifies as a fight, don't you?" She smiled wickedly.

Butch could feel the trap but didn't know where it lay. "I don't know if I'd call it a fight. Maybe a tussle."

Kate laughed. "You have too many muscles to use the word tussle. And you knocked a guy on his ass. It was a fight."

He rolled his eyes. "What's your point?"

Her gaze focused on his mouth. "Makeup sex."

Butch came out of his corner like a boxer at the bell. He wasted no time circling but moved straight in, opening an all-out assault on her senses. He'd learned the places that excited her, the ones that made her weak. He exploited as best he could through the cotton that separated them. Her knees buckled. Butch caught her, carrying her to his truck. There would be no driving home. His hands were everywhere. He pulled the dress down, her bare, firm breasts peaked in the night air. He suckled as his hands found the damp heat beneath her panties. His hands rode over her hips, down her butt, savoring the smooth expanse of skin while stripping the panties from her legs.

She parted her legs, inviting him to settle against her core. She pulled his shirt from his jeans, her fingers digging into his back. In the narrow space, she wrapped her legs around his back. She held his head to her breast, pushing into the heat of his mouth.

Butch used his teeth, nipping the sensitive bud. Kate thrashed her head from side-to-side, cursing him in one breath and moaning deep, throaty in the next. "I need you. Now."

"Yes, you do." He shoved his jeans until his cock sprang free then slid into her overheated body. Hot and wet for him. Only him. His strokes were short and fast, matching his mood. The passion and raw emotion beat off of him, beat into her. Kate wrapped her arms around his neck and held on, meeting him stroke for stroke. His pace quickened and his teeth sank into her shoulder. She cried out as her body locked down on his with wave after wave of tremors.

She squeezed him, torturing him with hot friction until he followed her into the oblivion. His dead weight collapsed on her. Nearly fully clothed, buried deeply in her naked body, too exhausted to go anywhere, Butch rested his head on her chest. He caught his breath, watching her breast rise and fall, his tongue within easy reach of her tempting nipple.

Kate ran her fingers through his hair, arching as he pulled her breast into the heat of his mouth.

Butch took his time savoring her body. He pressed a kiss over her heart before pulling her dress into place, covering what he wanted no other man to see. "I hope I don't have to make it a habit of fighting other men off of you."

"You're so silly." She traced his lower lip with her finger. "Those guys weren't interested in me."

"Baby, every man in that bar was interested in you."

Pure mischief showed in her crooked smile. "Well, if they were interested, it ended after I won the first fifty. Let's get a midnight breakfast. On them."

Butch hitched his pants and climbed into the driver's seat. "Lord, give me strength."

"You're going to need it."

Sunday morning started late and slow. Butch kept Kate in bed hours past her normal rise time. To his mind, she had started coming around to his side of life. Hot nights, simmering mornings. Butch left Katie soaking in a hot tub to start the coffee. He'd just poured a cup when Jeb and Tom stumbled in through the door.

"Well, don't you boys look like you were rode hard and put away wet?"

"Clyde," Jeb said with a big toothy grin as he looked his brother up and down. "That is the pot calling the kettle black."

Butch raised his eyebrows at Jeb. It had been a long time, a really long time, since he saw that goofy grin. He belted out a big belly laugh, thinking all Jeb had needed was a good roll in the hay. "Clyde, you have no idea."

"Clyde and Clyde, we need a party." Tom patted them both on the backs.

Tom invited Waters, who invited the crew.

Jeb invited the girls who invited the Sly Dog.

Butch left the party planning to the boys and walked across the field to the Big House. He had his own planning to do. While he was there, he invited his parents to the party. They invited the church.

Butch walked back across the field an hour later with a whistle on his lips and a spring in his step. Trudy sat on the small pier fishing in the McCormicks' pond. "Catching anything?"

"Just sunshine." Trudy climbed to her feet and ran her hand up and down Butch's arm. "You disappeared awfully quick last night. Did you find Kate?"

"I did. You in the mood for a party, Trudy?"

Trudy flashed him a smile as bright as the sun. "You know I'm always in the mood for a party, Butchy."

"We're having one at the old house. Starting now."

In a matter of hours, a good old-fashioned barbecue had sprung up at the old house. For all of the pain and loss of Angie and Fawn's death, they had a lot to celebrate. The project was back up and running, keeping men at jobs that paid a hell of a lot better than unemployment and felt better, too. Butch was no longer a person of interest in Angie's murder, with no motive and no evidence suggesting he wasn't sleeping away the morning when Angie died. Kate had been cleared of involvement with Fawn's death, thanks to Jeb's tenacity and Tom's attention to detail. Hyde was in a coma, but he was alive. And where there was life, there was hope. That was worth celebrating.

The potluck-style feast had enough to feed the whole town. Jeb roasted chops and burgers on Tom's homemade grill. Emily made more fried chicken and Tom bought out all the beer and soda pop from the nearest store. Watermelon was cut, potato salad was scooped, and laughter was shared. Butch ate twice as much as he should have and sat down at the piano to keep from having another piece of chicken. Friends and family moved his few pieces of furniture out of the way and danced into the evening.

The sun edged toward evening when Kate slipped away to celebrate in the quiet of the barn. She took apart the riding mower to give it a tune-up, needing time to herself. So many people to meet and greet, so much food to eat, Kate needed a bit of quiet. When she found it, her mind filled with Butch. He had fast worked his way into being a big part of her life. Over the past few days, her feelings had only grown stronger as he stood by her when she couldn't stand for herself. She had told Butch she loved him. And she did, but was it enough? Her mother had loved her father at the beginning. But it didn't last, love hadn't been enough. Kate had no experience with long-term relationships. The few boyfriends she'd had had whined that she didn't spend enough time with them, that she had too many projects. How did people balance real life with a love life? Kate had no role models. How did you know when the feelings were enough to build a life on?

Kate stroked the steel frame, petting it like a dog. With a sigh, she drained the oil from the motor.

"There you are," Butch said, his grin a little too wide. "Are you hiding from me?"

Kate's heart stopped at the sight of him, with his hip cocked against the doorframe. In jeans that fit tight across his hips and a soft cotton shirt that draped off of his strong shoulders, Butch looked like something out of a magazine. Her rugged, sexy, country boy. And he wanted her.

Kate's feelings boiled over. Her body, mind, and soul craved him. "Never."

He walked to where she sat cross-legged on the floor and played with the ends of her hair, the cocky grin still curled on his lips. "Then what are you doing?"

"Messing around." Kate watched the oil drain from the engine. "Things just got…overwhelming. I needed a place to breathe."

Butch inhaled deeply. "I know what you mean. A smelly, old barn is my first choice." He leaned in close to her, inhaling the nape of her neck. "You always smell like strawberries. It makes me so damned hungry."

"Don't bite me." Kate giggled. "You left enough marks on me last night."

Butch nipped at her throat and wrapped his arms around her when she squirmed. "It's never enough. I want everyone to know you're with me."

Kate giggled again. "They all know we're together, you big goof. It's pretty hard to miss the way you slobber on me all the time."

"I do not slobber. It's drool, and it's not my fault you get my juices flowing." He teased her with a nibble on the ear. "Come on back inside. There are some people I want you to meet."

Kate rose to her feet but stayed firmly in place facing Butch. "I think we should do it."

Butch grinned and took her shirt by the hem. "I knew you liked the hay loft."

"Not sex." Kate laughed, wrapping her arms around her waist to keep her shirt in place. "Your house. We should stop talking about it and do it. We can bring the equipment over and give the crew some overtime. We should start building your house. I'll give you a good price."

Butch tugged at her hem and eventually gave up, cupping her breasts over the thin cloth of her shirt instead. "You're gonna live here. With me."

"I'll stay here. At least until the project is done."

"Coward."

Kate's eyebrows arched high. "I'm no coward."

"Then you are staying here with me. In-def-in-ate-ly." Butch nodded, satisfied with himself. "We'll start building *our* house but not today." Butch swung Kate into his arms, easily tossing around her light weight.

Kate laughed and kicked her legs. "I can walk, you know. I haven't been drinking."

"I have been drinking, and I'm feeling very affectionate right now, and I want you right where I've got you. Stop fussing before we're both on the ground."

Butch nipped and teased as he carried Katie into the living room. Trudy slid over on the couch to make room for Butch, but he chased a boy off the armchair instead and sat down with Kate on his lap.

"Reverend Marcus, this is Katie. The Reverend has known me since I was in diapers."

The kindly man with the puff of white hair grinned. Laugh lines surrounded twinkling eyes. "And all that time, I've tried to offer him advice, even when it wasn't welcome."

Butch grinned down at Kate with a glow that had nothing to do with alcohol, and Kate looked back at him the same way.

"So this is the next Mrs. McCormick? Over my career, I figure I've married close to a thousand couples. Me and the missus were together over thirty-five years when she passed away. I have a knack for recognizing the real thing, and I see it here in front of me."

Butch smirked at the old man. "One correction, Reverend. This is the last Mrs. McCormick."

Trudy tisked her tongue at him. "You've only been on your own a few weeks. You aren't really thinking about getting married again?"

"I've been on my own my whole life." Butch looked into Kate's eyes and rubbed his chin thoughtfully. "I'd marry Kate today if I thought she'd have me. But, she's going to build us a house and live in it with me. I'll take that for now."

Reverend Marcus shook his head. "Living in sin, Butch?"

Butch grinned back. "Living in love, Reverend. Living in love."

Kate pulled Butch's chin to her. "Why would you think I wouldn't have you?"

Butch kissed the tip of her nose. "My independent Kate once screamed that she didn't need a man."

Kate looked into those warm, soft-blue pools and fell for Butch all over again. "Well, I don't *need* a man, and I don't want a man, or just any man."

Butch's grin stretched into a lovesick smile. "But you want me, and you'll have me."

Kate fought her answering smile. "Maybe I would, if you did a few things first."

The smile fell from Butch's lips as he pulled away from Kate. "Like what?"

"Well, I'm traditional. You would have to ask my father first. And then, you would have to ask me properly. I'm only going to get married once. I want a real proposal."

The smile flashed back across his face as Butch relaxed. "That's it?"

Kate's voice went up an octave. "That's a lot. Especially the part with my father." Kate gawked up at him. "On second thought, maybe you shouldn't ask him. Maybe ask Tom. He likes you."

Butch yelled across the room to Tom, who was working on another go around with the tall Amanda in another short skirt.

Tom escorted the pretty woman into the living room. "You shouted?"

Kate gasped as her heart skipped a beat. "What are you doing?"

"Do I have your blessing to ask Kate to marry me?" Butch asked.

That got the attention of the whole house. John grinned at his son, his hand on Emily's shoulder as her eyes teared. Jeb grinned like an idiot while he whispered to the blonde he had met the night before. Trudy's wide eyes blinked repeatedly.

Tom took a swig of his beer and looked very serious. "I have to think of Kate's best interest, you understand that?"

"No, Tom," Kate interrupted. "Butch, I didn't mean now. I meant later, in a few years."

Butch raised an eyebrow to Tom, ignoring Kate. "Sure," he said warily.

"So, what are your prospects?"

Butch frowned. "My prospects? What kind of stupid question is that?"

"It's a good one. How do I know you can provide for her?"

Kate rolled her eyes. "I provide for myself."

"Hush, Katie," Tom said. "The men are talking."

Kate launched herself at Tom, but Butch's arms snapped down like steel bands. "I have two houses and enough money for us to live on for the rest of our lives. And I have fast enough reflexes to keep her from kicking your ass."

Tom tipped his bottle to Butch. "That is worth bonus points. Where do you stand on kids?"

"Definitely pro."

"How many do you want?"

"Oh, five or six would be fine."

Kate clutched her arms protectively over her flat stomach. "Five or six? Are you nuts?"

"You know she's a little crazy, right? And she can't cook. Are you prepared to handle her?"

Kate whipped her head back to Tom. "*Handle her?* I'll handle you, you sorry excuse for a cousin." When Kate tried to come off the chair again, Butch shifted his legs, trapping her legs and leaving them uselessly kicking in the air.

"I can handle her," Butch said. "This woman is pure trouble, and I'm looking forward to each and every minute."

"I want a wing in the house. If my nephews and nieces are going to be here, I need a place nearby."

"Done."

Tom winked at Kate. "Well, as long as you know what you're getting into. And you understand if you break her heart, lots of pieces of you are going to get broken."

Butch nodded. "I would expect nothing less."

Tom laughed. "Fine, go ahead and marry her."

"No." Kate squirmed on Butch's lap, trying to find some purchase to push herself up. Furious, her blood boiled. How humiliating! Butch and Tom haggling over her like she was the runt of the litter. They were mocking her about one of the most important decisions of her life.

"Where are you going?" Butch pulled her back against him. "I haven't asked you yet."

"I don't want you to ask me. You're a pair of idiots."

Tom looked to the woman under his arm. "Don't pay any attention to her. She's always bitchy when someone is going to propose."

Kate glared at Tom, but her response was cut short when Butch took her chin in his hand and turned her to face him. "Katie—"

Kate slapped at his hand. "No, this isn't asking me properly. You aren't taking me seriously."

Butch slid out from underneath her and went down on one knee. He took her hand and kissed her fingertips. "I take everything about you very seriously. I'm here, on my knees, in front of all my family and friends, telling you I didn't know what love was until I met you. I've never had anyone love me the way that you do. I've never had anyone willing to stand beside me, to stand in front of me the way you do. My life had no color, no texture before you. In the short amount of time we've been together, you've become such a part of my life I can't imagine a single day going by without seeing your smile, without tasting your lips. I love you with everything I am. If you love me the same way, please do me the honor of marrying me."

Poetry, Kate thought. Butch gave her romance and laughter and everything beautiful in the world. And she wanted it, just as he did, every day for the rest of her life. Butch filled the holes she didn't know she had. With him, she was happy and complete, and she realized in that moment, it was enough. Kate knew her love for Butch was enough for her today, and she knew it would be enough for every day for the rest of her life.

While she stared, Butch pulled a ring from his pocket

and slid it onto her finger. Kate's mouth fell open as she stared at the glittering square diamond nestled between two smaller stones in a simple, elegant setting. She choked up.

"You carry a ring in your pocket?"

Butch smiled and tucked her hair back behind her ear. "My granddaddy gave this to my grandma on their thirtieth wedding anniversary. They were together fifty-two years. I'm betting we can beat their record. What do you say?"

"It's beautiful. It's so beautiful." Kate's eyes welled up, and she bit her lip. "We shouldn't, you know. We haven't known each other very long."

"I've been looking for you my whole life, Kate. I understand why you would doubt me. I've had three wives, but you're my first love. I love you with all of my heart, Kate."

John, Emily, Jeb, and Tom all nodded their approval. The love and acceptance of the people who were important to Butch, important to Kate, made her brave.

She brought Butch's and her joined hands to her lips and looked into Butch's eyes. "I have longevity in my genes. I'm betting we make sixty years easily."

Butch closed the distance between them, smiling. "That means 'yes,' right?"

She fell into his arms, burying her face in his throat while she fought back tears of joy. "That means yes. I want you, Butch. Only you. I need you, but most of all, I love you very much."

A round of applause welcomed the committed lovers' first official kiss.

Chapter Nineteen

Kate slept with her ring on, afraid the fairy tale would disappear if she didn't. She woke completely happy and wrapped around the man she loved. The sparkle of her ring in the early morning sun mesmerized her. She turned into him, kissed his chest, and worked her way up along his throat to his jaw. She felt so much and wanted to share it all with him. So she woke him, using her body to express the depth of the emotions that drowned her. She ended face down on Butch, both of them purring contentedly. He quickly morphed into a soft snore while Kate lay wide awake.

Kate bounded into the kitchen behind schedule but uncaring. Tom and Jeb sat at the kitchen table enjoying the box of Cheerios Jeb bought when he shopped.

"Fruity Pebbles," Kate said. "They were my absolute favorite when we were little."

Tom shook his head. "Give me Count Chocula any day."

"Never had them," Jeb said. "Mom always made us

breakfast. Monday was scrambled eggs, Tuesday pancakes, Wednesday oatmeal, Thursday hard-boiled eggs, Friday raisin bread."

Tom drained the milk from the bowl and set it down. "I don't know if I feel sad for you that you've never had Count Chocula—one of the finest breakfast cereals ever created— or jealous that your mama made you a real meal every day of your life."

Kate rolled her eyes. "You didn't miss out on anything, Jeb."

Butch stumbled into the kitchen. Just like every morning, he found Kate, pulled her onto his lap, buried his face in her hair, and breathed her in. "What did Jeb miss out on?"

"Count Chocula and Fruity Pebbles," Kate said.

Jeb sipped his coffee. "Mom never would let us buy those. She said they were boxed sugar that would rot our teeth."

"I had Honeycombs a few times when I slept over at Hyde's house," Butch said.

Kate leaned back into Butch. "I'm going to go visit him today. We didn't get over yesterday with everything going on."

Butch lifted her hand and kissed the ring on her finger. "You ready to become Mrs. Katie McCormick?"

"Wow. That would take some getting used to. Maybe I should keep my name."

"Hmmm. You could do that, or consider sharing mine with me."

"Is that important to you?"

"It is. You said you were traditional. Well, I am, too. I want us to be together. One house, one family, one name."

Kate hadn't anticipated how she would feel about giving up her name. She'd spent a lot of time and effort making something of Kate Riley. But this was important to him, more than he said. "Maybe. I'll work on it. I mean, it's not like it's changing next week. I'll have a long time to get used to the idea." Kate laced her fingers with Butch's, admiring how nicely they fit together.

"Why would you have a long time?"

"Well, it will be a while before we actually get married. So no need to panic yet."

"Uh huh. How long is 'a while' to you?"

Kate pulled his arms around her waist. "A few years."

Butch crossed his arms over her and spoke softly. "In my book, that's quite a while longer than a while. I was thinking we'd get married when I finished my tour in the fall."

Kate's feet turned to ice. The fact that her heart stopped might have had something to do with it. "That's only, like, five months away. What's the rush?"

Butch didn't quite fight down the smile that crept onto his lips. "I love you."

Kate jumped up, bumping the table hard enough to rock the coffee cups. "I love you, too, but what's the rush? We can live together, build the house, you do your thing, and I'll do mine, and then when everything's good, we can get married." She back-pedaled until the counter brought her up short.

Butch stalked her, the kitchen island providing her only shelter. "If you ask me, everything's good right now. We can talk to Reverend Marcus and see when he's open before I leave."

"Before you leave?" Kate's voice was too high, her air

choked off by the lump in her throat. "Everything isn't good. Hyde. Hyde's still in a coma. You would want him there, right? You haven't finished settling Fawn's estate. You'll have to go back to California, and then you have a tour."

Butch walked after her, his long, slow strides navigating around the chairs she put in his path. "Any more excuses?"

"Reasons. Hundreds of reasons to wait." When his smile just grew, Kate knocked over two chairs and skirted by him.

Tom went to the sink and washed his bowl. "You do know how to keep her on her toes. I've never seen her run scared before."

"I'm not running." Kate kept the island between her and Butch.

Jeb raised his coffee in salute. "It'll be nice to actually be at one of your weddings."

"My last wedding. You'll be my best man, right? Whenever we have it?"

"I'm here for you, little brother."

Kate made a break for it, skirting by Tom for the door. "You plan your Mad Hatter Tea Party. I'm going to work."

Kate's palms sweated as she drove along the country roads. It was crazy to get engaged after knowing Butch for just a few weeks, but did he really think she was nuts enough to marry him in months? They loved each other, so she didn't see the hurry to make it legal. They did the important part. They committed to each other in front of God, family, and friends. She didn't really give a rat's ass whether the government recognized it or not. They could take the time to get to know each other, to build a house and a life together. If or when they were ready for kids, well, then they could get married. It wasn't like getting married made things permanent. Butch was living proof of that. So were her father and uncle.

Kate turned into the site to find the crew gathered around the main trailer. Every window was broken, and the white walls bore the ugly scars of hate. "Die Bitch" was scrawled in black spray paint. The shaky letters proclaimed that "I know what you did" and threatened "An eye for an eye."

Kate stared with unseeing eyes at the repulsive graffiti. Her face warmed, and her fingers flexed around the steering wheel. She was being threatened. Her. Personally. Somebody came onto her site and threatened her. They didn't even have the balls to do it to her face. Well fuck that.

Kate slammed out of her truck and barked at the crew. "Get me new glass now. I want those windows replaced by noon. And get me paint. Dark blue like our logo. Paint it today. We are not looking at this one minute longer than we have to. This is our house. Nobody comes in and messes with it. How did they get in? Didn't the alarm go off?"

Waters came toward her with his hands out. "I was first on site this morning. The gate was closed, but yes, the alarm on the trailers was going off. I shut it down and called the police. If they came through the gate, they closed it when they left. Could have come over the fence, I suppose."

Kate flung her hand out at her violated trailer. "Look at that. I want it fixed. Now."

"We'll get it fixed, Kate, but the sheriff needs to see it first."

"The sheriff can—" She cut off when Jeb's SUV turned in with the lights flashing. "The sheriff can get to work now, because that shit isn't staying there."

Tom had pulled in behind Jeb, and the two men stood looking at the damage.

"I'm spending a lot of time out here, Kate. 'I know what you did,'" Jeb read the accusation. "Any idea what it means?"

Kate kicked a stone, sending a plume of dust into the air when it landed a good fifteen feet away. "If you are asking literally, no. I could speculate that somebody still thinks I had something to do with Fawn's death, which I didn't. But whoever it is has no concept whatsoever of what I'm going to do once I get my hands on them. I'm going to sit up in that tree with a rifle and the next time they set a toe on this property, I'm blasting it to kingdom come."

"You're going to do nothing, Kate." Jeb spoke plainly, sternly. There was no give in his tone, no room for negotiation.

Kate growled her frustration to the sky, spinning in a slow, controlled circle that was very much the opposite of the out-of-control rage consuming her. "You can't expect me to do nothing. This is personal."

"You're damned right it is. Somebody is baiting you. You rise to the bait, you're going to be caught. If you won't think of yourself, think of Butch."

Kate bit down on her lower lip hard enough to leave marks. "That's not fair."

"I don't really care about being fair right now."

Kate kicked three more rocks before stomping off.

Kate walked calmly into the trailer some twenty minutes later. A sweaty sheen covered her. Tufts of hair pulled from the band and matted to her face.

Tom cocked his head. "You hit the rock pile?"

Kate pulled a bottle of water from the full-sized refrigerator. "Yeah."

"That's what I guessed. It do any good?"

"Took the edge off. How bad is the damage?" Her voice matched the calm in her body. Her hands didn't clench or flinch as they hung at her sides. She didn't dance, shifting from one foot to the other. She stood with her shoulders back and chin up in an exhausted calm.

"Minimal. The stuff inside was moved around but nothing broken. I talked to Jeb about beefing up security around here. He has some ideas. Good ones."

Kate picked up a folder from her desk and poured the glass shards into the trash can. "I'm going to call home."

"I can call, Kate. My father won't flip out the way yours does."

"I'll take care of it, but I will call your father instead of mine."

"I'll be outside if you need me."

She picked up her desk phone and dialed the number. "Uncle Mike? It's Kate. We've had another problem."

Michael Riley was ice to her father's fire. He never yelled, and he seldom swore, but that didn't mean there were any soft edges to the man. She reported the incident, repeating the same answers she had given Jeb. She finished when her father had come into the room. She could hear him in the background, arguing with Mike. Her father wanted to bring Kate home and leave Tom down in her place.

Kate hung up before a sentence was rendered and pulled the phone cord from the wall. She turned off her cell phone and nearly ran out of the trailer, wanting to be legitimately unavailable when one of them called on a working line. Outside, three men painted the trailer white. Kate recognized them as the three she had nearly fired for dumping into the stream.

"They volunteered," Tom told her when she raised her eyebrows.

"Whoever did this, it wasn't one of us," one of the painters said.

Kate wasn't sure if he meant the vandal wasn't one of the three of them or, in a bigger picture, one of the locals. Either way, she appreciated the sentiment. She appreciated someone saw what they were trying to build when it felt like everything was working against them. The laborers prepped the paint.

"I wanted it painted dark blue."

"Not in Tennessee," the second painter said. "It'll turn into an oven come summer. White is better."

"An oven. Good to know. Thanks. I'll pay the overtime if you can get it done today." Kate turned back to Tom. "Where's Jeb?"

"He left while you were on the phone. How did it go?"

"Fine until my father walked in. I hung up before he could attempt to revoke my travel privileges and order me back to Michigan."

Tom's cell phone rang.

"You might not want to answer that."

Tom rolled his eyes. "He has a hard time remembering we have our own company and don't actually work for them anymore."

"I know. You'd think he'd be happy we're off the payroll." Kate ran her hands over her messy ponytail. "Maybe it was a mistake going after the design-build with them. It just seemed so…"

"Obvious," Tom finished. "Riley Brothers have always built some of the finest buildings around. It was a natural to think that matching our brains with their expertise would create something extraordinary."

"Yes. But so far, the only thing extraordinary is the pain in my ass."

Tom chuckled and stroked Kate's arm when she didn't smile. "I have some good news for you."

"You have video evidence that the rat bastard who did this fell face first into a patch of poison ivy?"

"We don't have cameras, so no, but hope springs eternal. Jeb said we can pick up your truck from the impound lot. You'll have your own wheels again. Let's celebrate the little things. I'll take you into town and buy you lunch, we'll swing by to visit Hyde, then I'll take you to get your truck."

Late for the breakfast crowd, early for the lunch crowd, Kate and Tom found themselves at the best table in the little restaurant. As they sipped coffee in a booth looking out over the street, Trudy happened by. She waved enthusiastically at the pair, and Tom beckoned her inside.

"Care to join us?" Tom invited with a beguiling grin on his face.

"I don't want to intrude," Trudy said when Kate scowled.

"Eating lunch with a beautiful woman is never intrusive." Tom slid over to make room.

"I believe you are already eating lunch with a beautiful woman."

"Kate?" Tom said mockingly. "She's not beautiful. She's family."

Kate huffed. "You see what I have to live with?"

The waitress came over to chitchat and take their orders.

Trudy took a long, slow drink of her sweet tea. "Jeb came by to see me this morning. I'm sorry to hear y'all had more trouble. I wish there was something I could do to help."

Katie sat up a little straighter. "What did Jeb want?"

"Oh, he asked me about going into Butch's house to straighten up. I didn't realize Butch didn't know it was me coming in and helping to keep things tidy. I swear I asked if he wanted some help. I never would have been so forward as to go into someone's house uninvited."

"Did you use my phone?" Kate blurted out.

"I didn't use it, but one day I was wiping the counters down and I noticed the charge was low. I plugged it in on the counter. I hate when I forget to charge mine. It seems like my battery is always dead when I need the phone the most, and I see how much you use yours."

"Thanks. I'd hate to have a dead battery in an emergency," Kate said skeptically. She wanted to see holes in Trudy's story. Holes so big you could drive a Mack truck through it. Kate didn't really want Trudy to be the killer, but it would have made things easy. If it were Trudy, the mystery would be solved, the culprit arrested, and Kate could get back to her regularly scheduled life.

Tom kicked her under the table.

Kate glared at him but spoke to Trudy. "That was very thoughtful of you. Really, thanks."

Trudy flashed Kate a bright, warm grin. "It wasn't anything. So, it seems your life just keeps getting more exciting. You're engaged to Butch."

Kate set her left hand on the table where the sunlight danced off of the stones. She still went soft and mushy inside when she looked at the ring. Butch knew her well. He gave her a ring that wasn't the newest or the biggest or the latest style but a ring that already meant something to him. Butch's grandparents' ring symbolized commitment and longevity. It represented a stable foundation they would build their lives upon.

"I still can't believe it. I look at the ring on my finger and have to touch it to make sure it's real."

"When is the wedding?"

When Tom snickered, Kate kicked at him. "We're still talking about that. I'd like to wait a bit."

Trudy waved her finger as though she knew what came next. "But Butch wants to get married right away."

Kate nodded.

Trudy laughed. "Butch has always been like that. It may take that man forever to make up his mind, but once it's made up, he wants it now."

Kate didn't comment. She'd been accused more than once of charging in where angels feared to tread. She certainly wasn't going to criticize Butch for loving her enough to jump in headfirst. She wished she had his confidence.

Trudy clamped her hand down on Kate's, covering the beloved ring. "We should go shopping. You know, register for stuff. Let's go."

Kate didn't have to feign the shock. "Now?"

"Sure, it'll be fun."

"I can't." Kate pulled her hand back. "Tom and I are going to visit Hyde and then get my truck out of the impound lot." The waitress came with plates stacked up both arms. Thankful for the change in conversation, Kate pulled her hands into her lap and ran her fingers over her engagement ring to make sure it was intact.

Trudy pouted but didn't relent. "Tomorrow?"

"I have to work. Things have been piling up."

Kate kept her mouth full to avoid Trudy's game of twenty questions. She didn't gossip, and if she had been inclined to talk, Tom's little conspiracy theory cured that. Tom picked up the table talk, asking if Trudy knew Amanda and Allison and then guiding the conversation through to the last bite.

"We should get going," Kate said as Trudy sipped her tea to the bottom of the glass.

"I owe. I owe. It's off to work I go." Tom misquoted the Disney song as he picked up the check and walked Trudy to her car, which earned him a kiss on the cheek. Kate sat on the truck's hood watching as Trudy wrapped her arm around Tom's and threw her head back to laugh. Tom said something else and earned another laugh.

"Men are so easy," Kate muttered.

Kate snapped at Tom when he came back with a smile on his face. "What was that all about? I thought you suspected her of all this nasty business."

"I don't have any proof, so I'm following some good advice."

Kate slid off the hood and climbed into the truck. "What advice?"

"Keep your friends close and your enemies closer."

Kate slid the chair close to Hyde's bed. "Has Nurse Cutie Pie been in to see you lately? As long as you're lying here doing nothing, you might as well think of something interesting to say to her. I know most people say you should be yourself, but I'm a firm believer in putting on a good facade at first." Kate hesitated. "Facade means a front covering. Like on a building, you can have a brick facade, but the building is still made of concrete and steel."

Tom dragged a chair to the opposite side of the bed and sat facing his cousin. "I'm sure he knows what facade means, Katie."

Kate ignored him. "Take me, for example. I put on a facade of being mellow and easygoing."

Tom choked on his tongue.

She ignored him again. "I wait until people see how brilliant I am before I show my rougher edges."

"Honey," Tom said, "your edges aren't rough, they're as blunt as a baseball bat."

"Don't listen to him, Hyde. You just think about what to say to that cute nurse and open your eyes when you're ready. We're gonna go. Jeb said we can pick up my truck now that the prosecutor believes I didn't kill Fawn."

"He doesn't believe there's enough evidence. That's not the same as he believed you didn't do it."

"Hyde? Do you have anything heavy I can throw at my cousin's rock-hard head?"

They walked out of the hospital together as Tom nodded

to the nurses.

Kate climbed into Tom's work truck. "I'll bet you five dollars it's the nurse that brings him out of it."

"I don't think it works that way." Tom drove over to the impound lot outside of town. Upbeat rock and roll poured out of the windows. "It's beautiful down here."

"I know. I always liked driving in the country, but the hills add something more. It's like something out of a book." The world seemed green and lush as crops reached up toward the welcoming sun. "They are calling for rain for the next few days. Maybe we can do some sightseeing."

"I'd like to get down to Lynchburg and tour the Jack Daniel's Distillery."

Kate nodded. "Consider it on the list."

Tom slowed the truck to bank around a turn made blind by a thick of trees. At the peak of the turn, they both realized a truck flew toward them on the wrong side of the road. Tom flung his arm out and slammed Kate across the chest and into the seat as he drove the truck off the road. The steep bank pulled the truck down even as Tom fought to keep the vehicle under some control. The airbags deployed as the truck grill planted in the bottom of a drainage ditch.

"Katie? Are you hurt?"

Kate mentally ran through her body, making sure everything moved the right way. "No, no," Kate said. "What about you?"

"I don't think so. I'm going to call Jeb."

"We're all just happy you both weren't seriously hurt." Emily filled Tom's plate, soothing his bruises with oversized portions.

Butch had called his parents after the near miss and welcomed the non-negotiable invitation to dinner. The big house gave them the space to wind down emotionally and physically. His mother had made her homemade lasagna. Her face brightened when Tom asked for a third helping.

Emily stood as she served another overflowing serving. "Is there any chance you're going to find who did this, Jeb?"

Jeb wiped his mouth with a napkin. "Not likely. We can't find anyone who saw the accident."

"It happened so fast," Kate said. "One minute, we were rocking out and the next we were in a ditch. I don't know how Tom avoided the head-on collision."

Butch reached out, providing the support she wouldn't ask for. Immediately, she interlaced her fingers with his.

Dinner conversation wandered, but the happenings of the past weeks were never far from the surface. Over peach pie, Tom and Jeb made plans to tighten security on the job.

"A guy I know has guard dogs," Jeb said. "Give him my name. He'll give you a good rate."

"I'll call him. We'll have the new gate in tomorrow and the new cameras. You're not the only one who has a guy."

"We can't catch a break. I'm not a suspect anymore, but nobody hears that. All they hear is someone threatened vengeance." Kate's voice broke. "This is bullshit. This is absolute bullshit. It doesn't matter how hard we work, how many people we hire, all people see is whatever perversion they want to be true." She paced the length of the room. In a matter of minutes, her strides changed from long and strong to short and coltish. She stopped near the doorway, her arms wrapped around her stomach.

Butch saw the shadow of defeat in her too-pale face. He remembered the way she retreated when questioned for Fawn's murder. He worried she would retreat from him—mentally or physically.

Kate hung her head. "I'm tired. I'm going to walk to the old house." She walked out the door.

Tom stood as if to follow.

Butch stilled him with a wave of his hand. "I have her. We'll see you there later."

The full moon and cloudless night were a blessing. Butch saw Katie on the path as clear as day. He ran to catch up, laced their fingers together, and kissed her ring.

"I don't want company," Kate said.

"I'm not company, I'm your fiancé. Or did you forget that?" His teeth bit at her knuckle.

"I didn't forget." She moved closer to him, which spoke volumes of the progress they'd made.

Butch wrapped his arm around her shoulders. "Let's just walk. It's a beautiful night out. Look at that big, full moon." Butch steered Kate to the right, away from the path and toward a small grove of trees on the edge of the property. He led her through the darkened woods by memory alone until they came out on a moonlit path next to the creek. Butch put his arm around her. It was like hugging the Tin Man. "You need to relax."

Kate took a deep breath and let it out slowly. "I am relaxed."

Butch looked at her and laughed. "You actually believe that, don't you? Honey, you are worlds away from relaxed."

Butch had a proven cure for her Tin Man Syndrome. He led her to the pier on the lake. "Come sit next to me, and I'll show you how to relax."

Kate sat next to Butch near the end of the pier, but she kept a wary eye on him.

"I'm not a snake looking to bite you. Give me your feet."

"Why?"

Butch wrapped his fingers around her ankle and pulled it into his lap. "So I can rub them. A foot rub is an excellent way to start relaxing. Morning, noon, or night." He took off her shoe and her sock and worked on her arch.

Kate made a sound somewhere between a moan and a sigh and lay back on the wooden pier. She arched and bucked as he stroked ticklish spots.

He took her other foot, stripped it, and began the same slow, intense process, letting her sink inch by inch into sensation. His hands wound up her calves and worked at the back of her knees. Kate threw her head back and moaned. Butch rolled her to her stomach and worked on the knots in her thighs. He knelt, straddling her legs and began a thorough exploration of her butt and back.

"What happened to the foot massage?" Kate gasped as his fingers wrapped under the underside of her breast.

"Shhh. You're not relaxing." He peeled her shirt over her head. Kate extracted her arms and turned it into a pillow. Butch unfastened the clip on her cream-colored bra and let his fingers play over the expanse of her back. Kate's trim figure curved under hands that easily covered her back. Her larger-than-life personality made it easy to forget how small a package she came in. Butch reached under Kate and undid the buttons on her jeans.

She lifted her hips to help him. "I knew you had ulterior motives."

Butch chuckled against her skin as he trailed kisses down her flawless back. "I deny that accusation, ma'am. There is nothing more relaxing than hot sex under a full moon."

Kate closed her eyes and grinned as she let him have his way. "Better than sex in a hayloft?"

"In the full moon, I can see every bit of you." Perfectly proportioned, her body had become his paradise. A siren's call beckoned in her dreamy little smile.

Butch pulled off his shirt, kicked off his boots, and stripped down to his skin. He lay next to Kate, his head propped on one arm. His free hand trailed up and down the center of her body, from the dip at the base of her throat through the valley between her breasts to the flat plains of her belly and past the fiery phoenix to the nest of tight curls. He loved her this way: open to him.

Butch lowered his head and kissed her. Kate wrapped her arms around his neck and held on when he pulled away. Butch wrapped a hand around each wrist and broke her grasp. He rose to his feet, taking her with him, keeping her mouth locked to his. He lifted her into his arms and swung her around in a circle. She broke the kiss and giggled.

Looking into each other's eyes, they had a moment of absolute clarity.

She scrambled to clutch onto his shoulders a second too late, and she was in the lake.

"You son of a bitch! It's cold!"

Butch laughed. He dove in head first, sailing over her and into the water. He came up swinging his wet hair. "That's how you know you're alive! Woo hoo!"

Kate treaded water with a scowl on her face that threatened trouble. His grin grew as he swam toward her.

"Stay away from me, you no good piece of shit!" Kate hit the water with her palm, sending a plume at Butch's face.

Undeterred, he dove under the water, slithering toward her like a water serpent. Kate screamed and swam back toward the ladder on the pier. Her fingertips had scraped the wood of the ladder when strong hands closed around her waist and yanked her away.

"I've got you," Butch said triumphantly.

Kate screamed and kicked desperately in the water. "We're going to drown, you idiot, let me go."

"We're not going to drown." Butch laughed.

Kate thrashed, fear palpable in her breathless gasps. Butch kicked strongly, bringing him to water shallow enough where he could stand. Her wet skin was slippery as an eel as she twisted and pushed to get out of his grip.

Butch wrapped his arms around her and tied her to his chest. "Relax, Katie. We aren't going to drown. I'm standing."

Kate stopped thrashing long enough to run her foot along his leg. She looked in his eyes, and he saw anger break into a sprint, blowing by panic and self-preservation. Kate thumped her fist on his chest. "You idiot! What were you thinking throwing me in the lake? I'm going to—"

Butch cut off the threat, opening his arms and letting her fall into the water. She swallowed a mouthful of lake before she stopped yelling at him.

She grabbed his arm and pulled herself up until she could wrap her arms around his neck. Panting, Kate rested her head against his neck. "You really are a son of a bitch. You know that?"

Butch laughed again and trailed a line of kisses from her hairline to her shoulder. "Nothing is more relaxing than skinny dipping."

"Hmmph. I was just fine on the pier."

"I've always loved the feel of the water on my bare skin." Butch ran his hands up and down the lines of her body as he had before, knowing the water played along with his touch.

Kate shivered. Butch lifted her higher in his arms and laid her back in the water to bring her lovely breast to his mouth. The water rippled along her body. The hands that were buried deep in his hair began to relax. He lapped at the valley between her breasts before shifting his attention to her other breast. Her fingers relaxed, releasing him to float on the water.

Butch watched as she gave herself to him. On the pier, he thought she had looked like a goddess in the moonlight. She had looked like a babe compared to the nymph he now held in his hands. Her long hair splayed in all directions, dark as the night itself. Her arms were spread wide and her palms up, floating, moving sensually with the water. Her generous breasts floated up to him, an offering he didn't deserve, a temptation he couldn't resist. His fingers nestled into the lines of her ribs as he held her body to his.

"Oh, God."

Kate smiled at his oath. "Is there a problem?"

Butch brought his mouth to the flat of her stomach and played with her belly button.

Kate arched and moaned under his touch, enflaming his desire.

"I want you. Now."

Kate laughed as he brought her against the line of his

body. The hard evidence of his desire pressed against her belly as he moved them back toward the ladder.

"I thought cold water, uh, inhibited a man."

"The water is cold? You've got me so hot, I hadn't noticed." Butch set Kate against the rung of the ladder. "Wrap your legs around me. Now."

"You're so demanding," Kate teased. "You need to relax."

Kate gasped out the last word as Butch drove up into her. His body pinned hers against the unyielding wood, his mouth demanding she keep his pace. Everything in Butch tightened until he thought he would explode. He fought for control, ensuring her pleasure before his. Her stomach convulsed, her core locked down on him. Desperate for relief, Butch grabbed onto the ladder as he thrust deeply one final time.

Kate whispered against his shoulder. "Are you relaxed?"

"Honey, I'm so relaxed, I'm not sure if I can get us out of here."

Kate closed her eyes and held on tightly. "Then don't. Let's just stay here." Kate sighed and turned into Butch's neck. Tears dripped onto his chest, searing his skin. Her shoulders shook.

Butch kissed her shoulder. "Tell me."

Kate took in a deep breath and held it. "I think I'm paranoid."

"It will be okay." Butch trailed kisses along her shoulder and ran his hands along her hip to soothe her.

"I don't think it will be. I've thought about this a lot, and I don't see how the outcome can be good."

"I'm listening."

"Someone killed off your exes. Now, it seems, he or she has me in their sights even though we aren't married. The way I see it, this can end one of four ways. One, I get killed before we are married. Two, I get killed while we are married, making you a bachelor again. Three, I get killed after you ruthlessly divorce me, breaking your promise and my heart. Or four, we split up now, and I stay alive but die inside, because I don't have you." She tightened her hold on him. "Do you know why I wanted to walk to your parents' house tonight? I was afraid to start the car. I was afraid there would be a bomb or something, and it would kill you and Tom and Jeb."

"Oh, no, honey. That would never happen."

"You don't know that. You can't say that. Maybe, I should go away, just for a while. Tom could run the project from here, and I can work on it from Detroit. With me gone, there would be no reason to hurt any of you or sabotage the project."

Butch took her face in his hands, tilting her head back and looking into her eyes. "No, Katie. No. We'll find another way. You're so tired. Come away with me. We'll go to my cabin in California. You'll have nothing to do but watch the wildlife, make love in front of a fire, and skinny dip in the hot tub. Come away with me."

Kate bit her lip and held on to him. "Let's pack."

Butch hadn't expected to accept, let alone so quickly. She worried more than he realized and it shamed him. "We can leave in the morning."

Kate climbed the ladder. Shivering as her wet skin met the night air, she fought with her dry clothes. Butch unfolded the wadded cloth and drew it down over her stomach. His hands drew farther down, running over the curve of her butt.

"You are the most beautiful thing I've ever seen. Have I told you lately that I love you?"

Kate shimmied her wet hips into the dry denim and stood to face him, topless. "You might have mentioned it a time or two. I wouldn't complain if I had to hear you say it again."

Somewhere in the shadows, the brush rustled.

Kate held her shirt over her breasts. "Did you hear that?"

Butch stared into the night. He willed the shadow to take form but saw nothing. "Probably just some animal looking for a meal." He hoped it was but feared it wasn't. Butch took her shirt from her hands, pulled it over her head. His gaze returned to the patch of night as he rammed his legs into his own jeans. Skipping socks, he shoved his feet into his shoes and tucked Kate under his arm. "Let's get home."

Chapter Twenty

Kate stepped into the afternoon sun wearing the light linen dress Butch had bought her the night before in the little seaside town. She shaded her eyes with a forearm as they tried to adjust to the bright light.

"There's my sleeping beauty. A few days away from the office, and you've come to appreciate the benefits of sleeping in." Butch hung onto the edge of the swimming pool, goggles pushed up onto his wet hair. "I like the dress."

Kate ran her hands down the white linen, fingering the embroidered flowers. "I can buy my own clothes."

"You can buy the practical ones. I get to buy the play clothes."

She rolled her eyes at him. "Not all my clothes are practical." She sat down by the edge of the pool and let her feet dangle in. "Don't let me interrupt you."

"I just have a few more laps to do. I hadn't worked out since I got home. I forgot how good this feels." He pulled his goggles back in place and dove.

Kate watched his long, powerful lines cut through the water. The man did have a body on him. Kate looked over her shoulder at the house. Butch called it his cabin. The only similarities between the structure behind her and a cabin were that they were made of wood and surrounded by trees. This cabin was a four-bedroom house with a gourmet kitchen, spacious great room, fitness room, and practice studio. It wasn't decorated but contained a collection of functional and related items. The great room featured a leather couch, a coffee table, a big-screen television, and a baby grand piano. There were no pictures on the walls, no curtains on the windows, no rugs on the floor.

Two bedrooms had actual beds and dressers. Butch's bedroom also had a bedside table that held a clock. A third bedroom was only recognizable as an office because of the computer set up on the card table. The fourth room had nothing in it but dust.

Butch had lived in the house for over a year, but it never became his home.

Kate's favorite space was this back patio, looking over hills and trees. This play-land belonged to the insects, birds, and squirrels. It would take years to absorb the beauty, if she ever could.

"Hey! Katie! You asleep?" Butch swam back to her side.

Kate pulled her feet from the water and lay on her stomach on a mat, propping herself up on her elbows. "No. Just daydreaming. I love the view here."

Butch smiled wickedly, keeping his eyes focused on her exposed décolletage. "The view is spectacular."

Kate followed his eyes down and promptly sat up. "I

meant the trees. Pervert."

Butch caught her ankle and pulled her toward him. "That's not what you said this morning. You're naked under that dress, aren't you?"

"Everyone is naked under their clothes. Don't you dare pull me in. This is linen."

Butch hooked a finger in her neckline. "You aren't wearing a bra. Or panties."

Katie swatted at his hand. "There's hardly a point with you around. I put them on; you just take them off again."

Butch smiled unapologetically. "Come on in. The water's fine."

"Don't you get my dress wet. The linen will wrinkle."

He tugged on her ankle until he could reach her knee. "I'll buy you a new one."

Kate swatted at him as she laughed. "You will not. This one is just fine as long as it stays dry."

"There's my practical Katie." Butch grabbed her hand and pulled her into the water with him.

Kate screamed. Butch captured the sound, covering her mouth with his. She planted her palms against his chest and pushed with everything she had.

"You're ridiculous. The water is cold." She meant to scold him but couldn't keep the laughter from bubbling up.

Butch pulled her against his chest and walked up the pool stairs. At the top, he set her on her feet long enough to strip the wet dress from her body, and he carried her into the hot tub. "Better?"

Kate smiled and nodded, snuggling against Butch. "Are you keeping this house?"

"My cabin? Absolutely."

"This isn't a cabin. What about the pink house?" Kate had thought Butch exaggerated when he said Fawn painted the house pink. He hadn't. Every room in the house was pink in some fashion. "I didn't know there were so many shades of pink. The pink striped room was dizzying."

"I'll sell it eventually. I'll have to have it repainted, or I'll lose my shirt on it." Butch kissed her jaw. "I decided to give Fawn's estate to her father, after taxes and expenses. Technically, since we were still married, all of it is mine. But I'm going to abide by the pre-nup."

Kate tipped her head up and kissed his chin. "You're a good man."

"He's a good man, and Fawn gave him a rough time. He doesn't want any of it—the house, her car, her jewelry. I don't want it either. I gave Trudy some, which will have to come out of my share. I'll sell the rest at auction or something."

"You met with her father yesterday, didn't you?"

Butch rested his chin on her head. "Yeah, we made the arrangements for her funeral. She's on her way now. We're going to have a private service the day after tomorrow." He closed his eyes and sat still.

Kate hugged him to her. "You don't want me to go with you, do you?"

"I want you with me more than anything, but…"

Kate kissed his chin again. "I'll be here for you when you get home."

"What did I do to deserve you? My practical Katie." He brushed his lips over hers tenderly, intimately.

Kate laughed against his mouth. "How practical am I? I agreed to marry a man I've only known for a few weeks. I should have held out for months. Years even."

Butch lifted her hand from the water and kissed her ring. "You aren't going to back out on me, are you?"

"Not a chance. You're stuck with me."

His body on Tennessee time, Butch had risen without an alarm in the late morning. More than the time change had him up. Jeb had called last night, letting him know there was no change with Hyde, someone had keyed Tom's truck, and Kate received some ugly hate mail at the trailer. Butch debated the best way to tell Katie but pushed that off for now. Today, he would bury Fawn. The ceremony would be small. No viewings. No public announcement. Just family and the friends she called by name. Butch used a mirror to knot his tie, something he did only on Christmas and at funerals. His black suit hung in the closet he hadn't emptied when he went to Tennessee. He used a product to tame his hair and splashed on a judicious amount of cologne. He didn't recognize the man in the mirror. When had he gotten so old?

A bark of laughter bounced down the empty hall.

Butch found Kate pacing the dining room she'd commandeered into an office, her phone pressed to her ear. It might be nine in the morning here, but at home, the day's work was nearly half done. "You don't really believe that?" She padded about barefoot in a pair of shorts and a T-shirt that said "Irony: the opposite of wrinkly." She laughed again. "You're so full of shit your eyes are brown."

Kate saw him standing in the doorway and blew him a kiss. When he caught it and held it to his heart, her smile broadened.

She spoke into the phone. "Of course I can do that. The question is, what are you going to do for me?"

Butch signaled her, pointing at the door.

"Hold on a minute." Kate set the phone down and went to Butch, wrapping her arms around his waist. "Are you sure you don't want me to go with you? You don't have to do this alone."

Butch held her tightly, wanting her feel, her scent, to carry him through the day. He needed to do this alone. He needed to take care of Fawn, to fulfill his obligation to her, and having Kate there wouldn't be right. Not that any of this was right. "We've gone over this."

Kate rose on her toes, waiting until Butch bent down. She pressed a light kiss to his lips. "I'll be waiting for you."

The miles between his cabin and the funeral home mirrored the path his life had taken with Fawn. Twists and turns. Detours. Traffic jams. He pulled into the parking lot of a stately funeral home on a quaint corner in the town where her parents lived. Only three cars sat parked in the lot. Butch had come early to stand with her family.

The plush carpet and gentle lighting intended to soothe knocked his morale down a notch. People weren't gathering today to celebrate a life well lived. They gathered to lament a life lost, a life taken. Just as they had with Angie.

"Hey, Butch." A thin man came around the corner in a dark suit. Randy Jordan, Fawn's older brother. "Sneaking out for a smoke."

Butch accepted the offered hand. "I thought you quit."

"I did. Don't tell my mother. I need air." Randy took a step toward the door then stopped. "If she says anything today, you know, she's just upset."

Butch nodded. Taking a fortifying breath, he walked into the room where Fawn Jordan lay.

Grant Jordan looked up from a flower arrangement. "Butch." Grant crossed the short distance between them. He pulled Butch in for a one-armed hug. "Butch, I just…oh. God. I'm sorry."

Tall with straight shoulders and salt-and-pepper hair, Fawn's father usually looked like a man ready to take on the world. The man in front of Butch, fighting back tears, was made of paper.

"I'm sorry, Grant. I don't know what more to say."

Grant smiled a brave, weak smile. "What is there to say? We both loved her. I know things didn't end up so great between you two. I had hoped, well, when she went to Tennessee I had hope it meant you two were getting back together. You were good for her."

Heat crept through Butch, acid in his veins. He wanted to hide in shame. He had not only not been good for Fawn… he'd been the death of her.

"She deserved so much more," Butch said. He didn't know what he meant, he only wanted to ease the pain of the father grieving for his only daughter. "She knew you loved her. You, Nancy, Randy. I know she didn't always show it, but she knew and loved you back."

Grant's mouth stretched into a strained grimace of a smile swamped with misery. "She was a handful, wasn't she? I didn't have a gray hair until she entered puberty. The parties and the drama and the boys." He broke down. "It all went so fast."

Butch stepped into his father-in-law, giving him a

shoulder to cry on.

"I never told this to anyone, but I always worried something would happen to Fawn. Her star was too bright. Stars like hers, they just don't last. I tried, so hard. I did everything I could think of to protect her from the world and from herself. When she married you, I hoped we'd gotten past the rough stuff. She had everything she'd ever wanted."

Grief radiated from the man Butch had come to respect and love. He deserved more than days of self-doubt and nights of what-ifs. "It was because of you and Nancy that she was able to have everything. You did a good job raising her. Despite what happened between Fawn and me, I have always been proud to call you my father-in-law."

Grant stepped back and straightened his jacket. "I know you filed the papers but they weren't final. You're my son. Today as much as yesterday."

Butch choked on the words. Invisible hands of guilt and responsibility squeezed his throat, allowing neither air nor thought nor reason past. *You killed his daughter. Her blood is on your hands.* "Y-you don't know what that means to me." *You fraud. You don't deserve to stand next to him.*

A woman in black and gray shuffled past, her skirt ruffling as she walked.

"Nancy," Butch said. "I can't tell you how sorry I am—"

"No, you can't, so don't bother trying." Nancy Jordan stood as tall as her husband, her blond hair styled to match her daughter's. "We gave her into *your* keeping. This is your fault."

"Nancy!" Apology strained Grant's already sad eyes as he issued the admonishment.

Do you take Fawn Margaret Jordan in sickness and in

health? I do. "Nancy, I would give anything to change what happened."

The downturn of Nancy's mouth telegraphed the depth of her grief and, at that moment, anger. "You left her. How could you do that? She thought the sun rose and set with you. How could you turn her out? She was just a child." Grief didn't want truth or facts. Grief wanted to rage. "I have only myself to blame. I bought her those tickets and the back-stage passes. It never occurred to me you would mislead such a sweet, young girl. You're a monster." She raged as Grant stepped in front of her. "An absolute monster. It should be you in that casket."

"That's enough, Nancy. That's enough. Excuse us, Butch." Grant held his now-sobbing wife to his chest as he walked her out of the room.

It should be you in that casket.

Butch stood alone. The pretty room with heavy drapes called attention to the open casket in the front of the room. A stand at either end held a large cascade of spring flowers while other baskets sat arranged artistically along the walls.

Butch bowed his head and shuffled to the casket. Death hadn't taken Fawn's beauty. Staring at her, Butch didn't have words. The songwriter, the poet who made his livelihood with words, had none to express his regret for her, for them. "I wish." What did he wish? "I wish…I'd made different choices. If I had known the path led here, I would have made a change. I would have come to California. We didn't love each other, but I would have done everything I could to protect you. I just…I didn't know." *So much worse the crime.*

Butch squeezed his eyes shut as he forced down the guilt that swamped him. He swallowed hard, opening his eyes.

Another face lay over Fawn's, a face with cascading red hair surrounding it. "Katie," Butch breathed, his stomach clenching. "No." He ground his eyes shut again and swallowed the bile that burned its way up the back of his throat. The threats. The framing. The vandalism. When he opened his eyes again, Fawn's peaceful face had returned, but Butch couldn't rid himself of the vision of Kate's face stilled in death. *You're a monster.*

B utch struggled with composure as he stood next to his father-in-law. He bore the weight of the stares and whispers as he greeted those invited to usher Fawn into the next life. His hand felt like glass. How many more hands could he shake before his just shattered?

Weeks before, he'd stood next to Angie's mother, accepting condolences and offering them in return. So many had come out for Angie, a person of no worldly consequence, while so few truly mourned for Fawn. *Who would grieve for Katie?*

A shiver ran through Butch as the minister called those gathered to take their seats. Front row, Nancy sat on the center aisle, Grant at her side. Then came Randy with Butch next to him. The minister began with a prayer and a reading. Butch winced as the words selected to offer comfort were like fingernails on a chalk board.

Grant was called forward to speak about his daughter. He stood but faltered. He looked to his son. Randy rose instantly, accepted the paper from the shaking hand and stepped to face the gathering.

He cleared his throat. "These are my father's words." Randy took a breath as he focused on the paper in his hand. "Fawn came into the world in the backseat of my neighbor's El Dorado. She wasn't due for another two weeks, but Fawn had other ideas. Little did I realize that would be the theme of her life. Fawn had ideas. I always admired the way she pushed for more, for better, even as she was driving me insane. As we gather today to celebrate her life, I wanted to share what her life meant, so we could all keep a little part of her with us. I think Fawn would agree life isn't the cards you're dealt, it's what you do with them. Whether you're eight or eighty-eight, life is to be embraced, lived for the moment that is, not saved for one that may never come."

Randy looked up from the paper, but in that instant, it was Tom's face masked in anguish. "For myself, I'll say I never imagined not having my sister. But as painful as today is, I'll take it over a life in which she never existed." Randy turned to the casket, removed a heavy bracelet that had been tucked up his sleeve and draped it over his sister's hands. "I love you, little sister. My world isn't the same without you."

Butch pushed out of his seat, muttering apologies as he lurched up the aisle.

Kate brushed her hair smooth and tied it with a band at the top of her head. She put on a dress, this one a fun, flowered print. It surprised Kate that she liked wearing dresses. Her body was free to move easily in the clingy material. They made her feel pretty. She was starting to get used to that, too. Kate applied a touch of pink to her lips then stood back to survey the results. The effect was simple but, she thought, attractive. Her only adornments were the diamonds in her ears, given to her by her family as a college graduation present, and the one on her hand, given to her by the man she waited anxiously for. She worried about him but hadn't texted, respecting that Fawn's funeral was something she couldn't be a part of. So she planned. She made a reservation at a high-end restaurant then routed a drive to a secluded spot she'd found on Google Earth.

A car drove up the long driveway, almost sneaking past her it rolled so quietly. Kate checked her hair one last time and ran down the stairs. She slowed down, opened the front door, and walked down the wooden stairs to the concrete drive below. Butch sat in the car, his head on the steering wheel.

Kate swore quietly and moved quickly to the driver's door, throwing it wide.

Butch turned his head, looking at her over hands locked around the steering wheel. "This is a mistake."

She pried his hands from the wheel and pulled his head to rest on her stomach. She stroked his hair gently. "I know. I should have gone with you. Come inside."

She led him into the house, sat on the corner of the couch, and held her arms wide. He needed to be held, loved, and she was just the woman for the job. "Butch, come here."

Butch shook his head. "You're right about me. I'm not a good bet," he said, his voice a low murmur. He closed his eyes. "I need the ring back."

Kate sat frozen, her arms drifting in space. A moment passed. He turned away. She dropped her arms, her brain hearing but not processing the words. "I don't understand."

"I'm saying you were right. It's stupid for two people who have only known each other for a few weeks to get married. It's a pattern I keep falling into. It's not good for me. It's not good for you."

She shook her head and came to her feet, forcing her voice to be stern. "You're not getting out that easily. You started this."

"I started this. I'm ending this."

Kate grabbed his arm and spun him to face her. "No. We are not over." She caught his face in her hands and kissed him.

But he didn't kiss her back. His lips didn't move. His eyes didn't close. His body didn't respond.

Kate wondered where the sound went. The room suddenly had no color. She rubbed her palm over her breaking heart. "Butch?"

"I'm sorry, Kate." He turned back toward the window. "A cab is here to take you to an airport. I've arranged travel back to Nashville or Detroit. Your choice."

Kate stared at the back of his head, psychically willing him to turn around and tell her it was a stupid, fucked up joke.

But he didn't turn.

She pulled the beloved ring from her finger and set it on the end table. Her sole focus became leaving as quickly as possible. In the bedroom she'd left minutes before, she scraped her toiletries into a bag. Clothes from her dresser were tossed haphazardly on top. She couldn't look at the closet, where those pretty dresses hung. The tears were too close. She picked up her pace, knowing that in moments she would be a hot mess. In the dining area, she shoved her papers and laptop into a bag, draped her small purse across her body, and walked out the door.

She moved without seeing, down the stairs, into the waiting cab. The tears fell. She couldn't stop them but didn't cry out. She didn't speak until a woman at the charter desk asked her where she was going.

"Home. I want to go home. Detroit."

Kate had once thought you couldn't die from emotional pain, but as she sat alone, thousands of feet above the ground, she understood you could. Life as she knew it had ended.

Hours and hours later, another cab dropped her at her office, the one she and Tom renovated themselves. In the dark of night, she let herself in, walked along the restored black and white tiles, and up the stairs. She ran up one final flight and out the door to the roof. She ran in a circle, wanting to escape the pain clawing at her heart. She stopped in the middle, dropping her head back and screaming at the top of her lungs.

Her legs failed and Kate collapsed to the rough roof, her throat burning as she cried out. On her side, with her knees pressed to her chest, Kate willed the night to take her.

Twelve hours did nothing to ease Butch's pain. Neither did the bottle of Jack he found in a cabinet and a guitar he kept on hand. It didn't help any more than telling himself over and over that he did the right thing for her. He paced the open floor of his cabin, guitar strapped to his body, fingers working the neck, but nothing except noise came out.

The shrill ring of the phone was a welcomed interruption.

Butch looked at the screen, for a second hoping it was Kate calling to cuss him out after seeing through his facade. But it wasn't.

"Clyde, you'd better not be drunk dialing me." Butch kept his voice light to keep all of the dark thoughts at bay. Hyde. His parents. His friends. Kate. At least he knew she was fine. She should be back in Detroit by now. Asleep in her own bed. Safe and sound.

"Clyde, after the night we've had, getting a good drunk on sounds like a great idea." Jeb sounded as exhausted as Butch felt. "We've had a fire. We lost the barn."

Butch held his breath. "Are you hurt? Mom, Dad, Tom?"

"The fire didn't hurt anything but the barn."

Butch kicked at a cabinet door. "What happened?"

"The girls Tom and I picked up at the bar were coming over for dinner. Tom set the grill up. I saw him do it. It wasn't close enough to the barn to be a problem. We were in the kitchen. Tom scrubbed vegetables for the grill to go with the steaks. I went upstairs to get some candles for the table. I'll tell you, Butch, I've never seen anything like it. The room was purple when the blue paint lit up with the red light from the fire. I raced downstairs. We got the tractor and some stuff out. It went up so fast. There was nothing to do but protect the house."

"How bad?"

"It's gone. Completely gone."

Butch's gut clenched, and bile rose in his throat. Whatever was going on, he'd done the right thing, chasing Katie away. He was right, no matter how wrong it felt. "All right. I'll be home tomorrow."

"Just you?"

"Kate and I broke up. She's home in Michigan. Tell Tom, if he doesn't already know."

"Yeah. I will. Shit, Butch. Shit. I'm sorry, man."

K ate stood in the late nineteenth-century building she and Tom had renovated with the help of their family. RILEY ARCHITECTS AND ENGINEERS was proudly displayed over the archway that led to the front door.

The place stood empty, except for Kate. Not unusual for a Saturday. Three floor-to-ceiling windows provided her second-floor office with intimate exposure to the hustle of the street below. Kate stood at a window in a thick sweater that did nothing to stop the chill that ran continuously through her.

In the week she'd been back, she'd slept here every night. She'd gone to the home she shared with Tom for clothes and moved into the small apartment on the third floor of the building. Tom's house was one of her favorite places, but without him there, memories made the space too small.

Kate found that work cleared her mind. When she worked, she didn't spend every moment wondering if Butch thought of her. Designing the new space for a not-for-profit gallery meant the tears stopped flowing enough for her to see. Her hands didn't tremble when she prepared a proposal for a multi-use complex in Cleveland. Her breath came in and went out without a hitch while she reviewed material specifications.

Kate had simplified her life. Wake. Work. Sleep. Repeat.

The phone rang. Eight-thirty Eastern. Right on time.

"Hey, Tom."

"How ya feeling today, Katie?"

"Kate. My name is Kate."

Silence stretched. "The weather has been great. Everyone is working overtime, and we've nearly made up the time we've lost." More silence. "It's been a week. A solid week with no accidents, incidents, or fires. Jeb can't explain it, but everyone is starting to relax and get back to normal."

"That's good."

"It's time for you to come back. As much as I hate to admit this out loud, you are better at managing the field work. We need you. I have a house for us, a cottage. It's quiet with plenty of space."

"I miss it, the everyday hustle." Office life didn't suit Kate. The quiet diplomacy of it gave her too much time to think. She liked being on the ground, where hours mattered and decisions needed to be made now. But could she return to Butch's home town? She picked up a photo from her desk. It pictured Butch and a woman in a red dress. They sat at a table, their heads together in conspiracy. She wanted more than his attention; he wore his little boy smile. The corner date was before they had been engaged but after he'd declared them "exclusive."

Kate set the picture down. "I don't think I can see him, Tom. Not yet."

"You don't have to," Tom said quickly. "He doesn't come around, and his tour starts soon. He'll be miles away for months."

Tom had been careful with the subject of Butch. Kate knew Tom had moved out of Butch's house into a cabin Jeb found for him. He, Jeb, and Butch had become friends in their own right, and it saddened Kate that Tom walked away from that because of her. She didn't expect him to. She just didn't want to be a part of it. Maybe in ten years they'd look back at this and laugh. Butch would be re-married, and she'd have her name on the most interesting buildings on the continent. They would survive. They would move on.

"All right. I'll come."

Butch sat on the piano bench, his guitar cradled in his lap, playing the lineup for his tour. His fingers played the notes but the sound wasn't right. He played them over and over but heard nothing but flat, deadened tones. He'd written the songs. If anyone should know how to play them, he should.

Butch's head snapped up at the slam of a screen door. This was hard enough without interruptions.

Trudy's heels clipped across the floor. "You will never guess who I saw at the grocery."

Butch dropped his head down, looking at his fingers and threatening retribution if they didn't get in the game.

Paper rustled from the couch where Jeb sat, reading the Sunday edition. "Was it Elvis?"

"No, Mr. Smartypants. It was that Kate Riley. I hoped we'd seen the last of her troublemaking ways." Her clinking heels faded into the kitchen.

Butch turned slowly, looking at his brother. His heart pumped in double time. "Did you know she was back?"

"I knew Tom was going to ask her to come back." Jeb dropped the paper on his lap.

God, the house felt empty. Could he live alone again? "How about you? Are you staying or going back to the apartment?"

"I'm staying. I've gotten used to seeing your face."

Butch released the breath he held. "Likewise. I'm going to go out for a while."

Jeb stood. "It's not too late, Butch. You can get her back."

Butch couldn't look Jeb in the eye. He thought to explain how he couldn't live with the thought of Kate in a casket, his hands closing the lid. He couldn't live with what it would do to Tom, to lose his sister the way Randy had. Butch would have to be a selfish bastard to keep Kate, knowing what stalked him. He couldn't do it to her, he wouldn't do it to her. But in the end, he just walked past his brother.

Trudy stepped out of the kitchen in a sunshine yellow dress and a white apron. "How do pork chops sound for dinner, Butchy?"

This was not his life. "I'm not hungry."

She stomped an indignant foot. "That's all you have to say? After I went grocery shopping for you?"

Butch took out his wallet, pulled a few bills and shoved them at Trudy. "From now on, don't." He took his hat from the hook, snagged his keys from the table, and looked at Jeb. "Don't wait up for me."

Walking out had been the easy part. Where to now? It didn't matter. One place was as good as the next. Butch drove without purpose or destination. He drove to escape the stone cold prison he lived in. After two hours, he stopped for a drink. Hat low on his head, he sat at a bar and nursed a beer, staring at a television showing an infomercial for a hair remover.

The bartender didn't pay much attention when he served Butch. He set the bottle and retreated to the end where his buddy lingered. The early-week night didn't pull the crowds in, so the bartender passed the time talking. The pair stared at Butch, then the bartender slowly worked his way closer. "Need another beer?"

Butch shook his head.

"Anyone ever told you, you look a lot like Butch McCormick?"

What the hell, Butch thought. If he couldn't be happy, maybe he could make someone else's night. It would be his good deed of the fucking day. Maybe if he did enough good deeds, he'd get out of hell.

Butch pushed his hat back with his thumb and smiled. "My mama says I look like my daddy. Pleased to meet you."

"Good to meet you, Mr. McCormick."

"Butch."

"Butch. This is Larry…and Mary Ann. Y'all come meet Butch McCormick."

The locals of this bar weren't so different from his own. Good people who didn't need to know about his bullshit. With them, he could forget about the bullshit.

"I saw you in concert two years ago," Mary Ann said. "You put on the best show. Would you sign something? For my mother?"

Butch took a cocktail napkin and borrowed a pen. "Who do I make it out to?"

Then came the pictures and the selfies and the spots burned into his eyes from the flashes.

The women gathered around him, near enough to touch. Competing perfume collided with latent beer and invaded his head. Eyes. Everywhere eyes looked at him. The room spun. Too many hands. Too many smiles. And still more eyes measured him up like he was a trophy. A trophy-man slut.

Butch needed some space. At the far end, an empty stage sat in the dark. "Does that piano work?"

"Yes, sir."

"How about a quick tune?" The entire bar—bartender and all—followed Butch to the corner. He ran his fingers up the keys. "A bit out of tune, but I'm betting we do just fine."

Butch played three songs from the concert lineup. He picked two he could do in his sleep and the one that had been giving him trouble. In front of a crowd, with the thrill of the performance in his veins, it played just fine. He'd given these good people a little something tonight, and they'd given him something back.

Butch pushed to his feet. "Y'all have a real nice place here. I appreciate your hospitality." Butch handed five times the cost of the beer to the bartender. "I have to be getting back."

"Are you sure? Butch?" The offer wore a white blouse and no bra.

Trophy-man slut.

"I am."

Butch dragged his body into his house an hour after Jeb left for work. In his bedroom, the closet door sat open. Her clothes were gone. The drawers she used sat starkly empty. The scent of strawberries he cursed each night had faded.

Left alone with himself, he couldn't stand it.

Butch ran to his studio and packed up his guitars. He'd go to Nashville. He'd go to Steel Strings or…or to the practice studio. Somebody always hung around with extra time on their hands.

Ten hours later hadn't changed the story…except Butch was too tired to care about the empty house.

"Where have you been?" Trudy stood in the kitchen doorway, hands on her hips. She was June Cleaver reincarnated, down to the flip of her hair.

"Working. What are you doing here, Trudy?" Butch was past dealing with other people's needs. Tonight, he just wanted to sleep, alone, without the dreams and regrets.

"Making you dinner. I made a nice meatloaf—"

"You have to stop this, Trudy." Butch's head pounded. The few hours of sleep in his truck had long worn off, his patience gone, too. "We are not playing house."

Trudy's demeanor stilled. She clasped her hands demurely in front and spoke softly. "This is because of Kate Riley, isn't it?"

He missed Kate. He loved her and wanted her back here, right in this house, because not having her here was eating him alive.

But.

But.

"I see." Trudy took the white apron off. "Well, the nice meatloaf is on the stove. Do yourself a favor and eat a vegetable with it."

"Trudy." Butch grabbed her hand when she walked past. "I'm sorry. It's not you, it's me. I just need to sleep. Forgive me?"

Trudy cupped Butch's face. "Always. Now, I'm going to go take care of a few things. You do the same."

"**B**itch! Bitch, bitch, bitch, bitch, bitch." Kate kicked a folding chair, thunder raging inside the trailer.

"Are you sure it's a woman?" Waters leaned over Tom's shoulder toward the grainy image. A figure in black used a baseball bat on the call-button stand outside the new gate. The figure tried to strangle the box and then kick in the post. When the gate didn't open, a bottle with a tail was lit and lobbed over the fence.

"She throws like a girl." Kate sneered at the screen as the figure threw two more.

The trailer door opened, and Jeb stepped in.

Kate wondered how she would feel seeing Jeb again. Here he stood, and all she felt was pissed that someone threw three homemade, cheap-ass fire bombs into her yard. "Look at that, Jeb! Right there. Vandalism and destruction of private property and…and…trespassing."

"Let me see what we've got." Jeb took Tom's seat and watched the video. "She couldn't have walked. Are there any cars on the footage?"

"Ha! So you think it's a woman, too."

"Moves like a woman," Jeb said. "No man I know throws like that."

Tom held a mug of coffee out to Jeb. "Except maybe you, Clyde."

Jeb accepted the cup. "Even in diapers, I threw better than that. Now, I didn't see any damage."

Tom took a chair at the table, the rest followed suit. "They landed in the middle of the parking area. There's nothing there to burn."

Jeb set his notebook on the table and sketched the scene quickly. "Did you call my friend about those dogs?"

Kate held up her palm. "I need to rethink the dogs. I liked the idea when it was graffiti. I'm not sure I want some psycho burning dogs alive."

"Any other ideas?" Jeb asked.

Kate and Tom rattled off a few.

"We could hire a sniper."

"We could electrify the fence."

"We could stay here, sleep here."

"More cameras."

"An alarm."

"Armed guards."

"A moat, with alligators."

Jeb looked between the pair. "Alligators?"

"Nobody messes with alligators," Tom said reasonably.

"Call Landon Finch. He handles all of Butch's security on tour. He'll have the kind of contacts you need for property security. I'll do what I can to have my guys drive by, but I don't have a lot of resources." Jeb scribbled the name and number on a sheet in his notebook, ripped it out, and slid it to the center of the table. "You two settle in to Hatter's place?"

Kate leaned back in her chair. "We appreciate your help. It's a good place. Just needed a little dusting. Mr. Hatter stopped by to check on us. I don't think he believed we were cousins."

Tom reached for the paper Jeb left. "Dinner's at the

usual time, if you're interested."

"Well…I…"

"No awkward moments," Kate said. "We'd all become friends over the weeks. I'm not asking either of you to take sides. There are no sides. What happened, happened. I'm moving on. Jeb, you're welcome at this house any time. Dinner included. Now, if you'll excuse me, I'm going to inspect the fencing and find a spot for the alligators."

"Kate?" Jeb crossed the room and hugged her awkwardly. "Don't do anything stupid. Okay?"

"Did Mom make this?" Jeb levered a thick slab of meatloaf out of the pan and onto his plate. "Did she make mashed potatoes, too?"

"Mom didn't make it. Trudy did." Butch sat opposite his brother, glad for another heartbeat in the house. "I took a bite out of her yesterday, one she didn't deserve."

Jeb paused a moment. "What happened?"

Butch told the story, explaining how he'd been going on little sleep. Jeb glossed over his sins focusing on one point.

"Did Trudy seem upset when she left?"

"No. She accepted my apology and moved on. She's good like that, Jeb. I can't ever remember having a fight with Trudy."

Jeb pushed the plate away. "Somebody vandalized the Riley site last night. A woman went at the gate box something fierce and tossed three Molotov cocktails over the fence."

Butch shook his head like a bobble doll. "That can't be

right." He'd done the right thing and walked away. He paid for Kate's safety with his misery. She was out of this. "Was anyone hurt?"

"Property damage. Call box is busted, but the cocktails burned harmlessly." Jeb scratched his chin. "She was there when I went to investigate. Kate. She looks as bad as you do. I don't know what happened out in California, but there isn't much in life that can't be undone."

Butch rubbed his eyes. "I don't want her in this, Jeb."

Jeb chewed slowly, his gaze on Butch's face. "That's why you broke it off? You're scared?"

Butch looked at his hands, picked at callous tips. "I can live alone, knowing she's alive. I can't live knowing she died because of me."

"It doesn't work that way, Butch. Don't you see that? We aren't in control here. Until we figure out who the suspect is, all we can do is play defense. The best way to do that is stick together. Call that woman up." Jeb ticked the items off on his fingers. "Tell her you were a dumbass. Tell her you love her, and beg her to forgive you."

"It's not that simple, Jeb. I wish it were." Butch looked out the window, and the night reflected his ghostly image. Since when had his cheekbones stuck out like that? His eyes sunken in? "Four more weeks. I'll leave for my tour, and she'll be safe." He couldn't talk about this anymore. "There's a game on tonight. Any interest in watching?"

Jeb sighed. "I could catch a few innings."

"Good. Eat up. I'll be in the studio." Butch climbed the creaky stairs to the large room. He picked up an acoustic that had been his go-to in his twenties. "You and I have come a long way, haven't we? You have any stories left for me?"

His fingers slid down the fret board, settling in around number seven. They moved like Irish dancers, quick strokes forward and back, up and down. With the first blast of energy burned off, he swung into a tune that sounded like something made thirty years ago. The twang touched him deep inside, soothing what hurt.

"Son of a bitch!" Jeb shouted.

Chapter Twenty-One

Butch set the guitar on the floor and ran, because Jeb rarely shouted. "What's the matter?"

Jeb buttoned his shirt over a bullet proof vest. "Those two boneheads are sitting in a tree with rifles."

Butch knew Jeb's job could be dangerous, but seeing him with a vest, going out into the night, scared the crap out of him. "What boneheads? You can't go alone."

"Kate and Tom are the boneheads, and hell, yeah, I'm going alone. That way there'll be no witnesses when I beat them to a pulp."

"I'm going with you." Butch fought to pull on a pair of boots while hopping across the floor, knowing if he wasn't fast, Jeb would leave him. "I can help you talk Tom down, and then Kate will come, too."

With his lights and sirens going, Jeb made the drive in nearly half the time. He drove around the site, his spotlight combing the fence line.

"Who called it in?" Butch peered into the trees, seeing nothing human.

"One of the local boys they hired. He's trying to keep the bosses out of trouble."

"Do you really think it's them? Maybe your killer is setting them up. Did you call Tom?" Butch woke his cell and called Tom's number on speakerphone. It rolled to voicemail.

"Let me try." Jeb did the same, but his call was answered.

"Hello?" Tom spoke in a deep whisper.

Jeb snapped the words. "Where are you?"

"Uh…"

Jeb threw the vehicle into park and stormed out. "Don't bullshit me. Where are you and Kate?"

"Kate? What makes you think she's with me?"

A shot came from behind the car. Butch followed Jeb along the fence line. They rounded a corner, walking across a grassy field. The thick foliage blotted out the lights from Jeb's truck. The only light came from the moon.

"Why did you do that?" Tom's voice.

"It was an accident," Kate answered.

Butch started to jog, a bad idea on dark and unfamiliar land. The idea of her in a tree with a gun…what happened when their target shot back?

Jeb crossed a small swale where grass reached past their knees.

"I've had enough of this. Get out here. Now." Another shot fired and Jeb fell to the ground. "Down. I'm hit."

"What!" Butch crawled to his brother, desperate to see the wound. He never would have believed it if he weren't there himself. Kate and Tom shot Jeb. He rolled Jeb, and an odor as pungent and offensive as he ever smelled filled his sinuses.

Jeb coughed, struggling to sit up. "Jesus, what's that smell?"

"It's you. I think. I can't find a hole, but there a wet spot on your shoulder." He inhaled deeply and instantly regretted it. "Oh yeah. You've been skunked."

"Son of a—" Jeb tore at his shirt. "Thomas Riley. Kate Riley. Get down here. You have to the count of five before I arrest you for assaulting an officer."

"I *told* you it was Jeb." Tom's voice. "Can't you lip read?"

"It's dark. I thought it was our bitch. It was a warning shot. I missed."

Butch followed the fence another fifty feet to a twisted willow tree. The trunk of the willow stood inside the fence, but many of the thick branches hung over.

"You said you knew how to fire it." Tom's voice again, annoyed.

"I do. You pull the trigger. Nothing to it."

"Yeah, that's what you said about the chicken parmesan."

Butch chuckled at the banter. God, he missed this. "Y'all better come down. Jeb is riled. You don't want him coming up for you."

A bear's growl came from behind him. "Did you find them, Butch?"

"Yeah. At the big willow."

Tom handed Butch the modified paintball gun and dropped to the ground. Butch reached to help Kate, but Tom bodied him out of the way and set her on the ground.

Kate moved away from Butch, keeping Tom between them. She couldn't breathe with Butch so close. She was over him, she reminded herself. He had the woman in the red dress, and she had her work. She told herself she was moving on and to act normal. Fake it if she had to.

Jeb stomped into view. "What. Were. You. Thinking."

Kate leaned toward Tom. "It's never good when each word is its own sentence."

Tom stepped forward. "We talked about taking added steps, Jeb."

Jeb pointed a finger in Tom's face. "Like getting dogs. Like hiring security. *Not* sitting in a tree and taking pot shots at folks. What the hell did you hit me with anyway?"

"It's a homemade stink ball." Tom sounded proud. "We took paintball shells and filled them with a skunk-sulfur-tuna fish mixture suspended in an oil emulsion. It'll take days to scrub off."

"What? This isn't coming off for days?"

Tom stepped closer to inspect Jeb. "It really does smell, doesn't it? Yeah, I think you have some splatter. Use tomato juice and Dawn. Treat it like you've been skunked."

"I have been skunked!"

Butch snickered and stepped closer to Jeb. "I'm glad we didn't take my truck. You probably should strip before you get in the car."

"You guys like cloth seats down here, right?" Kate avoided eye contact with Butch and hoped her voice sounded steadier than she felt. She fumbled with the gun, setting the butt on the ground. "You should definitely strip before—*pow*—shit, didn't mean to do that."

The rifle discharged a stink ball straight up. They

scrambled for distance, having no idea where the stink ball would land.

Plop.

Jeb grabbed the gun from Kate's hands. "Give me that. And your ammunition."

She handed over a small bag with a dozen balls.

"You, too." Jeb held his hand out for Tom's rifle. "Give." Tom handed it over.

"We are not done talking about this. Tomorrow morning. Bright and early. Both of you. Got it?"

"Fine," Tom said. "It would have worked, Jeb. We would have been able to find the woman in the dark."

"I'm done with this tonight. Go home, and stay put." Jeb arranged the rifles and ammo so he could still walk. "I may have to burn this shirt. Twelve years of college between you two, and you're sitting in a tree skunking people."

Kate felt like a chastised child. "When you say it like that, it sounds ridiculous."

"It is ridiculous. Big brains and overactive imaginations. God, this smell is never going away. Give me dumb, boring criminals any day." Jeb huffed out a heavy breath. "You need a ride back?"

"No. We left the truck close." Tom boosted Kate into the tree then climbed the fence.

Relief made Kate twenty pounds lighter. She worried she'd have to sit in a truck with Butch. She'd done her best not to look at him, but she felt his presence. Her heart squeezed at the familiar banter she'd not realized how much she'd missed. She loved him. She didn't know if there would ever be a time she wouldn't love him. But it didn't matter. He'd ended it and sealed the deal by cuddling up with the stranger. Her father was right, a man like Butch had a woman in every city.

"You were right," Kate said, needing lighter thoughts in her head. "We should have electrified the fence."

B utch lay in bed, the morning sun sneaking in around the edges of the window shades. A week ago, he'd had Kate satisfied and sprawled across his chest. He'd listened to her breathe, inhaled that scent. He'd followed her down the stairs for coffee with the family.

If he closed his eyes, he could still smell the coffee.

Actually, with his eyes open, he could smell the coffee now. Butch slid out of bed and went downstairs. In the kitchen, bright with sunlight, Jeb sat at the kitchen table.

Jeb crossed his legs and tied his boot. "I thought you gave up the early hours."

"I thought…" Butch looked around, but it was just the two of them.

"Tom gave me the recipe. Do I still smell to you?"

Butch walked behind his brother. Sniffed. "Do you want the truth?"

"Son of a bitch. I am going to get them back. I don't know where. I don't know when, but one day. Boom." Jeb tied his lace and stomped his boot on the floor.

Butch closed his eyes, holding back his laughter. Jeb didn't talk this much. Jeb didn't say "boom."

"I know you're laughing back there."

"I'm not," Butch denied, but the laughter fell out of him. "Did you see the two of them up in that tree?"

Jeb chortled, tying his other boot. "Tom nearly fell on his head. Now *that* would have been funny. What are you doing today?"

"Rehearsals. Finch has some details he wants to review. I'll probably grab dinner in Nashville."

Jeb stood, sniffed his own shoulder, and opened the back door. "I'll see you tonight."

Butch closed the door behind Jeb and took his coffee to the living room. Everything looked the same and nothing did. Then something caught his eye. A white tube sat propped in the corner between the piano and the wall. Butch opened the top and pulled out the sketches for his house.

He remembered Kate working on it on the table. Jeb made dinner than night, and Butch and Kate set the table. She rolled up the plans and set it aside. That was forever ago. Before he proposed. Before California.

Butch rolled the long sheet out. Three-feet wide by two-feet tall, the pages held ink drawn by Kate's hand. Pencil shadowed the background along with notes and figures by a different hand. Tom's. Butch laughed at a note that said, "Subject to gravity."

Over the front door, a small sign had been sketched in. The words were written on the bottom of the sheet with an arrow to the right place. "Live. Love. Laugh."

Pain racked Butch's system. An emotional pain as real as any physical one he'd ever had. Who was he kidding? Staying away from Kate wasn't keeping her safe, and it was killing him. He needed to talk to her.

Thirty minutes later, Butch stood outside the site gate and argued with a man on a chair.

"I'm sorry, Mr. McCormick, but you're not on my list."

The elder gentleman took his position as gate operator seriously.

"Kate Riley knows me."

"I reckon everyone knows you." He spit on the ground.

Butch could see the trailer and Kate's truck. All he needed was five minutes. Five minutes to apologize and win her back. "Can you call her? I'm sure she'll add me to the list."

The old man closed one eye against the sun. "Tom Riley made the list. Would he add you to it?"

Would he? "Of course."

Boots on gravel had both men looking into the sun. "Well, speak of the devil," the old man said. "Mr. McCormick was just asking to see Kate. I told him he wasn't on the list."

Butch hadn't noticed how intimidating Tom Riley could be. He had the size and the strength, and right now, he had hate in his eyes.

"Why don't you take a break, Mr. Anderson? Paula has some homemade lemonade in the trailer." Tom stayed quiet until Anderson departed. "You here to see Kate?"

"Yeah. Look, Tom, I made a mistake. I shouldn't have broken things off. I…I just need to talk to her."

"No."

Butch waited for a moment, waited for more, but it didn't come. "Come on, Tom. You can't tell me I can't talk to her."

"I can. She's my little sister where it counts. I told you when you asked to marry her that if you broke her heart, you'd have problems. You're a good man, Butch, and I still consider you my friend, but you're a bad bet. No way am I letting you within a mile of Kate. If you really care about her, stay away. It only hurts her to see you. Go on your tour, she'll be gone when you get back. Clean and simple."

The gate stayed closed, and Tom turned his back.

"Tom. Just…let me talk to her for five minutes. Three."

Tom turned around. "No."

"She'll have to come out eventually. I can stay here all day."

"It's your day." Tom stalked toward the trailer without another backward glance.

Butch wanted to be mad, but he couldn't get there. He needed to figure out how to get to Kate. "The willow tree."

K ate drove the perimeter of the project site. These little patrols were the newest part of her routine. She did it for the safety of the people working. She did it for her own sanity. Not that she had much sanity to protect right now. Seeing Butch last night had hurt. She didn't expect to see him, let alone when his brother was dressing her and Tom down like disobedient children.

Maybe she was wrong to come back. Being busy couldn't compete with the sights and sounds and smells she associated with Butch McCormick.

Kate parked the truck to inspect the drainage swale. This place, in her expert opinion, gave the easiest entry. The ground fell away eighteen inches in a vee, leaving a gap under the fence. She could wiggle through without much difficulty.

"Katie."

She froze. Her first hope was her imagination was viciously toying with her. She dreamed about Butch and him calling her name.

Then he appeared along the fence, traipsing over tall grasses. "Katie. We need to talk."

Kate stepped back. "There's nothing to talk about." She turned and walked quickly to her truck. She wasn't running, she told herself. She had no reason to run.

"I'm sorry. For everything. I'm so sorry."

Kate stopped and looked over her shoulder. He looked just as she dreamed him. Jeans, soft T-shirt, long hair blowing in the breeze. His fingers curled through the fencing.

"Yeah. Me, too." *Walk away. Turn and walk away before you cry.*

"Can we talk?"

Kate shook her head and ran for the safety of her truck.

"Katie? Katie, please."

Kate drove as fast as she dared to the most remote section of the site. Engine still running, she dropped her head to the steering wheel. The pain of rejection led the way. She did as he asked. Against her better judgement, she let herself care about a man she barely knew. Likely sex clouded her brain. Yeah, that had to be it. Orgasm-induced temporary insanity. Well, she was sane now. She wouldn't fall for the same trap twice. He wasn't for her. She pictured the image of Butch and the red-dressed woman. Not then. Not now.

Kate turned the radio on, blasted it, and cried.

Butch had gone into Nashville and worked. His sets were flat and uninspired. That happened when you didn't give a fuck.

"Snap out of it, Butch." Landon Finch sat on the leather couch with a concerned twist to his mouth. "You play like that on stage, and I might as well book you into Fort Nowhere's Funtime Jamboree."

"It wasn't that bad." He knew it was. "It'll be fine with a live audience. That bar near Chattanooga thought it was fine." Butch stood, stretching legs that itched to go somewhere. "Is there anything else you wanted to go over?"

Finch closed up the file he carried. "I think that's it. How about a bite?"

Butch's phone buzzed with a text.

Come to Sly Dog.

There was only one reason he would be interested.

K there?

Yes

Nashville traffic slowed Butch down, giving him time to rehearse. "Kate. I understand now that loving someone… no. Katie, I tried to do the right thing but, damn it." He still didn't have the speech down when he pulled into the Sly Dog's parking lot. He caught his reflection in the rearview mirror. "Act casual. We don't want her running again."

Casual was slow. Casual greeted people. Casual went to the bar and ordered a beer.

"Hey y'all. I need your attention for a minute." Butch knew the man on stage. He worked in a factory making tires during the week and arm wrestled on weekends. A mountain of a man without an ounce of fat, he looked nervous up there, hunched over a microphone set too short for his height. He cleared his throat, his deep bass voice resonated without the electronics. "I'm a little tea pot short and stout. Here is my handle. Here is my spout."

The bar lost it. Man, woman, young, old, barked out in fun-filled laughter at the big man's expense.

"Sing it, tea pot."

"I got your handle right here."

"I like my tea sweet."

The big man continued. "When I get all steamed up, I just shout, tip me over, and pour me out."

Clap clap clap. Whistle. Really, loud *whistle.* "Encore!"

"Hell no." The man leaped off the stage, landing with a thunderous noise. He stomped to the bar, determined to ignore the fans clamoring around him. "Cuervo. Straight. A double." He slammed the shot. "Damned woman."

Butch drank his beer, smiling about the "damned woman" who'd gotten the better of the big man. "What did you bet her?"

"A beer. I win, I buy her a beer and a table to drink it at. Gimme another Cuervo." He slammed it. "Bat shit crazy woman."

Butch stood tall. "She beat you fair and square. No need to insult her."

"It's not an insult. It's a fact."

Butch shoved the arm as thick as his leg. "Apologize."

"You dumped her crazy ass. What do you care?"

"Apologize. Now."

The mountain stood tall. "Or what?"

Butch figured he had one shot. Better make it count. The trainer he worked with was a former fighter and taught

Butch a thing or two. Butch struck fast, ringing the guy's bell. "Apologize."

The mountain sat hard on a stool, swayed a bit. "Shit. Sorry."

Butch shook his hand out, helping steady the man. "Appreciate it. Let me get you something for that. Cuervo on me."

"Butch. What the hell are you doing?" Jeb crossed the room fast, looking ready to back his brother up.

"It's on me, Sheriff. I said something I shouldn't have. We're square." The mountain looked at Butch. "Good luck, man."

Butch saw Kate through the crowd. A splash of red with startling blue eyes. "Yeah. 'Scuse me, Jeb." Butch moved quickly, but he lost her. He rounded a corner to the dart boards and came up on Tom.

Butch tightened his fist again. "Where is she?" Butch stepped to the right, and Tom mirrored him.

"She's not for you. I bet half the single women in here would go home with you. Let me buy you a beer. We'll find one for you." Tom spoke congenially but without flexibility.

Butch looked Tom in the eye. "I want Kate."

"You can't have her."

Butch shouted in Tom's face. "I love her."

Tom shouted back. "You should have thought of that before you fucked up. You made this bed, so you lie in it, alone. Leave her out of it."

Jeb pushed his way between the two. "Easy, boys."

Tom backed toward the door. "She's not for you."

Clarity did funny things for a man, Butch thought as he crouched behind the dumpster. Clarity showed him that his life would be a tragically empty wasteland without Kate. Clarity also showed him that if he bribed the guy at Kate's favorite pizza place, he'd know when she'd be picking up her twice-weekly order.

She pulled the Mustang into the lot, parked, and went into the restaurant. Butch crept behind her car, watching, watching, watching. Out she came with two boxes. She walked around to the passenger side and…

"Gotcha." Butch tossed the boxes aside and wrapped Kate up in his arms.

"Are you nuts?" She fought to throw the elbows pinned to her arms. "Let me go."

"Not until we talk. I've been trying to talk to you for days. Now is the time."

She fought again but got nowhere. "Fine. Talk."

"Not here. Where are your keys?" His hand slid around her hips, finding the keys dangling from her pocket. "Get in and stay. I will chase you down." Butch let her go slowly, expecting her to make a break for it. She wrinkled her nose and stuck out her tongue but got in the car.

"You didn't need to ruin my dinner."

He started the car and took off out of town. "I'll make it up to you."

"Don't bother." Kate put her window down and rested her elbow on the top of the door. "What is the point of all this?"

He'd practiced his speech for days. All the reasons she should forget about everything he'd said and listen to him now. "We're stuck in the middle of our story. We need to talk to move on."

"We're at the end of our story. The very end. The epilogue where the hero and heroine say it was fun while it lasted, have a happy life, etcetera, etcetera, etcetera."

Butch drove past fields, letting the quiet do its job.

"It wouldn't have worked." She spoke quietly, with a resignation that said she'd thought about this a lot. "It was one thing when we were two horny rabbits, but when things got hard, we collapsed like a house of cards. With the lives we lead, we would have just ended up hurting each other worse. Better to find out now."

"I love you." He needed her to believe he did.

"I think those words mean different things to us."

"What does it mean to you?" He turned off the main road to a cinder road barely wide enough for two cars.

She turned toward Butch, taking her time before speaking. "Loving someone means trusting someone completely. Knowing they'll be there for you. Willing to do what it takes to make them happy. Knowing what they need even when they don't. Putting them before you."

Butch turned onto a path with more grass than road.

"This car isn't made for this kind of road. Where are we going?"

"I have something to show you."

Kate dropped her head back on her seat. "Can't we just end this?" She looked out the window, staring at a house that looked a lot like the big house. The pond with its wooden pier came into view on her right. They were on the dirt road that went around the farm. "What are you doing?"

Butch drove around the scorched earth that had been the barn and around a broad, squat building to the front of his house.

"Oh. Oh my God. What did you do?"

"Come see." Butch ran to her side of the car, opening the door with a bow. "Welcome home."

"It's…it's your house." Kate's gaze poured over the house that matched her drawings. Her mouth opened and closed. She covered her mouth as her eyes swept over the details that had only existed in her imagination. "How?"

Butch led her through a door and into the courtyard behind, where she laughed.

"It's a movie set." Kate spun in a circle. Where the front was fully trimmed and painted, the back was plywood framed and braced on two-by-fours. "How did you do this? Why did you do this?"

"I want this for us. The real thing." Butch captured her hands and held them to his heart. "I love you in exactly the way you described. If anything, that was the problem. I couldn't stand the thought of you being hurt because of me. I understand now that the only thing that will keep you safe is finding who's behind this."

"What you did hurt me more than any crazy bitch could." Kate turned away. As much as this gift overwhelmed her, her heart still bled.

"Look at me. Please?" He waited until she did. "I know I messed up. I am sorry beyond words. Let me spend the rest of my life making it up to you."

Her soul leapt with joy, shouting a resounding yes, but her heart and her head hesitated. A tear ran down her cheek.

Butch knelt on one knee. "Love me again? Make a life with me?"

She retreated a step back. "I can't. I can't be happy in a relationship where I'm one of many."

Butch frowned, worry crowding between his brows. "One of many what?"

"Women, Butch. I know about the other woman."

Butch scrambled to his feet, his hand over his heart. "I swear, there has been no other woman since the moment I laid eyes on you."

"The one in the red dress. Someone sent me a photo." Kate walked away from him, thinking. She expected him to look guilty, caught red handed. Instead he looked confused and maybe a little desperate. "Looked like you and she were pretty intimate to me."

Butch chased her down, spinning her until she faced him. His narrow eyes and the color on his cheeks showed him as a little worried, a little desperate, a little frustrated. "I don't cheat. I don't know who was in a picture, and I don't care. This is about me and you." He rubbed a hand through his hair.

She wanted to believe him. Oh God, she wanted to believe, but it was hard when every breath still stung with betrayal and rejection. She refused to settle for being anyone's second choice. "Well, you looked awfully cozy with her in that booth, sitting side by side so close you were almost wearing that tight, red skirt with her. Her necklace had an *A* hanging between her breasts. Ring any bells?"

Recognition flashed in Butch's eyes. "Abbey."

Kate swallowed the sick lump in her throat. "Now you remember her?"

Butch laughed, his face free from the worry she had seen.

"And now this is funny?" The hurt flared. Kate resisted the urge to throw something and stomp her feet like a child. No matter what, she would act like an adult. She would leave with her head held high.

Butch reached out and tucked a stray hair behind her ear. "No, not funny, but in a way it makes me happy." He drew her closer. "You told me once if it looked like you were moving on, that you were just passing time, waiting for me to come back. You being jealous over Abbey McNeil means you haven't moved on yet. You still love me."

She didn't deny it, but loving him didn't change where they stood. "I may be stupid enough to still love you but won't spend the rest of my life wondering who is in line ahead of me. You insisted on the whole exclusive deal. Why? What did it do for either of us?" She tried to pull away from him, needing distance to shore up her defenses. He held her too close, smelled too good, felt too right. It would be easy to step back into life with him.

Butch tugged a squirming Kate fully into his arms. "I didn't cheat on you." At her snort, he softened his tone. "She was a reporter gouging me for material on my breakup with Fawn. Remember, we left the Sly Dog that night when she showed up. She was waiting for me after rehearsal the next day. Finch has been after me about keeping on the good side of the media, so I had a drink with her. That's all it was."

Kate blinked back tears, afraid to hope. "Really? Why didn't you mention it to me?"

"Because it…she is meaningless. The moment I stepped out of that bar, there was only one woman on my mind."

Butch released his hold on her and took her hands, planting kisses on both palms. "I may have my flaws. I'm stubborn, I like to sleep in late, and I can't fix a tractor, but I'm not a cheater. I didn't cheat on you that day, and I won't ever cheat on you. I just want the chance to make up for all my mistakes."

Kate's tears flowed freely, her heart and her head locked in a fierce battle.

Butch cupped her face, capturing her eyes with his own. "If you can honestly say you don't love me, I'll let you go. You will never hear from me again."

Her lips trembled. "It's not that easy. You hurt me. Badly. I don't know how to fix it."

"Let me." Butch again took her in his arms, kissing her with the desperation of a drowning man. Holding her tightly, he showed all he wanted to give her. "I broke us. Let me fix us."

Chapter Twenty-Two

Butch nearly wept with joy when she kissed him back. "Sending you away was one of the hardest things I've ever done."

"And one of the stupidest. Give yourself some credit." Kate snuggled closer, nuzzling against his neck. "No more protecting me. We're in this together, okay?"

"We're in this together, but I'm going to do everything I can to protect us. We'll put up a fence, start locking the doors. Start carrying guns. Hell, we'll move if we have to. Start a life of our own in a place of our own." Butch pushed her back until he could kiss her lips. "Will you wear my ring?"

"Let's take some time. We're together, and that's what matters. We can take our time with the rest." Kate leaned her head on his chest, looking toward the fields. "I can't decide which looks more out of place: the hole where the barn should be or that steel monstrosity with a grand piano sitting in the middle of it." She stepped out of his embrace and walked toward the oversized shipping container parked on a spot of flat land.

On a level piece of ground sat a thirty-by-twenty-foot, corrugated-metal box with a wide, sliding door. A forest-green, pitched roof sat atop straw-yellow walls. The furnishings from the California house Butch had tagged on that first trip with Trudy had made the long haul across the country.

Now that it was here, Butch didn't know what he was going to do with it all. "Looks like I wasted my time painting the barn."

Butch stood close, holding her hand.

"And you don't have a hay loft anymore."

He kissed her bare left hand. "Guess you'll have to add that to the plan."

Trudy came out of the back door to stand with the couple and linked her arm through Butch's. "I like the piano. It is so shiny. Can I take that little curio table?"

"What are you doing here, Trudy?"

"Checking on you, Butchy. You know I worry."

Butch looked down at Kate. "You can stop. I know where I am. But take what you like, whatever makes you happy. I have everything I need." Butch sighed, looking up at the scraps of his life. "Tom did me a big favor, getting that up so quick."

Kate frowned at the eyesore. "That's an engineer for you. Functional. Fast. Fugly. We'll do better. Good thing we have an expansion plan."

"Clyde, I hope you have sense enough to hold on to that woman this time around." Jeb stepped through the cutouts. "Might be harder than you think. Tom's on a rampage with Kate disappearing."

"Oh!" Kate dug into her bag. "I didn't think to call him."

"Looks a little late for that. He's behind me."

"Kate!" Tom's voice shouted from the other side of the facade. The cheap door opened, and Tom poured through, snorting like a bull. His gaze raked the scene until he found Butch. "I told you to stay away from her."

Tom ran at Butch. Kate jumped in his path, Jeb right behind her.

Kate planted her hands on his chest. "Stop, Tom."

"I'm going to kill him."

"Don't, 'cause then Jeb would have to arrest you, and your future nieces and nephews wouldn't have a daddy or an uncle."

Tom stopped dead and looked down at Kate. "What?"

"We're back together. He realized he was a dumbass, and I realized I love him anyway, so we're together. You going to be okay with that?"

Tom hugged his cousin. "It's going to take some time. I was all set to kick some ass." He released her and extended his hand to Butch. "It's a little bit of a let down to just shake your hand."

Butch accepted the offered hand then dropped to his knees when Tom squeezed his bones like they were toothpicks. "Christ, Tom. I'm sorry." Butch snatched his hand back when Tom relented. "Shit. That hurt."

"Good. Now, what's for dinner?"

Trudy flashed Jeb and Tom a friendly smile. "Looks like we're going to have a houseful. I'll get dinner started."

Butch looked down at the friend who smothered him by mothering him. "You don't have to do that. I can run into town and pick something up."

Kate leaned into Butch "Well I had pizza until someone went caveman on me."

Trudy wrinkled her nose. "You've lived in the big city too long, Butch McCormick. Dinner is something you make, not pick up."

"You know we're going to have to fill in the hillside." Tom stood with his hands on his hips, looking away from the setting sun to where the earth dipped under the mock house front.

Kate mirrored her cousin's stance and cocked her head. "We can excavate a pond in the front yard. Make it into a scenic feature with a fountain."

Tom nodded. "Or we can excavate around the pond in back. Enlarge it."

"That sounds like a lot of work." Jeb looked at the grass and fields.

"Not a lot of work," Kate said. "Just work. We'll need the dirt. We could bring it in from off site, but the less we have to haul it, the less it costs."

"What if we started from scratch?" Butch asked. "Bought a new piece of land and started from scratch."

Trudy gasped. "Butch, you aren't serious."

"Well," Tom said. "Retrofits are always challenging. Greenfield construction is generally less complicated and more efficient. What are you thinking?"

Butch looked at Kate and thought only about keeping her safe. He was coming to understand that home wasn't a place, but the people in that place.

"You think Dad and Mama would move?" Butch asked Jeb.

Jeb shrugged. "He'll worry about money. You may have

to commit to some grandbabies."

Butch nodded. "We can sell the farm. Parcel out the big house."

"If that's the way you're thinking, we can develop the property into nice housing. Cicada is going to bring jobs, which will bring people who need places to live." Tom did some quick math and named a number that dropped Jeb's and Trudy's mouths open.

Jeb shook his head. "Shit, Clyde. That is some serious manure."

"Just thinking out loud. I'd need the back of a napkin to figure it all out."

"Well, that is just awful." Trudy waved a finger between Jeb and Butch. "You two should be ashamed of yourselves, even thinking of selling off your family land for postage stamp houses. And you." She directed her ire at Kate. "You are what is wrong with foreigners coming in. You have no respect for our values. Our principals. You would destroy this beautiful land to make a few bucks. You are no better than that money-grabbing Fawn. I won't stand for it. Do you hear? I won't stand for it." Trudy threw her head back and stomped off down the path to her family's farm.

Jeb whistled between his teeth. "That was some exit. What do ya think she's going to do?"

"She'll call Mama," Butch said. "I better call her first and make it clear we were just talking."

While Butch dialed, Tom turned to Jeb. "Foreigners?"

Jeb laughed. "A true southerner thinks anyone not from the Deep South is a foreigner." He sobered. "For what it's worth, I want the house here. My job's here, and my history is here. I want my family here."

A week without Katie in his bed had taught Butch an appreciation for what had been his routine for mornings. When his cock awoke long before the rooster crowed, he took full advantage of the naked woman curled around him. He hadn't known the right word for the physical, mental, and psychological bliss that came with starting most days buried deep in a woman he loved as much as he lusted after. Ecstasy, a state of being beyond reason and self-control, not only now described his mornings, it was the title of a new song.

Butch stumbled down the stairs, poured the coffee, and found Kate by instinct. He lifted her until she settled into his lap. Yeah, life was good, again.

"You look used," Jeb said.

"Come on, man. We talked about this," Tom said, his voice edged with nausea.

Kate laughed. "You have sex all the time. I don't know why you get so freaked out when I do."

Tom covered his ears. "Lalalalala."

Butch grinned at Tom, waiting for him to pull his fingers from his ears. "Are you moving back here, Tom, or staying at Hatter's?"

"Both. You can't live in a place and do what we're planning to do. We can use Hatter's place until this one is inhabitable."

Kate wove her fingers between Butch's. "We'll break ground when you're on tour. You can sleep here until then."

"*We'll* sleep here. Non-negotiable."

Kate turned and kissed Butch. "Stay safe today."

"There has to be a rule about kissing in the kitchen," Tom said. "It's unsanitary."

Kate set her dishes in the sink. "Come on. It's time to go to work. When did you become a prude, anyway?"

"When did sex become a table topic?"

Kate snorted. "Since you were old enough to have it. With or without a woman."

Butch listened as they cat-and-dogged it out the door. Two engines started, gravel crackled, and the songs of morning birds took over.

"Those two are something," Jeb said. "Pushy, ornery, and don't take no for an answer. You gonna propose again?"

Butch frowned. "Don't want to jinx things."

"You know best, Clyde. It sure seemed wrong when they weren't here."

"I thought the same thing." Dust kicked up behind a truck that drove around the farm. Normally, Butch wouldn't see his father's truck from the kitchen, the barn would be in the way. Without it, he had time to pour his father a cup. "Dad's coming."

John opened the screen door and joined his boys in the morning ritual. "You boys in the middle of something?"

Jeb finished his coffee. "Just finishing breakfast. What are you up to this morning?"

"The wheat is about ready for cutting. I guess I'm glad I didn't get to it before the barn burned down. Bad enough we lost what we did. Thought you'd like to know Trudy came by yesterday and gave your mama an earful. You were smart to call first."

Jeb went to the sink and rinsed his cup. "What

happened?"

"Your mama assured Trudy it was just talk, and you boys were here for the long haul."

"Good. I'm headed to work." Jeb paused in the doorway. "Butch, I've never said anything about any of the women you've brought home, good or bad. I always figured it was your business who you kept house with, but this time I'm going to have my say. Kate is a keeper. All of us can see it. If you push her away this time, well, only a fool would expect her to come back again. Don't be a fool. And lock the door behind me."

Jeb left. So did their father. Butch was alone in a quiet house. He ate the breakfast his family always left in the microwave for him. Then he went to his piano and ran his fingers over all eighty-eight keys. The tune he'd been letting simmer, the one he called "Ecstasy," poured out of the upright. He hummed a melody, remembering her heels dug into his backside. His voice intertwined with the bass on the piano, as intimate as the act of making loving. Over and under. In and out. His tune soared to a crescendo.

"I sure did like it better when you kept the door unlocked," Trudy shouted through the picture window.

A proverbial bucket of water doused his musical cock stand. Butch rose from the piano bench, walked stiff legged to the old, oak door, and twisted the new deadbolt. Trudy wore hot-pink capris, a blouse of yellow and pink flowers, and white sneakers. Her blond hair was pulled into a thick tail bound with a bright-pink band.

"You look like spring. Pretty as a picture."

"Aren't you sweet?" Trudy pulled Butch down to lay a kiss on his shadowed cheek. "Want to see my new toy? It's a golf cart. Well, it was. It's retired now. Want to go for a drive around the farm?"

Butch shuffled back to the piano bench. "I heard you visited my mother."

Trudy nodded curtly. "I do what I have to do, Butch. Mama, you, my girlfriends. You mean the world to me. I can't stand by and not try to stop a disaster from happening. That's just good sense, isn't it?"

"I've known you forever, Trudy. You've always made sense to me."

"Some people are just in sync with each other, and others aren't. You and me, well, we've always been like two peas in a pod." Trudy gave a light chuckle.

Could Trudy think there was more to their friendship? She dated, he dated, and while she hadn't married, he was sure she had opportunities. Yet he suddenly felt like he needed to make clear that even if she was interested, he wasn't. "You've always been a good friend to me. Why hasn't some man swept you off your feet and made you his own?"

Trudy cocked her head and gave him a sexy smile. "Who says I haven't been swept off my feet? How about taking me out to lunch?"

"I just ate breakfast an hour ago. I'm going to go see Kate. She and I have a few things to clear up." Butch stood a little straighter. He knew what he wanted. He hadn't been stupid when he asked Kate Riley to marry him. It was one of the smartest things he'd ever done. Now she was his. He was going to do everything he could to love her, to protect her, to make her happy. She wasn't going to be afraid anymore.

"Well, before you go running out of here, Romeo, you might want to go take a shower. You stink. And flowers.

Women love flowers."

Showered, shaved, ring in his pocket, Butch ran into town and found Kate a pretty bouquet of flowers. He had debated about roses. He wanted to give Kate the romance of roses, but this bright bouquet of cheery flowers just fit somehow. Butch knew Kate seldom took time for lunch, so he stopped at the restaurant and picked up everything he needed for a picnic. He didn't have a blanket, but Kate had plenty of tarps and plastic they could use. Butch drove toward Kate, completely confident in himself once again. Completely happy with her.

He ran up the stairs to the trailer with a song on his lips. Tom's whole face fell when Butch walked in the door.

"What?" Butch asked. "She can't be mad at me. She was whistling when she left the house."

Tom shook his head. "You texted Katie to come home."

Butch shook his head, the smile still plastered on his face. "No, I didn't."

"Yes, you did. I saw it."

Butch felt his pockets. "I don't have my phone."

The color drained from Tom's face. "Oh my God."

"I'll drive." Butch hit the door at a full run. "Call Jeb."

Tom held on to the phone with one hand and the Jesus bar with the other. "Jeb, you've got to get to the old house quick. Somebody texted Kate posing as Butch to get her to go home."

Jeb swore vehemently. "Where are you?"

"We're on our way. Won't be more than fifteen minutes."

Every mile turned into five. Fertile fields flew by the window as they raced down the road but never seemed to end. Butch put the pedal to the floor and pushed the truck to its limits.

"Her truck is in the drive. I can see it from here." Tom said.

Butch banked the truck hard and threw it into park before the wheels stopped moving.

Tom leaped out of the truck and raced into the house. "Kate! Katie!" His shout reverberated off of the hard floors and empty walls, but nothing moved. Tom raced up the stairs without any thought as to what could be waiting for him.

Butch followed only steps behind. When Tom ran up the stairs, Butch raced into the kitchen. "Tom!" Butch's heart pounded as he stared at the mess on the kitchen table where two coffee mugs sat. One was upright and centered. The other was knocked over with its contents soaking the thin tablecloth. The chair was tipped over. The miscellany on the counter was strewn across the floor. The heart that pounded so violently stopped at the sight of the pink hair band lying under the table.

Butch scooped it up and held it on one finger. "It's Trudy's. She had it in her hair when she left here this morning. Oh my God, what has she done?"

"We need to find Kate. Now."

"Can you shoot a gun?" Butch ran to his grandparents' bedroom. The gun safe yawned wide open. "Shit."

Tom swallowed hard. "What's missing?"

"A handgun."

Kate landed hard against the earth. She rolled to her back to try to get her bearings, but the endless blue of the sky and painted clouds provided her no landmark. She heard barking. Chubsy was barking. Somewhere close. That wasn't his friendly bark. As if in a dream, she remembered him running next to her. But she hadn't been walking. She had been flying. Where was he? She rolled to her hands and knees and let her head hang for a moment. Her stomach rolled as the world spun. She braced her hands and let the contents of her stomach empty. Her abdomen cramped painfully, repeatedly until there was nothing left but the sharp, painful bite of bile. She looked up at the tall grass surrounding her. She needed to get out of here. The barking hurt her ears but gave her a bearing. Without understanding why, she knew it was imperative that she get out of there. She crawled toward the dog, toward her dog. The air shattered. Silence ruled.

Tom ran both hands through his hair. "She's not answering her phone. I've called at least a dozen times."

Jeb pulled keys from Butch's back pocket and tossed them to Tom. "Take Butch's truck, and get over to the big house on the off chance she's there. Call us the minute you get there. If she's not there, warn my parents, and get them out."

"Then go to Trudy's house," Butch said. "Search everywhere."

"Where are you two going?" Tom asked as they moved to the vehicles.

"The fields. She dumped Angie there and burned down the barn. My gut says whatever she did, she did it close by. If you find her, call us. She has a gun, and we know she'll kill. Call Waters and tell him to seal the property." Jeb swung the door of his own truck shut and started the engine as Butch jumped in on the other side. "I have men on the way. We'll find her."

Jeb drove as fast as he safely could around the fields.

"Damn it, Jeb. How did we miss it? Tom saw it. He saw it, and we blew him off."

"Trudy's family," Jeb said. "You never want it to be family. Keep your eyes out. The hay is long. Too bad Daddy didn't get it cut sooner."

Butch swallowed his heart. "Shit, Jeb. Shit. He's cutting it now. Drive faster. Cut through the field."

"I can't see anything. I could run over her if she's in it. We have to go around." Jeb pushed the truck faster as the road straightened out in front of him.

"Slow down," Butch said. "I'll be able to see more from the back."

Jeb stomped on the brake, letting Butch climb out of the door and into the bed of the truck. "Tom's calling." Jeb put the phone to his ear. "Did you find her?" Jeb paused, the spoke again. "We're circling the field. Call me back when you get there."

Jeb disconnected the line. "Tom says Trudy and Kate aren't at the big house, and Mama hasn't seen either of them. She's headed to Reverend Marcus's, and Tom's heading to Trudy's." He pointed out the window. "There's Daddy. Take my phone. Keep trying Kate. If she has her phone on her, maybe we can hear it."

Butch dialed Kate's phone while Jeb drove, closing the distance to their father's tractor. Abruptly, the sound of the tractor ground to a halt. They watched from a distance as their father climbed out of the seat, looking hard at the ground. "Faster, Jeb."

Butch tossed the cell phone at Jeb through the sliding window and leapt from the truck to run toward his father. In the silence, the wind carried an electronic melody. It was one of his songs. Butch veered east and followed the tones to where the battered phone lay in the freshly cut hay, just a few hundred yards behind the tractor.

Butch answered the phone. "She's not here." Butch watched as his father staggered away from the tractor and bent over to be wretchedly sick. "Jeb. Something's wrong with Dad." Butch tried to run, but his legs were too heavy. He gritted his teeth and pushed forward, feeling as though he were slogging through mud. He was going to be too late. Butch knew it. He was going to be too late.

Chapter Twenty-Three

Butch raced past his father to the front of the tractor to see the pile of bloodied, black fur. Butch rested a hand on the big head. The dog panted heavily as he lay still.

"I never saw him." John's hand shook as he reached to the tractor, needing the support to steady his shaking legs.

"You didn't do it. He's been shot. Help me get Chubsy up on the tractor. Dad, listen to me. You need to get out of here. Trudy has been the one behind the accidents, behind the murders. She has Kate somewhere."

John suddenly looked old to Butch, unsteady. "Not Trudy."

"I know. The world has gone crazy. Help me." Together, they lifted the dog onto the deck of the tractor. He yelped in pain but didn't fight them.

"Why?" John wiped a hand across his forehead. "For God's sake, why?"

"That's the first thing I'm going to ask when I find them. I sent Mom to the Reverend's. Get Chubsy to the vet. Please."

Butch jumped into the back of the truck and held on again to the light bracket to get a better view across the field. He slapped on the top of the cab. "There, Jeb. The hay is matted down. There's a trail. I'm going to follow it."

"There's something in the road ahead." Jeb brought the truck to a stop "It's a golf cart."

Butch leaned into the little window as Jeb scanned back and forth with binoculars. "It's Trudy. She was showing it off this morning. Do you see her anywhere?"

Jeb scanned slowly to the left and then the right, stopping at the pond. "She's on the fishing pier."

"Kate?"

"I don't see her, so I can't be sure." Jeb pulled the strap over his neck. "We'll leave the truck here. You follow the trail and hope to God it leads to Kate. I'll work my way in from the side."

Butch followed the trail of matted hay as it cut across the field. He studied the ground. There were no footprints, no boot prints, but he caught the impression of hands and deeper gouges. She was crawling.

The trail brought him back out to the road near the pond. Trudy sat on the edge of the pier with her feet in the water. He stayed low, hidden by the tall grass, but could find no sign of Kate. Over the pounding of his heart, Butch heard Trudy singing one of the love songs he had written. Her blond hair, hanging freely down her back, swayed as she rocked to the rhythm.

Butch took a deep breath. It took every ounce of his self-control not to rail at her for Kate's location. That wouldn't help anyone. Butch looked around but didn't see Jeb. He took another deep breath.

"Hey, Trudy. Enjoying the day?" He fought to keep his voice light.

"I enjoy every day, Butchy. Did you and Miss Kate have a nice talk?"

Butch shook his head. "She wasn't at work. You wouldn't happen to know where she is, would you?"

Trudy stood and walked around the edge of the pier, keeping her eyes on the water. "Now that you mention it, she did stop by our house. We had a nice cup of coffee, but she left in a hurry. She went to have a chat with your daddy. "

"My house," Butch said. "The one I share with Kate."

Trudy waved her hand dismissingly. "I'll never understand what you see in her. She can't keep a house. She can't cook, she can't dress. She's a social disaster. What kind of wife would she be for you?"

"She wouldn't be the kind of wife you would be?"

Trudy stood facing Butch, only the width of the pier between them. "That's right, Butch. That's exactly right."

"I'll make you a deal. You tell me where Kate is, we get her out of here healthy and strong, and I'll marry you." Butch held out his hand to Trudy.

Trudy beamed at him. Sunlight danced in her hair, and her eyes were glassy with happiness. She took a step toward Butch and saw him take a half-step back.

He swallowed hard, holding his eyes fixed on her.

"You're lying. You're lying, Butch McCormick. Shame on you!" Trudy pulled the gun from her pocket and raised her arm to his heart.

A streak of red shot out from the bush and hit Trudy. Trudy landed near the walking path, Kate in the middle of the pier. Trudy bounded to her feet, angry. Kate staggered, stumbling as she tried to gain her feet.

"Katie!" Butch lunged at her and caught her around the hips. She fell against him as he pulled her to her feet. "Are you hurt?"

Trudy stood on the pier with the gun firmly focused on Kate. "Get away from him. He's mine. You heard him."

"She drugged me. She put something in my coffee." Kate couldn't stand. She staggered like a drunk and repeatedly blinked, widening her eyes until Butch could see all the whites around her foggy, blue pools. "I can't find Chubsy. He was with me before."

"Stay behind me." Desperate, Butch shoved her behind him.

"She drugged me," Kate said again, leaning her head between his shoulder blades. "The world is spinning. Get out of here, Butch."

"Shut up, Kate. Do what I say. Hold on to me, and don't let go." Butch put her hands on his hips to steady her. He couldn't move, not without exposing Kate, and he wasn't doing that. He needed to stall until Jeb arrived. "Trudy, the deal was Kate leaves here healthy and in one piece. Then I'll get down on my knee and ask you properly."

Trudy paced and sweat broke out on her brow. She licked her lips, looking at Butch from the tops of her eyes.

The gun didn't waver as Trudy walked around the pier, her steps jerky and coltish. Butch tried to stand his ground, but Kate kept falling over, and he had to move to keep his body in front. Butch didn't think Trudy would shoot him, but his every instinct said if he stepped away from Kate, she would be dead.

"Katie. I need you to stand still."

"I am." Kate swayed and took another step to her right.

Butch pulled on her left hand until he felt her along the centerline of his body. "Wrap your arms around me."

Trudy railed as Kate's hands wrapped around his chest. "She shouldn't be touching you like that!"

"She's sick, Trudy. You know she is."

"Get away from her, Butch. I mean it. We're officially engaged, and I won't put up with any woman putting her hands on you."

Butch held his hand out, palms up. "You have always taken care of me, haven't you, Trudy?"

"Damned right, I have."

"You took care of Angie for me, didn't you?"

Trudy snarled at Butch. "She was making a fool out of you, and you just let her. She begged money out of you to buy those tits and then showed them off to any man that smiled her way. You didn't see them, laughing at you in the bar."

"I don't care what people think, Trudy. Not like that. Is that what happened with Fawn?"

"Did you see what she did to me? The pictures on the internet were horrible! She deserved what she got. You never thanked me, you know. Not that I expected it but, honestly, what she would have cost you."

"I'm thanking you now, Trudy."

"It was all so easy. Fawn walked right up to the front door and then let me drive her rental car. She called me her redneck chauffer. She isn't laughing now. And I knew the perfect way to kill two birds with one stone. I used *her* work truck." Trudy leaned around Butch, yelling at Kate. "I had to work hard to drag Fawn's skinny butt over to that wall.

Why couldn't you just GO HOME? After being arrested for murder, any sensible person would leave. But not you. You. Stayed. Right. Here." She stomped with each word, the wood vibrating beneath her feet. "Butch finally dumps you, and you *still* came back. Don't you care that he kissed up to that slut Abbey McNeil?"

Kate's head bounced off his shoulder. "The picture, Butch. She must have sent the picture."

Butch drew Trudy's attention back to him. "What about Hyde, Trudy? What did our friend do?"

"He found that bitch's hotel key in my car. He wanted to know who I was sleeping with. I tried to get it back, but he said he was going to give it to Jeb to dust for fingerprints. Then he fell."

Butch felt like he'd been hit with a sledgehammer. "Good Lord, Trudy. Hyde is like our brother."

"Ask her about your other wife," Kate said.

"Tessa? Did you have anything to do with Tessa's accident?"

Trudy lifted her chin. "I had to stop her. You were letting her take advantage of you, just like Angie always did. That's your problem. You're just too nice. Lucky for you…you have me."

"I have to agree with you, Trudy." Jeb stepped into the road. His eyes were flat, that of a predator, as he held the gun trained on Trudy. "Put the gun down."

Trudy stomped her foot in a show of temper. "I'm the one in control. You put your gun down, Jebediah, or I'll shoot Butch."

"You don't want to do that, Trudy. You love Butch. We all know you've loved him for a long time. Tell him. Isn't it about time you told him?"

Tears filled Trudy's eyes and raced down her face. She blinked hard. "I love you, Butch. I've loved you since Bobby Willard knocked the ice cream cone out of my hand and it splattered on the ground. Do you remember? I was sitting on the swing crying. I had to save for a long time for that ice cream. Then you came over with a double scoop."

"I remember," Butch said. "It was a scoop of vanilla and a scoop of chocolate with sprinkles. I didn't know which you liked, so I got you both. And who didn't like sprinkles?"

"You swept me off my feet. I never had nobody do something that nice for me. My daddy always said I was nothing. He was wrong. I showed him he was wrong. And so did you. You always did nice things for me. That's how I knew you loved me. I've been waiting for you to come home and realize it was me you needed all along."

Butch's gaze darted between Jeb and Trudy. He looked for some sign from his brother on what he should do.

Jeb kept his eyes on Trudy. "Butch does love you. That much is true."

Trudy's brows came together in exquisite agony. "He doesn't. But he could," she said softly. Then she hardened. "If it wasn't for her."

Trudy jerked her head back to Butch as Kate lost her balance and fell beyond the shelter he provided. Trudy pulled the trigger.

Butch dove to the right to shield Kate's body. A searing pain shot through his arm, and he pushed back, throwing himself and Kate into the pond. Butch went under, and the cold water stole his breath before he came back to his senses. He came up shouting for Jeb. "Where's Kate?"

The pop of the handgun had been echoed by the shot fired by Jeb. The bullet flew true. Trudy had collapsed to the wooden decking. In silence, the decades-old ache in Trudy's heart finally stopped.

K ate dug her fingers into Butch's chest, but still the world spun. She flew. She closed her eyes against the dizzy array of blues and whites that swirled around her. Then the cold engulfed her. She opened her eyes to a murky, colorless world. She tried to kick her feet, but couldn't tell down from up. She was exhausted. Simply too tired to care. She stopped fighting and drifted to sleep.

K ate's face stung as if bitten by a wasp. She rolled her head to escape. A quick sting hit the other cheek. Then another. Kate flailed her hands in front of her, protection from the invasion.

From far away a voice called her name.

Then it came closer.

"Come on, Katie. Open your eyes."

She tried to answer but couldn't remember how.

B utch stroked back her hair and kissed her lips. "Please, honey. Open those beautiful eyes for me."

Her lashes fluttered. "Butch?"

Her voice was weak and breathy, but he heard it. "That's right, baby. It's Butch. Open your eyes and look at the man you're going to marry. Jeb's calling the preacher. He's going to meet us at the hospital." He dug in his pocket and then slid the promise back in place.

Kate rolled her head side-to-side and forced her eyes to open. "Want a dress."

Butch looked down at her with tears of joy in his eyes. "Then you'll have a dress. We'll have an old-fashioned wedding right here at the house we're going to build."

The EMTs rolled a stretcher onto the pier. Butch held her head as she was lifted onto the cushion.

Kate frowned, her brows pressed together in confusion. "Where are we going?"

"To the hospital, honey. You just rest, everything is going to be fine." Butch let go of her hand as they rolled her into the ambulance. He went to where Jeb crouched over Trudy's body. Jeb's face was an unreadable mask, but Butch felt Jeb's loss as real as his own. "You tried to get her to shoot you."

Jeb nodded. "Didn't work. I didn't think she would shoot you."

"She didn't. I just got in the way." Butch looked down at his arm. "It's not much more than a scratch. I'm sorry you had to do that. I'm sorry you had to be the one to stop her."

Jeb looked down at Trudy's face, so serene in death it was hard to believe what she was in life. "Yep. I'm sorry, too, for all the good that does any of us." Jeb walked away from the body.

Something about it felt to Butch like Jeb walked away from him, too. Butch rubbed his throbbing arm as he walked to the ambulance. "Clyde, if that's what you think, you've got another think coming." He climbed into the ambulance, sat, and took Kate's hand in his. "Now about this wedding…"

Chapter Twenty-Four

The October sun shone down on the happy couple as they stood under the arbor and exchanged their vows. In Kate's mind, she'd been married to Butch for nearly four months now, but if he wanted a fancy party, who was she to deny him? He was handsome in a charcoal suit that matched his eyes. Kate's fingers itched to slip through his wild, untamed hair.

She looked around the courtyard of their home, the one they had built together. Today it was filled with family and friends. Kate cried when her father and uncle walked her down the aisle. She felt the tear on her father's cheek as he kissed her and put her hand in Butch's for the keeping. Tom stoically took on the role as her "man of honor." She had persuaded him by telling him there was no one she would want to stand for her except him. When she promised he wouldn't be in a dress or have to do the "girly" things, he had agreed, nearly breaking her ribs when he hugged her.

Jeb stood somberly next to Butch. At Kate's smile, he winked and smiled back, taking years off of his face. Trudy's death had cost Jeb, and he was working off the debt. He left the sheriff's department and started a security firm with Butch's agent, Landon Finch. Chameleon Securities had kept Jeb busy traveling over the past few months, but Butch made sure his brother knew where his home was. Butch had pushed to get Jeb's wing done first. They had locked themselves in Jeb's office for a whole afternoon. When they came out, they went to his rooms, and by that evening, Jeb was home.

While the Reverend Marcus's voice droned on, Kate looked around her and was overcome with love. John and Emily had signed over the old house to Butch, Jeb, and Kate, ensuring their sons would stick this time. One of Emily's dogs had given birth to a litter of puppies, the largest of which looked the picture of his father, Chubsy. Taylor, the broad-chested black Lab pup, leaned against Kate with unfailing fidelity. At four months old, he was over thirty pounds of un-conditional love that rarely left her side. Chubsy sat on her foot, tail wagging. The limp the vet said he would have the rest of his life slowed him down, but he didn't seem to mind leaving the running for the younger dogs. Hyde sat in the front row, laughing, with his arm around Nurse Betty. They had their own date set for the spring. The Cicada building was open for business, and CEO Chuck Allen had become a local celebrity with his outreach for women. He just signed the papers to have Kate and Tom design a distribution cen-ter for him in a distressed county that wanted the jobs every bit as much as Cicada needed workers.

Kate was happy beyond her wildest dreams. And right

there in the middle of the ceremony, well before the "I do's," Kate rose on her toes, and kissed Butch on the mouth.

Butch wrapped his arms around her and kissed her back. The guests giggled and hollered while Butch tucked Kate under his shoulder and proceeded to marry her. She wept with joy as Butch slid his ring over the finger of her manicured hand and proudly put her ring on him.

Under a painted sky, rich with red and orange and dappled with cotton-candy clouds, Kate laughed as Jeb spun her in a circle and brought her back against his hard body.

"Clyde, this is Tennessee, not West Virginia. You can't be making a move on your sister, and that's exactly what she is now that I married her." Butch grabbed Kate by the waist and spun her in a circle.

A thin smile crossed Jeb's face and lit his eyes for a quick moment. "Clyde, that's just sick." The phone in his pocket vibrated. Jeb absently pulled it out to check the text message. He frowned.

"What is it?" Butch asked.

"An old friend. I have to take this." Jeb left the couple to their guests and disappeared into the lower level of the east wing of the house as the band took a break and Butch's latest CD was put on.

Butch pulled Kate tight against him. "You're too good for me. Four top-ten songs all inspired by you."

Kate rolled her eyes. "You could write some nice ones about me. 'Stinkball Shotgun?'"

"That's a nice song about a girl who gets what she wants. It's especially popular in Texas, I hear."

She threw her head back and laughed. "What about 'In the Hay Loft?' And 'Chicken Surprise' is definitely not nice."

A voice behind Butch cleared. "Do you think an old man can get a dance with his best girl?"

Butch spun Kate and saw Jeb sneak out of the courtyard. "Absolutely." Butch delivered Kate into her father's hands, kissed his wife, and went after this brother.

"Sneaking out of my wedding? You know there isn't going to be a next one. You miss this one, you're out of luck." The wind blew Butch's long curly hair around his face.

"You mess up this one, and I'll have to attend your funeral after Katie kills you." Jeb stopped and looked into his brother's eyes. "Don't mess up."

Butch saw the pain in his brother's eyes—eyes which threatened that something cold and painful lurked behind the chiseled face. Butch worried about Jeb. He locked what happened that day on the pier inside an icy core, possibly for forever. Here at the new house with Kate and Tom, he saw glimpses of the man that was his brother, and that gave him hope.

"I won't." Butch smiled, high on life. "She won't let me. Pushy woman. Where are you going?"

"Helping a friend."

"You have a vest on. Do you have help yourself?"

Jeb climbed into the truck. "I just need to check on his little sister. I'm taking the chopper. I'll be back tomorrow. Next day at the latest. Tell Katie I love her."

Butch grinned at his brother. "The hell I will. Get your ass back here, and tell her yourself."

Butch trotted back into the courtyard a happy man. He

snuck up on Kate as she chatted with his mother's church group and nibbled her neck. He breathed in her scent. "The smell of wild strawberries always makes me so damned hungry. Come with me, Mrs. McCormick. I want to show you something."

Katie playfully held back, giving her apologies to her guests as he tugged her. "I think I've already seen that show, Mr. McCormick."

"Little woman, are you going to come peaceful-like?" Butch lowered his eyes and growled at her mockingly.

"I told you. I'm not the little-woman type." Kate giggled, dancing around Butch, playing hard to get.

Butch grinned. "I was hoping we'd do this the hard way." Butch shouldered his bride and ran into their wing of the house, nudging their dogs aside and locking the door firmly behind him. Once up the stairs, he threw her onto the bed and tossed the long skirt up.

Kate laughed as satin and lace covered her face.

"You have boots on."

"What else is a girl going to wear on her wedding day?" Kate tugged off her panties and rolled on top of Butch. With eager hands, she stripped him down to skin. Her long fingernails, painted white and trimmed with sparkles, teased over his tense muscles. She took her time, tasting him, savoring every line, every valley, every plane. "You have something for me, Mr. McCormick?"

Butch moaned with blessed torture and fitted her over him. He wanted to remember the sight of her this way forever: her face as flushed as her dark red hair, the swell of her breasts pushing at the sculpted dress, and that look on her face.

"Wait." He reached across the bed for his coat. He fished in his pocket and pulled out his phone.

Kate sat up straight. "You're calling someone? Now?"

Butch worked the touch screen and took her picture. "Put that sexy look back on your face. Yeah, that's the one."

Kate swirled her hips and teased him until he couldn't see straight. Butch tossed the camera aside and grabbed her hips with hard fingers, taking control of the situation. He drove up hard and fast, showing no mercy when her body convulsed over his. He wrapped his arms around her body and thrust into her until he exploded, filling her.

They lay locked together, both unwilling to have any distance between them. As the heat of sex wore off, Kate propped herself up and looked down into her husband's eyes. She kissed his chin and sighed. "I love you."

Butch ran his thumb along her jaw. "I know you do. I love you, too. You're everything to me."

"I believe you. I feel it." Kate kissed him gently, deeply, showing how much he meant to her. "We should get back before people think we've gotten lost."

Butch rolled with his wife, pinning her under his body. He moved his hips in a slow, languid rhythm that had her mewing like a kitten. "We're not lost, Katie. We're found, and I'm going to stay found with you forever."

Acknowledgments

Thank you to the many talented and patient people who helped bring Butch and Katie to life. Thanks to Kristen for teaching this city girl about farming, to Mitch from North Wells Service Center for helping me hobble Kate's Shelby, and to Laura Stone for bringing out the Southern charm in this story. Thank you to Kyra, Kristen, Anna, Sue, and Michelle for being the first to read my story and giving me the courage to go public. Thank you to my mother, Jane, and my aunt, Barbara, for your constant love and support. Thank you, reader, for spending your time with me. I first wrote this to entertain myself—to laugh, to daydream, to escape. Now I entrust it to you, hoping it lightens your day and brings a smile to your face.

About the Author

Anita DeVito is a Cleveland, Ohio, native who grew up on a diet of mysteries, rock-n-roll, and her nonna's homemade pasta. By day, she works as a Civil Engineer unraveling the mysteries of water challenges, while by night, she applies her talents to the vexing question of "Who dunnit?" Visit Anita's website at www.AnitaDeVitoWrites.com for more information on her fast-paced style of storytelling and to sign up for her news-less newsletter, Equinoxious. Start every season with short stories, games, puzzles, and some brain teasing fun. Anita lives with her husband, two sons, and two ornery dogs.